A STATION
IN THE DELTA

A STATION
IN THE DELTA

A NOVEL

John Cassidy

CHARLES SCRIBNER'S SONS / New York

Copyright © 1979 John R. Cassidy

Library of Congress Cataloging in Publication Data

Cassidy, John R.   (date)
  A station in the delta.

  1. Vietnamese Conflict, 1961–1975—Fiction.
I. Title.
PZ4.C3423St   [PS3553.A7956]   813'.5'4   79–9819
ISBN 0–684–16156–7

1 3 5 7 9 11 13 15 17 19 O/C 20 18 16 14 12 10 8 6 4 2

Printed in the United States of America

To Mother,
who listens

A STATION
IN THE DELTA

1

The little plane banked for the approach, and Toby Busch peered across the cockpit and out through the window on the pilot's side at the airstrip among the rice paddies, and at the town beyond, which was to be his home for the next two years. He tried to shift his weight in the narrow seat to get a better view, but the Browning 9mm pistol kept getting in his way. The holster was new and stiff, and usually ended up on the seat under his hip. The pilot noticed his struggles and gave him a faint smile, but said nothing.

Throughout his career Toby had always arrived at new posts by air, but never before in a plane as small as this three-passenger Helio, nor at a landing field such as this one, which consisted of nothing more than a dusty strip of packed earth, palm trees at the far end, and a small shack, a revetment made of wooden ammunition boxes, two abandoned sheepsfoot rollers, one jeep, and two sport-shirted Americans at the near end.

This was his second flight with this pilot, in this plane. The pilot was Dino Gallup. The Helio was such a noisy plane that they had not been able to talk very much. Toby knew little about him except that Gallup was the Americanized version of Bacigalupi, and that Dino enjoyed flying and being Italian-American, and was good at both endeavors.

"You'd think," Dino shouted at him above the noise, "that when they make a landing strip they'd study the wind currents. This strip here at My Tho always has a ninety-degree crosswind. Should have been built *this* way." He took one hand off the wheel and gestured across the front of his chest. "I keep telling Air Ops in Saigon that for these short-takeoff and -landing planes, it would be easier to land *across* the runway when you've got a fifteen-knot crosswind, but they won't let me try it!" He laughed. The prospect obviously intrigued him.

"Would it really do it?"

"Almost all of these STOLs would come pretty near it. But because they're so moss-backed up there in Saigon, we always have to wedge into My Tho like a goddamned crab."

Toby squinted at the pilot's face, whose tone said that if he had been in Air Ops in Saigon, he would also have refused permission for such an insane action.

Toby was not a pilot, but he could sense the balance of forces at work on the airplane, and he noted with amusement that his right foot was already twitching in search of a brake pedal.

Dino brought them out of the turn, eased off on the throttle, and nosed the plane down sharply until it seemed that he would skim off the tops of the heads of the waiting men.

"Always like to make a steep approach in Vietnam," he explained. "There are uncouth persons on the ground who like to sit around on approach paths and shoot at airplanes."

In a motion like the rocking of a board swing, the airplane swung back to level flight from the quick descent, and Dino skimmed it steadily along a few inches above the runway. The nose was pointed wildly off to the left of the direction they were moving, but at the instant that the wheels touched the dirt with a gentle tap, Dino deftly swung the nose back toward the palm trees without a bounce or a lurch.

"Outstanding!" Toby exclaimed.

A smile curled Dino's lips, but he did not look away from his task. He reversed the pitch of the propeller, applied the throttle, and brought them to a stop. More adjustments, and he whirled the plane around until it pointed back toward the waiting men. He locked the brakes, left the engine idling, and turned to Toby.

"Toby," he said, "you and I are going to be seeing quite a bit of each other from now on."

"Yes, I suppose I will be flying with you once in a while. All of this is new to me, so I can't tell how often."

"It's not new to me, and I guarantee it'll be pretty often."

"You think so?"

"Yep. Not always with me, of course. Depends on where you go, or whether they give me assignments outside of the Delta Region. Some of the places you'll need a chopper, or if you got a lot of cargo it would need a Porter instead of one of these little Helios. But anyway, I'm going to be a good friend and tell you something right here at the start, even though it's none of my business."

"What's that?"

"That pistol you got on your belt there."

"Yeah?"

"You know who wears the Browning 9mm in Vietnam?"

"No, who?"

"The CIA."

"Yeah?"

"Yep. Nobody but the CIA. It makes you stand out a mile. I knew the minute I saw you at Than Son Nhut the other day that you were CIA—before I ever met you."

"Well, but you're an Air American pilot, so you would know. Who else would figure it out?"

"Everybody," said Dino evenly.

"Well, you know the reason." The reason was that the Browning ammunition was compatible with the Swedish K machine gun, and that all the province offices had been supplied with both weapons, which were judged to be superior to the Colt .45 pistol and its machine-gun counterpart, the famous grease gun.

"I know the reason," Dino said. "Of course, it's no skin off of my ass, but all of us round-eyes in Vietnam already run enough risks as it is—getting shot by a sniper or degutted by some kid with a grenade. But you, you're doubling your risk by telling the whole world you belong to that bad old intelligence agency. So, I just thought I'd give you a tip."

"Thanks."

"Excuse me for butting in?"

Toby laughed at the mild contrition in the dark eyes. "Dino, my business is collecting information. When somebody gives me valuable information without me even asking for it, I'd have to be a damned fool to get mad at him for it."

Dino's face recovered its expression of insouciance. "You're gonna be one of our good ones, Toby," he said happily, and eased the throttle forward.

They fanned up a cloud of dust behind them as they rolled along the strip to the other end. "That's Ski there with Ben," Dino shouted. "Guess he wants me to take him back home, although Can Tho didn't say anything to me about it. John Kunowski's his name. Stationed in Moc Hoa. Doesn't have much to do up there, and he gets lonesome, so he visits around."

Toby had never heard of Ski, but he did know about Ben Compton from the briefings and conversations in Can Tho. The two men came to the side of the plane, Ski carrying a small airline bag.

"Hi, Dino," said Ski, when Dino had throttled back. "How about a ride to Moc Hoa?"

"I'm supposed to go over to Cao Lanh from here. Did you check with Can Tho?"

"Yep. Called Jerry on the sideband a few minutes ago. He said to call in as soon as you're airborne, and he'll adjust your schedule for you."

"Hop in."

The man waited until Toby had removed his own luggage from behind the seat, two large suitcases, battered and labeled by much travel in Europe and South America.

"You're Toby Busch," he said, tossing his little bag into the plane.

"That's right."

"I'm Ski Kunowski." He extended his hand and Toby gripped it.

"Glad to meet you."

"I'm up in Moc Hoa. Come up and see me after you get settled in."

"I may do that," Toby replied. He was being polite. He didn't know whether he would have the opportunity or the desire to make such a visit. Ski wedged himself into the plane and closed the door, and half a minute later Dino had lifted them off the runway and left a welcome silence behind.

"I'm Ben Compton," said the other man, extending his hand.

"I've heard a lot about you," said Toby, returning the firm grip. He knew that Ben was an army major, detached for special civilian duty with the CIA for the pacification program. He had served in the Special Forces, the 82nd Airborne, and had been in Korea and many other insurgency areas in Southeast Asia.

He was tall, slim, blond, and blue-eyed. Pleasant-looking. Might even be called handsome by some, and he moved with the lightness of an athlete. He was neat as a pin, in spite of the dust and heat, and Toby thought that he did not look much like a professional warrior.

They stowed Toby's luggage in the back of the open jeep and clambered into the front seats. "You've kind of got the advantage of me," said Ben, "because I never heard of you until a couple of days ago, and nobody around here knows much about you."

He said this in a cheerful voice, as if he were looking forward to the process of getting acquainted.

"I'm not surprised," said Toby. "I didn't know I was coming to My Tho myself until a couple of days ago."

"Par for the course," murmured Ben. He started the motor

and swung the jeep off the end of the runway to the dusty road, heading toward the town.

"All this is new to me," said Toby.

"You mean the Far East?"

"Well, yes, the Far East is new to me—but what I was talking about was the system of assignments. It's the first time in my whole career that I didn't know what job I would have, even before I left my previous post. You know how it is. You're stationed in Athens, and your tour is about up, and they ask you if you want to go to Cairo as . . . well, on some specific assignment." He remembered that this man was military, under contract to the CIA, and that he had no need to know any details of the organization of a station. Ben looked at him curiously.

"But here in Vietnam," Toby went on, "it's different. You arrive in Saigon, just a warm body, with some intelligence operations experience, they hope, and then they shop you around."

"Did they shop you long?"

"No, sir, they sure as hell didn't. I didn't let them. All the section heads at the station there were lined up to interview me, and they all said how good a job they knew I could do in their sections, but I had a good look at that station, and I said to myself, My God, this is just like a headquarters in the field, and I can do without headquarters duty. So, when they said My Tho needed a P officer, I said: 'I accept! Where's My Tho and what's a P officer?'"

Ben laughed delightedly.

"And here I am," Toby concluded, with an expansive sweep of his hand.

"My new boss."

Toby looked at him quickly, but saw that Ben had made the remark with a matter-of-fact good humor. Toby began to relax in the presence of his new associate.

He looked around at the countryside as they bounced down the road. It was flat delta land, with rice paddies, an occasional clump of trees, small thatched dwellings. A little child was sitting on a water buffalo off to their left, and brought him a flashback of a picture he had seen in his sixth-grade geography book. Cochin China.

"So, how are things in Can Tho?" Ben asked.

"Well, I guess they're all right, but I don't know what standard to use. I've never been there before. In fact, I've never been on this side of the Pacific before."

"You're a clean slate."

"Right."

"That can be an advantage."

"I suppose so."

"How do the people in Can Tho think we're doing out here in the provinces?"

"You mean in the pacification program and things like that?"

"Yeah."

"They seem to be fairly optimistic. Not too good, but not too bad."

Ben nodded thoughtfully. "And what do they think in Saigon?"

"The Saigon people seem to think we've got the VC on the run out in the provinces."

"That figures. Saigon says we're winning, Regional Offices in Can Tho say we're doing fairly well. The picture seems to be colored by the distance."

"And what does the Provincial Pacification Officer from My Tho say?" asked Toby.

"I say we're gettin' our butt waxed."

"The hell you say."

"They're just kickin' the shit out of us here. And not only here, but all over the delta. I can't speak with any authority about the other regions, but the delta, Region Four, is in trouble. Ski is the only guy in the region that isn't as uneasy as hell, and that's because he's got almost no VC up there. Hell, Kien Tuong Province doesn't have much of *anything!*"

"Have all of you been reporting these things to Saigon and Can Tho?"

"They've got the same facts we have. They just interpret them differently."

"It doesn't seem possible that people would put such different interpretations on the same set of facts."

"They look at the statistics. They're at a distance. Statistics is a poor way to estimate your position in unconventional warfare. The closer you get to the action, the less the statistics mean to you."

"Well, they get action in Saigon too, don't they?"

"Oh, sure. They get grenades and bombs and things like that. But there's no doubt about who controls Saigon. And Can Tho, too. Can Tho gets mortared now and then, but they've got the Ninth ARVN close by. But we're out here trying to reclaim towns and hamlets from the VC. The statistics say we're doing it, but a ride around the countryside says like *hell* we are!"

"I've got my work cut out for me, then. We've got to get good intelligence in to Can Tho and Saigon."

"Right."

The countryside certainly didn't look like a battlefield. He saw a man and a woman squatting at work in a large vegetable garden. It was a big enough plot to be a supplier for a town market. The conical straw hats hid the laborers' faces, and gave them the appearance of motionless symbols of the peace that seemed to pervade the land. From the air he had seen lines of craters made by the B-52 bombs, but from ground level among the rice paddies and vegetable gardens he saw none of the ravages of war. Saigon had seemed to be laced together with barbed wire, and Can Tho looked nearly as besieged as Saigon, but here, where the action was, there seemed to be no trace of it, no fear of it, and no preparations for it.

"You've not only got your work cut out for you, Toby, but you've got an obstacle in Can Tho. Did you know that?"

"You talking about Chet Wolleson?"

"Uh-huh."

"News travels fast." Toby had not known Chet was in Can Tho until he arrived there on his way to My Tho. He wondered whether he would have asked for the My Tho assignment if he had known that Chet would be in the chain of command between him and Saigon.

"Well, I don't really know much about it. The fact is, it's really only a kind of gossip. Little Jack, the PRU adviser, was in Can Tho yesterday. Maybe you saw him?"

"Not that I know of. I don't know the man."

"Well, he heard by the grapevine that Chet doesn't exactly think you're God's gift to the Far East."

"That's putting it mildly."

"How come?"

"We were stationed together in Frankfurt. Chet was my supervisor. A young German agent was killed in one of my operations, and Chet thinks I was either stupid or deceitful, or both. I'll tell you about it someday."

"Well, it's lucky he's just the Deputy Regional Officer in Charge. How does the ROIC himself feel about it?"

"I don't know, but he seems like a bright guy and a nice enough fellow. I have an idea he'll want to make his own judgments about me."

"From what I know of Bill Voigt, I think you're right."

They entered the edge of the town. Toby noted that My Tho was no more oriental in appearance than Saigon or Can Tho, although for that matter he had no idea what would make a city appear to be oriental. Ideographic signs on streets and shop windows? The Vietnamese used the alphabet introduced to them by the Portuguese. Pagoda roofs? One did see an occasional pagoda, and these were classically oriental, but most of the other structures could have been lifted out and placed in any other tropical city he had ever been in, without changing the appearance of the city in the slightest.

They turned in at the gate in a high masonry wall. Two massive panels of steel swung inward as they approached, and the jeep drove through without having to stop. Ben waved to the uniformed guards at the gate, and at the corners of the wall, and they saluted him respectfully.

"Nung guards," said Ben.

"Yeah. I noticed people were always talking about Nung guards in Saigon, as if I would know what they are."

"They're ethnic Chinese," said Ben, "that have lived in Vietnam for God knows how many generations. They're supposed to be more loyal to their families and who knows what else than they are to Vietnam, and very few of them ever join the Viet Cong. So we hire them as guards for our buildings and compounds."

"Are they good at it?"

"Seem dependable. You have to keep your eye on them or they tend to goof off, but they're pretty good."

There were sandbag bunkers at each corner inside the outer wall, and similar bunkers were placed strategically near doors to the main building.

"Looks like the place is expecting an attack," Toby commented.

"We get mortared now and then," Ben replied. "You never know when some sapper squad will come in after a mortar barrage and try to blow you up with a satchel charge."

Toby made no further comment, afraid that he might betray the sense of foreboding that had begun to gnaw at him. They took the luggage through the front door of a building that reflected a kind of Latin or Mediterranean style—plain, even severe, on the outside, but spacious, colorful, and artistic on the inside: the old Roman atrium, or the Latin American patio.

The room they now entered had a high ceiling, from which hung big fans that brought to mind Sidney Greenstreet and fezzes and restless natives. The fans were turning slowly. The air was noticeably cooler inside than it was outside. The floor was tiled in blue, and there were columns, pilasters, and ceiling moldings that spoke of its French colonial origins.

Placed neatly about the room were sofas and occasional chairs that Toby recognized as typical USAID bamboo-and-foam-rubber styles, with tables, lamps, and magazine racks to match. It was comfortable and clean, but far from cozy.

"This is a sort of common room," Ben said. "Then we've got the bar over there in that corner, and stereo equipment, and a movie setup, when we can get the film."

The bar corner relieved the severity of the decor to some extent. The bar was of dark wood with high stools. Small easy chairs and cocktail tables nearby gave the scene an appearance of intimacy and comfort.

"We don't try to air-condition this space," Ben went on. "It's too big, for one thing, and the way it's built, high ceiling and fans and all, it stays fairly cool."

"Seems very nice."

"Out in back there's another building. Used to be servants' quarters, I think. We built a breezeway that leads from that door over there back to the other building, and made that building into our office. Living spaces are upstairs."

There was a stairway to the right of the front entrance, and they ascended it to the second floor. Ben and Little Jack had rooms opposite one another at one end of the corridor, and shared a bathroom. There was a guest room farther along, and at the end was the room that T. C. James had occupied. That room would now be Toby's. It had a private bath.

Ben opened the door to Toby's new room, and a wave of chilled air struck them. There was a large window on the far side, but Toby could not see through the heavy, translucent curtains. The panes, he knew, would be made of Plexiglas, as most windows were in this warring land. An air conditioner throbbed in its niche at the base of the window, and beyond that, somewhere in the rear of the building, he could hear the persistent muffled roar of the diesel generator, a sound he had heard wherever he walked or stayed since he had arrived in Vietnam. The American presence was peppered through the country, and no local power supply, however adequate it might be for the modest needs of the Vietnamese, could begin to satisfy the American appetite for light, refrigeration, air conditioning, appliances, and gadgets. Wherever they settled, the Americans brought their appliances, and the power to run them.

They put the luggage on the low double bed and Toby looked around. There was a desk against one wall, a small table, an easy chair with a floor lamp, a big steel wardrobe, a chest of drawers, and a large mirror affixed to the wall. On another wall were a number of hooks, from which hung a Swedish K, with several magazines of ammunition in a satchel beneath it, a steel helmet, an M-2 carbine, a flak jacket, and miscellaneous web gear.

The sight of this battle paraphernalia made him uneasy again. He had coped with danger many times, but it had never been the danger of open combat. His was a profession of wits, and if your wits were sharper than your adversary's you could foresee the risks and avoid them. If you used your wits to avoid combat, you would be a coward. What would combat be like? How would he handle himself if it came?

"You've got your own bathroom, through that door there," Ben said. "Little Jack and I have got a big one at the other end of the hall."

"How is it between you and him?" Toby asked. "You being a major and him a sergeant, and both of you living in the same quarters and sharing a bathroom?"

"For this work we're civilians. He hasn't been here long, and I haven't been able to get a good judgment of his professional skills, but we get along OK. It's 'Ben' and 'Little Jack' while we're in this situation. The minute we got back in uniform, of course, we'd be military again."

"That makes sense."

"I'll leave you to get settled," Ben said. "When you're ready, or if you need anything in the meantime, I'll be in the office."

"Thanks. I'll be down shortly."

Ben went out and closed the door.

Toby had had the impulse to say to Ben that he had impressed him very much with his simplicity, directness, and intelligence, and that he had a conviction they would get along well and probably become fast friends. In the Tau Kappa Epsilon house at Iowa University years ago, he would have said so to a new friend. But in his years of clandestine operations he had had to learn to resist such impulses. There would be plenty of time for Ben to discover that Toby was well impressed with him, and was pleased to be associated with him. If, in the meantime, it turned out that Ben was not quite what a first impression showed him to be, Toby was not committed to him in any way.

He began to unpack. Gregarious by instinct, he hated these restrictions on human relationships. It was one of the parts of his profession that he found unvaryingly distasteful. His entire career was one of dealing with, and using, human beings, and he had had to train himself away from his instinctive reactions to them. He had seen too many cases, some of them involving himself, in which a charming agent, who seemed to be such a kindred spirit in ideas and philosophies, sincerely dedicated to the free and messy political life of nontotalitarian governments, would turn out to be nothing more than an expert con man who would give you false information, run nonexistent collection nets, and embezzle your money, at the same time slapping you on the back. If you had become close friends with the agent, you found yourself excusing him, justifying him, defending him— maybe even lying about him to headquarters, a deadly mistake in the intelligence business.

He smiled a little sadly as he put away the neatly ironed clothes. Mary Lynn was meticulous about keeping his clothing neatly arranged and spotless, and this care for his things had been so consistent and unfailing through the years that he had almost ceased to notice it. He noticed it now. Those swift and efficient hands reached all the way from Iowa to touch his heart with a little pang of loneliness as he unpacked. He wondered, with guilty amusement, if he had been married so long that he would miss her attention to his clothing as much as he would miss her attention to his sexual needs. No, it hadn't reached that point yet.

He did miss her already. She had gone with him through all the years and had borne up well under the pressures of secrecy and the irritations of making a home for a man who could never discuss his work, even with his wife, and who did a great deal of that work at outlandish hours of the night. He had depended on her, as well, to bring the children through the first years, when they could be told only his cover story, to an age where their watchful eyes and youthful curiosity would at last become more dangerous than their knowledge of the truth. Then, they were told the truth—just enough to satisfy their curiosity and compel their silence.

She had had the choice: a safe-haven residence in Taiwan or Hong Kong, or a separation allowance and residence in the United States. She did not hesitate. She was now in a small rented house in her hometown in Iowa. It had been a joy for her to move back to that tranquil town, a few blocks from her parents, their polyglot children adapting to Iowa schools as they had adapted to European and South American schools in the past.

He would now see them twice a year. He had never been away from them for such a long time, but they were comfortable and safe, and they were learning what it was like to have a grandma and grandpa. That was good.

He showered and put on one of the clean sport shirts, tan slacks, and brown loafers. Mary Lynn thought this had been a directed assignment. When you got a directed assignment, which was often talked about in the CIA but rarely happened, you had your choice. You went or you resigned. You agreed to those terms before you were ever hired.

But this assignment had been directed, not by the CIA, but by his own inner compulsions. He had volunteered for the duty. Even as sensible a woman as Mary Lynn would never have understood why. This was where the action was today, and a man in this business wanted action. The days of the cold war, when he had cut his operational teeth against the clandestine power of the Soviet bloc pushing against the eastern borders of Europe—those days were gone. The power was now pushing, indirectly but relentlessly, in Vietnam, and he wanted to be there.

Mary Lynn was afraid for him. She had cried when he left. He had not seen tears in those lovely hazel eyes in a long time, especially tears shed about him, and they had touched him deeply.

Another reason for volunteering was the question of his record. So far as he could tell, the Frankfurt incident, although a serious setback, had not blighted his career. He was sure that there were some big, unanswered questions in his file, and that in a pinch, where a promotion or a choice assignment might hang in the balance, that unresolved difficulty might swing the balance against him. If he could turn in a good performance, under conditions of danger and hardship, having volunteered for the duty, that would also be in his file, and would tend to resolve in his favor any doubts from previous duty.

He went down the stairs and across the common room, elated and vaguely apprehensive. He was about to plunge once more into the tangle of the work he loved, and this time the tangle was to be complicated by an oriental setting and a vicious war.

2

Toby opened the door to the breezeway, walked across the short distance to the other building, and entered the office. Ben was seated at a desk on one side of the large room, and there was an empty desk on the side opposite him, which Toby surmised would be his own. Behind those desks, in one corner, amid a clutter of file cabinets and typewriter tables, was a third, slightly smaller desk. It had manuals, ammo magazines, a carbine, and other oddments of military equipment on its surface or leaned against it. That one had to be Little Jack's desk.

One wall of the office was almost completely covered by a large relief map of the province. One thing a war did for a country, he thought, was map it down to the last detail.

In the other far corner was a secretary's desk, where a woman was seated with her back to them. She was slender, and had glossy black hair that flowed down her back to her waist, accentuating the pale blue sheen of her *ao dai*. Toby noted the perfect curve of her waistline under the garment, and could see why the *ao dai* was often called the best legacy the French had left to the Vietnamese. American women, who could look so ravishing and luscious in other garments, usually succeeded only in looking vulgar when they put on an *ao dai*.

The woman was concentrating on a long document in her typewriter and did not stop work. Something about her posture made Toby think she would be pretty, but then he thought once again about how wrong impulsive judgments can be, and he

16

inwardly prepared himself to see a broad, coarse face, perhaps pleasant, but unrefined and plain.

"Get settled?" Ben asked.

"Yeah. Room seems fine. How about drinking water?"

"Mrs. Chao boils it for us. She's our cook. You'll find bottles of drinking water in the refrigerator in the kitchen, and in the one behind the bar too."

"Good."

Ben explained the office arrangements briefly, identifying desks and safes. It was expected that Toby would use T.C.'s desk.

"Where is Little Jack?" Toby asked, as they came to the cluttered area.

"He's out at the PRU compound. They're going out on an operation tonight. A VC printing press in a village to the north of here. They're going to try to capture it if they can—or destroy it, if not."

"Little Jack is infantry?"

"That's right. Master Sergeant John Horner. He was in Korea, and he's knocked around quite a bit since then. Special Forces, and so on."

"Is he good?"

"Well, let's put it this way," said Ben with a laugh. "Little Jack doesn't hide his light under a bushel. If you ask him, he'll tell you he's damned good, although he'll say it in a real modest way."

There was no rancor in Ben's voice, but Toby realized that his direct question had been evaded.

"And back here in this other corner," said Ben, leading Toby to where the woman was still busily typing, "is Therese. Therese, I'd like for you to meet our new boss, Mr. Busch."

The woman turned in her swivel chair, and Toby was barely able to suppress a gasp of surprise. Therese was beautiful. Her complexion was impeccable, her mouth soft and full, and her eyes had just enough of the oriental to make them the most inviting and bewitching eyes he had ever gazed into. When she arose, unsmiling, and bowed to him ever so slightly, the lines and movement of her body completed the picture of perfection. She was slender, but there was nothing boyish about her body.

"How do you do, Mr. Busch," she said. Her English seemed fluent, but there were traces of Vietnamese tonality in it.

"I am happy to meet you, Therese. But shouldn't I call you something besides a first name? You are obviously not a little girl."

She did not laugh or smile. She did not seem surly or even timid, but rather sad, and perhaps worried. "Yes," she replied, "I am not a little girl, Mr. Busch." He liked her voice, too. It was soft and sweet. "I am a war widow. But most Americans cannot pronounce my Vietnamese name, so I ask them to call me Therese. It is my Catholic name."

"You are Catholic, then?"

"Yes. I am from Hanoi. One of the refugees."

Hanoi! thought Toby with a start, then cursed himself. Why did he have to pin everybody to an ideological board the minute he met them?

"All right, then," he said. "Therese it is."

"I believe we do not worry so much about names as Americans do," she said quietly, and Toby thought there might be an ever-so-gentle rebuke in her tone.

"Perhaps not. Anyway, I'll let you get back to your work." She nodded politely and returned to her typewriter.

"Now, why don't I show you the rest of the establishment?" Ben suggested. Toby nodded, and Ben led him off to the other rooms and outbuildings of the little compound. One was the small warehouse where Ben kept the supplies for his pacification teams—black pajamas, weapons, ammunition, foodstuffs, first-aid kits, books, office supplies. Off in one corner of the main structure, heavily bunkered with sandbags, was their main storage area. It contained boxes of ammunition, jerry cans of fresh water and fuel, boxes of C rations, racks of rifles and submachine guns, grenades, helmets, and other equipment.

Seeing the weapons reminded Toby. "Dino told me I'd be better off without the Browning pistol," he said.

"Dino is absolutely right," Ben replied laconically. "Here." He handed Toby a Colt .45 pistol in a leather holster. "You can find yourself a web belt for that over there on that rack."

"I've already got the belt."

"There's plenty of ammo in that case over there, and extra clips. Ever handle one of these cannons before?"

"A few times. Years ago."

"We can go over to the police firing range as often as we like, to keep ourselves sharp. I can refresh you on stripping and cleaning it."

"Thanks. I feel less like a billboard for the CIA already."

"Not everybody's sharp like Dino, but he's right. You're better off without the Browning. It's a great pistol, and packs a wallop, but not the wallop *that* big old monster does. That baby will stop a man cold."

"I hope it doesn't come to that," Toby said unthinkingly, and Ben gave him a puzzled look.

They climbed a small stairway to the roof of the house. The roof was flat, and the outer walls of the structure came up to form a parapet about a foot high all around it. The center was bare, but at each corner there was a small, low revetment of sandbags. In and around these revetments were various weapons, one fifty-caliber machine gun on a tripod with a canvas cover, a 57mm recoilless rifle, two M-2 rocket launchers, with boxes of rockets and grenades.

"Little Jack scrounged most of this stuff," Ben said with a mixture of amusement and exasperation. "You'd think he was getting ready to defend Fort Donelson against Grant."

"It looks like he could do it."

"Who knows, maybe it will come in handy some time. Anyway, we've got a drill in case of attack. Little Jack stands by the switches till I get in position on the roof. When I give him the signal, he turns on the floodlights. Then he mans that corner over there. You'll take another corner, and I'll have this one."

"That leaves one corner unmanned."

"Yep. But, hell, the best military units in the world are never up to complete strength in combat. There's always a corner unmanned somewhere. You just fight the battle as it develops."

Toby thought that the floodlights would be as much of an advantage to the Viet Cong as to the defenders, but Ben reassured him. The lights were halfway up the outer walls, and would not silhouette the men on the roof. They would give the defenders a first look at the area in case of an attack, and would destroy the enemy's night vision for the first crucial minutes. An assault force would shoot out the lights as soon as they could, but while they were doing so, the defenders would be shooting at *them*.

There was a house directly across the street, another at some distance on one side, a vacant lot on the other side, and a small canal or irrigation ditch along the back. The sides of the canal had been sloped in such a way that it offered no concealment from observation from the house.

Toby looked at the area, and at the weaponry and the emplacements, lost in thought for some time. "Jesus!" he exclaimed at last. "Is this house in that much danger?"

"How much danger do you mean?"

"So much that all this is necessary?"

"Toby," said Ben slowly, "I think I have kind of the same reaction in a way, because I'm not much on defensive warfare. But where you've got to centralize your activities in one spot in a combat zone, you just naturally prepare as much as you can for *anything*. It would be suicide not to be ready . . . and that may be one value of having all this stuff. They probably know we've got it, and they have to take it into consideration in any plans they may have for this place. They'll know that an assault against us is going to hurt a lot of people."

They went back down to the office, where Ben showed him through the files and extracted from the safes a number of briefing booklets, operational records, chronological files of cables and dispatches.

"I don't want to try to teach an expert how to suck eggs," said Ben, "but I have an idea that if you go through this material first, you'll find that seeing people and places around here will fit in a lot better. And here is one file you ought to study harder than anything else, because this is something that is going to be in our hair for a long time around here."

He handed Toby a thick folder, labeled YENAN BATTALION.

"Oh, yes, I've heard them talking about this in Saigon and Can Tho," said Toby. He sat down at his desk.

Ben perched on the edge of it, placed the folder on the desk, and tapped it with his finger. "This is a main force battalion, and it's usually about four hundred strong. And I wish to God I had an outfit like that fighting under *me.*"

"Good, huh?"

"Any way you look at them. Tough, savvy fighters. Elusive. Well led. They're tearing one part of this province to shreds, and we can't ever pin them down with a big enough force to destroy them."

"They don't operate anywhere except in one part of this province?"

"That's the way it looks. And they're so famous on both sides that they don't have any trouble getting local force battalions to cooperate with them when they need it."

"But I thought main force battalions are like regular army, and the local forces are a kind of militia."

"Yep."

"So how come the Yenan Battalion confines its operations to just one area like this?"

"Damned if I know. It sure isn't normal. The only thing we can figure out is that they're getting ready for something big. We're not sure what it is, but we know that an outfit like that, operating in one particular area, sending local forces on minor operations, ambushing people, assaulting our pacification teams —we know they're workin' on some kind of a plan. They're harassing us, and at the same time they're training themselves."

"What for?"

"I wish to God I knew. I guess that'll be your department—finding out what they're up to."

"Thanks," said Toby drily.

"We've got some ideas, though. It's pretty certain that they'll have to do whatever it is before the next monsoon season. The pattern of their operations doesn't center on anything in particular, although in this province it's heaviest against My Tho. I don't know details about other provinces, but they all seem to have similar patterns. Personally, I think something big is going to happen around Tet."

"What makes you think so?"

"Rumors. A report here and there that Tet is the target date for something. Some people say that the VC wouldn't dare violate the sacred New Year celebration . . . but I don't know. The tempo of their operations seems to point that way."

Toby remembered that his first home leave came about a month after Tet. He made a mental calculation. "That's less than five months away."

"Right."

"Have we got any collection operations at all?"

"Intelligence collection operations?"

"Yes."

"You'd have to look in the files. I don't know much about intelligence operations. My guess is that we haven't got a thing."

"And only five months to go? My God, you can't start with nothing, without even knowing the language, and expect to set up a good collection operation and get anything authenticated and reliable out of it in less than five months. You might do it in peacetime in a European situation, but not here in a combat zone."

"If you don't, we'll be fighting blind," said Ben.

"Does Saigon know about this? Nobody up there mentioned it to me."

"They've probably got some indications. But a lot of what I've told you is something I've just sensed in my gut. How do you report that to Saigon? A lot of the other fellows around the country have got the same feeling, but it's just a feeling. Something big is coming. If we're not ready for it, we're going to get wiped out."

"Five months." Toby stared at the folder.

"This Yenan Battalion is under the command of a guy they call the Tiger. He is also sometimes referred to as Tu Binh, but that's not likely to be his real name. It's like Therese says. The Vietnamese take names kind of casually. But, anyway, the Tiger has got good collection operations, all right. He knows every move we make. Almost as if he had somebody sitting here listening to us."

With a jolt Toby thought of Therese, typing away busily, well within the range of their voices. He must speak to Ben about this casual discussion of confidential information.

"Most important," Ben was saying, "is that he is one of the best tacticians and combat leaders I've ever been up against. He's great, and if he lives through whatever it is that's coming, he'll be one of the military leaders of North Vietnam eventually."

"A pro, huh?"

"Yes, sir. That man plans and executes military operations without a flaw. He swoops in, tears his target to pieces, and gets away fast, without losing more than one or two of his men at the most."

"Well, I'd better get to work then," said Toby.

"Yeah. I'll leave you to your reading. Tomorrow, I suggest we go over to meet the Province Senior Adviser, and then go on over to the Special Police Office and meet the head man."

"That's Colonel Manh?"

"Right. Your counterpart. You'll be in liaison with him, and he knows who you're with. He's a decent guy, and his men seem to be pretty good, but they're up against experts, and they don't know shit from Shinola about intelligence operations."

"They don't?"

"Nope. Neither do I, Toby. We sure have been needing somebody around here that does."

"But you had some training before you came here?"

"Yeah, but most of it was on the pacification program. Which, of course, is my job here. But I ought to know something about intelligence, too. We can't put these teams in contested villages blind—or anyway, we *shouldn't* do it. The VC can come in on them at will and cut them to pieces. Even a sloppy bunch of local forces can do it if they catch them by surprise."

"I can believe it."

"That's why I think the new ICEX program is so important."

The utterance of those secret initials, with the beautiful Northerner in the room, caused Toby's skin to prickle. "We'd better talk about that later, Ben," he said peremptorily, so as to cut off the talk immediately, and he sensed the instinctive military response—obedience. Ben stood up.

"If you need anything, let me know," he said quietly, and went back to his desk.

Toby spent the rest of the afternoon delving in the records and files of the office.

He was perplexed at much of what he saw. Nothing like this had ever happened to him before. A small office, deep in a country that, under other circumstances, would have had only moderate interest for his agency. In liaison with a Special Police force whose functions were an odd mixture of military and police operations. Collecting order-of-battle intelligence, which was outside the charter of the CIA and to a great extent beyond its competence. That was what the Defense Intelligence Agency was for.

Most worrisome of all was the prospect of working in clandestine operations in a culture that was new to him and a language that he could hardly count to ten in. He would have to work through an interpreter, or through agents who spoke English. European languages were only a matter of time and concentration, for they shared a common pool of origin. Oriental languages were different, and there would not be time for him to learn the language well enough to operate in it. French was becoming less and less helpful as years passed in Vietnam, so that even his rather pedestrian French would be of little use to him.

And not one single going operation for the collection of intelligence!

Whatever intelligence was in the files—and there was almost nothing worthy of the name—had come from casual informants, whose authenticity and worth were not established, or had been passed to them from the Special Police, derived from their own collection operations, about which this office knew almost nothing.

Well, he'd have to change all this.

At five o'clock Therese put away her work, closed and locked the safe by her desk, and moved toward the door. She paused by his desk.

"Will you need me for anything more today, sir?"

"No, nothing, thank you."

"You come to our country at a bad time," she said, "but I hope you will like it."

"I like it already, Therese."

"I hope you will be pleased with my work, also."

"I'm sure I will. I notice you don't waste time."

"Vietnam has no time to waste," she said, and with a slight bow she turned and walked out the door.

"She seems so solemn," Toby commented to Ben. "Doesn't she ever smile?"

"Not very often. She's a troubled young woman."

"Where does she live?"

"She lives in a kind of a slum or tenement district across town a little way. She's got a little motorbike she rides."

Even as he spoke they heard the buzz of a small motor, and the gates clanked as she was let out of the compound.

"She sure is a knockout," Toby mused.

"I figured you would notice that."

"The reason I clammed up a minute ago is that ICEX is a restricted program, and I'm sure she hasn't been cleared to hear about it."

"I guessed as much," said Ben, shortly.

"I don't know even whether she's been cleared properly for the job she does have. Do you?"

"All I know is that T.C. hired her. I guess he had her cleared. You could look it up. I never had access to the security papers."

"I'll look tomorrow. If there's any doubt about her, I want to get it cleared up right now, because if we have to let her go for some reason I want to do it before I fall in love and try to run away to the jungle with her."

Ben laughed gleefully. "Yes, sir, she sure makes the old juices run."

They went into the main building, and Ben put a record on the stereo while Toby mixed drinks. They sat at the bar talking quietly of inconsequential things until Mrs. Chao, a slight, rather wrinkled and graying woman, announced that dinner was ready.

The dinner was delicious, although Toby did not recognize most of the dishes. Ben named them for him. "Vietnamese. You can't get it in a restaurant, even in Vietnam, because Vietnamese cooking doesn't adapt itself well to restaurant service. This is Mrs. Chao's way of saying welcome."

Toby thanked Mrs. Chao and complimented her on the meal, and she beamed at him.

After dinner they sat at the bar again and talked, getting acquainted. From force of habit, Toby got most of the information and gave very little. His evasion of questions he did not want to answer was as smooth as it was unconscious on his part, and it did not dampen the cordiality of the moment.

Ben had been in Vietnam in one capacity or another for many years, and had been about to return to military duty in the United States when he was contacted by a CIA representative. He was signed up under a contract program, trained in the United States and in the pacification school at Vung Tau, and now had forty-two pacification teams under his supervision in Dinh Tuong Province. He had made one attempt at marriage, but his wife had found no way to domesticate the man or to steer him into a different profession, and the divorce had been amicable.

They spoke of Little Jack and the Provincial Reconnaissance Units. Armed intelligence collection squads. Night fighters. Man for man the best warriors in Vietnam, on either side. Many of them ex–Viet Cong, who had "rallied" to the government side, as the peculiar English of the war described it, under the Chieu Hoi program. Each province in Vietnam had one of these units, about a hundred strong, "advised" by an American.

Ben had no authority over Little Jack, since the PRU program was not within the structure of his pacification operations. They collaborated in the defense arrangements for the house, but did not work together. Little Jack would be Toby's responsibility to supervise.

Toby was interested in combat experiences, but on that subject Ben's evasive skill matched his own. He merely steered the conversation away from tales of battle. Toby wondered why.

A nightcap, and Toby noticed the first, familiar rumblings of a coming diarrhea. He was not surprised. It never failed. In fact, he was surprised that it had not come sooner. A couple of days of intestinal upset, perhaps with some medication to ease it if it got too severe, and his system would be adjusted to the intestinal flora of his new location. He was glad he had a bathroom to himself. He knew he'd spend some time there tonight, often in waves of nausea that would make him want above all to be alone.

He said good night to Ben, who was sitting pensively in an easy chair, toying with a glass of whisky and water, listening to a tape of Roger Williams. Toby was not sorry to leave. The arpeggios and filigrees of Roger Williams distressed and bored him. Amplified and purified as they were by this high-quality electronic equipment, they filled the room from wall to wall with cascades of sterile syrup. Ben obviously was lost in pleasure among them.

Toby's room was cool, so cool that by the time he had brushed his teeth and prepared for bed he was slightly chilly, and he pulled the light woolen blanket over him gratefully. The Vietnamese must think the Americans insane, to spend so much fuel and machinery to cool a room down in the tropic night, and then put on a blanket to keep warm. The diarrhea had not yet come, and he drifted pleasantly into sleep.

He knew that he had not been asleep long when the wrenching of his gut awoke him. He turned on the light by the bed, slipped his feet into two plastic zoris, walked to the bathroom, switched on the light there, and sat down for the first of what he knew would be several convulsive evacuations that night. This first one was violent enough to make him feel justified in taking Lomotil, and he resolved to get a couple of pills from his kit before he went back to bed.

The twisting and heaving of his bowels subsided and he turned to get paper, and cursed the empty cardboard tube on the roller. He would tear the hide off whoever was responsible for this. He looked around the room. There had to be spare rolls. Where would they be?

There was a cabinet on the far wall, and he got up and waddled over to it.

He felt, rather than heard, the tremendous explosion, and the next thing he knew he was lying flat on the floor, halfway out of the bathroom door, which had been blown from its hinges by the blast.

For several seconds he lay there, trying to collect his thoughts, taking a mental stock of his body.

Ben burst from his own room, carrying a carbine. His eyes darted here and there, and he stepped across Toby's prone form and looked at the bathroom.

There was a gaping hole in the outer wall, beside the stool, and another one in the opposite wall where the projectile had exited. The air was cloudy with plaster dust and the smell of explosive.

"B-forty," said Ben tersely.

The B-40 rocket, hand-launched. The old German *Panzer-faust,* smaller than the American bazooka, but with astounding powers of penetration. A favorite weapon of the VC—light and powerful.

Ben turned off all the lights in the room and bathroom, and shouted something in Vietnamese down the inner corridor.

"I sure hope that's the right word for floodlights," he muttered, "and I hope Mrs. Chao knows what switches I mean." He stepped into the bathroom again and flung open the window and stood waiting. The area around the house was suddenly bathed in a brilliant light. Toby staggered weakly to his feet and looked out the window in the direction Ben was staring. Ben had calculated the trajectory and knew exactly where to look.

There, on the slope of the canal, was a small figure clad in dark clothing. The figure was standing upright, intent upon fitting another round into his rocket launcher.

"I've got to remember to get a heavy rifle in my room," Ben murmured. "This thing will have to do for now." He raised the carbine to his shoulder, fired one round, and the figure in the ditch crumpled silently to the ground.

They waited for a time, motionless.

"What are we waiting for?" asked Toby.

"To see if any more of them are around."

"Oh."

Ben called something in Vietnamese through the open window, went back into the bedroom, and turned on the low bed lamp. "Are you all right?" he asked, coming back to where Toby was crouched in the bathroom.

"I think so," Toby replied. He was nervous to the point of making inane jokes. "It's a hell of a time to try to kill a man, right when he's taking a crap. I thought there was some kind of a gentlemen's agreement in war that that was one time you didn't fire on the enemy."

"Were you sitting on the can?" Ben asked, astonished.

"No, I was looking for toilet paper. Some idiot had left the paper holder empty."

Ben burst out laughing, and Toby glowered at him.

"Frankly," he said, "I don't see anything so goddamned funny about it. Ridiculous and stupid, yes, but not funny."

"I'm sorry, Toby. I couldn't help thinking that Chi Hai has just saved your life."

"Who?"

"Chi Hai. That's Mrs. Chao's daughter. She takes care of the bedrooms. If she had put paper there, half of you would still be sitting on that stool. Look." He switched on the light.

Toby saw with horror that he had been sitting squarely in the rocket's path. If he had not moved at that precise moment, it would have caught him slightly above the waist, and would surely have cut him in two.

Ben turned off the light.

"Are you going out to get the body?" Toby asked.

"The guards will handle things from here on."

"What will they do with it?"

"They'll take the weapons and leave the body."

"Leave it?"

"Yeah. His family will come to pick him up. No sense making

it worse than it is. They'll come in the dark and they'll take care of him."

"His family? Do families travel with the VC?"

"This was a local kid. I've seen him before. Probably a member of a local force battalion or a sapper squad."

"Just decided he was going to come and shoot at us?"

"Make no mistake about it, Toby," said Ben, "that wasn't just a little adventure. The VC don't operate that way. It had a purpose. Probably just wanted to let us know that they knew you had arrived. Kill you if they could, but even if they didn't we'd know that they know who you are and where you sleep. It's part of the terror."

"You mean that rocket was really aimed at *me,* and not just the house?"

"No question about it. Why would he aim at the corner if he was just aiming at the house? That fellow has probably been out there in the shadows for some time getting ready to fire. When your light came on he knew what was up, and knew he shouldn't miss the opportunity."

"Christ, what a thing to tell a man that's already got the shits!" It had never occurred to him that the enemy might zero in on him, personally. As a part of their composite foe, yes, but as a single, personal enemy—it was frightening. Frightening, hell! It was terrifying!

"Yes, sir," said Ben lightly, "it is some initiation to Region Four."

"If it wasn't for the honor of the thing . . ." Toby began, but couldn't remember the rest of the quip. Then he remembered his condition. "Ben, will you get the hell out of here and let me clean myself up?"

"OK, Toby. Just don't turn the lights up any higher."

"I won't. But Ben . . ." he looked earnestly at Ben, who had turned at the door to face him, ". . . are you sure that kid's dead? Maybe . . ."

"He won't fire at you again, Toby."

"That's not what I mean. I mean, if he's only wounded, and out there on the ground."

"He's dead, Toby. I hit him right in the heart."

"How do you know?"

"That's where I aimed. At that distance, and with a stationary target, I don't miss."

Ben left, and Toby stood for a long time as if in a trance. His mind could not cope with, could not even accept as real, the events of the past five minutes.

Slowly he went back into the bathroom and drew some water and washed. He climbed back into bed, knowing that sleep was far away.

3

Bill Voigt sat in his office in the somewhat dilapidated building assigned to the CIA's Regional Officer in Charge within the CORDS compound in Can Tho, and studied the latest ICEX outline from Saigon. Groups of capital letters were peppered liberally all over the page, initials so pervasive and familiar that the people who dealt with them rarely pronounced the letters separately, but simply spoke most of them as the words they appeared to be.

A faint smile played about his lips as he began to read. Here he was, a ROIC sitting in a CORDS office studying an ICEX paper detailing a program to attack the VC by coordinated work between the MACV and the ARVN with the CIA doing the coordinating. Newcomers ought to be given a course in acronyms before they studied Vietnamese.

Come to think of it, you would need more than just a course in acronyms, because sometimes the full title told you no more than the initials did. Military Assistance Command, Vietnam, and Army of the Republic of Vietnam were straightforward and simple. But what in hell was meant by Civilian Operations and Revolutionary Development Support? Bill knew what CORDS was and did, but that title certainly didn't say it. Maybe just U.S. Civilian Operations, Vietnam?

As to the Intelligence Coordination and Exploitation program, whatever its name or cabalistic sign might be, it was one of the first really sensible approaches to the intelligence business he had seen since arriving in Vietnam. Here at last was a plan, something he and his fellow operations officers could put into effect in a logical and organized way. Not that he had many experienced operations officers in his region. None of the other regions did either, for that matter, but he thought he had a more valid complaint than the others, since the delta had about 40 percent of the population and more than half of the VC in South Vietnam. That was the reason he had been so pleased with the assignment of Toby Busch to Region IV, and the reason he had forthwith confirmed Toby's assignment to My Tho, in the province of Dinh Tuong. Dinh Tuong was the worst trouble spot of all the fourteen provinces in the region.

Toby would know what to do, or would soon learn. Of course, the other province officers would learn too, but they were not instructed by the years of previous experience that Toby had. Most of them were nonstaffers, contract men, hastily recruited, trained, and placed. But astonishingly good men for such a large and hurried effort. Ex-smoke-jumpers, ex–Green Berets, ex-policemen, almost any active, physically demanding profession might provide grist for the CIA's pacification mill.

He shook his head slowly as he read. Even the best schemes in the world have got to suffer the ministrations of the bureaucrats. Words like "neutralization," "dichotomies," "interface," and "thrust" leaped out at him from places where simple words would have sufficed, and he rubbed his forehead wearily.

Chet Wolleson poked his head in the door. "That pouch just came in from Saigon," he said. "We got the file on Busch."

"Good. Let me have a look at it."

Chet stepped in and placed a folder on his desk.

"It's a shame it can't be his complete personnel folder," said Bill.

"Yeah. But I've never known headquarters to trust a complete folder to a pouch or a field office."

"No. Will this one contain an account of the Frankfurt incident?"

"I doubt it. Most of that was never put in writing, anyway. But I can fill you in on it."

"Are you going to be able to give it to me without bias, Chet?"

"Yes, I can," said Chet in a cold, even tone. "I don't make any secret of the fact that I don't like him, but I wouldn't give you any account that wasn't true and factual."

"All right. Let me go through this, then we can talk."

Chet left, and Bill opened the file. He folded the top documents over and began reading from the bottom of the pile, which was the beginning.

Tolliver Busch. Bill smiled. He had wondered when he first saw that name in the cable the other day if the man would be nicknamed Tolly. He liked Toby better.

Graduate of Iowa University. Joined agency in 1954. Training records excellent. Cold war days. Tours in Athens, Budapest, Frankfurt, and Bogotá. One short assignment to headquarters. Frequent TDY assignments throughout Europe and Latin America. Temporary duty assignments of such frequency indicated that the man had something rather special in the way of operational skills and drive. People knew him, knew what he could do, and asked to have him sent to them when they needed to have it done, whatever it was. Languages: German, native fluency. Greek and Spanish good. Adequate French, and some Hungarian.

Fitness reports. Bill frowned. Annual fitness reports could be the most misleading documents in a man's file. The natural decency of most rating officers, and the requirements of the form, made for a lot of high-blown rhetoric. Few officers were rated below the *excellent* category, because the erosion of the ratings over the years had brought about a situation where any man who was rated *good* was really poor, and if he was rated *fair,* he was an unmitigated disaster. When a supervisor wanted to show a man to be truly and exceptionally good under this system, he had to use words and phrases that indicated a da Vinci–like mind, and a Christlike character.

Tolliver Busch's fitness reports showed that his supervisors had had an especially high regard for him, until one report from Frankfurt, which damned him roundly with some seemingly mild criticism. Subsequent reports were undoubtedly colored by that one. Supervisors were not supposed to see previous reports by other supervisors before making out their own, but it happened, and a bad report would naturally tend to soften or deflect the impulse to praise.

Or perhaps Busch *had* gone into a slump—a decline?

". . . in this instance showed operational judgment that was not as carefully reasoned as it might have been, and caused serious disruption in one particular operation, with repercussions in other operations of this station."

In the language of the fitness report, that phrase said that Tolliver Busch had done something incredibly stupid.

That report was signed by Chester Wolleson.

Names of other supervisors. Some of them Bill knew personally, some of them by name only, and some of them not at all. Fitness reports never included any operational details, however. He could not tell exactly what it was Toby had done.

He closed the file, drummed nervously on the desk for a moment, leaned back in his chair, and lit a cigarette.

Toby had volunteered for assignment to Vietnam. That could mean any number of things. Chet had been the key supervisor who had given him his bad fitness report. Had probably brought delays to otherwise merited promotion. Perhaps had set a ceiling on Toby's career that might never be lifted.

Chet Wolleson was a good operations officer. He came recommended highly, and Bill had been pleased at the way Chet had taken hold of his responsibilities. Chet wanted and demanded action, and he gave as good as he got.

On the other hand, he had less tact and sensitivity than a person needed in a supervisory position. Energetic himself, and dedicated to the job during every waking hour, he could not understand anyone who could take his mind off work for a time to relax. He tended to be impatient with associates who were not as unrelentingly serious about the job as he was.

Admittedly, his blunt and often brutal treatment of those in his charge was accompanied by an equally fierce loyalty to the same persons when outsiders were involved. He could flay a subordinate alive, and five minutes later send an acid cable defending that same subordinate against any questions or insinuations from headquarters.

Toby Busch might be an exception. He detested Busch.

What a can of worms! Bill crushed out his cigarette and pressed a button, and Laura came to the door. She was plump and dark, a pleasant young woman, and a surprisingly good secretary. The best ones were not usually offered, or would not accept, assignments to Vietnam.

"Will you ask Mr. Wolleson to come in, please?"

"Yes, sir."

He leafed idly through the file as he waited. He wondered what kind of an impression his own file would make on somebody higher up the line. Again the faint smile tugged at the corners of his mouth. It would certainly be a bigger file than this one, old-time intelligence whore that he was. OSS in Burma and the Philippines. Changeover to CIA, cold war, Korea, Japan, Thailand. For a man from Massachusetts, he had certainly managed to get his life hopelessly entwined and identified with the affairs of the Far East. And here he was in the latest of the seemingly endless oriental wars, trying to do the right thing.

In this one, however, his own son was also involved. The smile turned to a frown as he thought of Will. A lieutenant in the 25th Division, stationed in II Corps. Probably a good soldier. Had Bill's passion for Far Eastern affairs guided the boy inexorably to his present occupation and location? A man wants his son to be a good citizen, and a good soldier if it came to that, but in Will's case was it necessary?

Chet opened the door.

"Let's talk about Busch," said Bill.

Chet sat down in the bamboo-and-foam-rubber chair opposite the desk. He waited for Bill to begin.

38

"His file isn't really bad," Bill said.

"No, I suppose not," Chet replied noncommittally.

"Except for that report you gave him in Frankfurt."

"It was justified."

"He's had a lot of TDYs all over the world. He apparently has got something people know about and need. Know what it is?"

"Yeah. He's a recruiter. That fellow could recruit Mao Tse-tung if he could get ten minutes alone with him."

Bill whistled softly. No wonder they asked for him! If there was one single virtue that the agency coveted it was the ability to recruit agents. Everything the agency did was based on re-cruited agents.

"You bring Busch into a station," Chet continued tonelessly, "and give him a couple of hours with a file on the prospect, and then turn him loose. If the man is recruitable, he'll get him. If he isn't, he cools the approach out in such a way that there aren't any unpleasant repercussions."

"Sounds pretty impressive."

"It is."

"And yet you don't think much of him?"

"I would not have accepted him for the Delta Region if I had been ROIC."

"All because of something that happened in Frankfurt?"

"That, and his attitude at the time, and ever since."

"What happened?"

"Well, he came to Frankfurt out of Budapest. I was Foreign Intelligence Ops Chief in Frankfurt at that time. Operations are a bit different in a denied area, of course. He was pretty critical of some of our operational procedures in Frankfurt, but I figured it was just because he had come from a tight situation, and that he'd relax a little bit when he got used to Frankfurt. He was replacing Ernie Free, and they just had two weeks overlap before Ernie had to leave. I don't know whether you know Ernie?"

"No, I don't think so."

"Well, Ernie's principal operation was one he was pretty

proud of, and he'd been working for a long time to get it started. I thought it was damned good. It was a net based in Bad Neustadt for cross-border operations into East Germany, and it looked like it had good chances of developing operations into Soviet territory too, although that was still pretty far in the future.

"So, when Busch arrives he looks over this file, and Ernie starts making arrangements to hand over the principal agent, but Busch right there dug his heels in. He didn't like the sound of the principal agent, and said he didn't want to meet him personally, but wanted to work with him through a cut-out until he could test him and authenticate him.

"Now, this was an old ex-Gehlen man, and that's what bothered Busch. He said he didn't see how we could ever run a unilateral operation with an agent that used to belong to Gehlen. How could we be sure the guy was ours now, and not still Gehlen's? But Ernie had ironclad proof that the guy had really broken with Gehlen, and in fact, the Gehlen people sent us a mildly derogatory report on the guy when we sent his name buried in a list for name checks.

"So Busch and Ernie and I sat down and talked it over, and I said I didn't think we ought to waste time testing the guy any more. And so Busch said all right, he would do it, but he wanted me to know he didn't like it one bit, and he thought the operation had holes big enough to drive a tank through."

"Did he put that in writing?"

"No."

"That says something in his favor, it seems to me."

"Frankly, I don't think he would have dared to put it in writing, because Ernie Free is one of the best ops officers I've ever worked with, and the way he built that net and handled the paper and administrative processing was a classic. Perfect. He looked into every danger and every possibility of a flap, and either eliminated it or resolved it as well as possible and made the situation a matter of record. We were beginning to get some preliminary take from it, and it looked good.

"Now, after Ernie was gone, Busch came to me and said he still wanted to test this operation, even if he was already blown to the principal agent, and so I said all right, go ahead and test it, but for God's sake get the goddamned thing going and keep it moving.

"Busch had recruited a young German university student, and was going to put him into the net to report back directly to him. I thought it was a waste of time, but I gave him the OK, and he went to work.

"What I didn't know, and what he never told me, was that he intended to *dangle* that kid. He wasn't going to introduce him to the principal agent and have the agent put the kid to work. He was going to set him up so that the principal agent would 'discover' the kid and bring him into the net without knowing that Busch had anything to do with it. He was going to penetrate his own operation at the middle echelon."

"Well, Christ," said Bill, "there's nothing wrong with that. It's a pretty good way to test an operation if you've got the time and the operation is important enough. I've done it myself."

"Yes, but in this case he used an inexperienced kid, up against an old pro, and sent him in without enough training."

"What happened?"

"Busch found the kid on his front doorstep a few weeks later. The kid's body was a pulp from bullets. Busch was never able to contact the principal agent again, not even by emergency or fallback arrangements. That agent was telling us that if that was the way we wanted to play, we'd have to play without him and his friends."

"Maybe Busch was right? Maybe the net was an East German or a Soviet operation against us. Or maybe just a paper mill, pure and simple?"

"No, sir! During a couple of years after that, our people managed to pick up an agent or two who had been members of that net, and there is no question that it was legitimate. They weren't sure exactly what had happened, but they did know that the principal agent got pissed off as hell at the Americans and called the whole thing off.

"So Busch not only succeeded in getting the kid killed, he also wiped out a chance for our station to set up what might have been one of the best collection operations in Europe."

Bill sat and stared into the distance for a time. At last he sighed, got up, gathered the papers out of his in-box, put them in his safe and twisted the knob to lock it. He tugged at the drawers to make sure they were locked, inspected the office carefully for stray papers, then went to the door.

"It's past quitting time," he said. "Let's go have a drink."

"I'll have to secure my office first. See you down there in a minute."

Bill stopped at Laura's desk. "I'll be over at the bar, Laura. There are some papers in my out-box for you, but the rest of the office is secure."

"OK, Mr. Voigt."

He walked down the stairs and paused at the air operations counter, near the front door of the building. Jerry Burkholder was sitting there surrounded by his big wall charts, his communications equipment, clipboards, schedules, and other paraphernalia.

"What's up, Jer?" Bill asked.

"Nothing much, Bill. Dino took Ski back up to Moc Hoa, and then he had to make an emergency run over to Chau Doc to pick up a wounded PRU and bring him to the hospital here."

"Jesus, that little Helio isn't much of a thing to haul a wounded man in."

"It was the only thing we had within range, and he couldn't wait for anything bigger."

"Anything else?"

"Nope. Everything's quiet. Quieter than I've seen things for a couple or three years. I don't like it."

Bill shook his head resignedly. "I don't either." Chet joined him. "I'll be over in the bar for a while if anything comes up," Bill told Jerry.

"Right."

They walked across the paved driveway into the little space that served the Americans living and working in this compound as a bar and mess hall. The bar was dimly lighted, and the walls were covered with woven reeds, giving it an atmosphere of South Pacific informality. They sat at a table near the far wall. Bill ordered his usual gin and tonic and Chet his usual CC and water.

"Chet," Bill said as they sipped their drinks, "I'm going to give Busch every benefit of the doubt. I'm not going to restrict him in any way in his operations. I'll keep my eye on him, but officially I have no reason to doubt his abilities or his judgment except for that one fitness report, which has been followed by some other fitness reports that neither refute yours nor bear it out."

Chet nodded. "I hope you won't be sorry."

"By the way, where is this other guy, this Ernie Free, now?"

Chet hitched forward in his chair excitedly. "That's another thing that pisses me off. You see, I persuaded Ernie to come out here when I came, because I wanted him with me. He works like a demon and he's one of the best ops officers I know, as I told you. But when he got to Saigon they ignored my request to have him assigned down here, and sent him up to Nha Trang."

"What's he doing up there?"

"He's the P officer up there. Last I heard, he had set up a penetration of the Provincial Committee of Kanh Hoa Province. It's one of the few we've got anywhere in the country, and maybe the best. And to think we could have had him down here, if those bastards up in Saigon had done what I wanted."

Two USAID nurses came in, and Bill motioned them to the table beside him. They were followed almost immediately by Dino, and Jess Theodorides, a helicopter pilot for Air America.

With Dino at the table, serious conversation was almost out of the question. He leered ferociously at the tiny barmaid and made her laugh. He kidded Cynthia and Sheila, the nurses, deplored everything Greek, for Jess's benefit, and spoke scornfully of flying anything that had an upside-down ceiling fan sticking out the top.

Everyone joined in the banter except Chet, and Bill was mildly uncomfortable for him. Chet had no fund of small talk. He seemed not to be able to talk to anyone about anything except his work. When he had at last finished his drink and left to go back to his office, Bill wondered if he had any inkling that the cordial farewells from the table reflected nothing more than relief at his departure.

Bill sipped his drink and sat back happily. These gatherings occurred regularly, and he was glad. In Can Tho they had little else to do during leisure hours. They drank more than they should, but he knew of no alcohol problems among them. It was overindulgence, but it was civilized. It helped shut the door for a time on the grim things that were going on in the country around them.

He had lost the thread of the conversation.

"I was just saying," Dino informed him, "that King Agesilaus here agrees with me on one thing."

"What's that?"

"When you fly, the most likely place to get shot is right in the ass," Dino said, serious now. "But Jess and I signed contracts to fly civilian aircraft for a civilian organization. When there is combat going on, I don't fly where it is."

"Right," said Jess.

"The army can do the combat flying."

"Right."

"If the Charlies ever shoot *me* in the ass, they're going to have to get under an easy chair or a bar stool to do it."

4

Toby came downstairs to breakfast, and found Ben already seated at the table with a cup of coffee before him.

"How'd you sleep?" Ben asked.

"I won't lie to you. I was pretty tense."

"Gut still rumbling?"

"I took a couple of Lomotils, and they fixed me up, I think. From long experience with this kind of thing, I would say that my insides feel like it's all over."

"Good."

"Is the body gone?"

"Yeah."

"That bothered me more than the diarrhea, I think."

"What, getting shot at?"

"Well, sure, but mainly thinking about that kid out there dead, and his family, and all."

"Oh." Ben nodded, but Toby sensed that he did not understand.

Mrs. Chao came in, immaculately clean and cheerful, and set a cup of coffee before him. It wasn't bothering her, obviously, although she had seen the action too. "Bacon and eggs . . . soon," she said, nodding vigorously. He smiled his thanks and she went back into the kitchen.

"Minnie'll be back pretty soon, and we'll get him to arrange for repairs to the bathroom."

"Who's Minnie?"

"Tran Van Minh. Not our famous friend, 'Big Minh.' This one is our general manager, and handyman, and interpreter, and adviser on things Vietnamese. He went out with Little Jack on last night's PRU operation."

"Is that part of his duties?"

"No. Nobody makes him do it. I think he senses that the PRUs would turn into a gang of chicken thieves pretty quickly if they aren't led right, and he likes to be along to help out. He wants the Vietnamese to fight their own war."

"Sounds like quite a guy."

"If we didn't have Minnie around we'd have to hire six other men to do the things he does."

"Tran would be his family name, and Minh would be his given name, if I remember the Vietnam familiarization course correctly."

"Right."

"So you would call him either Minnie, or just Minh, or Mr. Tran?"

"Wrong. There aren't that many family names in Vietnam. Once you've used Tran and Hoang and Ho and Nguyen and a dozen or so others, there aren't any more. All a family name does is tell you what ancestral tribe the person claims to belong to. The given name is the one that separates him from other people, and so they say Ong—Mr.—Minh, not Ong Tran, and we round-eyes follow suit in our various languages and say Mr. Thieu, for example, instead of Mr. Nguyen."

"And Mrs. Chao," said Toby with a smile, as that small person came in and laid plates of food on the table.

She smiled back at him, ducked her head quickly, and returned to the kitchen, and the two men began to eat. The bacon was crisp and the eggs done just right. This part of the duty, at least, was not going to be a hardship.

"That thing doesn't seem to bother you, Ben, even if it did kind of get to me."

"What thing?"

"Killing that fellow last night. It doesn't seem quite real that a person could kill a man and not have the slightest impulse or desire to talk about it afterwards. Do you know what I mean? It made a big impression on me, but it doesn't seem to have had any effect on you at all."

"It's part of my profession," said Ben quietly.

"Yeah. Sure."

Toby ate in silence. Ben's attitude was right and normal, of course. In a war you shoot to kill. You aim at the heart.

But his mind rebelled against it all. Even though that kid was an enemy, there was something immensely sad about the crumpling of that young body so swiftly and silently in response to the crack of the carbine. Seeing it huddled there, lifeless, alone in death, he had remembered young Gerd, huddled on his doorstep that morning.

"I didn't mean to sound like a preacher or a saint," he said.

"You didn't."

"I guess it must sound crazy to you, but I couldn't help feeling a little sorry for that kid."

"No, it doesn't sound crazy. But while you're feeling sorry for him, don't forget that he was trying to kill you."

Toby shook his head. "I guess I'll never forget that."

The noise of the gates opening brought them both to their feet. They went to the door and saw a dusty jeep pulling into the space beside the other two under the shed roof that slanted down from the inner side of the compound wall.

A big muscular man climbed from behind the wheel, picked up an M-16, pouches of clips, and a pair of binoculars from the back of the vehicle, and came toward them. His passenger, a slight, erect Vietnamese, dressed in fatigues, retrieved an M-2 carbine from the vehicle and followed him.

"How'd it go, Little Jack?" asked Ben.

"We got ambushed," said Little Jack wearily.

"Bad?"

"No, we saw the situation before we were fully committed,

and pulled out. One of the men got a couple of fragments from a claymore. That's all."

"That's lucky."

"Damn right."

"Little Jack, this is Toby Busch. Little Jack Horner, Toby."

"Hello," said Little Jack. "I saw you from a distance down at Can Tho the other day, but didn't get a chance to say hello." He crushed Toby's hand in a big paw. Toby could see why the nickname stuck. The name of the Mother Goose character was wildly inappropriate for this giant. He was about six feet four inches, and must have weighed two hundred twenty pounds, all of it bone and muscle.

"And this is Tran Van Minh," Ben continued.

The Vietnamese extended his comparatively small hand, and now it was Toby's turn to feel like a bear.

"How do you do, Mr. Busch," Minh greeted him.

"Everybody around here calls him Minnie," said Ben.

"Well, I . . . er . . . Mr. Minh . . ." Toby began.

"If you wish to call me Minnie, I will not mind," said the man.

"All right, then: Minnie."

Minnie had the smooth complexion of the Indochinese. His hair was cut short and parted on one side, with deep indentations on either side where the hairline was receding, although he seemed fairly young. His ears stuck out from his head, his teeth were large and perfect, and when he smiled a mass of laugh lines radiated from the corners of his eyes. The big ears and the big teeth would have given him a comical, perhaps even a clownish, appearance were it not for something in his eyes that spoke of a keen intellect and a serious character.

"What happened?" Ben asked, as they trooped through the house to the office.

"You know the village we were targeting?"

"I've never been there, but I know where it is."

"Well, we was coming up along this canal that leads in from the south, and we got to a place where a big high footbridge goes across it—right at the edge of the village. It was dark, and I couldn't see clear to the head of the line, but the point man tripped a claymore that was someplace close to the end of that footbridge."

"The man that tripped it was the one that was wounded?"

"Yeah. And then we come under fire from three sides all at once, but we bugged out before they could close the door behind us."

"They knew you were coming."

"They sure as hell did. It was that goddamned Yenan Battalion is what it was."

Ben frowned. "Doesn't sound like it to me."

"Whattaya mean? I was there. That ambush was set up by professionals."

"That claymore sure wasn't rigged by any professional."

"How do you figure that?"

"Figure it out for yourself. When a professional rigs a claymore, the man that trips it gets blown to pieces, not just nicked with a couple of fragments. If you were in my platoon and you rigged up a claymore that didn't do anything except nick the point man and alert the enemy and let them escape, I'd have you digging latrines for a year. The Yenan Battalion doesn't work that way. Sounds more like a local force battalion to me."

"It wouldn't of if you'd a been there," Little Jack huffed, and went into the dining room.

They heard the clank of the gates and the buzz of the motorbike. Therese came in, clad in a different *ao dai* from yesterday's. This one was a tunic of soft pink over trousers of satiny white. They were spotless.

She greeted them politely and went directly to her desk. Toby caught a faint fragrance as she moved past him, and suddenly realized that he was staring intently at that perfect body and the lovely, melancholy face. He looked away quickly.

"You can see what we're up against, Toby," said Ben, himself seemingly caught in the same trance as Toby. "Whatever it was that hit those guys last night, it was certainly a trap, and it was prepared before the PRUs ever got near them."

"Does it always happen that way?"

"Not always. Sometimes an operation will go off without a hitch, but when it does I always figure it wasn't because the VC didn't know about it, but probably because they just couldn't get forces in place in time to ambush them. Or maybe because they knew the operation wasn't worth ambushing."

"It's a hell of a note."

"Yeah, and Little Jack has got an almost unbroken string of these ambushes. I feel kind of sorry for him, in a way."

Toby sat at his desk and drummed on its surface with his fingers. "Ben," he said, "any way you look at it, there's only one answer to this problem. We've got to find out how the information is leaking out."

"You'll know how to do that," Ben replied. "I sure don't. Let me know if I can help."

Toby nodded and Ben left. Toby turned in his chair and looked at Therese, who, with her back to him, was working at her typewriter. Might as well start on the most obvious suspect. But it wasn't going to be easy or pleasant. He got up and walked back to her desk.

"Therese, may I interrupt you for a minute?"

"Certainly, Mr. Busch," she said, turning quickly to face him.

"I want to find out something about the files that are kept here in the office."

"Yes, sir." She rose and opened the safe by her desk. "This is my safe." She flicked through the files, her fingers precise and delicate. He steeled himself against the nearness of her body and looked over the tabs on the file folders. Intelligence reports from the Special Police. PRU reports. Pacification reports, requisitions, records.

He was relieved to find that none of the material in her safe was exclusively agency material to which she should not have had access.

"Will you come and sit up here for a moment?" he said. "I want to talk to you about the office routines and procedures, especially about security."

"Very well." She moved behind him to his desk and sat down in the chair beside it, facing him.

"Is the office ever left empty during working hours?"

"Only during lunchtime."

"But you lock everything up when you all go out to lunch, don't you?"

"Yes."

"And it has been a rule that the office is never left untended with the safes open and papers out on the desks?"

"Yes, sir, that has always been the rule." She was obviously disturbed and apprehensive about this line of questioning.

"In other words, when the safes are open, either Mr. Horner or Mr. Compton is here?"

"Yes. Or me."

"They leave you here alone when their own safes are open?"

The concern in her eyes deepened. "Yes."

Toby felt as guilty as if he were physically abusing her. "Did Mr. James give you any instructions about security when he hired you?"

"Yes. He told me about the need-to-know, and locking safes, and security checks before leaving, and those things."

"And you understand that *all* of us are subject to security rules, including me?"

She nodded.

"And being in charge of this office, it is my responsibility to see that the security of the office and its work is protected, and that means that I must question and watch everybody who has access to our papers and conversations?"

Again she nodded.

"You have had access to almost everything in the office, more than you are authorized to have, and perhaps more than it is good for you to have."

"And you do not trust me?"

"I didn't say that."

"But it is true."

"In a sense it is. Until I can see proof that you are trustworthy, it *must* be so. I have no choice."

"I see."

"Therese," he said gently, "this is a part of my profession that I dislike very much. If my personal feelings in the matter could govern things, I would never question you. But I cannot report to my superiors that the office is secure because my personal feelings tell me that it is. I hope you understand that?"

"Yes," she said, looking down at her hands, "but I cannot prove anything about myself to you. I come from Hanoi, and all my records are there. I was married there, but my husband was . . . my husband was killed soon after we came south, and there are no records of us in South Vietnam."

"I see," he said. "In a sense that may be one point in your favor."

"I do not understand."

"Look at it this way. If the North Vietnamese or the Viet Cong were using you as an agent, they would certainly have fixed you up with some kind of documentation, wouldn't they?"

"I think so, perhaps," she said hesitantly.

Ben came striding rapidly into the office. "Toby," he said, "I just got word that the VC hit my team at An Loi last night and hurt it bad. I gotta get down there as soon as possible. Can we cancel the meeting with the PSA and Colonel Manh this morning so you can go along with me?"

"Sure."

Therese rose. "I will call them to cancel the appointments if you wish, sir."

"Thank you, Therese," said Ben, and turned to Toby. "Would you get on the sideband to Can Tho, while I load up the jeep?

See if Jerry can get us a couple of choppers up there. There's going to be some wounded to be brought out."

"That's An Loi, right?"

"Right."

"What about a plane if they don't have choppers?"

"No good. There's no landing strip."

Toby went to the single sideband transceiver, which glowed and hummed twenty-four hours a day just inside the breezeway door. He looked up Jerry's call sign, unhooked the microphone, and called for Butane, identifying himself as Buffalo. Burkholder from Busch. Silly system that the VC would figure out almost as soon as it was instituted, if they thought it worthwhile.

"I've only got one chopper," Butane responded, "and he's in the air right now. I'll divert him to you as soon as possible."

"OK. Can you try to get another one, too?"

"I'll do what I can."

"Thanks. Buffalo out."

"Butane out."

An Loi was worse than Toby could have imagined. There were few buildings left standing, and bodies were scattered among the ruins, many of them badly cut up by bullets and fragments. Dozens of wounded had been gathered in the hot interior of the only building left relatively intact, a structure of concrete and corrugated iron.

Jess landed in his chopper shortly after Ben and Toby had arrived, with Minnie along to help. By the time the chopper was loaded with wounded, a second one had arrived, this one with a Vietnamese doctor and two nurses. Gritting his teeth, Toby helped load the wounded on board, hurting them as he did so, not being able to avoid hurting them. All afternoon they worked.

When the last of the wounded were airborne, on their way to the Ninth Evacuation Hospital, Ben stood and talked with the team leader for some time. They gestured toward a large mound of mud some hundreds of yards away, beyond the edge of the devastated village. Ben was highly agitated, and the team leader, exhausted and still in the grip of the violence of the night's action, shook his head and replied in a low voice.

At length Ben patted the man on the back, and returned to the jeep.

"The team really didn't do so bad," he said, "considering that it was the Yenan Battalion that hit them in full force."

"What's the problem about that mud thing?" Toby asked him.

"That's a mud fort. You see the goddamned things all over the country."

"What do they do with them?"

"They commit suicide. Those walls can't stop a B-Forty round, but there's always a few damned fools that just won't give up the habit of taking cover in them, or using them as strongpoints. It might have been all right before shaped charges and rockets, while the French were here. They learned it from the French. Came from Africa and the Foreign Legion, I suppose. But they're death traps in this day and age.

"A lot of those wounded we just loaded had taken cover in that one over there. But most of the people inside it were killed. Two B-Forty rounds is all it took."

"Were any of your team members in there?"

"One. He was trying to persuade all the others to come out. He was killed."

"For nothing," Toby commented softly.

"For nothing. Bill Voigt will blow up when he hears about it. He's a fanatic on the subject. He had a couple of experiences with that kind of a defensive philosophy in Burma. He thinks mud forts do something to the psychology of a people."

Minnie climbed into the jeep and Ben started it up. "Bill wrote a paper on mud forts," he continued. "Headquarters was impressed with it, I understand, and circulated it to the Pentagon. His idea is that the South Vietnamese seem to be getting more and more of a mud fort attitude about the war—you know, go inside where it's safe and maybe the enemy will go away. Bill's even seeing signs that the Americans are being infected by it. He says if he had his way he'd blow up every mud fort in the country, and then pull the fingernails out of anybody that ever built another one."

He put the jeep in gear and they moved slowly along the littered street. There was nothing more they could do here. Already the villagers, although still showing signs of shock, were at work clearing away the wreckage, collecting their belongings, and preparing meals over small fires here and there.

"Not all of them are mud fort enthusiasts," Ben said. "You'd be surprised at how soon these people will have this village put back together."

"You gotta admire them, don't you?" Toby replied, watching a small man hauling mightily upon a large wooden pole, to begin clearing away the wreckage of his home.

"Guts."

"That's it."

"North or South Vietnamese, Viet Cong or ARVN, or just villagers like these, they're a feisty people, aren't they, Minnie?"

Minnie leaned forward in his seat. "The word is new to me, sir. Feisty?"

"Yeah. Feisty. It means pugnacious. It means they never run away from a fight, and they fight hard. Maybe even that they get a certain kind of fulfillment, a certain joy, out of fighting."

"And the word for that is 'feisty'?"

"That's right."

"Then I would say yes. The Vietnamese are feisty."

"You see what I was telling you, Toby?" Ben continued, as they reached the edge of the village and picked up speed on the rough road. "That Yenan Battalion is tearing us apart in this area. They did lose four or five men, and that's a lot for an attack on a little village like this one, but it isn't an unacceptable loss for them."

"There's no question that it was the Yenan Battalion?"

"Nope. Some of the dead had the insignias. They knew exactly where to hit and when. They knew this team was new and still pretty weak. They figured they could hit it without much damage to themselves, and that news of what happened in An Loi would demoralize a lot of other teams."

"Will it?"

"It'll scare the shit out of them for a while."

"It sure as hell would make *me* nervous," Toby said fervently.

"The Viet Cong secret weapon. Terror."

"You understand it . . . after you see something like that."

"And these little villages have been the center of the war all along. The war is *about* them, and it's *in* them. Not the cities. Right from the start you could see what the Viet Cong was up to. What they wanted was to destroy the government of South Vietnam, and they knew they could do it without even touching Saigon. All they had to do was cut the lines of authority and communication from Saigon to the villages and hamlets. They didn't even have to destroy the middle echelons, the regional and provincial governments.

"I saw it happen time after time at the beginning. They would come into the villages, like An Loi, in the middle of the night, haul the village chief out of bed, along with the chief of police, the schoolteachers, the educated people—anybody in a position of respect or authority—shoot them in the back of the head, and line the corpses up in the street with notes pinned on them, so the villagers would have no doubt about who had done it.

"If anybody was crazy enough to try to take the place of any of the murdered people, they'd be laying out in the streets the next morning themselves, with a note pinned on them. That's terror as the professionals build it and use it.

"They did that to each village, and each time the central government lost contact and authority over one more unit. The VC didn't even have to occupy or police the villages. The terror was enough. Saigon was losing the war. There was nothing

Saigon could concentrate its big army and firepower on. There still isn't."

"Yep," said Toby. "I wasn't here to see it, but I've read about it a lot. And I was briefed on the techniques and situation by everybody you could imagine—"

"And now by me," said Ben apologetically. "I'm sorry."

"No need to apologize. You're the first one I've talked to about it who has seen it from the start, down at the level where it happened. It's like reading about a famous battle, and then visiting the battlefield. It comes to life for you."

"It does for a fact," Ben said.

"For example, I remember the figures they gave us. Forty thousand people killed that way in these villages in less than a year."

"That's right. That was the main push. It's still going on, but not as many each year now."

"Forty thousand is just a figure when you get briefed on it. You hear the figure, but you don't . . ."

"You don't think people, you think numbers. When you're sitting in an office or in front of a television set, it's just a number. But when you see it happen on the spot, and know the people it happens to, then it means something. And even then, my God, forty thousand!"

They drove in silence for a time through the gathering dusk. "In spite of it all," Ben said thoughtfully, "the villages seem to welcome our teams when they come to try to reestablish the government structure. They know that having a team in a village may provoke an attack like this one today, but they welcome the team just the same. They don't give up, except for the few that duck into the mud forts. If you give them some help and a little bit of hope, they come back. Feisty people."

"Feisty," echoed Minnie, pleased with the new word.

5

Toby transferred some papers from the files to his leather brief-case and locked his safe. Ben was busy at his desk, preparing a report for Saigon about An Loi.

"I hope you don't mind me not going with you, Toby?"

"No, you go ahead with your work. Minnie knows his way around over at the Special Police Offices, I'm sure."

"Sure. Better than I do, in fact."

Toby went out to the jeep, where Minnie was waiting, dressed in slacks and open-collared shirt.

They drove first to the office of the Province Senior Adviser, an army lieutenant colonel who had no desire to become involved in Toby's affairs, and let the fact be known in a wash of great cordiality. "Please let me know . . . All the best of luck. . . . It is extremely important . . . If there is ever anything . . . You fellows over there have no idea how much . . . Good to have talked with you. . . . Appreciate your call."

So much for him. It was like calling on the ambassador at an overseas post. Great puffs of wind that mean nothing at all. No complications here.

Under Minnie's directions, he drove to the center of town, to a large, square compound that occupied a city block. It was enclosed on all sides by a fence of vertical iron bars, on a base wall of concrete about three feet high. It would keep out intruders, but was not fortified against military attack, so far as his nonmilitary eye could discern. Guards were at the gates, and some sandbag bunkers here and there.

"This is the compound of the provincial government," said Minnie. "Almost all of the provincial government offices are here. Special Police Offices are on the second floor, and that small building behind the main building is the Revolutionary Development Office."

"Revolutionary Development." The name must be an awkward translation of something meaningful in Vietnamese, or else had been dreamed up by somebody who knew Vietnamese psychology better than he; but to Toby's ears, "revolutionary development" was no more satisfactory or descriptive than "pacification," and both referred to the same thing. But then, the strange and illogical language probably reflected quite accurately the minds that produced it.

"The Revolutionary Development Office is where Ben comes to meet his counterparts, I guess?" he said.

"Yes."

They parked the jeep inside the compound and went up to the second floor, past a reception desk in the corridor, and were ushered into a large office that overlooked the front of the compound. A squarely built, stocky man, with close-clipped hair, arose from his desk to greet them. He was neatly dressed in the dark trousers, white open-collared shirt, and shoulder boards that were the official working uniform of the Special Police. His mouth was straight and rather severe, his nose broad and flat, and his eyes were framed by steel-rimmed spectacles with slightly tinted lenses.

Minnie introduced them, and Colonel Manh motioned them into comfortable chairs around a low table in one corner of the office. *Good manners,* Toby thought. Around a table, rather than across a desk. Minnie interpreted for them so skillfully and unobtrusively that they were soon talking directly to one another, almost as if Minnie were not there at all.

"You have come to replace Mr. James," Manh said. "We liked Mr. James very much."

"I did not know Mr. James," said Toby.

"He was a charming man."

"Did you find your joint work with him to be successful?"

Manh seemed puzzled by the question.

"It was most pleasant," he replied.

"And was it productive?"

"Oh, yes, quite productive."

"Colonel Manh," said Toby, "I believe I should tell you here at the beginning that I hope to do more with you and your office than just be cordial friends." Manh nodded and waited for Toby to continue.

"It is my idea that our governments have put us into liaison with one another to work together, not merely to exchange papers now and then."

Manh was cautious, but interested. Toby went on.

"Our two organizations are working on a new program that is going to involve you and me in a lot of hard work together."

"I have heard something of the program."

"I want to anticipate the start of it by getting Dinh Tuong Province ready now."

Colonel Manh smiled. "I would be pleased by such an early beginning. What do you propose?"

Toby opened his briefcase and extracted a sheaf of papers. "These are intelligence reports from your department."

Manh looked at the papers in Toby's hand, and waited.

"However well they may have served in the past," Toby went on, "they are not good enough for the new program."

"Not good enough?"

"No. Let me show you."

Toby motioned Minnie to inch forward a bit so that he could read and interpret as they went through the reports, but before he began, Manh stopped him and called a subordinate to bring the original Vietnamese reports from the files.

With these two versions of the reports, Toby proceeded to show Manh what was wrong with the Special Police reports. He was impressed by Manh's quick understanding of his criticisms, and he was sure that Manh would see through the fiction that the reports "may have been good enough in the past." Those reports were never good for anything.

At length Manh sat back. "You have shown me enough. What do you propose?"

Toby was elated at the attitude of genuine interest on Manh's part. He was sure that this was the first time Manh had ever had any contact with an American adviser who intended to work hard at the liaison, and bring to it some experience and expertise.

"I want to train your people, Colonel Manh," he said.

"You want to train them?"

"Yes. I want to ask you to make them available to me for a course of instruction in the collection of information, and in the preparation of reports."

Manh was thoughtful. "It would be difficult to allow the men to be away from their work."

"I know the difficulties. The decision is yours, of course. But the need is great, and it is urgent. I want the intelligence from Dinh Tuong Province to go all the way to the top of the ARVN command and the American MACV forces, and to be respected and believed."

Manh gave him a broad grin. *That* was the kind of talk he obviously liked. "Before we go further in this, let me call Major Thieu," he said. He indicated by a gesture that Minnie should tell Toby who Thieu was.

"Major Thieu is the officer who sees that Manh's orders are carried out, and makes sure that everything is done, and acts for the colonel. There is a name for it in English." Minnie searched for the word.

"Executive officer?"

"Yes, executive officer." Minnie continued speaking in a tone and manner that would indicate to Manh a dispassionate description of Thieu. "I believe I should tell you about Thieu. He is a . . . a positive man. He believes that he speaks good English, and he will not use an interpreter. He is difficult for Americans to work with because of that, but if you want to work well with the Special Police in this province you must work with Major Thieu in whatever way he wishes to work, because he is in a powerful position. I will try to help all I can, but it must never appear that I am interpreting for him. You will see."

"I'll follow your lead, Minnie," said Toby.

Major Thieu came in. He was about Colonel Manh's height, but less sturdily built. He had large protruding eyes, which gave him an expression of mild and perpetual astonishment.

After the introductions, Thieu sat down in a chair next to Toby and drew it uncomfortably near.

"You wish to teach men?" he asked, and Toby was tempted to move back from him, because Thieu spoke with his face close to his own.

"Yes," Toby replied. He spoke slowly and as distinctly as he could form the words. "I want to teach them two hours a day."

Thieu nodded, but Toby was not sure he had understood.

"Here?"

"Yes."

"*You* will teach?"

"Yes."

"When?"

"As soon as possible." Toby had the sensation of being in the midst of a classroom drill in a foreign-language course.

"How many men?"

"All of them who are engaged in intelligence work." He realized that this was probably too complicated a sentence for Thieu, but Thieu looked at him wisely and smiled.

"Impossible," said Thieu politely. "Too many. But it is not important. I will bring all men who get information and all men who write information. They require teach. Others not."

Toby smiled. Thieu had agreed with him while believing that he was disagreeing. "How many will that be?"

Thieu made a mental calculation. "Twelve men."

"I would like to begin about a week from now."

"Yes, we have them," replied Thieu promptly.

Minnie stirred uncomfortably and Toby glanced innocently at him.

"What about blackboards, chalk, desks, paper, pencils?" Toby asked, certain that these words would be as familiar to Thieu as they are to any beginning student in any language. Thieu fielded the question with ill-concealed pride in his skill, and replied that such things would be easily provided.

"We will also need a four-drawer safe, but I could provide that; and we will need the names and some biographical information on all the men who will be involved, because they will be handling secret information, and our regulations require that they be cleared before we can give them that information."

Toby made this statement with the realization that Thieu would not understand it, but hoping that Minnie would notice that he was also directing his remarks toward Manh. Minnie did. Thieu made as if to study the question seriously, and Minnie translated for Manh. Toby could see that Thieu was listening intently, with a somewhat condescending expression for his superior officer, who did not understand the language. Thieu then spoke at some length with Manh, and Minnie translated, as if from Manh. "If you will give them a written list of the preparations they should make, they will attend to it."

"I'll have it over here to them this afternoon," Toby said. "That's the kind of response I like." They all arose and shook hands, and Toby and Minnie left.

"Minnie," Toby said, as they drove out of the compound, "you do an excellent job of interpreting. I'm not used to dealing through interpreters, but I can recognize an expert job when I see one."

"Thank you, Mr. Busch."

"I call you Minnie and you call me Mr. Busch. It doesn't seem right."

"Friendship does not depend on such things, does it? One can be equally charming with formality as with informality."

"But others who hear it might think I had a kind of contempt for you."

"They might also think that when I call you 'Mr. Busch,' it is because *I* have contempt for *you.*"

Toby grinned at him ruefully.

"I am not disturbed by the names as we use them," Minnie went on. "If I am not troubled, I believe you do not need to be troubled."

"OK," Toby gave in. "So be it."

Back at the office, Toby called Can Tho on the single sideband and asked for a plane to take him down the following day. Jerry promised to give him a pick-up hour later that evening, when tomorrow's schedule would be firm.

Now to start the process of defining his security problems. He called Little Jack into the common room for a conference. It was inconvenient that he did not have a private office where he could discuss confidential matters, but there was no use worrying about it. He would just have to get accustomed to using the common room for that purpose.

He laid a tablet of yellow foolscap on the low table before him. "I want you," he said to Little Jack, "to name all the people who have access to the information about your operations ahead of time."

"All of them?"

"Every single one you can think of."

"Let's see now. There's me, and Ben and Minnie and the PRU sergeant, and you and Therese and Colonel Manh and Major Thieu. And then, there's a Special Police officer they send along with us, and he certainly would have to know ahead of time."

Toby was jotting down names and drawing lines as Little Jack spoke. He shook his head in dismay.

"Look at all these people and all the loose ends," he said. "Not only have we got too many people who know about these things in our own office, but we have no control over where the information goes after it reaches Manh's office." He doodled on the pad, lost in thought.

"What about the Province Senior Adviser's office?" he went on.

"Oh, yeah," Little Jack admitted with a start. "We have to send a written notice of each operation to the PSA office before we go out."

Toby remembered his meeting with the PSA, and decided that this particular gap would not be difficult to close. He could delay sending the reports, or just neglect to send them at all. Dangerous, if a flap occurred, but perhaps a risk he would have to take.

"Think of anybody else?"

"Not offhand."

Toby leaned back in his chair, studying his list. "Well, that's a start.

"That all?" Little Jack asked, getting up to go.

"One other thing, Little Jack. In questions of security, there is one hard and fast rule. *Don't talk.* Don't even mention the problem to anybody without checking with me first, OK?"

"Sure."

"And that means, don't say or even hint to anybody that we are even talking about the *leaks,* or plans to find the source of the leaks. You understand? If you alert the guilty person, he's going to start laying low, and we'll never catch him. We've got to make sure he keeps on operating while we're looking for him."

"Well," said Little Jack, "of course you can automatically eliminate anybody that would get hurt by the leak."

"I don't automatically eliminate anybody," Toby replied coolly. "I don't eliminate the PRU man, or Minnie, or Therese, or even you."

Little Jack bristled. "Me? I'd have to be some kind of a stupid son of a bitch to leak the information and then walk into the ambush."

"Yes. Pretty stupid. Or very brave."

"Well, in this case—"

"About half of the security leaks that are found turn out to be people you would automatically eliminate, if you were using that kind of logic."

"Yeah, but for Christ's sake—"

"You could be giving out information without realizing it, you know. Have you got Vietnamese friends you talk to a lot? Any girlfriends?"

Little Jack perceived that he was being coolly interrogated. "Well, hell," he said, "a man's gonna have women if there's women around. But I sure as shit don't talk about military operations when I'm in the sack with a broad."

"No, I don't suppose you do. But you can see what we have to think about when you consider how many people have the information as a matter of course?"

Little Jack nodded slowly. Then, seeing that Toby had dismissed him, he returned to the office.

Toby next called Ben away from his work, and showed him his list. "I think you've got everybody down," Ben told him. "It's a big enough list, at that."

"What about your own operations? Who knows about them?"

"Everybody in the country knows about my operations, at every stage of the game," said Ben. "I've been giving this a lot of thought since you got here, and I've come to the conclusion that the least likely place to get information about my pacification teams would be here in this office. The teams are known about, by everybody, from the very start—Vung Tau, the villages they're going to, the Revolutionary Development Offices, the Special Police. Everybody."

"But didn't you say that the Yenan Battalion knows everything about your teams? How good they are? Which ones are weak? Things like that?"

"That's right. But they could get that information from their own sources in the villages."

"I suppose you're right. We'll go on that assumption."

"I don't want to try to tell you how to run something like this. You're in the business, and I'm not."

"Things like this are more a question of study, and common sense, than they are of any special skill, Ben. Now I've got to sit down and make some kind of sense of this, and come up with an idea of what we ought to do—write up something to take down to Can Tho with me."

"That reminds me, are you going to be coming back from Can Tho tomorrow?"

"If Jerry gets me down there early enough in the morning to get all my business done, and then gets me a plane back after lunch, I'll be back. Why?"

"We're planning a kind of welcome-aboard party for you."

"Who's we?"

"Couple of nurses and a secretary from the PSA office. All Americans."

"That sounds good."

"Would you go to the PX while you're there and bring us some things?"

"You bet. What do you need?"

"Nuts and crackers, and things like that for the bar. Some booze. Mrs. Chao may want some things for the kitchen, too. I'll have a list for you."

Toby returned to his desk. He found it difficult to concentrate, and realized with some disgust that the reason was a vague sense of elation he felt about the party. It was sophomoric, really. A party with unattached females, and he was reacting as if he were preparing for his first high-school date.

It didn't take much introspection to discover the reason. It was freedom. He had, by coming to Vietnam, regained the freedom of the single male. He had consciously and willingly given up that freedom when he took a wife, but he had never quite forgotten it, or ceased, it would seem, to regret losing it.

6

One of the tasks Bill Voigt had as Regional Officer in Charge was to deal with the press when Washington or Saigon so instructed him. That was why he was now squinting worriedly at Wilbur Hamilton, the PRU adviser for Bill's Phong Dinh Province, who was sitting in the chair across the desk from him.

This was a new experience to Bill. Intelligence officers should not, by the very nature of their profession, give interviews to the press, or even maintain any contacts with the press, except where it was firmly understood that the information exchanged was not to be published. This was the way it had always been, and journalists he had known in the past had understood and accepted the situation as natural.

In Vietnam, however, with six hundred reporters on the scene, the press was too overwhelming a presence to be safely ignored or fended off. Bill had already been back to the States on home leave once, and had been dismayed at the picture of the war that television was showing the American public.

"That isn't the same war I'm involved in!" he kept repeating to family and friends, but he could see that they didn't believe him.

The cable on the desk before him spoke volumes in few words: ". . . Miss Alice Christopher . . . Midwest News Syndicate . . . all phases of our counterinsurgency operations which can be securely . . . your own judgment . . . refusal would prejudice . . . desirable she draw favorable conclusions, but no attempts to distort or falsify . . . frank and candid without . . ."

It was enough to make a veteran clandestine operator panic. Sort of like walking out your front door naked. Without any restrictions, reporters had seen the Pacification Training Camp at Vung Tau. They had seen pacification teams at work in the villages. They had rejoiced in playing with the word "pacification," which was a goddamned stupid way to name or describe what the program was really trying to do.

Now here came Miss Alice Christopher, who was the Vietnam War correspondent for a small Midwestern chain of papers, and she wanted to go out on a PRU operation!

And Saigon had authorized it. *Authorized?* Hell, they had *instructed* him to do it. And the only reason they would do that was that Washington had sent *them* the same instructions.

"It's crazy, Chet," he said, looking over at his deputy, who was standing in the door with a copy of the same cable in his hand. "Sending a woman out with a bunch of night fighters into a VC-controlled hamlet. She won't be able to see a thing, and she'll probably get herself killed, and maybe you think *that* wouldn't make the CIA popular in the States!"

"I wouldn't do it if I were you," said Chet. "I'd tell Saigon to stick it up their ass."

"I can't do that."

"The hell you can't! You know as well as I do that nobody in headquarters is going to dare question a decision of the man on the spot, if he puts it on the record that he can't do something securely. If they go ahead and order him to do it anyway, and things blow up, who gets the blame? *They* do, because he didn't want to do it and they made him. They know that. They sure as hell won't order you to do it if you cable a refusal for security reasons."

"But don't you see that Saigon is on the spot? You've read this cable. Put yourself in the place of the guy that wrote it, and figure out why he would have said things the way he did. They want us to handle this a certain way, and you can bet they've had instructions from headquarters, maybe even from the White House. They can't put into an official communication exactly what they want to tell us about this situation, but if you read it from Saigon's point of view you can get the message. And they're trusting us to read between the lines and do the right thing. Know what I mean?"

Chet nodded, but Bill knew that he did not understand. It was a flaw in Chet's mentality that he was going to have to deal with in a fitness report that would be due in a few weeks. Chet considered anybody at the other end of a line of communications to be an adversary. Chet believed in calling a spade a spade. Chet was an excellent deputy—he had been a deputy in his last three posts. He would be a calamity as a chief of anything. He would have told the reporter to get lost, and would have sent a cable to Saigon with unanswerable objections to the request, thus forcing Saigon to look for other means of accomplishing a delicate and difficult task. And Chet would have indelibly impressed himself upon the minds of a number of upper-level officers as being an intractable and inflexible officer.

Bill stared at the cable.

. . . TAKE THIS WOMAN OFF OUR HANDS. GIVE HER A STORY THAT WILL SATISFY HER, AND WILL MAKE HER A FRIEND OF OUR AGENCY. DO NOT SHOW HER OUR WORST OPERATIONS, BECAUSE SHE WOULD REPORT THEM AS THE NORM. DO NOT SHOW HER ONLY THE BEST, BECAUSE SHE WOULD SUSPECT A SNOW JOB, AND WOULD LOOK FOR WORSE, AND WOULD FIND IT. BUT BE HONEST. THE WHITE HOUSE IS WATCHING. WHEN YOU REPORT ON WHAT YOU DO WITH HER, MAKE IT A ROUTINE, FACTUAL, EVEN DRY, ACCOUNT. WE REALIZE THIS IS A TURD WE ARE

HANDING YOU, BUT DON'T TELL US YOUR OBJECTIONS
TO IT, BECAUSE WE'VE ALREADY THOUGHT OF THEM
ALL. WE ARE DEPENDING ON YOU.

Bill would have liked to send her to Toby Busch, because
Busch was at least an experienced agency man. But he couldn't
do that. Busch was still somewhat of an unknown quantity, and
anyway his province was too much of a problem.

He had finally settled on Phong Dinh Province, the province
in which his own regional office was located. She was going out
with the PRU that night to a hamlet that was VC-controlled, but
not far away from Can Tho. The Special Police had a report that
a VC commo-liaison cadre was living in that hamlet. If you
could get a commo-liaison cadre it was like plugging into their
phone line, or reading their mail, or breaking their code. The
Special Police wanted this man, and wanted him badly, to interrogate him about operations in the province. The PRU was
going to try to capture him.

Chances were that they would run into a firefight in the
hamlet, too, because these VC villages were always on their
guard.

Wilbur might not understand the problems of upper-level
bureaucracy, but Bill trusted his judgment and his abilities. A
navy lieutenant (jg), member of Seal Team One, he was an
educated and articulate man and a good leader. Most important
of all, he loved combat. If he had not, he would never have
volunteered for duty with the Seals, that offshoot of the old
Underwater Demolition teams, who were trained in unconventional warfare, in fighting on and under the sea, on land, and in
the air. Parachutists, divers, warriors.

Wilbur would keep her safe if anybody could.

Laura ushered into the office a young woman who was visibly
relishing her appearance in baggy fatigues. "This is Miss Alice
Christopher," said Laura, and the others introduced themselves
to the reporter.

"We're not very used to this sort of thing, Miss Christopher," Bill began uneasily.

"Everybody calls me Chris," she said.

"All right, Chris."

"I'm sorry to put you to so much trouble."

"I'm going to be perfectly honest with you. We want to show you a good PRU operation, but we don't want you to get hurt or killed. So the one we're showing you isn't the most dangerous one you could imagine, but it isn't a walk in the moonlight, either. There is likely to be some shooting, maybe a lot of it."

"I understand."

"I'd be a fool if I didn't want to show you our best, but I'd be even more foolish if I tried to convince you that we never do anything that isn't brilliantly conceived and executed."

"Don't worry," she said. "I didn't come to do a sensational exposé of the CIA or the PRU. Unless what I see looks crazy or stupid, the story won't put you in a bad light. What I want is a story that will show the PRU in action. I think I've got to see it to be able to write about it."

"You won't carry a weapon?"

"That's right. My only protection as a journalist."

"It's going to be dark," said Wilbur. "The VC may have trouble seeing who is a journalist and who is a PRU. You sure you want to get into that kind of a situation?"

"I won't tell you I'm not scared, because I am. But I won't back out. And I won't get in your way, and I don't expect any special protection."

Wilbur stood up. "I don't approve of it at all, Chris," he said, with a disarming smile, "but your bosses and my bosses seem to think it's OK. So, if we're going to do it, we better get going right away. We've got a lot of preparations to make before dark."

They moved toward the door.

"Good luck," Bill said.

As they filed out into the anteroom, Wilbur paused at the

door and said in a soft aside to Bill, "Relax if you can, sir. She's my little chicken now, and I'll take care of her."

Bill put his hand on Wilbur's shoulder and gripped it in a gesture of gratitude. Wilbur understood.

"Mr. Busch just came in," said Laura, as he was returning to his desk.

"Oh, I'd almost forgotten he was coming down today. Tell him to come on up, please."

Toby came through the door a moment later, briefcase in hand, and Bill waved him into the chair Wilbur had just vacated.

"I didn't expect to see you again so soon, Toby."

"I didn't expect it either, but it doesn't take long to see the problems we've got in My Tho, and I need to touch base with you because I intend to start on them right now."

"Good. Cup of coffee?" Bill signaled to Laura, who brought them coffee from the urn near her desk.

"Ben is convinced there's something big brewing for about the time of Tet," said Toby, taking a tentative sip of the coffee.

"I've heard that from a lot of people, but we've got nothing solid on it, and Saigon discounts the rumors heavily."

"Why?"

"Their theory is that the VC are not so stupid as to try something they can't possibly accomplish. The VC aren't really strong enough for anything big, and they know it as well as we do."

"I see. The old theory that you can judge a Communist's intentions by finding out what his capabilities are?"

"Right."

"It makes me uneasy as hell."

"It's worked pretty well in Europe. It's a cinch that anything the Russians *can* do against us, they *will* do."

"I know," said Toby. "I've heard it all before, but it still seems to be a pretty unsatisfactory way to find out what an enemy's intentions are."

"How else could you do it? Hell, we don't even know what our own intentions are ten days in advance!"

"That's a fact." Toby grinned. "Well, anyway, I doubt if My Tho intelligence is going to help you even find out the VC capabilities, because we've got a total lack of information about anything that's going on in the province, except for what Ben's pacification teams pick up in the course of their work—and you can hardly call that intelligence. Can't evaluate it. So, in reality, we know nothing. Zilch!"

"That's the way I've seen your problems from here."

"And to add to the problem, we've got a bad security leak somewhere."

"What kind of a leak?" Bill was alarmed.

"Oh, it's none of our agency classified information, so far as I can tell. It's information about PRU operations mainly, and about our locations and comings and goings in My Tho. The PRU information would carry over into the ICEX operations when they get started."

"So, what do you intend to do?"

"I've got some tentative plans for both problems, and I want to start working on them right away," said Toby. "I wanted to let you know what I'm going to do before I start."

"Good."

"Seems an awful waste of time to have to fly up here to tell you. I guess there's no other way we can communicate securely, is there?"

"We do have pouches."

"Not often enough."

"That's the only other way."

"Well, we'll just have to cope with it," Toby concluded, reaching for his briefcase.

"Before you start, Toby, I think we ought to talk about you and Chet."

"About me and Chet? Why?"

"I know you'll understand my position. I have fourteen P

officers, like you, and fourteen O officers, like Ben, in addition to fourteen PRU advisers. I can't possibly handle them all personally, so I've got a regional officer for each category. Chet is the regional P officer."

Toby was dismayed.

"You understand," Bill went on, "that I couldn't make an exception and deal personally with your operations?"

"Sure," Toby replied hesitantly.

"The fact is, I would have less excuse with you than with the others because you're an old hand, and wouldn't need all that much supervision."

"I understand."

"I'm sorry I didn't make this clear to you before you went up to My Tho. I guess I just assumed that you would see the situation."

"I certainly should have seen it. I've been around long enough to know how things have to function."

"Toby, I've read your file, and I've heard Chet's story of the Frankfurt incident. As far as I can tell, that episode doesn't need to enter into our professional relationships here. But I haven't heard your side of the story. You didn't write any comment on the fitness report. You knew, of course, that you had the right to add a comment?"

"Certainly."

"Do you want to tell me your version?"

"No. And for the same reason that I didn't comment on that fitness report. You know what the propaganda analysis people always say—that if you get somebody in a position where he has to deny something, you've already got him convicted."

"Do you believe you've been convicted?"

"No. I just don't want to be put in the position of making excuses or alibis, and I don't know how to tell it without running the risk that it will sound just like an alibi."

"I think I could handle the distinction."

"Maybe. But you've got both of us in full view for a while, and

I'd rather you would judge me by actions, and not explanations."

"All right. It's your decision."

"It may make my job a little harder, to have to deal directly with Chet, but we'll manage."

"So," said Bill, leaning back in his chair, "what have you got in mind for your problems?"

"Oh, do you want to hear my ideas anyway?"

"Sure. It's not all that rigid and formal. I always like to be up on what you fellows are doing, and I want you to come in and shoot the breeze whenever we've both got the time. The actual management of things will be Chet's responsibility."

Toby, visibly relieved, gave Bill a brief account of his problems, and his plans for dealing with them. Bill listened with interest, and with the understanding of a man who has been through similar experiences.

"Have you got any of this on paper?" he asked.

"All of it," Toby replied, patting the briefcase.

"Good. Why don't you go give it to Chet right now? Whatever you may think of him, he won't let your papers sit in his in-box. He'll work on them for you."

"I know. I don't worry about that part of it." Toby got up to go.

"By the way, I hear you almost got your ass shot off," Bill remarked as Toby reached the door. Toby turned and looked at Bill's twinkling eyes.

"It was a real welcome," Toby said with a crooked smile.

He found Chet in his office, and sat down and opened his briefcase.

"Bill said that all my work goes through you."

"That's right."

"OK. I've got a rough draft of a message I'd like to send to Saigon."

He handed the draft to Chet, and Chet read it slowly.

"Let me get this straight, Busch," said Chet, after studying the paper intently. "You say here that the office has got a security leak, and you want to verify the clearances of all these people and then test the operations for a leak?"

"That's right," Toby said steadily. "How else would you do it?"

"You sure are a great one for testing. This sounds just like a replay of Frankfurt."

"Except that I *suspected* that Frankfurt net. I *know* I've got a leak in My Tho."

"You were pretty goddamned positive about Frankfurt, too, as I remember."

"I had no proof, but I was certain. I still am. That principal agent was a double. You could look at that operation and see, you could smell it a mile off. The Soviets were setting up a penetration of our operations in Frankfurt, and that agent was their foot in the door."

"Horse shit! Ernie Free set up that operation like a model. Damned near perfect."

"Naturally. If you were setting up a double agent against *them,* wouldn't you see to it that everything fell into place perfectly?"

"Busch, we've been through all this before, and there's no use doing it again. But I want to get something straight right now. Because of you, and that stupid operation of yours, I've been a deputy for my last three assignments. Never a chief. Never the head of anything. 'Chet Wolleson?' they all say. 'Experienced man. Got some good ops in his background. But, wait a minute. Don't forget Frankfurt. Yeah, don't forget Frankfurt. We better not promote him just yet. And we better not give him his own station yet. One more tour as a deputy to a strong officer. Can't have things like Frankfurt!'

"The Frankfurt flap wasn't my fault, but it happened when the operations there were under my supervision, and the Chief of Station wouldn't go to bat for me.

"Well, let me tell you something, Mr. College Boy. It isn't going to happen again, because I'm going to watch you like a hawk. There's gonna be no half-ass school solution operations here, because they'll never get past me. Every plan you submit, every cable you send, every proposal you make, is gonna be looked at very carefully, and if I have the slightest reason to doubt, I'll stop you. Cold."

Toby looked him steadily in the eye. "I don't have to tell you that there are ways the lower echelon can put the upper echelon on the spot," he said.

"Are you making threats?"

"I'm just reminding you that you're not dealing with a junior officer trainee who doesn't know how the system works."

"All right then, I'll tell *you* something. I may not have a college degree, and of course that's another thing against me, but I got where I am by work, not by wavin' a goddamned sheepskin. And in those years of work I've learned a few things about the system, too. Don't try any out-of-channels crap on me, Busch. You do everything by the book, or by God I'll blow you right out of the water!"

7

Dino angled the plane into the usual attitude for a landing at the My Tho strip, and squinted in the late-afternoon sun. "I didn't mention it this morning," he said, "but I notice you changed your hardware." He looked down at the Colt .45 on Toby's belt.

"Yeah. Ben said you were right."

"Ben is a brilliant fellow."

"I'm sure he will treasure your good opinion."

"They all do."

Dino dropped the plane lightly to the ground and taxied up to where Ben was waiting.

"Hi, Ben," he shouted, as Toby unloaded the bags of PX supplies. "How's things here in My Tho?"

"The VC still seem to be kind of unfriendly, Dino," said Ben.

"You don't say. Imagine that!"

"But we're still trying to win their hearts and minds."

"That's the way to handle 'em. If they won't be friends, take an ax handle to 'em, is what I say." He leaned across the cockpit to secure the door. "Well," he concluded, "keep a tight asshole!"

"Same to you."

"I got a request in for a steel plate to put under mine."

He secured the latch, waved gaily at them, and had soon lifted his little plane free to fade into a faint dot and a mutter in the sky.

"Party still on?" Toby asked Ben, as they headed toward town.

"Yeah. I'm gonna pick up the girls about seven. It'll just be drinks and dinner. Maybe put on some records and dance."

"Coat and tie?"

"No. We never do for parties around here."

"Good."

"How'd things go in Can Tho?"

"Pretty good. I have to deal through Chet, of course. That may cause me a lot of extra worry and work."

"I wouldn't be surprised. When do you expect to start training the Special Police?"

"As soon as possible."

"Can I sit in on the classes?"

Toby was surprised. "Sure, but it's going to be pretty elementary. I'm sure you've already had courses that were more advanced than what I'll be teaching these people."

"I've got a reason for asking." Ben said. "The way I see it, this is probably going to be the last real war of any size we're going to fight for a long time. But we'll still have the same power against us, and we're going to have to fight it by other means —the means *you* know how to use. . . . So, I'm thinking about trying to get the CIA to hire me and resign from the army."

"They can't, Ben. You've got it backwards. You'd have to resign first, and then apply to the CIA. There's a rule about proselytizing among the services, you know."

"Yeah, I know. What I've got in mind is to do things in such a way as to get a hint about whether the agency would be interested in hiring me."

"It would have to be an awfully broad hint, because that's just as much proselytizing as giving you a signature on a piece of paper. Our personnel people handle things like that as if they were walking on eggs."

"Well, I think I'll give it a try."

"But why do you want to sit in on these classes?"

"It's like being a soldier. You know, you can take the best recruit in the world, and train him for months in the United States, but no matter how you train him, he still isn't a soldier. He becomes a soldier when he gets into action. Now, a soldier learns more about being a soldier in a few hours of combat, watching and learning from experienced combat men, than he could ever learn in a training camp."

"Yeah, I've always heard that."

"I have an idea the same is true for your profession. Now, here I am with an opportunity to watch an experienced intelligence officer at work in the field, and I don't want to miss it."

"You want to study *me*, instead of the course, is that it?"

"Exactly."

"I'm flattered."

"And I promise that if we get into a combat situation, I'll let you come along and study me."

"That sounds like a fair proposition." Toby laughed. "But I know you'll understand when I tell you that collecting on a deal like that would not be one of my favorite pastimes."

"Then it's all right if I sit in on the classes?"

"Sure."

Toby had just enough time to shower and change clothes before the guests arrived. Minnie's workmen had patched the brickwork of the bathroom wall, but had not yet put the finish on it. Ben had spoken of putting a heavy wire mesh as a stand-off net along the sides of the house, to detonate any future projectiles before they reached the walls of the building itself. They still had not made a final decision about that. The psychological impact of such a cocoon around the house was something to think about, both for the inhabitants of the house and for the VC. Ben thought that it might be best just to place the guards somewhat differently, and have them patrol the canal area every hour or so.

Whatever the solution, Toby thought, inspecting himself in

the mirror before going downstairs, it wasn't going to guarantee anybody's safety or really solve any problem. It would be just coping; and just coping in a combat zone left an empty feeling in the gut.

Mrs. Chao and Chi Hai had prepared hors d'oeuvres and placed them here and there on the bar and the cocktail tables. There were festive arrangements of napkins, flowers in small vases, and bowls of fruit. Toby liked the looks of it. It was understated, but it was special and somehow just right.

Ben left in the jeep to pick up the women, and Little Jack came into the common room dressed in slacks and sport shirt. His clothes had probably been neatly ironed and folded five minutes ago, but they had now acquired the rumpled look that was characteristic of the man. He did not seem to be looking forward to the party.

"It ain't gonna be any go-go dance, Toby," he said disconsolately.

"Well, I don't know that I had a go-go dance in mind."

"I guess it depends on how you like your women."

"How do you like them?" Toby asked.

"I like to have fun with them, and then lay 'em," he said.

"And if you start out knowing that you won't be able to lay them, then you don't have any fun?"

"Oh, I guess it ain't quite that simple. As long as there's a *possibility,* it's fun, you know what I mean? I guess the most fun in the world is a woman that will just barely let you lay her."

Toby laughed. "I think you've got hold of a universal law there," he said.

"But in this case you know there's no possibility," Little Jack went on gloomily. "In this case it's gonna be feed her, give her a couple of drinks, maybe dance a little bit, and then take her home. Some fun evening!"

Toby was surprised at the vague feeling of disappointment Little Jack's comments had evoked. He realized that although he had laughed at the man's crude statement, he shared Little

Jack's philosophy about women to a greater extent than he liked to admit to himself. Of course, Little Jack's seductive skills would probably confine his successes to a certain type of woman, a type that would be of little interest to Toby.

Moreover, there was no sense in doing himself an injustice. He did like to be around women just to talk with them, even if he knew that they wouldn't even barely let him lay them. He hoped that there would be some good man-woman talk tonight.

The jeep came through the gate, and they went to the door to meet the guests.

Little Jack pointed out Louise Kenney, who would be Toby's dinner partner. He looked her over, and was surprised and pleased to find that she was pretty. Her blond hair was done in a neat, fluffy style that set off her soft blue eyes. Those eyes had a gentle, but lively, quality. She had splendid curves, much too exuberant for the blue *ao dai* she was wearing.

Little Jack's partner was Marie Claire, and as near as he could tell from Little Jack's pronunciation, her last name was Renondeau. She had a slender, Gallic look about her, although her English was perfectly colloquial American. Her hair was straight and cut in a boyish style, which accentuated her long and graceful neck. She was not a beautiful woman, but her body was more petite and better suited to the *ao dai* than Louise's.

The tomboy was for Ben. One could see from the first moment that Peggy Hall was fun to be around. She was slightly below medium height and build, and she had on slacks and a blouse that, while feminine and clean, were nevertheless not selected or worn with any idea of half-concealing and half-revealing the good things underneath. Her hair was in some disarray, and she either did not notice it or did not care. She was chattering away at Ben, her eyes dancing with fun and mischief, and Ben was grunting a reply now and then, enjoying the chatter. Peggy and Louise were nurses, part of an American medical team that had volunteered to come to Vietnam to help improve the medical services here. They worked in the Vietnamese hospital near the edge of town. Marie Claire was the secretary of the Province Senior Adviser, and it was only after they were introduced that Toby realized he had seen her before.

They mingled comfortably, and soon were gathered around the bar. Little Jack found relief for his own unease by serving as bartender.

"So you're Toby," said Peggy. "The man who had such a narrow escape on his first night in My Tho."

Toby looked at her sharply, and saw that she was teasing.

"Peggy," said Louise, "you're embarrassing the poor man."

"Does it embarrass you, Toby?" asked Peggy.

"Well, it's not the kind of a war story I'll be able to tell my grandchildren, that's for sure."

"Maybe you could dress it up a little," said Marie Claire. "Have it happen in the kitchen, or the bedroom."

"That's it," said Peggy. "You could say you had been frying an egg, and had just turned around to get a spatula when the rocket came through right above the stove."

Toby sipped his drink and frowned at her. "Brilliant!" he muttered. She obviously knew the entire story. All the embarrassing details.

"But," she went on, raising a hand in warning, "then one day this rather gray-haired, bent old ex-nurse comes to the door and says to you, 'Busch, I know about your past. If you do not pay me ten thousand dollars immediately, I will tell your grandchildren about that rocket.' "

"Not a dime!" Toby exploded. "Not a thin dime. Remember, gray-haired old ex-nurses are not that big an element in our population. Who would notice if one of them disappeared without a trace? In fact, who would notice if one of them disappeared *before* she got gray-haired and old and bent?"

"I'm going to arm-wrestle him later on," Peggy said in a loud aside to Ben. "He needs to be taught a lesson."

"Watch her, Toby," said Ben. "She's little, but she's wiry."

Mrs. Chao announced that dinner was served. They trooped

into the dining room, and Ben commanded Mrs. Chao and Chi Hai to stand nearby as they gathered around the table. Before they sat down, Ben handed each of them a glass of wine and lifted his own toward Toby.

"I am not a speechmaker," he said. "But I know everybody here feels like I do. When we say welcome, we really mean it. Welcome to My Tho, Toby!"

They drank the toast with smiles and words of approval. Toby sat down with them, suffused with the glow of cocktails and friendship.

Mrs. Chao and Chi Hai served a delicious meal of dishes and names that were new to him. Wine added its warmth to the easy talk; and even Little Jack was making rough attempts at sophisticated chatter, which were amusing to everybody, including himself.

After dinner, Ben put on some records, and they dutifully danced two or three numbers; but the surfeit of food and drink had unfitted them for even slow dancing, and they drifted back to the pleasant darkness of the bar to sit and talk. Toby realized that he had not relaxed this much since coming to Vietnam.

"I suppose," said Louise quietly to him, "that you have noticed how Peggy feels about Ben?"

"No," he admitted, "I hadn't noticed anything special."

"I'm surprised. I had an idea that people in your business would be quick to catch on to people's feelings."

"In my business?" he asked her with studied casualness.

"Yes, my dear," she said gently. "Don't be upset. Everybody knows."

"What about Peggy's feelings?" he said abruptly. He wanted to get her off the subject of his profession. It did not surprise him that everybody knew, but he did not want to confirm it, or talk about it. The experience and training of years forbade such talk on an occasion like this.

"She's so hopelessly in love with that man that she can hardly think of anything else, and the big lunk hasn't got a clue."

Toby looked at Peggy, chattering softly to Ben at the table near them. *What a charming picture,* he thought, realizing at the same time that the euphoria of the drinks could make almost anything charming to his foggy eyes.

"Let me fix us another drink," said Toby with a judicious air, "and as I do it, I will observe them. And then I will give you an opinion."

"Good," said Louise. "The thing needs a trained observer to observe it. So you go and observe it."

Toby went behind the bar and mixed the drinks, watching the other couple all the while with meticulous discretion. He spilled some liquor on the bar, and mopped it up studiously, then walked back to his own table, taking elaborate precautions against colliding with chairs and tables on the way.

"Well," he said carefully, "I will admit that there is a certain sparkle to the eye, and a certain amount of touching and giggling, but it looks more like high spirits than love to me."

"It's love," said Louise, taking a drink from her replenished glass. "L–O–V–E, love." She was impressed with the solemnity of her pronouncement.

"Are you sure of that?"

"I live with her."

"Oh, I didn't know that."

"Yes. All three of us live in a house on the far edge of town."

"By yourselves?"

"Well, there's a Vietnamese couple who serve as housekeeper and caretaker, and we have guards."

"But you don't have an American man living with you?" he asked, in a tone of shock and disbelief.

"Well, really, Mr. Busch!"

"You know what I mean."

"It's just the way I told you. We've got to live somewhere, and there is no American compound around here, or any dormitory. The Province Senior Adviser lives in a house not very far from us, so . . ."

"Well, it seems to me—"

"Let's not talk about our domestic arrangements. Let's talk about Peggy."

"All right." He drank some more. He gazed at her and felt the tug of that voluptuous body, so near his own. He forced the thoughts back with an effort. *Get thee behind me, Little Jack.*

"We worry about her," Louise went on. "Ben doesn't care for her in the same way. You can see that. She's bound to get her heart broken. And underneath that joking and playfulness is a very sensitive woman." She looked at him earnestly, but seemed to have a little trouble keeping her eyes focused on him.

"Really?"

"Yes. It's so sad." Louise sipped her drink, and her gentle blue eyes began to cloud over, as if she might cry.

"Hell, Louise," he said, "I don't see how a person can be that much in love with somebody that doesn't return the affection at all."

"I don't know about men, but it can sure happen to a woman. In fact, one of the surest ways to attract some women is to ignore them completely."

"He's a great guy, but somehow I don't think I would figure him as a romantic type."

"He's not. He hasn't got the slightest idea of what's going on. If you ever get the chance, let him know, will you? I know he wouldn't want to hurt her."

"Never advise other people about their love life," said Toby pompously. "You'll never be thanked for it, and you may get punched in the nose."

"Don't be silly! That's not what I mean. I mean, if you ever see a chance just to put in a casual word . . . don't you see? I don't mean to collar him and give him a birds-and-bees talk."

They sat and sipped their drinks, and Toby looked at her intently.

"Louise," he said, with the careful concentration of the

slightly drunk. "I suppose you and I will be thrown together quite a bit in the next year or so."

"You make us sound like a mulligan stew. But I know what you mean. I'll be here at least a year. I think I'd go crazy if I couldn't get together with Americans now and then."

"I haven't had much experience with platonic relationships with women."

She smiled mysteriously.

"In fact," he went on, "I have never had any *desire* to have a platonic relationship with a woman."

"I suppose not."

"Anyway," he went on, "I can tell already that weeks and weeks without talking seriously to a woman, talking about things that matter, you know, and being in company with a woman . . . Well, what I mean is without the atmosphere of a woman's company . . ." He stopped and looked at her as if he had made a statement, and was awaiting, and expecting, her approval of it.

"Go on," she said quietly.

"Well," he said with great deliberation, "I just wanted to say that I'm glad you are around. You are a sweet woman."

"How nice!"

"I want to be good friends with you."

"I'd like that."

"You are not going to be easy to be just friends with."

"I think that is rather nice to hear, too," she said.

"I am a little drunk, and I'm going to shut up before I say something stupid."

"I think I must be in the same position—I mean condition . . . myself," she said, "because I have an urge to tell you something I probably wouldn't say otherwise."

"What's that?"

She leaned close to him, to emphasize the weight of her words. "Let's be friends!"

What a profound observation! He took another drink and

blinked. It almost brought a lump to his throat. Here was a woman with a brain. He took another sip. As well as a body. He glanced quickly at her body, then beyond it as if his gaze were intended to encompass other things as well.

"Well!" he said.

They sat and beamed at each other, certain that the warmth they were basking in was platonic.

The party broke up about midnight. Ben explained mistily to one and all that while it might seem unchivalrous for just one male to escort all the ladies home, nevertheless to troop across town in three vehicles would be pointless, and he suggested that he be the escort, since everybody else was drunk.

There was some discussion about who was and who was not drunk, but in the end Ben drove out the gates with his precious cargo, and Toby climbed the stairs to his room.

He was unbuttoning his shirt when the first mortar projectile he had ever heard in his life exploded about a block away. The adrenalin flowed and brought a chill of sobriety to his brain. He did not know what the explosion was, but memories of the rocket still loomed large, and he knew that whatever it was, it was hostile. He stood fixed to the spot, undecided. Then the second round hit, no nearer, but in a slightly different direction.

He heard Little Jack burst from his room. "They're mortaring us, Toby!" Little Jack called, as he went by the door. "Get a weapon and get down to the common room."

Toby grabbed the grease gun from its peg on the wall, picked up a satchel of magazines, and sped down the stairs as the third round went off, this one significantly closer than the first two.

Little Jack was sitting in an overstuffed chair in the middle of the room. He was naked to the waist, and he had an M-16 lying on the floor beside the chair. He motioned to a chair near him.

"Mortar fire would come right through that roof if it hit directly," he explained. "We always come down here during a barrage. The windows are up at a level so that we're out of line of any fragments that would come from a ground detonation."

Toby sat down. He was under attack by an enemy, and his heart was pounding. He did not count the explosions as they came, but he could perceive that this house was evidently not a target. Only one round fell close. The rest of the explosions seemed to center three or four blocks away. He noticed with some surprise that he could hear a faint, deep pop before each explosion, and wondered if it was the sound of the mortar being fired.

Little Jack said that it was. "You can't always hear it. If the night is quiet and the wind is right, you can. You get so you know the sound, though, and once you do, the first one you hear of an evening will start you toward cover before the round ever arrives."

"When do we go up to the roof?" Toby asked, forcing a casual tone to his voice.

"As soon as they quit firing," said Little Jack. "They wouldn't try anything with troops or sapper squads while the firing is in progress."

"Firing is in progress" was not a natural phrase for a man like Little Jack, and Toby found it amusing that in the midst of this kind of violence, the man would utter such a ponderous phrase —the prescribed military terminology.

They continued to converse quietly between explosions, strangely detached from the world of noise and fire outside.

"I suppose Ben will take cover somewhere?"

"Sure. You'd have to be a goddamned fool to drive through the streets with this going on, unless you had to. He may be still over at the girls' house. Wherever he is, you can bet your ass he's under cover."

Little Jack's tone was strangely sharp.

"Sounds like you've got kind of a low opinion of Ben," said Toby.

Little Jack returned his gaze steadily. "No, it ain't that. I just don't have much of an opinion at all."

"What does that mean?"

"I don't know much about him."

"Well, you know his rank, and where he's been, and what he's done."

"I know what the record says."

"Could the record lie?"

"Can CIA's records lie about a man?"

Toby winced inwardly. That had hit a nerve.

"In the army," Little Jack went on, "a man's personal record can make a real hero out of a chicken shit."

"He's got medals, hasn't he?"

"All that takes is friends that will write up and endorse the recommendation, and when you're an officer you can get friends like that easy. Medals are cheap in the army. Shit, I've got some myself. They don't mean a goddamned thing."

Detonations a bit closer now. Toby was uneasy. He was astonished that two men could sit under fire, even sheltered as they were, and talk about something other than the attack itself. But he also realized that the conversation helped keep his nerves under control.

"You think Ben may not be much of a soldier?"

"I don't know one way or the other. He talks real good, but talk is cheap."

He lit a cigarette and leaned back in the chair. There was only one dim floor lamp to give them light, but Toby noticed a long scar that slashed downward from Little Jack's left shoulder across his chest.

"That's some scar," he said.

"Yeah," said Little Jack carelessly.

"Is that a combat wound?"

"Bayonet."

"Jesus!" Toby laughed nervously. "Somebody sure wanted to kill you!"

"He tried."

"Where did it happen?"

"In Korea."

The firing ceased, and they climbed to the roof. "You watch

that side, Toby," said Little Jack. "I don't look for anything against this house, because nothing was aimed at us, but we'll watch for a few minutes."

Toby peered over the low parapet. He could see the shadowy forms of the guards as they came out of their sandbag bunkers and repositioned themselves around the wall.

They watched for about ten minutes, and then felt their way slowly back down the steps.

"I'm going down and wait for Ben, Little Jack," said Toby.

"I think I'll go down myself and have a drink before I hit the sack."

They went to the bar and sat on the high stools, a nightcap in hand.

"This is the first time I've ever had any association with pro-fessional soldiers in action. I've always thought that a guy would have to be a little bit out of his mind to be one, and looking at you and that scar makes me all the more certain. What is it that makes you stay with it?"

"Damned if I know. It's my life, that's all. I move around a lot, I see a lot of the world, I'm usually where the action is, you know what I mean? A man likes to be where the action is.

"Right now, for instance, the whole goddamned world is watching this war, and I'm right in the middle of it. Sounds like I'm a conceited son of a bitch, but hell, a guy wants to be important in something. I haven't got much in the way of other talents. You've seen my PRU reports, and you can tell I ain't ever gonna win no prize for writing."

"Yes, I have to admit that," said Toby, without malice.

"I couldn't stand going back and holding down some kind of a job in the States."

"Sure," Toby teased him. "It's a hell of a lot better to run around getting sliced up with a bayonet."

Little Jack laughed. "Hell, that's really just a scratch, Toby. I got scratches like that all over me. See this one here?" He indicated a white line up the back of his hand, which looked like a tendon ridge until one inspected it closely. "I never did know what caused that one. We was holdin' a line during those first days around Pusan, and there was so much going off all around us that the first thing I knew I felt a real sharp sting, and looked down and saw that something had creased the back of my hand. I got a couple of fragments in one leg, and a place down low on my belly where a bullet went clean through me."

"And you still want to keep on being a soldier?"

"Yep. There ain't any other life I'd want to live."

They sipped their drinks in silence.

"I'll admit," Little Jack said after a time, "there is one thing that I'd never want to go through again."

"What's that?"

"Gettin' captured. I was a prisoner of war in Korea. The Koreans are mean son of a bitches and when they saw my size they figured they'd have to break me down."

"Did they do it?"

"No, but they came closer to killing me than I ever been before or since."

"Didn't seem to do you any permanent damage."

"No. I got three of my front teeth bridged over. Got the real ones knocked out with a rifle butt. And I had the amoebas so bad I damned near had my gut eaten through."

Ben drove in. During the barrage he had stayed at the women's house, which had been some distance from the target area.

"Could you see what their target was, Ben?" Toby asked.

"Most of the fire fell in two separate places, as near as I could tell. One area was just up here in the next block or so, and the other was across town, somewhere around where Therese lives. Nothing military in either area. It was just harassment, I guess."

"Jesus, I hope Therese is all right."

"Yeah."

"Seems strange that they would harass the people they're supposed to be trying to win over."

"Yes, it's hard to figure out. Everything all right here?"

"No damage."

"Good." Ben turned his head and listened. "Here comes Spooky."

They went back up to the roof to watch. A C-47 had arrived over the area, and it now released flares that lighted the scene and the aircraft in a pale, intense glow.

"That old airplane may be as much as thirty years old," Ben mused.

As if squirting a stream of golden water, the plane fired lines of tracers into the area from which the mortar fire had come.

"Six thousand rounds a minute!" snorted Little Jack.

"Mini-guns," Ben explained to Toby. "They got 'em on those Spookies, and on the helicopter gunships, too."

"Hell of a way to fight a war," said Little Jack.

"You can say that again," Ben agreed.

"What's wrong with it?" Toby asked. He had already sensed that something about this lumbering old airplane pouring fire at the ground was not quite right, but he couldn't say what it was.

"Shit, the VC know the routine better than those guys up there with the guns," said Little Jack. "They know exactly where that plane is parked, and how long it takes to get it in the air, and they know how long it will take to get it over whatever target they're gonna work on. So, they just time their fire. If they figure it will be ten minutes before the Spooky can get there, they figure on eight minutes of mortar fire, and two minutes to move over a couple hundred yards so they can watch them guys make fools of theirself."

"This one is a little late, though," Ben pointed out.

"Half the time they are," said Little Jack. "But they're never early, that's for goddamned sure."

"Well, they gave our friends a chance to get a good seat over in some other treeline to watch the show."

"You mean all that fire is not hitting anything?" Toby asked.

"Not any VC, that's for sure. They'll fly around up there for five or ten minutes and fire off twenty-five or thirty thousand rounds, and all they'll do is fill a little patch of ground with lead," Little Jack said.

"If we lose this war," Ben said in a low, troubled voice, "it's going to be because we fought it wrong. There's something insane about firing twenty-five thousand rounds at a squad of men with three or four mortars."

"Especially if you don't kill a one of them!" Little Jack added.

"But how can we help it?" Ben went on. "The generals know it's crazy. Or at least some of the generals do. But they've got all the firepower our country can produce, and so when they have to make a choice between sending in men or sending in fire, there's only one choice they can make. Even when they know, and their own soldiers know, that it would make more military sense to send in the men, they've got to send the Spookies and the B-Fifty bombers instead."

"Because otherwise they'd get men killed?"

"Yep."

"My God, I thought it was routine for generals to send men into combat to get killed."

"Routine's hardly the word for it, and they don't send them in with the idea of getting them killed," Ben said. "But usually they send them in with a clear conscience, because they know that war kills men, and they know that sometimes getting four men killed now may save fifty men later on. But in this war, their hands are tied by television."

"Television?"

"Ever see that TV scene where American soldiers are setting fire to a Vietnamese village?"

"Everybody has."

"You saw them setting the fire?"

"Yes."

"Do you know *why* they set it?"

"Well, they were . . ." Toby began, then stopped, puzzled. "No, I guess I don't know."

"Neither did that television crew. And what's more, they didn't give a damn. They're in a competitive industry, and they were beating the competition with a sensational film."

"That's a fact. They don't conceal their motives very well. They don't even try to conceal them."

"Say some colonel sends in a platoon of men after a mortar squad, and six of them get killed, and here comes a TV crew and shows shots of the six body bags there on the ground, and then pans over to some gunships or Spookies sitting still on a ramp, and the announcer says something like, 'And so, this officer had to make a command decision, whether to oppose the enemy with American flesh or American firepower. He chose the flesh.' Then they pan the picture back to the body bags."

"That's the way they do it, all right."

"And he hasn't given a fact that wasn't true, but he has assembled a whole set of facts so that they tell a lie."

"It's a hell of a situation, isn't it?" Toby mused.

"I'll tell you something else about those television crews. Some of them are the gutsiest men I've ever seen. Give me a platoon of *them,* with rifles instead of cameras, and I'll take on any three platoons in the world. But their guts is causing more bloodshed . . . Oh, hell, what's the use talking about it?"

They watched the Spooky cruise back and forth, hosing down the area with its torrent of fire and metal.

"You gotta admit it's quite a show," said Toby. The Spooky released another flare. More jets of fire at the ground. Six thousand rounds a minute was one hundred rounds a second. At that rate, you couldn't hear the individual reports, as you did from a normal machine gun. You could only hear a one-hundred-cycle tone, a low hum. The lowest sound the human ear could perceive, as he remembered it, was about thirty or forty cycles per second. What note were the mini-guns playing, he wondered? He'd have to remember to look it up someday.

He grinned in the darkness, and thought that what Spooky was doing was not shooting the enemy—he was trying to hum the enemy to death. Toby was on the point of mentioning this to his companions, but then considered that they would think him drunk or frivolous, so he kept the thought to himself.

The last flare sputtered out. The big plane turned and lumbered away toward its home, and the three men felt their way back down the darkened stairs.

8

Chris Christopher sat huddled in the sampan, a little forward and to one side of Wilbur, her eyes staring at the black water of the Bassac rushing past the side of the boat. They had come about eight of the ten miles they were to make under the power of outboard motors. Two more miles and they would head up a smaller stream, propelled by poles and paddles. The last mile to the target would be on foot. There was no moon, but the zodiacal light was sufficient for a dim perception of objects and persons.

Wilbur said something in Vietnamese in a low tone, and a small man came aft from the bow and squatted beside them.

"This is Xuan," said Wilbur. "He's going to take care of you."

"But I don't want to interfere with your operations."

"That's why I'm giving him this job. I'm going to be too busy to stick with you myself. He'll watch you. He's got eyes like a cat. It'll be easy for you to panic in the dark, but just remember the enemy can't see any better than we can. At first, they won't even be able to see as well, because all of them except the perimeter guard will be in lighted houses.

"If you get separated for some reason, don't move. Stay exactly where you are, because Xuan will find you, or if he doesn't, somebody else will. If you're moving around in the dark, we'll lose you as sure as hell."

"I'll remember," she said, now thoroughly frightened by the whole prospect. When she had persuaded her editors to send

97

her to Vietnam she had assumed that being in combat action would be frightening, but she had not imagined how fearful it would really be.

The boats turned into the mouth of a small tributary of the Bassac, and the motors fell silent. Silently, dark figures arose in the sampans, and they were propelled by poles against the sluggish current.

They did not talk now. When at last they squished into a reedy bank, the men, though heavily armed, climbed out with hardly a clink of metal. Xuan led Chris to a small clump of saplings at the water's edge, where he cut a small wand with a sheath knife that was razor sharp. In pantomime, he showed her that she was to hold one end and he would hold the other, so that they could stay together in the darkness. They moved off down a path in single file.

She wondered at these slight, wiry men, who seemed to have the eyes and feet of cats. She stumbled repeatedly where they walked steadily.

There was a whispered exchange among them, after which some of their number left the path and disappeared into the blackness, as if they had been snuffed out of existence.

The lights of a small village appeared ahead of them. Xuan struck out to the left, dragging her through tall grass that whipped about her and sawed at her hands and face. They came to a mound of earth that loomed above the grass, and after circling it carefully, Xuan pulled her to the top and signaled her to keep down.

She crouched and looked about her in the dim light. She recognized the appearance of the mound. It was a grave, and the large bulky object before her was a concrete tomb.

Squatting beside her, Xuan used his carbine in a vigorous pantomime to show her that if firing started she should take cover on the side of the tomb opposite the village.

They waited. She marveled that he could sit so calmly in the darkness. She tried to relax. Maybe this operation would be uneventful after all. She hoped so. It wouldn't make a very good story, but she would at least live through it.

But no, she must not think that way. What she must hope for was action—hot, bloody combat. She wanted, she had to have, a story that would get a big play in her papers, and perhaps be picked up for publication elsewhere. Chris knew that she was reasonably attractive, at least as pretty as any female television correspondent she had ever seen, and prettier than most of them. She had the looks. All she needed was the breaks.

Television news. That was the career she wanted, the career she had been dreaming of since her high-school days. This small newspaper syndicate was the best she could do for now, but she was determined to make it the stepping-stone into television. It could be that. It would be, if she could get stories with real action, sensational coverage, the kind of human interest that television craved and devoured.

There was a shout from one of the houses. A woman screamed. Xuan remained motionless, while the crack of rifles split the silence of the night and tiny points of flame stabbed the darkness from several of the houses.

The firing intensified. Chris noticed that the sound came to her ears in waves, or surges, as the battle progressed. It was punctuated by shouts, and what must be Vietnamese oaths.

A ghostly figure hurtled toward them through the grass, and with a little cry of terror Chris started to rise. Her nerves tingled with fright, and her heart was pounding as if it would burst from her breast.

Xuan grasped her arm and held her down with an iron grip. The fleeing figure rushed by the mound with a loud snort and a grunt. It was a hog. Xuan patted her hand and released her.

The firing gathered and concentrated around three houses at one end of the village. Xuan shook his head in dismay. He held up a grenade and pointed it toward the village. She guessed that he must be saying that grenades would be used now, but she had no idea which side would use them.

As if on cue from Xuan, there came an explosion near one of the houses, followed in quick succession by two more. Then there was a lull in the firing. Xuan became tense, she could not tell why. He muttered something to her in a barely audible whisper. She did not know what he had said, but knew that he was expecting something.

The pop of carbines and the angry snap of heavier rifles resumed, now much closer to them, and Xuan suddenly grasped her arm again and shoved her roughly around to the other side of the vault, just in time to escape the bullets that began to smack into the earth and concrete of their position. The battle had moved from the village into the grassy field around them, and it intensified into a storm of sound and darting light.

A figure appeared at the base of the mound. Chris thought at first that it must be one of the PRUs, but Xuan's reaction showed her that she was wrong. Again her heart pounded wildly. The figure made as if to climb the side of the mound, and she realized that only Xuan stood between her and a swift death.

Xuan drew his knife. Why didn't he use his gun? She resisted an impulse to reach for his carbine. Silently he slipped down the side of the mound. She heard a startled exclamation, a scuffle, and then a strangled groan as Xuan's knife came up from below into the man's heart.

The firing was still swirling around them, but gradually it died out in the distance in little spasms of sound. Xuan climbed back up to where she was, wiping his knife with a handful of grass. He replaced it in its sheath and held out the wand for her to grasp.

The village was now quiet, and they found Wilbur standing in the doorway of one of the thatched houses that had been at the center of most of the fighting. The interior was lighted by oil lamps.

"You all right?" Wilbur asked her.

"Yes. Is it all over?"

"Yeah," he said, in a tone of heavy irony. "The operation was a success, but the patient died."

"You mean the cadre was killed?"

Wilbur pointed to a body on the floor beyond the door. "I think that's him."

She peered into the interior of the house at the body lying sprawled on the dirt floor near the far wall. Two other bodies were nearer to the door. She caught her breath in an involuntary start at the sight of the bodies, bodies that had only minutes before been alive and unaware of impending violence.

Some of the PRUs, their carbines at the ready, were moving purposefully about the village, going into houses, searching the exterior parts of the area. The villagers clustered warily in small groups. They were frightened. The PRUs were questioning some of them sharply, but were not harming them physically.

One by one the black-clad figures came to gather around the door where Wilbur stood, and reported to him, while Xuan went through the pockets of the dead man by the far wall.

Xuan had finished when the last of the PRUs had reported in, and he gathered the papers and pocket litter into a small bundle and brought it to Wilbur. The two men examined some of the paper and talked in low tones.

"Yeah, he was our man all right," Wilbur concluded with a sigh. "God, I wish we could have taken him alive. What this guy could have told us!"

Xuan then wrapped the papers in an oilcloth and tied a string around them. He handed the bundle back to Wilbur, who tucked it under his belt.

"This is all we got out of the operation," he said disgustedly.

"Not the way you planned it," said Chris.

"Sure wasn't. We got through their perimeter without any problem, but before we could get to the house something happened to alert the whole place. I think it was a pig."

"It was," said Chris, laughing nervously. "We saw it."

"They took us under fire, and after that it wasn't likely that we'd ever take the guy alive. They knew what we were after. They backed up in the village, and then most of them got away. They found a gap in our blocking force that shouldn't have been there. Tomorrow I'm going to find out why."

Chris remembered that she was a professional reporter, and she forced herself to act the part, keeping her voice calm with great effort. "Many people killed?"

"Two of the VC were killed out there in the street, besides these in here. Some people were hurt, too. I don't know how many yet. I don't think we lost any. Maybe a nick here and there."

"That's good."

"I don't know if we got any of them after they bugged out."

"Xuan killed one," Chris said, suddenly remembering, the shock of the memory showing in her voice. Wilbur spoke to Xuan, and Xuan gave a laconic reply.

"Yeah, he did," Wilbur said.

Chris looked once more at the bodies in the room, and felt her lips quivering and the sting of tears in her eyes. This was not the way she had imagined it at all. This was so calm and ruthless. A rush of pity for those young men and their families had destroyed her pose of journalistic detachment. For a moment she hated these cool, efficient killers, whose assault had left those bodies so battered and lifeless.

Wilbur was regarding her thoughtfully. "I'm sorry," she said. "This is the first battle I ever saw. I didn't know it would be exactly like this. I don't know what I expected."

"We killed them because we had to, Chris," said Wilbur. "When an enemy starts a firefight in these cases, your plan to simply arrest a man goes down the drain. You fight because you have to."

"Of course," she replied, squaring her shoulders. "I understand. I'll get used to it."

They made preparations to leave. "Sometimes the fact that the PRUs are so good and so well known works against us,"

Wilbur went on. "The enemy is so scared of them his actions are unpredictable."

Xuan finished a perfunctory search of the other corpses, and shook his head at Wilbur.

"OK," said Wilbur. "That's it. Let's move out." He put a hand on Chris's arm. "Be sure to stick with Xuan, will you? This could be the most dangerous part of the operation, because the whole countryside knows we're here now, and they may ambush us or set booby traps."

Xuan extended the wand to her, and they filed out of the village and back along the path through the tall grass. It seemed an eternity to Chris before they reached the sampans, but they did so without incident, and were soon moving downstream.

Wilbur was relaxed now, and in a more conversational mood. "Ask anybody in Vietnam about the PRUs," he said, moving his arm in a broad gesture toward the men in the sampans, "and they'll tell you that they're the best fighters in the country. It takes all the training and discipline we can give them to make them understand and operate on our primary objective the way we want them to. It doesn't make sense to them to move in against an enemy just to pick up a man for questioning, or to capture a communications center intact, or to collect the papers and files of a district committee. The war isn't a question of papers and information to them. To them, it's men and guns, and when they make contact with men and guns, they want to fight."

"So I notice."

"They are strictly ordered not to fight unless there is no way to avoid it on these operations. We're teaching them slowly but surely. This one is a good unit. They're smart and unflappable."

Xuan moved back to where they were seated, replacing his knife in its sheath. He extended his hand toward Chris, and she grasped what he was offering without at first realizing that it was the wand. He spoke to her in a cheery voice.

"He stripped the bark off and carved the name of the village and the date on the stick," Wilbur told her. "He thought you might like to keep it as a souvenir."

Chris was touched by the gesture from this slightly built man, who had led her through the night and protected her from its dangers.

"Yes, I would," she said. "Thank you, Xuan, for taking care of me." She extended her hand to him, as Wilbur translated. Xuan took her hand in his own in a friendly grip, then patted it lightly with his free hand, as he had done by the tomb, and returned to his seat in the bow.

9

While he was awaiting Saigon and headquarters action on the clearance documents and training materials, Toby instructed Therese in his own methods of office management. He tightened filing systems, updated logs and records that had been ignored or poorly handled in the past, and purged great quantities of material from the files.

"I want you to handle these things so that I won't have to worry about them," he told her. "If the typing load is too great, we may have to get a typist to help you out, but I want this office run with good routines and lean files. Do you think you can do it?"

"Yes, Mr. Busch."

"There is one rule that we must follow strictly from now on. In my safe there are some documents that pertain only to our agency's work, and should be seen only by authorized persons. Mr. Compton and I are the only ones authorized, and I have changed the combination of my safe, so that he and I are the only ones with access."

She was troubled.

"You do not trust me with everything?"

He smiled reassuringly. "It is because of strict regulations of my agency, which have been established as a result of long experience, and which seem to have been ignored in this office for a long time. Except for those things, I am trusting you with every part of the office. Most important of all, I want to be able to depend on you to handle deadlines, tickler systems, and routines of all sorts. If it turns out that you can do all this, you will be doing me the greatest service you can imagine."

He did not add, of course, that she would in so doing also be maintaining her access to the information that had been leaking out.

In her grasp of office management, Therese proved to be the equal of any secretary he had ever had or worked with. She watched his changes with approval, often making suggestions for more logical and simplified procedures. She voluntarily took tasks off his hands, always leaving him the means of assuming the work himself without embarrassment to either of them, if he desired.

He visited the Special Police Offices regularly to check on the preparations for the classes. He was surprised when Thieu gave him a list of the participants without delay. He had never had such a quick response to a bureaucratic procedure, even in the most advanced countries of Europe, and certainly not in Latin America.

Minnie hovered in the background during the meetings with Thieu, but Thieu did not try to conceal his distaste for the presence of an interpreter, and Toby found that by speaking slowly and searching for uncomplicated ideas expressed in simple phrases, he could communicate with the man. He did wish that Thieu did not feel compelled to stand so close to a person to talk. He found himself slowly backpedaling during each conversation, inexorably being forced into a chair or a corner before he gave up and allowed Thieu to set the distance between them. He had known Frenchmen who did this, and wondered if Thieu had caught it from the French.

The room that was to serve as a classroom had been supplied with a portable blackboard and writing tables and chairs. It had only two windows, which looked out into a shady portion of the compound, and was rather dark.

"It seems to me," he said, gesturing toward the windows,

"that there is hardly enough light in here. We may want to ask for some additional lamps. Do you have any available?"

"Yes," Thieu replied without hesitation. "That is Mekong River. But only one part. Other parts go by Truc Giang and Phu Vinh. Can Tho river is Bassac."

"Ah, I see," said Toby wisely, and added, as if making a quip that only he and Thieu would appreciate, "Then we will assume that our budding spies are to carry out their lucubrations by the light of the Mekong?" He gave an unobtrusive laugh that invited Thieu to join in, which Thieu did with alacrity. Minnie looked at them blankly, and Toby blessed him for it. Thieu would not have appreciated peasant participation in their sophisticated badinage.

Toby went with Little Jack to the PRU compound, and looked over the living arrangements and the men. The arrangements were spartan. These men did not decorate their barracks with *Playboy* pictures, although much of the rest of South Vietnam seemed to be papered with centerfolds. In fact, the PRUs did not decorate their quarters at all. Simple cots, pegs and racks and shelves for weaponry, small lockers for clothing. Toby noted that there did not seem to be any undercurrent of communication or sentiment between Little Jack and these men. They seemed almost indifferent to him and to Toby, and Little Jack apparently returned the indifference. Toby was uneasy, but told himself that he must withhold judgment in a situation so new to him.

Bill Voigt flew up and spent three hours with Toby. Mrs. Chao prepared a delicious lunch, and Toby felt that the inspection, if that was what it was, had gone off well. Bill said that he was calling a regional meeting of all P officers one week from that day, to discuss the ICEX program. It had been approved, and had been given a different name. It would be called the Phoenix program from now on.

"Why Phoenix?" Toby asked. "Somebody just draw it out of a hat, or does it have some significance?"

"I wasn't there," Bill said, "but as near as I can tell, it was selected with some care. They wanted something that would appeal to the emotions and the imagination of everybody, Americans and Vietnamese. They wanted something that would imply a successful campaign starting from nothing. Well, they thought of things like Bootstrap, but the Vietnamese have no tradition of the self-made man, and no history of boots with straps. They tried a lot of other things—slang, mythology, and so on—and then somebody thought of the phoenix, and came to find out the Vietnamese have got a legendary bird something like that. It didn't rise from the ashes, but there is something extraordinary about its origins, and so that's what the program is called. It's Phoenix in English, and Phung Hoang in Vietnamese."

"Phung Hoang?"

"Right."

"My God!" Toby laughed. "How can you get serious about something called 'Phung Hoang'?"

Bill smiled. "The Vietnamese apparently can, and we have got to do it, too."

"This meeting in Can Tho will be the first time I've had a chance to meet any of the other P officers, except for Ski," Toby said.

"Yes, and my son is going to be in Can Tho at the same time," Bill said. "You'll also get a chance to meet him." He made no attempt to conceal his pleasure at the prospect.

"On leave?"

"Three days. You can imagine what a joy it will be for his mother to have me write to her that I've been with him."

"The joy obviously won't be confined to his mother."

"Nope."

There were no mortarings during those days. Little Jack took his PRUs on an operation to find a Viet Cong rice cache. The operation was uneventful. They found no rice, and Little Jack concluded that the tip had been false.

The An Loi replacements were flown in, and Ben took them in a small convoy down to An Loi. He spent the night there, and returned the next day full of optimism for the little village and its team.

"You wouldn't recognize the place," he said. "They've got it pretty well rebuilt, and you can hardly see any traces of the attack. I think the team has got itself back together pretty well."

Toby was beginning to feel some optimism himself. He had prepared for, or had already begun, the major tasks that would occupy his time during this tour of duty, and he found that operating thus independently, at a distance from the corporate structure of the agency, gave him a sense of freedom and exhilaration he had never had in his work before.

There were two problems he had not yet even begun to attack. One of them was the Yenan Battalion, whose file he took from the safe time and again, for study and analysis. There had to be some way he could get a handle on it.

The other was his lack of any intelligence collection operations of his own. Such operations were, after all, the core of any intelligence officer's work, and lacking any of them at all, he could never feel right. To make the problem worse, he was in a new culture, hemmed in by unusual elements of security, language, and war, and he did not have the slightest idea how he was going to go about acquiring agents within the Viet Cong. He didn't even have the necessary elements to do a target study.

On this latter problem, help came from a totally unexpected source.

"Mr. Busch, may I speak with you alone?" Therese asked him one morning.

"Certainly. Shall we go in the house?"

They sat in the big chairs by the coffee table in the common room, Therese perching uneasily on the edge of hers, made to look tiny by its dimensions.

"Mr. Busch, I know that my position here is only to do work of the office, and not do any of the plans or other things."

"Well, of course—"

"Please, I am not complaining. I am apologizing if what I am going to say is not proper."

"Go ahead."

"You have only my word that I hate the Viet Cong," she continued, and Toby's face softened.

"Therese, I do not doubt your word." He realized that he meant it.

"I could not help hearing you mention sometimes that you do not have informants in the Viet Cong."

Toby's breath quickened. He knew from experience that this kind of a preliminary meant some prospect for recruitment. Therese misinterpreted his agitation.

"I cannot help hearing things in this office," she said. "Even those things you would not want me to hear."

"Never mind that. What is it you have in mind?"

"Where I live . . . it is a place in town. . . ."

"Yes, I've driven by that area. They mortared it the other evening, I think."

"Yes. That is the Viet Cong way."

"Go on."

"A family that lives in a house near mine, they have a son who is in the Viet Cong. He is not often at home, because he belongs to a local force battalion. But his mother has told me that her son has come to hate the Viet Cong."

"And you think he might be willing to . . . ?"

"Perhaps to be your informant."

"What I am looking for is an agent, not an informant," said Toby.

"I do not understand."

"It's really just a question of the meaning of words," he went on. "An informant would only tell me what he knows already. An agent would go look for information I want."

"I see."

"I ought to tell you that I wouldn't be very interested even in an agent, if he is nothing but a soldier in a local force battalion. What could he tell me or find out for me that would be worth the time and effort? He might be a way to get to other higher-level people, but operating that way has only a modest chance of success, and it takes a lot of time. Time is something we have very little of, as you said yourself."

"But he is not just a soldier. He is the commander of the battalion."

"The commander! Hey, that's different."

"He is visiting his mother now. He will leave after midnight. Do you wish to meet him before he leaves?"

Toby was elated, but he was now confronted with a dilemma. There were no hard-and-fast rules about approaching agent prospects, but every officer was expected to remember certain maxims that had proven valid in action. Before ever making a personal meeting, find out who the prospect is, what he knows, why he might be willing to tell it, where to meet him, and how to make certain that the meeting is secure and unobserved. Above all, have contingency plans in case it is a trap.

He could not possibly fulfill these requirements on such short notice.

But there was only one response he could make. He must meet the man tonight.

"Yes, I want to see him."

"You understand that I would be there," she reminded him hesitantly.

"I not only understand it, I want it. I *must* have you there." She already knew about the prospect, and Toby would have to assume that she would know much that went on eventually, even if he tried to cut her out of future operations. He needed an interpreter. She could be the interpreter and it would be unnecessary to bring an additional person in. His instincts approved of that.

"Very well," she replied.

"Furthermore, if this works out I will want you to continue in the operation with me at all times, to interpret. And to help."

"Very well. Then I will go home at lunchtime and make arrangements for the meeting."

"Has he told anybody else?"

"His mother knows that he is not happy."

"He must not tell anybody else. About that, or about the meeting tonight. Get that across to him, will you?"

"Very well."

"Even his mother should not know about this meeting, or his decision, or anything else."

"I will tell him."

"Now, about the meeting. It must be arranged so that it cannot be seen or heard by others. But it must be in a place that it would be natural for me to go. That is going to be difficult for a round-eyes like me in My Tho."

"Yes," she said thoughtfully. "That will be very difficult."

"Do you live alone, Therese?"

"Yes. I have a small house that is joined to another one. You would not call it a house in America, I think. I live alone, but my house is fastened to the house of another family. They are friends."

"How would you feel if your friends and neighbors got the idea that you were my mistress?"

"Your mistress?" She was unfamiliar with the word, but her confusion and hesitation showed that she sensed its meaning.

"My lover."

"I do not know." She was confused, embarrassed.

"Here is what I have in mind, Therese," he went on, with such enthusiasm and lack of guile that she relaxed and listened with interest. "I brought a little SONY television set with me from Can Tho the other day. Do you have a set in your house?"

"No. There are no television sets in any of the houses near there. Television sets are very expensive."

"But you do have electricity?"

"It is not constant, but we have electricity."

"Good. Here is what we could do, if you are willing to put your reputation on the line, Therese. I'll go with you this evening with the television set. We will let people conclude that it is a gift from me, but we won't *tell* them so. People believe something that they conclude much more firmly than something that you tell them. You will see to it that everybody in the area comes to know that you have the set. Let them watch it. You'll know how to handle things so they'll draw the conclusion. I'll also give you other things—"

"But Mr. Busch, I could not accept gifts from you."

"They will not be gifts from me. I will charge them to operational expenses, and they will be accounted for all the way to Washington. Since you are an employee, they will be officially on loan to you, and will appear on the records that way, but you will keep them in your possession as long as necessary for the operation. Do you see what I mean?"

"Yes."

"I am asking for a great deal from you," said Toby, checking his enthusiasm for a moment at the sight of her thoughtful eyes. "I will certainly understand if you refuse. Perhaps we could figure out another way to do it." His tone clearly said that no other way would be nearly so satisfactory as this one.

"I will do it," she said.

"Someday, perhaps, we can explain to your friends and neighbors the real truth about what we are doing."

"Does it mean that you now trust me?"

Toby paused and searched for the right words. "Therese," he said slowly, "in my work I have been deceived and even trapped by people I liked and trusted. Trust is the golden key in this business. Once a person wins the trust of an intelligence agency, he is in a position of great power. So, intelligence agencies are always careful about bestowing that trust."

"Yes, I see," she said, an edge of sarcasm in her voice.

"Therese," he said, pausing for a moment until her eyes

were directly on him, "I am violating the standard procedures of my agency by going to a strange place with you tonight, to meet an agent prospect, without knowing anything about him except what you have told me. If it is a deception, it could be the end of my career; and if it is a trap, it could be the end of my life. But I am going. Does that say anything to you about trust?"

She looked down at her hands. "Yes," she said faintly, and then raised her eyes to his again. A bashful smile had come to her lips, almost banishing the sadness from her eyes, and he knew that he had been forgiven.

"All right," he said brusquely, "now let's get the meeting arranged. First off, can this man get into your house without being seen?"

"I believe so."

"When you instruct him, tell him that we will be in your house alone at seven o'clock. He must wait at least fifteen minutes. Fix up a signal that will tell him if everything is all right for him to come in—something natural like a door being ajar."

"I could leave my shoes in the door."

"Good. If he doesn't see those shoes, he is not to come in. If the shoes are there, he must come as soon after seven fifteen as he can without being seen. All right?"

"Would it not be better for him to be there already?"

"No," said Toby gently. "Psychology is extremely important, especially at this stage. He comes to see *me*. I do not go to see *him*. It may sound silly, but it is important."

Again she smiled. "It does not sound silly. It sounds like a Vietnamese."

"Then the effect won't be lost on him."

"No."

"Now, here in the office, only you and I will know about this. Nobody else, American or Vietnamese, must be told."

"Very well."

"It means that Mr. Compton and Mr. Horner will both draw

the same conclusions that we expect others to draw about you and me."

"I understand."

"A good name is a great sacrifice to make."

"Mr. Busch, I will not worry about my good name. Other things are more important."

It was growing dark when he loaded her little motorbike into the back of the jeep, placed a cardboard container with the television set alongside it, and drove her across town. He drove without looking to right or left, as if he were making an unsuccessful effort to act naturally. Therese sat woodenly beside him. They came to the entrance to her area, a narrow path, passable to a motorbike being pushed but not to larger vehicles. He parked the jeep at the curb and lifted the motorbike out. She grasped the handlebars and headed along the path, pushing the bike as she moved through the gathering dusk. He followed her with the cardboard carton under his arm.

It was a slum by occidental standards, but it was not filthy. He could hardly believe that so many human beings could live in such a small space in such seeming order and harmony, and with so little refuse to litter public spaces. The pathway curved and turned to accommodate the haphazard placement of the tiny structures of thatch or wattle. At one point, he had to set his foot down on the path within about eighteen inches of a large bowl of rice around which a family was preparing to squat for their evening meal.

Expressionless eyes followed their progress down the path. Therese exchanged low greetings now and then with some of the onlookers. There were smiles on these occasions, somewhat formal, he thought, showing neither cordiality nor mirth, but not hostile either.

At last they came to a wattle-and-daub structure with a corrugated-iron shed-type roof, which had been built against another somewhat larger structure of the same material. The tin roof extended out beyond the front wall to form a narrow, porchlike shelter, supported by wooden posts at both corners. Therese fastened her motorbike to one of these posts with a chain and padlock. The door was secured by a simple warded lock, to which she produced a key from her purse. She opened the door, stepped inside, and motioned Toby to enter.

With a quick, graceful motion, she bent and removed her shoes and placed them precisely in front of the door. Toby could not suppress a smile, a smile of delight and affection, at the sight of those small shoes, so carefully positioned by their owner. By American standards, they were almost child-size.

The interior was in almost total darkness, until Therese switched on a bare bulb that hung on a dropcord from the ceiling. The bulb was small and did not light the room very well. Two lizards, conditioned to expect a meal of insects when the light went on, scurried across the ceiling.

The room was sparsely furnished. A low table, two chairs, a benchlike platform near the window at one end, which he realized was a Vietnamese bed, and a wardrobe against the wall near it. In another corner was a small oil cookstove, some modest utensils hanging from nails on the wall, and a jerry can that probably contained water.

Against the back wall were two shelves that were filled with books. He could make out French titles, English titles, and Vietnamese. There were hardcover and paperback books.

The floor was of wooden planks. It was spotless.

The air of the neighborhood was heavy with the odor of dishes being cooked in *nuoc mam,* the sauce of fermented fish that is Vietnam's national condiment. Although not exactly foul, the odor was sharp and persistent, even penetrating this home to some extent. Here, however, it was almost displaced by a faint fragrance, an elusive aura of the woman who lived in the home.

Toby set the carton on the table, opened it, and lifted the television set out. He pulled out the telescope antenna, unwound the power cord, and began to look for an outlet. Therese pointed to the dropcord, which had a European-style receptacle. Fortunately, the television set had come with an adapter. He plugged it into the receptacle and turned it on. A Can Tho station came in, broadcasting a Chinese opera, and he beckoned Therese close to him so that he could speak into her ear.

"We will leave this on, fairly loud, so that the conversation won't be overheard," he said. He noticed, with a rush of sensation over his whole body, that his lips were nearly touching that satiny cheek, and he drew back quickly.

"We should go on conversing," he went on, trying to keep a normal inflection in his voice, "just as if what everybody is thinking is true. Does anybody around here speak English except you?"

"I do not think so. But today one cannot be sure."

"We really ought to have the table to meet around, but with the television set on it . . . ."

"Mr. Busch, may I suggest something?"

"Go ahead."

"Vietnamese do not sit in chairs very much, and do not eat off tables like this. This man will feel more at ease if we sit on the floor."

"I can sit on the floor," Toby said, grinning, "but my legs are not in any shape for squatting as a Vietnamese does. But first, I want to check some things." He walked to the door and peered out slowly and unobtrusively. Then to the window to examine the shutters, which she had not opened upon their arrival.

"Can one see inside through these shutters?"

"Perhaps through a crack. I do not know."

"We may want to turn the light off during the meeting."

"Yes."

Toby sat down on the floor and hugged his knees to him. Therese dropped lightly to the floor beside him, but on her knees, geisha-style, rather than squatting on her heels. He wondered if a French education had taught her that Occidentals do not perceive squatting to be very ladylike. Not that he knew anything about her education.

"Si vous êtes catholique, du nord, vous . . . devez parler français . . . n'est-ce pas?" he asked, aware of how hesitant and awkward his French was.

"Oui," she replied. "Je parle français mieux qu'anglais." Her French was automatic and graceful.

"Well, now you *have* got me on the spot," he said.

"What do you mean?"

"If I say no, that your English is better than your French, you may be offended, and if I say your French is better than your English, you may be offended. So, what do I say?"

She laughed, and rang little bells of pleasure all through him.

"I'll just settle for this," he said. "Your English is better than my French, so I think we must stick with English."

"Very well."

"How long have you been in the south, Therese?"

A faint veil of distress clouded the lovely face, and he smiled reassuringly at her. "I am not questioning you. I am making conversation. And I *am* interested in knowing about you just for my own pleasure, not for official reasons."

"I have been in the south for a little more than one year."

"You escaped from the north more than a year ago?"

"Yes."

"When was your husband . . . killed?"

"About six months ago."

"Was he killed in battle?"

"No."

"You don't want to talk about it?"

"Yes."

"You *do* want to talk about it?"

"I mean, yes, I do not want to talk about it."

"Is it because you don't trust me?"

At first she was surprised by the question, and then she was delighted. Once again she laughed aloud, and he thought that she must have the most contagious, bubbling laugh he had ever heard.

"I didn't intend to make you laugh, but I'm glad I did. I'm not sure what it is that is so funny."

"I had thought that you do not trust me, but about me trusting you, I had not thought," she said. "I brought you to my home without any question, because I did not doubt you."

"Do I seem so harmless to you?"

"You would not harm me."

"No."

"But you do not trust me. And you do not trust yourself, either, I believe."

"You may be right."

The door opened noiselessly, and a man in dark shorts and an open-collared shirt came in. He appeared to be about forty years old, although Toby could not be sure. His hair was graying slightly at the temples, and there were lines under his eyes, lines of fatigue. His mouth was a grim, straight line, his face otherwise an expressionless mask.

They stood up, and Therese introduced the newcomer, Hoang Duc Dang. Toby had considered taking the customary precaution of using a pseudonym in this first exploratory meeting, but had discarded the idea. He was already widely known in My Tho, and certainly to the Viet Cong. There was no point in complicating matters needlessly.

Toby and Therese resumed their seats on the floor, and Dang squatted beside them.

"Who are you, Mr. Dang?" Toby asked abruptly.

Therese interpreted. "He says he is Hoang Duc Dang, and he is commander of the Determination-to-Win Local Force Battalion."

"How do I know that? I have only his word."

"He says that your own intelligence reports will verify that he is the commander of that battalion."

So they believe we have good intelligence on their forces? He is sure I already know about him. Well, no need to destroy that illusion.

"That is not what I meant," Toby said suavely. "What I mean is, how do I know he is *that* Hoang Duc Dang?"

Dang sat and thought about this question. Then he said something brusquely to Therese.

"He says he carries no documents."

"I would not have expected him to."

"He asks how he can be sure you are Tolliver Busch?"

"He can't," said Toby, without batting an eye. He looked at Therese. "Let's turn off the light, Therese, and turn up the volume on the television."

Therese did as he asked, leaving the room faintly illuminated by the small screen of the television set, which was facing away from them, and filling the air with the sounds of the Chinese opera—unmelodic, cacophonic to Toby's ears.

"Now," Toby continued, "why has he come to meet with me? Does he want to work with me?"

Therese exchanged several remarks with Dang. "He says for two reasons he has come. First, his family have been asking him to rally to the government side under the Chieu Hoi program for some time, but he does not want to rally. He says that as a Hoi Chanh he would be nothing but one who gives up. He does not want to give up . . . to quit. He wants to be useful. He wants to work for Vietnam."

"Well, just between us, Therese, I think he may have a false impression of the Chieu Hoi program, because a lot of the Hoi Chanhs *are* working for us. But that's all right with me, because if he did become a Hoi Chanh, I couldn't touch him. He'd be lost to me. Not only that, he'd stop getting any new information the minute he rallied. Now that I think of it, why keep this between you and me? Tell him what I have said."

Therese did so.

"Now," Toby went on, "he gave me his first reason. What is the second?"

Therese consulted Dang.

"He says that he does not believe in the mass . . . the mass . . . I do not know the English word for this. In French it is *soulèvement.*"

Toby wracked his brain. That would have something to do with rising, leavening, lightness, a . . . an uprising! He caught his breath.

"Uprising is the English word, I think," he said. "Let's see if what he says about it fits that meaning." He realized that Dang would note his surprise and excitement. It didn't matter. Dang should have the satisfaction of providing him with *some* information he didn't already know.

"He says that all the Viet Cong military units and civilian cadres are preparing for a mass uprising of the South Vietnamese people during Tet. This is to be the final struggle that will overthrow the Thieu régime and drive the Americans out of the country."

"And he doesn't believe in it?"

"He says that the Viet Cong leaders are making a bad interpretation of history. He says his own experience with the masses makes him believe that they will do nothing but wait. It will be a waste of Viet Cong soldiers, and will gain nothing."

"He knows history, it seems," Toby mused, "history beyond what the gospel of Marx and Lenin teaches."

"I believe so."

"Then in reality he is not disillusioned with the Viet Cong; only with these particular plans?"

Another detailed exchange between Therese and Dang. Toby cursed the difference in language. This was the guts of a recruitment, the exploration of motives and emotions, the search for a solid common ground.

"He does not wish to try to deceive you. He believes the Viet Cong programs are better than the Thieu and American ideas. But he believes that the Tet plans will be such a disaster for the Viet Cong that he wants to prevent them."

"How can he do that?"

"He says that if the ARVN forces and the American military

become convinced that the plan exists and will be carried out, they will take actions to prepare for it. If they do that well enough, even the most fanatical Viet Cong leader must see that they cannot succeed, and will cancel the plan, or change it."

Toby gazed at the dim figures of the other two, his mind racing with details he must remember, actions he must take. This man was a walk-in—an agent prospect who seeks out the Americans to join their side. Walk-ins almost invariably admit only a partial dissatisfaction or disillusionment, not a total break. The human heart resists such total breaks with the faith of the past. But Toby felt that Dang's disillusionment was probably more profound than he was admitting, even to himself. The most impressive thing about him was that he assumed what most walk-ins do not even consider until they are asked—that is, that it was his duty to stay in place and work for what he thought was right. Most such agent prospects just wanted *out*.

"Tell him," Toby said to Therese, "that I am going to proceed on the basis that what he has told me is the exact truth. I want one more meeting with him here as soon as he can make it. Ask him when he can come back to My Tho."

Dang replied that he could return in two weeks. They set a date and time.

"Next, I want him to bring me all the information he can get about his own battalion, and about the Tet uprising."

Dang grunted his assent, but added that he intended to be selective about the information he gave. This was also standard for the new walk-in.

"That brings up another item," Toby continued. "I want him to think carefully about the implications of what he is doing. How will he continue with the Viet Cong after Tet? What if they win? What if they lose? He is going to have to make a hard decision sooner or later. I believe this first step may be really only the beginning of his disillusionment with the Viet Cong and its methods and ideas. I think he should study seriously what is really in his heart, and should face all the facts, no matter how unpleasant or disturbing they may seem to him."

Therese passed along this short homily, and Dang stared silently in the direction of Toby's dim figure, but Toby could not see his eyes.

"At our next meeting," Toby continued, "I will give him some instructions in clandestine work, especially communications. He and I cannot meet regularly. The danger is too great. I am much too visible. On the other hand, I do not want any third person between him and me. The fewer persons who know about this, the safer he and I will both be. So we will set up systems so that we can pass information, but will not have to meet personally, except in an emergency."

Therese was translating these remarks piecemeal, and Dang received them without comment.

"I am sure I need not tell him that he must not reveal to anybody, to his family—not even his mother—that we have had this meeting. So far as his family knows, he should continue to procrastinate about rallying."

Dang understood, and said that he had already resolved on just that course of action.

"And finally, we need an interim emergency communication system. So here is what he must do. There is a revetment at the airstrip made out of ammunition boxes. Starting from the end nearest the road, he should look for the fourth box from the end, and the fourth box counting up from the ground. That box has a loose end. He should slip whatever information or message he has in that box. After he has loaded the box, he is to make a scratch or a slash with a knife on the wooden pole at the northwest corner of the block our compound is in, like this." Toby drew out his penknife and lightly scratched a curved slash on the floor for Dang to see. "He should make this mark about shoulder high, so that it is visible from the sidewalk without my having to search for it and attract attention. I will look at the pole each morning, so that the material will not be in the box too long."

Dang asked if he would have any difficulty knowing the pole he was to mark. Toby took a three-by-five card out of his pocket and sketched the location of the pole for him, and Dang studied it carefully, then handed the card back.

"Does he understand?" Toby asked.

"Yes."

"Have him repeat the instructions to me, step by step, please."

Dang repeated the instructions exactly. Toby was encouraged by this sign of an incisive mind.

"Now, Therese, we've got the housekeeping done. I want him to tell me everything he knows now about this uprising, and the preparations that are being made for it."

For the next hour they sat in the semi-darkness while Dang described the Viet Cong plan as he knew it. Toby made notes as best he could in the dim light, and occasionally questioned and probed to get the full picture. Dang explained that he had obtained what information he had in a series of orientation talks for local force leaders, in Tay Ninh Province. He gave the dates and the names of the participants in these sessions. Toby's professional doubts were further allayed by this information. Dang was intelligent enough to know that specific dates could be checked. If these facts checked with other information, Dang was probably exactly what he said he was, and could be a source of a wealth of intelligence about the Viet Cong.

When Toby saw that Dang was beginning to get restless, he arose to signal the end of the meeting.

"Before he goes," Toby said to Therese, "I want some personal data about him so that I can submit a clearance request on him, to see if he is on record as being used as an agent by anybody else, see if he has ever been used before, if he has ever lied to us or deceived us, things like that."

Therese spoke to Dang, who replied abruptly, in a way that told Toby the answer before Therese interpreted the words.

"He will not tell you anything about himself," she said.

"I will trust him that much less."

"He says he regrets it, but it must be so."

They reconfirmed the meeting for two weeks from that night in this same location. Toby held out his hand; Dang grasped it fleetingly, and slipped out the door.

"We will wait for a while," Toby said to Therese. They sat down at the table in the dim light.

"How did you know about the box at the airfield?" she asked.

"Force of habit," he replied. "We call that a 'dead drop.' In this business you never know when you'll need one, and when you need one it's too late to go looking for one."

"Dang admired that."

"Good." Toby peered closely at her in the dim light. "Therese, I have a task for you, and it may be difficult, but I hope you will try."

"I will try. What is it you wish?"

"I need all the information I can get about Dang. I can't get it from him directly, at least not yet, but I can't really work properly with him until I can be reasonably sure he isn't a double agent for the Viet Cong, or a provocation, or that he isn't already working with somebody else and just wants to make a little more money."

"He has not asked for money," Therese pointed out.

"No. An intelligent man would not ask at the first meeting. And if he is good he will never ask, and won't accept it if we offer it. At some stage in our relationship we may offer him some, and he might accept, who knows? It's possible he has some desperate financial problems. Anyway, I have to check up on him as well as I can."

"Of course."

"You know Dang's mother. I want you to talk casually to her and find out whatever you can about him, but without letting her know what you are doing. This is more for precise information about him than to test him. No telling how many Hoang Duc Dangs there are in Vietnam. I need to know exactly where he was born, and what the date was. His mother's name and his father's name. Anything else you can get about him."

"Very well, sir."

"Thanks." He stood up and turned on the light, then resumed his seat and began going over his notes. He corrected the sometimes illegible scrawl while the conversation was still fresh in his memory, and he probed Therese's memory on points that were not clear. Satisfied, he put the cards back in his pocket and rose to go.

"Thank you, Therese, for everything," he said. "For putting your reputation on the line, for spending your time. If Dang works out, we may have begun the recruitment of a first-class agent, a really important one, and the credit will be mostly yours."

"I am happy if I have been of help."

Toby took her hand in both of his own, and held it for a moment. "Poor Therese," he murmured. "You have such sadness and pain in your eyes."

"Yes," she said softly. "Someday it will pass."

He opened the door reluctantly, illuminating the area before the little dwelling with the faint light from the bulb within. "Perhaps we ought ot put on an act for prying eyes, here in the lighted doorway."

"An act?"

"Do Vietnamese lovers . . . do they kiss, as we Westerners do?"

"Yes."

"Then, Therese, if you will stand very still, I will now make a public demonstration."

She stood still, looking up at him. He leaned down and kissed her on the lips. He tried to make it look like the last, light punctuation to an hour of passionate lovemaking. Her lips were soft and slightly parted, and he realized that she was not simply receiving a carefully staged kiss. She was kissing him back.

He knew that the act was unnecessary, and was sure she must have realized it too.

"Good night," he whispered.

"Good night, sir."

10

Toby stood in the hot mid-morning sun, leaning against the revetment of ammo boxes. His pilot today would not be Dino. The gathering of all the provincial intelligence officers at Can Tho had forced Jerry to mobilize every one of his aircraft for several intensive hours, and Dino's little three-passenger Helio would be joined in the effort by a seven-passenger Porter and by Jess Theodorides's helicopter. Jess was to pick up Toby.

He looked at his watch, and began to pace casually about the end of the revetment as if he were lost in thought. A sidelong glance at the box satisfied him that his dead drop was still exactly as he had described it. There could not be anything in it yet. He did not go near it.

He would be gone for two nights, and he had charged Therese with the task of watching for the scratch signal on the pole during his absence.

He went back to the end of the revetment and stood by his luggage: a small airline overnight bag and a thin attaché case. Travel in this informal situation in the tropics was uncomplicated—shirts, slacks, socks, and underwear, shaving gear, an extra pair of shoes.

He hitched the .45 to a more comfortable position on his hip. He still hadn't gone to the firing range to practice. He must remember to do that when he got back. If he could find time. He thought of the things he had to do within the next month, and was contented with the burden and the challenge.

128

He had ached to go directly to his typewriter the moment he returned to the compound from his meeting with Dang. But he had resisted the temptation. Everybody in the household would know that he had driven out with Therese, and everybody would draw the conclusions he had planned for them to draw. If he had gone directly to his typewriter they might have modified those conclusions, and he must avoid that at all costs.

The following morning, when the moment came that it would look altogether normal, Toby had set to work on the task that fascinated him, one that he excelled at: the task of turning rough notes and recollections of an agent meeting into reports that would succinctly and completely deliver the information he had, and put on the record the details of what had happened at the meeting.

The operational report first. Details, precautions, checks, systems, times, schedules, and comments about the demeanor of the agent. He had set up a log for meetings with Dang, and wrote the first entry, and the first contact report. He prided himself on his contact reports. From them, any newcomer could reconstruct a complete and accurate history of any operation he had ever run.

He had hesitated about writing the intelligence report. He had been given extremely valuable information, but he had no approved or authenticated source and could not evaluate the material except by his gut instincts. The agency was not so rigid as to ignore the instincts of its officers, but it was extremely reluctant to circulate intelligence reports based on those instincts. The times when circumstances dictated such a dissemination were few and far between, and were invariably the occasion for an accompanying disclaimer that the source was new and untested, and that the accuracy of the information could not be judged.

He had written the report in spite of the difficulties he could foresee. It did tell of a massive plan by the Viet Cong, of strategic significance to the whole U.S. involvement in Vietnam. If the customers believed the report, they could begin preparing for the event at an early enough stage so that they could cope with it when it came. He was sure that any army commander with a feel for the situation would sense the truth of it. Ben and Little Jack and Dino and Bill Voigt had already shown him that they were uneasy, that something big seemed to be brewing. So far as he knew, his report was the first solid information from a Viet Cong source that seemed to confirm their suspicions. The Viet Cong were preparing to blow the lid off. He couldn't prove it, but he knew it.

The rattle of the big fan of a Huey helicopter came to his ears, and he squinted into the sun to find the silhouette of the Air America chopper. Jess came in steeply, and gently settled the skids of the aircraft close by. Toby set his luggage on the floor and climbed into the seat just behind Jess. There were two Filipino technicians and a Vietnamese soldier sitting on the other side. They exchanged friendly nods with him, but did not speak.

"Hi, Toby," said Jess. "Haven't seen you since An Loi. How's things down there?"

"Pretty good, I guess," he replied. "I haven't been back down. Ben took replacements down and he thinks they'll do better than the original ones did. Of course, the VC probably won't hit that village again, at least not for a long time."

"Probably not," Jess said, craning his neck to inspect his surroundings before lifting his ungainly machine off the ground. "They sure as hell kicked the shit out of it when they did, though."

He broke the skids free of the runway, set the helicopter in that peculiar scooping angle of the takeoff, and they zoomed forward, rattling and shaking. When they had cleared the treetops at the end of the runway, Jess quickly veered to the right in a sharp bank.

"They got some F-104s operating between here and Can Tho," he explained, "so we gotta give them a wide berth."

"What are they doing?"

"They've spotted a new battalion that's just moved into the My Tho perimeter," Jess replied. "They think they've got it cornered along a canal off there to our left, and they're working it over."

Toby could make out the darting jets against the sky off to his left, and could see puffs of smoke from the ground when they streaked toward the ground and fired their rockets. He could not hear any explosions over the sound of the big rotor over his head.

"They sure it's a new battalion?" he asked nonchalantly. There was no feeling of nonchalance in the pit of his stomach. This could not be Dang's battalion, because Dang had located his on the opposite side of My Tho.

"Yeah, but I don't know how they know. They sure as hell can't tell from up there in those jets. They might be rocketing a fishing party for all *they* know."

"I suppose so."

"But there's no question about it, the VC is moving around My Tho. You guys are in the bull's eye."

"It sure looks like it."

"Lots of other province towns are in the same boat, of course, except I don't think they got as much around them as you guys have got."

"You've made my day, Jess," said Toby drily.

"Thought that would interest you." Jess grinned back at him. "Of course you fellows can always call on the Ninth Division over there in Dong Tam."

"Yeah, but the Ninth just got in from the States not too long ago. They tell me it's still pretty green and body-count conscious. Ben thinks they might be worse than no help at all."

"Maybe Ben's right." Jess shrugged. "But as far as I'm concerned, anybody with a pair of shoes and a canteen and a gun is a help."

Again he banked the helicopter abruptly. "Christ, they're

over here now!" he exclaimed. He unhooked his microphone and called the Can Tho tower, giving them his position. "There's some 104s working on a treeline right here," he said indignantly, "and nobody told me a goddamned thing about it! Isn't Paddy Control talking to you guys anymore?"

"Sorry," came the answer. "I guess you were on the ground when those planes were diverted."

Grumbling to himself, Jess switched back to Jerry's frequency and gave Jerry his estimated time of arrival in Can Tho.

"I still say a helicopter is not made for warfare," he said, replacing the microphone on its bracket. "Hell, they go so slow and maneuver so slow, you could hit one of them with a sling-shot. They can put Mickey Rooney in one of them, and send him into some real heroic film situations in Korea, but they're not gonna get old Theodorides flying around in the bullets. I'm strictly a mercenary civilian. Passengers and freight. No guns. No combat."

Toby was not listening to Jess. His mind was racing back over the meeting with Dang, to see if he could remember any hint that Dang might have known about this new battalion. No new recollection came to him. He must remember to include some questions about it in his list for the next meeting.

Dino and the pilot of the Porter had already landed their first loads at Can Tho and were taking off for another load when the helicopter approached the airfield. Bill had sent members of his office force to the airport to drive the visitors to the CORDS dormitory, in the same building that housed the bar.

Toby recognized Ski among the group, and spoke briefly with him. He did not know any of the other province officers person-ally. That could be because he was in an area of the world he had never visited before, but it was more likely because all these province officers were contract men, with only one or two years of work with the agency.

He put his overnight bag on the bed in the cramped room assigned to him and hurried across the driveway to the ROIC office spaces. Chet was at his desk. Across from him sat a figure that was familiar to Toby. They both got up when Toby entered, and Chet greeted him with an unusually bluff and hearty manner. Chet was feeling expansive.

"Toby," he said, shaking hands, "you remember Ernie Free."

"Sure. How you doing, Ernie?"

"He's down here partly to relax and partly to sit in on our conference. Nothing official. Just cruising around."

"Good to see you again, Toby," said Ernie. He was skinny and slightly stooped, and wore glasses with heavy black frames. Toby was sure they were intended to give him a studious, intellectual appearance.

"Haven't seen you since Frankfurt," Toby said. "I think we nearly crossed paths a couple of times there at headquarters, but somehow always missed."

"Yeah. Boy, I sure was sorry to hear about how that Frankfurt operation turned out."

"It was a real blow."

"I just couldn't believe that agent would do such a thing," Ernie said, his eyes wide with innocence. Toby caught an almost feline bite behind the words.

"Chet," Toby said, "sorry to break in on you like this, but I had a meeting the other night that may turn into a good operation. I've got the operational report in rough draft right here, and I've also got an intel written up on the information. I'd appreciate it if you'd have a look at them as soon as you can."

"OK," said Chet, taking the papers from him absently. He was more interested right now in talking with Ernie Free, but Toby noted that he had put the papers on the desk before him, rather than in his in-box. It implied that he would attend to them first, and Toby was sure that he would do so. As Bill Voigt had said, Chet would move papers when they came to him.

"Have you seen Laura yet?" Chet asked him.

"No."

"Better go in there right away. She'll give you a schedule and all the material you'll need for the meetings."

Toby joined a small group of recently arrived officers in Laura's office, and picked up a sheaf of papers. The schedule told him that he was free until one o'clock. He went to the admin offices and found several province officers there. He decided to wait until later to check on supplies for My Tho. He ambled by Jerry's counter, and Jerry greeted him cordially.

"The clan is beginning to gather in the bar," said Jerry.

"Where else?" Toby laughed. "Guess I'll go have a beer before lunch."

He entered the bar and ordered a beer. As he started to drink it, sitting on a stool at the bar, he caught inviting glances from a table nearby and went over to the group that was seated there. They introduced themselves. Walt Dewey, from An Xuyen Province, Delbert Cumber from Kien Phong, men from Bac Lieu, Chau Doc, and Kien Giang.

"You're a staff man," Cumber commented.

"Yep. An old whore."

"All of use here are under the contract program," Dewey explained.

"So I understand."

"We were just talking about the new informant Saigon is supposed to have."

"New informant?"

"Yeah. The guy that came down to talk to us about the Phoenix program was telling Chet that Saigon has just made a real breakthrough. They've got access to an informant on the COSVN staff."

The Central Office for South Vietnam ran all the VC and North Vietnamese operations in the south. Its composition and location were unknown to the ARVN and the American forces, although nobody doubted that the office did exist, and that it was located not far from Saigon. If Saigon did have a penetration of COSVN, it was a real victory.

"Did Chet say it was an *informant?*" Toby asked gently. "We

don't use that word very much. Agent, or source, maybe
but . . ."

"Christ, I don't remember the exact word," said Cumber.
"Shows you what a pro *I* am. Whatever Chet called it, Saigon
is excited about it."

Toby was uneasy about discussing a sensitive operation in a
group like this. He was relieved when the Bac Lieu man
changed the subject.

"How's things in My Tho?" Bac Lieu asked.

"Compared to what?" Toby said with a laugh. "We've got no
intelligence collection operations. We've got a main force battalion that is out there worrying the province like a dog with an
old rag, and we seem to have a lot of local force battalions
gathering around My Tho for some reason or other."

"You could give just about the same speech for Rock Jaw,"
said the Kien Giang man, and Toby remembered that the capital of Kien Giang Province was Rach Gia.

The others agreed. The Viet Cong were slowly gathering
forces for something, and seemed to be concentrating around
the provincial capitals.

"They're not even in a staging position yet," said Cumber,
obviously a man of military experience. "In fact, they seem to
be training, more than anything else."

"But you don't *know?*"

"Hell no. We don't really *know* hardly anything at all. We've
got rumors and some eyeball reports that are pretty definite.
Those battalions are there all right, but how many of them, and
what they've got, and what they're getting ready for, we
haven't the slightest idea."

"All the other Americans around An Xuyen are laughing at
us and razzing us all the time," said Dewey. "They say the CIA
has got a special weejee board and things like that. They don't
believe anything special is going on. Even the Province Senior
Adviser's office feels that way."

"So, they're not getting ready?"

"Nope. They couldn't hold off a squad of Boy Scouts, and they couldn't last a day without going to the grocery store."

Ski walked in. He bought a beer and joined the group.

"Tanks, by God! I'm seeing tanks."

"Come on, Ski," the Rach Gia man laughed. "Even if the VC had tanks, why in hell would they put them in Kien Tuong? Nothing ever happens in Kien Tuong. There's nothing there to happen."

"Who the hell said they were VC tanks, and who said they were in Kien Tuong?" Ski snorted. "These are North Vietnamese, and they're across the border in Cambodia."

"The hell you say!"

"Yes, sir, by God. I got a guy to take me up in one of those little forward observation planes, and we could see the goddamned things just as plain as day."

"You should have got some pictures of them."

"I tried," said Ski, "but I don't know a goddamned thing about any camera, and the Japanese job I had was so complicated that the pictures came out with those tanks looking like bushes in a cow pasture."

"That's probably what they were, Ski. Maybe Moc Hoa's getting to you at last."

"OK, you bastards," Ski growled good-naturedly, "go ahead and laugh. You'll have a great big thigh-slappin' belly laugh the day those bushes start coming across the border and shooting at you."

"Don't worry about it, Ski," said Dewey seriously. "If they are North Vietnamese tanks, they're going to have a hell of a problem operating. Tanks can't live off of the land. They can't swim in Mao Tse-tung's sea of the people. Tanks have got to have support, especially supply lines of fuel."

Cumber joined in. "Yeah, and anyway, they wouldn't attack you there in Moc Hoa. They won't be headed south, they'll be going east, right through the Parrot's Beak, right to Saigon. Saigon may not be very good at unconventional warfare, but one thing ARVN has got the equipment for is conventional warfare, including tanks. Right down their alley."

"We hope," Dewey muttered.

"Well," said Ski, "I told Chet about it, so Saigon will know."

"You *told* them about it?" Toby asked.

"Yeah."

"What are they supposed to do, telephone the information to Saigon?"

"Well, they'll do whatever—"

"If you saw those things with your own eyes, you've got the makings of an important intelligence report, but the people that need it can't use it if it doesn't come to them in complete detail, through channels, from the guy that knows."

"Well, Christ, I gave it to Chet, and he never said nothing about it like that."

"Have you ever written an intelligence report, Ski?" Toby asked.

"No."

"In Kien Tuong?" Cumber laughed.

"After the sessions today, if you want to get together with me," Toby went on, "we'll find a typewriter and rough out a report to turn in to the regional reports officer. I'll show you how to do it."

"OK," said Ski. "Let's do it." He looked triumphantly around at the group. Here was one man, a professional, who didn't laugh at what he had seen.

At one o'clock the province officers convened in the conference room for the first session. Their enjoyment of the situation was almost juvenile. The work of the province officer, while unlike that of any other intelligence assignment that Toby had ever heard of, was a solitary task. It was not that the officer was isolated from other human beings, or even from his own countrymen. The aloneness came more from the lack of anybody to talk shop with.

These fourteen province officers, privileged on these rare occasions to discuss their work with others who had the same assignments and the same problems, reveled in the camaraderie and self-importance of the occasion.

"How's things in Chuong Thien?"

"Some days a fellow thinks things are in good shape, and then they hit one of our villages, and we can see they're gaining on us."

"Got any penetrations of the VC?"

"Special Police say they got some, but I don't know what they are, and I sure haven't seen any good information out of them."

"Hey, An Xuyen! They tell me you got a new ARVN regiment stationed down there."

"Sure have. Damned good one, too. It's Colonel Thanh. He's a wild man, and he doesn't want any of this horse shit about Spookies and B-Fifties. He goes in after 'em, and his regiment acts like a bunch of Texans, they're so proud of themselves."

". . . and so if you want a little vacation, just go visit Ski. . . ."

". . . the sons of bitches come in and kick the hell out of Chau Doc for about a half an hour or so, and then zoom right back across that canal into Cambodia, and the only thing we can do is sit there with our thumb up our ass and watch 'em relax. Can't even shoot at them, because by that time they're out of small-arms range."

". . . I disseminated ten reports last month. . . ."

"Ten? You wrote ten reports?"

"I didn't say that. I disseminated ten that the Special Police sent me."

"That's a pretty useless exercise, isn't it?"

Disseminated ten reports, thought Toby uneasily. Nice guy, but he didn't know what the word "disseminate" meant in this business. Who would he have sent those reports to, to call it that? Not anybody along official CIA channels, because they would not conform to CIA requirements for dissemination. He was tempted to look into it. But no, what the hell, he couldn't tidy up the whole country. He had his hands full in his own province.

The more he mingled with them and talked with them, the more he was convinced that this was an exceptional group of young men. Better, in many respects, than an equal number of staff intelligence officers. There were no prima donnas among them. They were humble about their intelligence skills, but it was obvious to Toby that they had military skills that few of his fellow intelligence officers could boast. They knew what to do to make their little establishments as militarily strong and safe as possible. If rumors and reports about a Tet uprising were true, those military skills might be many times more important than intelligence collection capabilities right now.

A mumble of voices began to pour into the room from two heavy speakers at opposite corners—a "cocktail party" tape, several voices taped simultaneously and replayed to form a background of sound in the room. It would not prevent normal conversation, but to a bug that might be planted in that space anything that was said would only add one more voice to the confusion.

Bill Voigt came in and sat down at the head of the big table. A murmur of greeting came from the assembled men, and Bill returned it with a quick smile. Ex-OSS as he was, experienced in insurgency and paramilitary operations, he had a high regard for these men, and they returned the affection. Now his face grew grave.

"Is there anybody here who hasn't heard about Saigon's new source?" he asked. They had all heard.

"I had an idea that was the case," Bill said, looking straight at Toby. "How does that information strike you, Toby?"

Toby shifted uneasily, and looked around at the other men apologetically. "It worries the hell out of me."

Bill had expected the response. The others were surprised. "Why?"

"Well, if *I* had laid on an important operation like that, I'd hate to think everybody in the whole agency was gossiping about it in bars and offices."

Bill nodded, and looked slowly around at all the faces turned toward him. There was a dead silence, except for the muttering of the speakers.

"Think about that, gentlemen," Bill said. "Think about the case officer that is running that operation. Think about the agent he's got, in a situation where that agent is going to get killed if the VC begin to suspect him; but remember that he won't have the privilege of dying easily or quickly. He'll be leaned on very, very hard, first.

"I am not going to tell you or confirm to you any information you believe you've got. I realize that this business is still a little new to most of you, and that you figured it was all right to talk with each other because we're all cleared, and that the hours and hours of drilling you on security procedures seemed just like a formality. But, gentlemen, let me tell you, it is no formality. This is not a girls' boarding school. We can talk shop as long as we keep it general. But don't talk about specific operations, either your own or anybody else's, not even to a fellow province officer, unless the person you're talking to has got to know, for official reasons. Is that clear?"

There were nods and grunts of assent.

"All right. That's all I intend to say on the subject, and I am confident it's all I will ever have to say from now on."

Toby glanced around the room and thought that Bill was probably right. His message had sunk in.

Bill dealt with some minor administrative matters, and then called in their guest from Saigon, who would be in charge of training them for the new program.

The Saigon man set up an easel with a flip chart of chains of command, and areas of responsibility. He passed out instruction sheets. He lectured the men on what they must do to initiate the program, and how they were to keep it going. PRU advisers would be given a training program a week or so later, and the PRU men must be held closely accountable to this new program. It was a hard, rational, coordinated attack on the secret Viet Cong structure within the territory and society of the south. It would be the major CIA contribution to the war effort from this moment forward.

Toby was fascinated. In all his years of collecting intelligence, this was the first time he had ever been involved in an enterprise where the collection would be in large part done by armed teams of men who would move at night through the countryside. He wished that there had been a more liberal salting of experienced staff officers among this group, men who would know better what to do with the information once they got it. On the other hand, these men would know how to *get* the information in the first place, which was also of primary importance.

He was not the only one to have thought along those lines. Much of the time in the two-day course was scheduled for training the men in the processing of the information once it was obtained. It was all elementary to Toby, but he realized that it was new to the rest of them.

But he was also sure that these young men, who knew so well how to survive and function in an insurgency situation, were bright enough to learn quickly the skills of intelligence work.

Except, perhaps, for Ski.

In the interim between the last session and an informal reception on that first day, which Bill Voigt had organized in his quarters, Toby worked with Ski to produce a draft of an intelligence report on his sighting of tanks. They went with the draft to the office of the regional reports officer, who read it with interest and said it could be submitted pretty much exactly as it had been written.

Ski was jubilant. What would be a modest task to a man reasonably adept at assembling and writing down facts in an orderly report was a major triumph to this veteran rifleman, who had earned his sergeant's stripes by combat, not by literary efforts. Toby had found him to be so inept at organizing and writing down what he knew that there was never any likelihood he would produce intelligence reports on his own in the future. This would perhaps be his only real production for the entire tour in Kien Tuong, and he could have had a right to be elated. But there was no doubt that Kien Tuong, where nothing ever happened, was the place for Ski.

At Bill's reception, to which the Regional Senior Adviser and a number of his staff had been invited so that they could meet the province officers, Toby had only a brief opportunity to speak to Chet.

"I read your material," Chet said coolly. "I want to talk to you about it tomorrow. Come to my office during the sessions on reports writing. You don't need that training."

"OK."

Toby stood and watched Chet move off, with Ernie Free in tow, introducing Ernie to guests, and leaving no doubt that he thought the gaunt, bespectacled man was a paragon of all the important virtues. Toby wondered at the strange friendship. He knew of nobody else who considered himself to be a close personal friend of Chet. Chet was so abrasive and defensive that other men were not tempted to exchange gossip or intimate thoughts with him. It was almost as if Ernie had tapped an unsuspected well of regard and affection in the depths of that prickly personality, and Ernie seemed to soak up the results without tiring. He cracked jokes and made Chet laugh. He listened to Chet's talk with shining eyes.

Toby would have thought that a man as basically cynical as Chet would have caught on to Ernie's act—and Toby was certain that it *was* an act. Ernie either didn't care, or didn't know how, to disguise his sycophancy. His mental stature was reflected in the object of that adulation, Toby thought. What could Chet ever do for him in the agency? If you're going to be a brown-nose, you ought to pick somebody who can do something for you.

Bill passed around a clipping from a newspaper account written by Chris Christopher. It was a lively and laudatory account of the PRUs, organized on a framework of a typical PRU nighttime operation against a Viet Cong village. Toby had a chance to talk it over with Wilbur, whose name appeared in the story, and Wilbur was pleased with the results of his operation.

"She didn't care very much for the bloodshed," he said, "and I was afraid maybe she might concentrate too much on that, or maybe even blast us for it, but she didn't. It's a good story. I'm having it translated and circulated to my PRUs here in Can Tho. They're always so proud of any kind of recognition like this in the American press. This is going to be better than a raise in pay. Say, would you like to have a copy of the translation to show to your own unit down there? I imagine Little Jack would like that. If you think so, I'll send you some copies."

"Thanks. I'd appreciate that."

During the reports-writing session the following day, Toby went to Chet's office. Ernie Free was there. He made no move to leave. Toby would have preferred to discuss the matter alone with Chet, but did not want to raise an issue that would get in the way of his main objective.

"Busch, I'm not going to send in this intel," Chet began tonelessly. "You've been had. This information goes absolutely against what Saigon is getting from its new source, and we've got nothing to justify sending this in. You don't even have any positive identification of your source. Nobody has ever heard of any series of orientation lectures for local force battalion commanders in Tay Ninh, and frankly I doubt that the VC would do such a thing."

Toby fought to keep his temper. "But the Saigon source is the only thing you're basing this decision on?"

"Let's put it this way," Chet said. "What they've got is a

high-level penetration—a hell of a lot higher level than a local force battalion commander, *if* that's what you've got."

"That's what I've got."

"Well, the reports from their source say that all these so-called preparations for the big offensive at the time of Tet are just for the purpose of keeping the country off balance, keeping the pressure on the Thieu government. They know they haven't got the strength to take on the ARVN and the American forces in conventional battle."

"How come this battalion commander doesn't know that?"

"Hell, Busch, use your head!" Chet glanced at Ernie, as if inviting him to share in deprecating Toby's obtuseness. "If you were planning that kind of a deception, would you let all your people in the field know it was a deception?"

Toby's gorge was rising, and he gripped the arms of the chair to control himself. It was true that the information agreed with Dang's assessment of Viet Cong capabilities; they couldn't succeed in such an uprising. But a deception operation on such a massive scale, involving the mobilization and disposition of so much of their military strength, merely to intimidate their enemy, didn't make sense to him.

"You mean they're doing all this just for show?"

"Well, no, the source never said that. He has said that they intend to carry out a series of local attacks, one right after another, starting after Tet. You know, Tet is a sacred holiday to these people and the VC aren't likely to mess it up with an offensive on that day." Chet sat back smugly in his chair, as if he had delivered the final blow.

Ernie hitched forward in his chair. "I can sympathize with you, Toby," he said unctuously. "I've got a penetration of the provincial committee in my province"—he said this with such studied matter-of-factness that it came across as blatant boasting to Toby—"and even *they* don't know about these plans of COSVN, although I think they suspect something like it."

Toby looked for a moment at the innocent eyes behind their heavy black frames, then turned away.

"What you're saying," he said to Chet, "is that you are basing your decision not to disseminate this information on the fact that the report disagrees with other information?"

"It disagrees with information from an established and tested source, yes. Your information comes from somebody we haven't even identified yet."

"Well, let me tell you something. I don't believe the information from your 'established and tested source.' "

"Oh? You don't believe a penetration of COSVN knows what he's talking about?"

"I'm out in the province, and this thing just doesn't look like a bluff to me." Toby realized that he had allowed himself to be led into a position of defending his information from the strength of his emotions about it. Not a very professional way to deal with intelligence matters.

"Another one of your gut feelings?" Chet sneered, glancing at Ernie. Ernie shook his head and smiled.

"Not just *my* gut feeling. The gut feelings of everybody that gets out into the provinces. The pilots and the province officers and the PRU advisers and the pacification teams."

"What are we supposed to do, make an intelligence report by majority vote?"

"No, but we ought to keep our minds and our ears open."

"That includes your own mind and your own ears, I suppose?"

"It ought to include everybody's."

"The report doesn't go."

"I could ask . . ." Toby began, then paused.

"Ask Bill?" Chet retorted sharply. He was waiting for that. Toby knew that he did not have a solid enough case to warrant putting the decision up to Bill, and Chet knew it, too.

"Forget it," Toby said, and rose to leave.

"The operational report will go in, of course," Chet said. "But this one either goes back to you or into the burn bag."

"I'll pick it up before I leave," Toby said. The operational report was mainly for the record. It would be read with some interest and filed away to await further developments from the field. Not even a hint of it would ever reach a customer.

He walked out and went across the driveway to the bar. It was almost time for lunch anyway, and he could have a beer and get his nerves back under control before he did or said something foolish.

Dino and Jess were sitting at the bar, glasses of beer on the dark wooden counter before them, engaged in a Greco-Roman skirmish.

"Hey, Toby," Dino exclaimed, "reinforcements! This Balkan won't admit that he doesn't know a thing about wines."

"You think *I* do?" Toby asked, signaling the girl behind the bar that he wanted a beer.

"Well, only a little bit, maybe, because with a name like Busch you gotta be classified as a *tedesco;* but after all, the Germans have got *some* wines that are all right."

"On behalf of Germany, I thank you," said Toby, raising his glass.

"Fact is," said Jess, picking up his own glass and peering through the amber liquid at the lights behind the bar, "beer is what started the argument. Caesar Augustus here was just saying that it's a shame we live in a culture dominated by the northern European influence, because beer is their drink, instead of all those great eyetalian wines. He thinks eyetalian wines are best. Better even than the French."

"I know they are," Dino volunteered. "And I know something else. Nobody in the world puts turpentine in their wine, except the Greeks."

"Turpentine," said Jess disgustedly. "Only a dumb eyetalian can't taste the difference between turpentine and a good retsina."

"Jess," said Dino slowly, rotating his glass of beer in the light, "to speak of a good retsina is like talking about a pleasant plane crash. There ain't no such animal."

"Too bad that bullet didn't hit you in the head instead of the wing," said Jess. "It wouldn't have done any damage there."

Toby was interested. "You get hit by a bullet?"

"Yeah," said Dino, becoming serious. "I don't know where or when it happened, exactly, but from the looks of it it was heavy stuff. Maybe fifty-caliber."

"That's something new, isn't it?"

"Well, in a way, yes. Our planes have been getting shot at now and then all along, but it's always been when they went low near VC territory."

"Which is where I never go," said Jess.

"But now it seems to be happening in places you never would have expected before. Jess damned near got racked by some tracers a couple of days ago."

"Boy, that stops being fun pretty quick," said Toby.

"Damn right," said Jess. "Much more of that, and I may just turn in my Texaco road map and go home."

"We don't agree about wines," said Dino, "but we agree about bullets."

But Dino could not be serious for long. He ordered another beer, and when the girl brought him his change he caught her tiny hand in his.

"I know you're saying to yourself that I'm drinking too much," he said fiercely. The twinkle in her eye revealed the extent of her fright.

"I do not say," she said.

"Do you know why I drink too much?"

She shook her head.

"Because"—his voice descended to a rasping whisper—"because I love you, and you will not run away with me. That's why. You don't love me, do you?"

"Yes."

"You do?" Dino was incredulous.

"Yes, I do not love you. My husband would not like it."

They all burst out laughing, except Dino, who could not

credit what his ears had heard. "Your husband? Do you mean that a little bitty girl like you, practically a baby, is married?"

"I am twenty-seven, Mr. Dino," said the girl, lifting her chin high, as if it would make her diminutive body taller and more impressive.

"Your husband is a lucky man, darling. He must love you almost as much as I do."

The girl went back to her work, glancing now and then in fond amusement at Dino. He finished his beer and he and Jess went into the dining room.

The door opened, and the province officers trooped in for drinks and lunch. Ernie Free was among them. He sat down on the stool next to Toby.

"Havin' a little brew before lunch?" he asked, with that forced bonhomie that seemed to characterize his dealings with other men.

"Yeah," said Toby shortly.

Ernie ordered a beer.

"This new program looks awfully good to me," he went on, looking for a subject that would open communications between them. Toby relented. His anger had subsided, and after all, his quarrel wasn't with Ernie, no matter how the latter's mannerisms might irritate him.

"Yeah," he said, "it makes a lot of sense. First thing we've done in this country that does make sense, it seems to me."

"You can say that again," said Ernie, paying for his beer and lifting his glass. "You know, I guess you and I are among the three or four staff men in the provinces in the whole country."

"Sure looks that way. It's no wonder we haven't got much in the way of collection operations."

"I know what you mean! Even though it does look like operating here isn't so hard for anybody that knows how to do it." He pushed the heavy black-framed glasses up on his nose and took another drink of his beer with a studied nonchalance. Toby stole a glance at him. Whatever his operational skills might be, he was certainly no actor. He could not conceal his eagerness to tell Toby of his triumphs in Kanh Hoa Province. He was a man who could not live without the approval of everybody around him.

"You may be right," Toby replied. He could not bring himself to play the game.

"I hadn't been in Nha Trang more than a couple of days before I found a way to get access to the Kanh Hoa Provincial Committee." He spoke in a low tone that could not be over-heard in the noisy bar, but he was nevertheless violating the rule about talking shop. The tone implied a modest judgment that this operation of his was such an elementary piece of business that any other operations officer would have done exactly the same thing if he had been in Ernie's shoes.

"Have you got an approved project on that?"

Ernie nodded. "It's a going operation. Producing good info."

"Congratulations."

"Thanks. I must say," he continued, with a transparent attempt to be disarmingly frank and professional, "that the info I get coincides with what Chet was saying. These preparations are a deception, an intimidation, not real preparations for battle."

"My source says the opposite."

"But you don't know yet if he—"

"No, he hasn't been cleared or approved yet."

Toby had the uneasy feeling that Ernie was trying to needle him rather than seek his approval, and he was relieved that just at that moment young Will Voigt came in. Toby beckoned him to a seat on the opposite side of him from Ernie. The young soldier bore himself proudly, his uniform spotless and starchy, his boots mirror-like.

"You've met so many of us these two days," said Toby, "that you won't remember our names, I know. I'm Toby Busch, and this is Ernie Free."

"You're right, Mr. Busch," he said, shaking hands with the

two of them. "I remember seeing you and hearing your names, but I couldn't have called the names right at this minute."

"I think we're close enough together in age," said Toby, "that I'd feel comfortable if you called me Toby."

"Same here," said Ernie.

"All right," said the soldier.

"I'm province officer in My Tho, and Ernie is up at Nha Trang."

"Things pretty hot down here in the delta?"

"Tense is a better word, I think."

"I think you're right. That's what you feel in the air up in Two Corps, too. A lot of tension."

"Personally," said Ernie, "I think it's just a ploy of the Viet Cong. Keep us uptight. Doesn't cost them much to do it, and it wears our side down."

Will looked at him curiously and shrugged. He did not seem to share Ernie's opinion.

"I've been looking forward to meeting you," Toby said. "Your father is so proud of you, it's all he can do to keep from telling every one of us we're not half the man his son is."

Will's eyes softened. "Yeah, I know. The old man is a dedicated patriot and flag-waver."

"You don't believe in waving the flag?"

"I'm even worse than he is."

"Very few men your age feel that way these days, it seems."

"Very few men my age have been raised the way I have, Toby. Ever since I was born I've been traveling and living all over the world."

"Yep. That's life in the CIA."

"I guess the son of an operations officer, ex-OSS, would have more travel under his belt when he reaches high school than almost any other kid in the world. I've been all over the Orient with the family, and in a way I'm more at home in this area than I am in the United States. I speak Japanese and pretty good Mandarin, and Tagalog, and I can get around in some other languages, too. I've grown up with Asians, and I know something about how they feel. All these kids beating their breasts in the States give me a pain in the ass, because they don't know a goddamned thing about the world they're so shook up about."

"That's what we CIA men do to our children," said Toby thoughtfully. "We make cosmopolitans out of them. Linguists. World travelers. World citizens. And maybe unhappy?"

Will pursed his lips. "Oh, it can be tough sometimes, but there are compensations. I know that when I used to go back to Dad's hometown and meet some of the kids, I'd wonder how they could be so ignorant about the world, and how they could ever be happy confined to a little old town like that, with nothing but their dads' cars and drive-in movies, and dragging Main Street. That was when I appreciated the life I've had."

Toby turned sideways abruptly and looked at the young soldier. "You volunteer for this duty?"

"How could I stay out, with the old man in it this way?"

Toby stared at the rings on the bar. "I wonder if I ought to find another profession before my own son reaches military age?"

"He might just get killed in a drag race on Main," Will laughed.

"Then you don't think we give our kids psychological problems?" Ernie asked him.

"Oh, I don't know. Maybe so. But who doesn't have some kind of psychological problems? Spook kids are different, that's all."

"I suppose so."

"Other kids have nightmares about falling, or about trying to run away from something and not being able to move their legs."

"Yeah."

"You know what the bad dream is of most kids that have moved all over the world all their lives?"

"No, what?"

"Ask your own kids sometime, maybe after they're in high school, and I'll bet they'll tell you they've had some variation on this dream. I've asked friends of mine, spook kids and diplomatic kids, and lots of them do. It's a dream where you leave your house in the morning and go to school, or go out to do something, you know? And then when you come back . . ." Will paused and looked at Toby intently, ". . . home isn't there anymore. The house isn't there. Nothing is there."

"It sounds worse than being chased."

"You wake up sweating."

They drank their beer in silence for a moment, then Ernie spoke. "What do you do up there in Two Corps?"

"I'm adviser to a platoon of Vietnamese Rangers."

"What're they like?"

"They're good. Give them good leaders and they fight. But giving them good leaders seems to turn out to be a pretty hard thing to do."

"It's the story of Vietnam, apparently," said Toby.

They finished their beer and went into the dining room. They sat down at the table with Dino and Jess, who were already halfway through lunch, and partway through a heated discussion of why the Italians had not been able to subdue the Greeks without Hitler's help.

11

The inauguration of the Phoenix program made it all the more urgent for Toby to begin the training of his Special Police class. He got prompt security clearance on the students, and although he had not received all the materials and equipment he had asked for, he convened the class and began to teach them with what he had.

They were young, neat men, of slight stature, attentive and respectful. One of them Toby immediately nicknamed Gabby to himself, because he kept the entire class amused during their leisure moments. Another one reminded him of a Charlie Chan movie, and he dubbed him Number One Son. Whatever their personalities, they were serious about the training. Ben sat among them, and they accepted him without question.

Minnie sat on one edge of the little platform, perched on a high stool, and interpreted with his usual speed and self-effacing skill.

These men had already had some training in intelligence work, and Toby did not waste time in preliminary orientation. He plunged directly into the first subject.

"Clandestine communications," he said, "are the thread, the cord, that all of our work is bound together by. Without communications, intelligence has no value whatsoever. In this course, I intend for you to learn how to communicate messages clandestinely in the presence of the enemy.

"Now, that does not necessarily mean to communicate with-

153

out being seen. In fact, perhaps the best way to communicate clandestinely is in full view of the world, doing things the on-looker can observe without any idea that what he is seeing or hearing is a message from you to somebody else.

"When our adversary becomes suspicious of us, he has taken the first step toward uncovering us, and destroying us. There-fore, it is better for your adversary to be confident that he knows everything you are doing, rather than have him wonder-ing about some gaps in your day, or some equipment you have that doesn't look right. In other words, keep your enemy happy while you go about kicking him in the ass."

He hoped that Minnie would be able to put that into Viet-namese with some effect, and he was not disapointed. There was a burst of appreciative laughter, and he grinned his thanks to Minnie. He was off to a good start.

He worked them hard. He taught them the techniques of surveillance, neighborhood checks, target analysis. Agent selec-tion, assessment, development. Recruitment techniques.

He hurried them. Tet was beginning to loom.

He wrote a skit on recruiting, and used Minnie and Therese in it, with the students participating to learn. There was little enthusiasm or comment about the skit, and he wondered if role playing was a good way to teach them.

He read scornfully the comment from one of their own office's intelligence reports, in which the reporting officer had urged the military reader of his message to "destroy the battal-ion" which the report had described.

"Your function is to give information," he told them, "not to take or recommend action about that information. You can tell your customer what the battalion is doing, how big it is, how many guns, who belongs to it, and how you got the information, but you have no authority to tell him to attack the battalion or ignore it.

"Suppose you were selling eggs in a stall in the municipal market. You have the moral obligation to tell the customer, if he wants to know, when the eggs were laid, whether they are chicken eggs or duck eggs, and what your price is. After he buys them, you have no authority to tell him that he must go home and make an omelette with them."

Toby thought this analogy would be mildly amusing to them, but he was disappointed. The students looked more puzzled than amused.

That afternoon, Minnie approached him after the class. "May I speak with you for a moment about the class, sir?"

"Sure."

"Let me invite you to have a beer."

"It'll be a pleasure."

They went to a small bar on the main street of the town and sat at a table on the sidewalk with bottles of San Miguel before them.

"You teach very well," Minnie began.

"It's nice of you to say so."

"Interpreting, I believe, ought to be more than just changing words from one language to another. It should make communications move between persons with full and correct meanings."

"No question about that."

"Then, I hope you will not be offended if I offer you some advice you have not asked for, and perhaps may feel that you do not need?"

"Go ahead. I won't be offended."

"I think perhaps some things about the Vietnamese mind, about his soul, have not yet become clear to you. Most Americans see the world from a very American point of view, and they cannot even conceive that there may be other ways to look at ordinary things. Of course, the same may be said of the Vietnamese. When this happens, I believe it to be the obligation of the more educated one to make the bridge between them."

"I certainly can't quarrel with that."

"Some of the things you teach are very American, or you teach them in a very American way. These men do not have backgrounds that help them see the difference, and so sometimes the communication is absent."

"I've had a feeling about that several times."

"Your class on recruitment, for example."

"Not very good? But they seemed attentive."

"They would not be ill-mannered."

"But, Minnie, believe me, I know something about recruiting. That part of the instruction is the part I feel the most confident about."

"I do not doubt that your techniques would succeed in Europe. If Therese had been a German or a French woman in our little drama, I believe you could have convinced her that dictatorship is bad and democracy is good; but I do not believe you would ever succeed in approaching and recruiting a Vietnamese for these reasons, the theories of democracy against dictatorship or totalitarianism."

"My God, Minnie," Toby exclaimed, clearly skeptical. "Our experience all over the world through all the years, as far as I know, is that ideology is the most important motivation of all. I don't mean that other countries ought to imitate the United States. But men naturally want freedom and justice, and will usually fight for them. Money is important, but not the most important. Blackmail is the worst, and we don't use it."

"Blackmail is bad anywhere in the world, I believe," Minnie agreed, "and money is important, even to the Vietnamese." He smiled and took a drink of his beer. "But if you want to recruit a Vietnamese, look for connections and levers in his family."

"His family?"

"Yes. Family is what makes a Vietnamese fight, or become emotional, or join one side or the other."

"Nothing but family?"

"Of course, it is not that simple. Other things do matter. But the most important, the first consideration of all, is his feeling for his family. This I believe you do not have in the European societies."

"No, certainly not in that sense."

"Another thing is the story about the eggs."

Toby scratched his head ruefully. "What was the matter with that story?"

"It is that the Vietnamese mind and the American mind seem to be on two separate roads in this matter."

"How do you mean?"

"In this respect, I am very Vietnamese myself, Mr. Busch. I confess that I do not understand the value of the story. I have been told that it is because of our reaction to what you call 'the what-if.' You suggested that we think what we might do if we were sellers in the marketplace. But you see, we are *not* sellers in the marketplace. How can we know what a seller feels? I am sure the class were all thinking that what they would need to do would be to find a seller in the marketplace and ask *him* about these things."

"But it's just a question of using your imagination."

"Perhaps. But a Vietnamese does not use his imagination that way."

Toby studied Minnie's words. "You mean that I can never successfully illustrate a point by asking the students to make believe they are somebody else?"

"Yes."

"Yes, I cannot?"

"Yes, you cannot."

"That's another thing," Toby said with a grin. "I notice that when you ask a Vietnamese a negative question, and he wants to give you a negative answer, he says yes."

"I do not understand."

"If I ask you, for example, 'Minnie, you are not a secret Viet Cong agent, are you?' what would you say?"

"I would say yes."

"Meaning you are not a Viet Cong agent."

"Yes."

"Americans would say no. 'No, I am not a Viet Cong agent.' "

"Vietnamese would say, 'Yes, I am not a Viet Cong agent.' "

"Now I wonder why that is?"

"For the Vietnamese, it is impolite to disagree."

"Can't you disagree in a polite way?"

"No. You must give your opinion in such a way that it will not be a disagreement, or appear to be a disagreement. It is a matter of form, but it is important."

"Well, I can understand that. Form is important, sometimes even in our pragmatic old United States."

"There is another thing, Mr. Busch," Minnie went on. "I have seen you come near another thing that must not be done, and I wonder if you know about it. From the way you speak, I think not."

"What's that, Minnie?"

"It is the power of words. To say the words sometimes makes a thing happen."

"Now *I'm* the one who doesn't understand," said Toby.

"If you asked one of the students what he would do if the Viet Cong captured and threatened his wife, he would be very frightened."

"He would? Why?"

"Because he believes that saying the words can cause the thing to happen. He thinks words have substance . . . force . . . power. So he does not say them, and does not want to have them said."

"But surely that is a superstition?"

"Call it what you like, it is very real. The Vietnamese believe that words have physical power."

"I appreciate your concern, and I won't forget," said Toby. He looked at his watch. "It's getting late."

Minnie put a hand on his arm to delay him. "That is one more thing, Mr. Busch, if you will pardon me for just another moment."

"OK," said Toby, resuming his seat. "What is it?"

"Time. You hurry the students on. You tell them time is short."

"Sure. You have to have some kind of a time framework."

"That is true. But the framework is different for a Viet-namese."

"How?"

"You must have heard that the oriental concept of time is circular, the occidental concept linear? To you, time moves in a straight line, and never repeats."

"That's right. And I have heard of the circular concept, but I don't understand it at all."

"Neither can we Vietnamese understand your linear con-cept. To us, time is eternal and repeating. A man, a soul, does not just begin at a point and end at another point on a line. He moves from one existence to another, in a circle of thousands of centuries. What he does in this one is not final or irrevocable, because this is not his only chance, his only existence."

"That, Minnie, is completely beyond my understanding," said Toby.

"I believe that neither people can completely understand the other in this respect. But it is important for us to know about the concepts we do not share."

"You are a thoughtful man, Minnie."

"Vietnam needs men to be thoughtful as well as brave. After this war we must make a society that will be just and free, and Vietnamese."

"Amen to that."

"We must be able to withstand and throw off the American influence."

Toby was startled. "Throw off . . ."

"Mr. Busch, the French have gone, but now the Americans have come. It is not the same thing, and their intentions are good, but their power and wealth are very great in a small country like Vietnam, and the Vietnamese admire and imitate and envy what they see. Especially the youth. But we cannot *become* Americans. Someday the Americans will leave, we hope"—Minnie smiled good-naturedly—"and when they do, we must be prepared to be Vietnamese once again. That is why our country needs thoughtful men. I want to help. I would even like to be one of the leaders when the time comes."

"I have an idea you will be. But if what you say is true, then it would mean that death shouldn't matter to a Vietnamese?"

"No, it does not mean that. You Christians believe in heaven, which is a glorious place, many times better than this earth, and yet death is a tragedy to Christians, is it not?"

"I see what you mean."

"You have seen death in Vietnam, Mr. Busch. Death is all around us, constantly, but no matter how much death is around, it is always tragic to those who remain behind."

"Yes."

"Someday we will look back at this time and see that we were just episodes, and that the war is just one episode on that circle of thousands of years." Minnie traced a large circle in the air with his index finger.

"Or," said Toby with a twinkle in his eye, "an episode along that straight line of thousands of years that stretches from there to there." He traced a straight line in the air with his finger.

Minnie grinned broadly at him. "There we have you," he said. "You will fall off the end of your line someday, and disappear into nothing. But we will still be here." Again he traced the circle in the air. "Moving around in our circle of time."

12

"You know, Toby," said Ben, "if I conform to the normal schedule of my tour here, I'll be home on leave from about the middle of January till the second week in February."

"Yes, I know," Toby replied. He had been planning to bring the matter up with Ben, but had hoped that he would have some more reliable information about the Tet uprising.

Ben sat down across the desk from him, obviously exploring the subject, rather than making a request. "The same rumors and the same feelings are around about trouble during Tet, you know?"

"I know."

"Well, you also heard about the information Saigon has that it may be a bluff?"

"Yes."

"The VC are certainly capable of such a trick."

"I suppose they are."

"I sure as hell hate to think of postponing my leave, too. My folks are going to be expecting me, and all. After all, the only thing we've got is just kind of a feeling or a suspicion. A fellow can't plan his life just on the basis of feelings like that."

"Certainly not. But we do have to use our judgment," said Toby, trying to make his voice sound casual and neutral. He did not want to force a decision. It would be better if it came from Ben.

"I agree. The thing that bothers me is that it could happen

that I would postpone my leave, and *then* when I did go on it, all hell would break loose."

Toby remembered the predictions of Chet and Ernie about a delayed offensive. They troubled him. "Ben, I know you're in a hell of a spot on this decision."

"I sure am. If I'm not here and my teams get into deep trouble . . ."

"It's a hell of a prospect, isn't it?"

"Have you got a preference about what I do?"

This was the direct question. Ben was leaving the decision to Toby.

"Yes," said Toby. "I want you to postpone it."

"Any particular reason, except for our feelings?"

"Yes."

"Can you tell me what it is?"

"No." Toby wished he could tell Ben about Dang, but steeled himself against the temptation.

Ben got up. He seemed disappointed, but also somehow strangely relieved. "So be it, boss. I'll put it off. I don't have to tell you that I sure would like to know anything you can tell me . . . whenever you can tell me."

"You can count on it."

"One thing more. If everything seems to be hanging together all right, will you mind if I arrange to take a few days around Christmas up at Vung Tau? Get out on the beach a little bit, and there really is quite a bit of legitimate work in the training camp that I can be doing."

"Go ahead and plan it," said Toby. Ben went out whistling tunelessly, and Toby returned his attention to the agenda he was preparing in his small notebook.

If only Ben and Little Jack could both be away from My Tho *tonight,* he thought. Once again he must drive out that gate with Therese, to make the second meeting with Dang. He knew what they would think, and he hated it. He had rehearsed all kinds of casual remarks to himself, to explain lightly to them that he was just taking Therese home because he had to go that way for this or that reason, or because she was going to help him select a gift for Mary Lynn in one of the shops in town; but he knew that such a casual remark, volunteered out of the blue, would be more likely to arouse their suspicions than allay them.

And so he did not even try to dissemble. He and Therese drove out the gate as if it were the normal and customary thing to do. He had no briefcase, although the little notebook was tucked into the pocket of his trousers, to help him maintain an efficient structure for the coming meeting with Dang.

Again they walked down the path, Therese ahead, wheeling her motorbike, and he self-consciously carrying a small package. It contained some items of toiletry and perfumes, which Therese had agreed would be good gifts for their act.

"But soaps and perfumes are not like television, Mr. Busch. One consumes them."

"Don't give it a thought, Therese," he said. "Let's just say that these are payment for the overtime. You're not collecting any money for all these extra hours, you know."

How graceful she was, even at the awkward task of wheeling the bike down a crooked path. The flowing lines of her *ao dai* undulated enticingly from the waist outward over the woman-curve of her hips, and made a delightful contrast with the hard, ungainly lines of the bike.

She locked her bike to the post, put her shoes just outside the door, snugly together, pointing precisely at the door frame.

They sat on the floor in the light of the television screen and waited. Toby sat close to her, but at this point his mind had blanked out all thoughts except for the coming meeting.

He went over his agenda with her, questioning her on some parts of it, letting her know what he intended to do at certain points so that she would be prepared for the interpretation. For this business he wished that he could have had Minnie. He would have been more confident of the communications, and communication was everything in the case of an agent under development, such as Dang. Therese did well enough, but she still had not caught the ability to take herself completely out of the conversation, the ability to avoid the "he says" locution that makes the interpreter a part of the conversation instead of simply an impersonal channel for it.

He closed the little book and tucked it into his shirt pocket. He was ready now. Now, when he looked at her, she was a woman again, the girl on the path with the bike. Her eyes returned his gaze for a moment, then she looked away shyly. There was something so appealing, so irresistible about the sadness in those lovely eyes. He realized that he was coming to trust her without any substantial reason for it. He also realized that no matter how unprofessional such an attitude might be, he was not uncomfortable about it.

Dang came in. This time he was purposeful, unhesitating. His eyes looked tired, perhaps more tired than they had at the first meeting. He held a small bundle of papers, and Toby's hand darted out and grasped it the moment Dang stepped through the door. Toby prodded and poked the packet, and then handed it back to its owner. Dang understood.

"Mr. Dang, what have you brought me to prove that you *are* Hoang Duc Dang?" Toby asked, as they assumed their places on the floor.

Dang untied the string from around the bundle of papers and extracted two sheets from it. "I have thought about this for a long time," he said. "To fight against a bad cause is good, but to betray comrades is bad."

Therese had benefited from the experience of the first night. Her interpreting was smoother now, and usually omitted the "he says."

"I understand," said Toby. "These are difficult decisions for a man to make."

"I have decided that it is more important that you should believe me now, without delay, than it is to avoid danger for my comrades. Our whole country is in danger."

"I believe that," said Toby. But the remark made him slightly uneasy. His experience with clandestine agents was that, probably because their lives of secrecy provide them with few other emotional outlets, they have frequent urges to harangue their case officer with long patriotic speeches. He is an outlet. He is the only one to whom they can say these things. Toby had always felt that these moments were good for the agent, and helpful to the case officer–agent relationship, and he listened sympathetically. But in this case he did not have enough time to let Dang ramble on and was searching his mind for a way to stem the tide before it began, when Dang himself seemed to awaken to what he was doing.

"We do not have time for explanations," said Dang. "I believe you understand."

"I understand."

"Here," said Dang, extending the document, two sheets of paper covered with closely written words, "is a list of all the men of the Determination-to-Win Battalion. That will show you that I am Hoang Duc Dang, their commander."

"It will help, Mr. Dang. But I must point out to you that even if you were merely a clerk, you could have brought me such a list."

Dang nodded. He had been expecting this reaction. "If you wish to select any single name on that list," said Dang, "I will see that he goes on a visit to his home at a certain time. You may set the date, although you must allow time for him to travel. You may arrest him and interrogate him. You will find that he is what the list says he is."

Toby nodded. "You would be willing to have one of your own men arrested?"

Dang smiled. "The sacrifice would be mine, not his, because we do not have men to spare. As to his own feelings, if he knows that he has not done anything to betray himself, that his arrest is only a misfortune and not his own fault, and of no shame to him or his honor, he may even be glad to be arrested. There is no war on Phu Quoc Island, and the food and conditions in the prison camp there are in many ways better than they are for the men of the Determination-to-Win Battalion in the field."

Toby looked at the list and consulted with Therese. He pointed to a name, and she circled it and noted the village the man came from.

"Have this man," said Toby to Dang, pointing to the name, "at his home on Saturday and Sunday of next week. We will find out if he is a Viet Cong soldier, but without arresting him." He did not know how Manh's men handled prisoners, and did not want to subject the man to torture just to establish Dang's bona fide.

Dang looked at him quizzically. *Good,* thought Toby. *He believes our intelligence on his battalion is good; let him think we also have capabilities along other lines that he is not aware of.*

"Mr. Dang," he went on, placing the list on the floor beside him and pulling his notebook out of his shirt pocket, "can you make it back here for one more meeting?"

"Yes."

"When can you make it."

"One month?"

"That is a long time. You cannot make it sooner?"

"No. It would be dangerous."

"All right. It will be the last meeting between us, unless an emergency comes up. At that meeting we will take a great deal of time to establish systems of communication and alert."

They set the time and date for the meeting, and changed the safety signal from the shoes by the door to one shutter slightly ajar.

"Mr. Dang, we will keep that box at the airfield as our principal dead drop for the time being. The signal will be the same."

Dang nodded. Toby then gave him two other dead drops as fallbacks, and systems of signals whereby they could alert each other to the need for a meeting. Dang would have to carry all these things in his memory, so Toby kept the arrangements simple.

"Now, one more item of housekeeping," Toby continued. "We need to set up an escape plan, a bug-out plan, for you, in case they—" Toby paused abruptly: *Remember, Mr. Busch, words have power. Saying the words sometimes makes a thing happen.* "In case you ever decide that you want to leave your battalion," he finished lamely. "Do you understand what I mean?"

Dang understood exactly what he had not said. "No plan will be necessary. I would never run away."

Nor would Dang take any electronic gear with him, for signaling or communication. Toby had known that this would be the case. He asked the question so that his records would show truthfully, not that he had assumed that Dang could not do so, but that he had asked Dang and that Dang had refused.

Dang showed that he understood the necessity for all these odds and ends of clandestine operations, and he helped get them out of the way quickly. When they were ready for the substance of this meeting, he began, "Will the ARVN and the Americans take action to stop these plans for Tet?"

"They will if we give them sufficient detail, and can convince them that the plans are real."

"I know much of the details for this province, and some of the general plan, but I cannot tell you details for other provinces, or for Saigon."

"I understand that. But something else has come up, Mr. Dang. We have reports that all the preparations you are talking about are really taking place, but that they are only for the purpose of deceiving the Thieu government and the Americans . . . that the Viet Cong know the plans are unrealistic, and do not intend the big attack to take place."

Dang's tired eyes followed Therese's interpretation intently. He nodded grimly, and replied at some length.

"He says that one of the men at the training session in Tay Ninh gave them indications that COSVN would try to deceive the Americans and Thieu exactly that way. He does not know how it was to be done, but he says they intended to have the deception reach the highest levels of both governments, and they were confident that they could do this."

"And so," said Toby thoughtfully, "it will boil down to this: Do we believe Dang, or do we believe the other story?"

Therese interpreted, and Dang looked steadily in Toby's direction.

"Well," said Toby, "we should not waste our time here by worrying about that. Let's get down to information and requirements."

Dang gave Toby other papers, some in his own handwriting, some lifted from battalion records. They contained information on the present disposition of troops in the province, and plans for bringing in other forces. The new battalion on the other side of My Tho, at which the planes had been firing the other day, was the 23rd Local Force Battalion. Its target would probably be the South Vietnamese Ranger Battalion stationed on the outskirts of the town. Although all of these forces were highly mobile and could not carry heavy weapons, they were equipped with good lighter ordinance: the AK-47 assault rifle, grenades, B-40 rockets, mortars, and some 90mm rockets and heavy machine guns.

"That doesn't seem to me like a peasant army swimming on the sea of the people," said Toby. "Surely they can't bring weapons like that on foot down the Ho Chi Minh Trail!"

Dang smiled. "The Ho Chi Minh Trail is more for propaganda and for men than for weapons," he said. "The weapons come by ship to Cambodia, by truck from the port to our border, and by sampan from the border to us. Thousands of tons every month."

"Can you get me details of who is involved in that traffic, and the exact routes and transfer points?"

"No. You would have to find that out in Cambodia, or near the border. A border liaison cadre could tell you, if you could find one."

"Keep that in mind, will you? It is of the utmost importance that we find out how this transportation system works. If we could interdict it at a crucial moment, it would help in our primary objective of preventing this uprising. Anything you can give us, or any names you find out about people we could recruit to help us . . ."

Dang nodded.

The agenda took an hour and a half to cover.

"That's all I have, Mr. Dang," Toby said at last. "Is there anything you believe we should talk about?"

"No."

They arose.

"When the time comes, you will be required to join in the offensive?" Toby asked.

"Yes."

"What will your task be—the task of the Determination-to-Win Battalion?"

"We will attack My Tho. The exact battle plan is not yet ready. I will inform you of details when I get them."

"You will attack My Tho with your mother and family living here?"

"Yes."

For the first time, Toby saw a sign of real distress in Dang's response. But he must be careful. *Words have . . . force . . . power.*

"Is there anything I can do to help them be safe?"

"No. Help from you would be more dangerous to them than military action."

"You cannot move them out?"

"No. All our soldiers have famlies in the towns and villages. These families are to be part of the general uprising. It is their safety and protection."

"Safety and protection in the battlefield won't be easy," Toby began, and then was fearful of saying more. He changed the subject. "Mr. Dang, you are risking your life, and I believe I can understand something of what has made you do it, but only *you* know what this decision has cost you in peace of mind. Nobody can help you in this inner struggle, but I can at least assure you that I believe you, that I am convinced that you are doing a good thing, and that I will do my best to see that your information does good for Vietnam. And I also want you to believe that if the time ever comes when I can help you in any way within my power to do so, you can depend upon me."

He waited for Therese to interpret these words, then held out his hand. Dang grasped it firmly, and the grip told Toby more about Dang's response than Dang could have expressed in words.

Therese peered out the door and nodded. Dang slipped out quickly and silently.

Toby and Therese sat down on the floor once more to wait. His knees were aching from the unaccustomed position, and he now stretched them out and lolled on one elbow. Therese sat easily, her legs tucked under her. The tension of the meeting was dissipating slowly.

"Interpreting uses more muscles than laboring with an ax or a shovel," said Toby. "I know, because I have interpreted for others in other languages."

"It is true," she said. "At the time, one does not notice. But now I feel very tired."

"You did well."

"I am glad."

"The meeting went well."

"Yes. Mr. Dang is confident now. He knows that you are experienced in these things, and so he is not so afraid for his safety."

"I think you're right. And he is beginning to understand himself better, and understand exactly what it is he's doing. He was still deceiving himself to some extent at the first meeting."

"Yes. He is thinking."

They sat quietly. A lizard on the ceiling scrabbled for an insect. A dog barked in the distance. The night was otherwise still. He caught a faint fragrance in the still air.

"I've been wondering about something, Therese," he said idly.

"What is that, Mr. Busch?"

"It may be indiscreet of me to ask, and I hope you will not be offended."

"I will not be offended."

"I have noticed all over Vietnam something about the women who live in conditions that are frankly primitive by modern standards. This, for example," he gestured to the room about him, "is primitive, isn't it?"

"Yes. It is primitive."

"In other parts of the world, when people live in primitive conditions, they usually look rather primitive themselves, more or less untidy—sometimes just plain dirty. But here in Vietnam I have not seen that. Even living in such conditions, the women of Vietnam always seem to be spotless, as if their clothing had never been near anything that would soil them, as if they had just been put on fresh about five minutes before. How do you manage to do that?"

"We work hard to do it, Mr. Busch. We do not feel right unless we are clean. One should be tidy, whatever the circumstances."

"Do all Vietnamese women feel that way?"

"I believe so."

"Most Americans would agree, I think, although whether they could do it under these circumstances, I can't say. We do have huge industries devoted to nothing but keeping people clean and sweet-smelling."

"Yes. You brought some of those things tonight."

"Coals to Newcastle."

"I do not understand."

"It's an old English saying. It means doing something that is unnecessary, something that has already been done, like putting a scent on a woman who already smells like a flower."

"Oh."

"I must go," he said, realizing with uneasiness the direction he had given to the conversation. He got up and extended his hand to her, although her lithe body needed no assistance.

She stood before him, close to him, her hand still held tightly in his own.

"I hate to leave you alone," he said.

"I am not afraid. Nothing will harm me here."

"That's not what I mean. I mean that to leave you here by yourself in this room, so full of grief and loneliness . . ."

"I am accustomed . . ."

". . . and so beautiful." His free hand brushed lightly over her hair and came to rest on one flawless cheek. He raised her chin and she stood quietly.

He kissed her, and held her tightly.

"Therese," he whispered. "Oh, Therese!"

"Yes. Yes, Mr. Busch," she whispered.

"Stop calling me Mr. Busch!" he growled.

He felt her laughing. "But it sounds . . ." she said, "Toby is . . . I cannot . . ."

"Nevertheless, when I have you in my arms I forbid you to call me Mr. Busch." He kissed her again, his hands caressing and exploring, finding the young, bare flesh. She kissed him back.

"Toby . . . Toby . . ." she murmured, tentatively, testing the sound. "No, it must be Tho. I will call you Anh Tho."

He was unzipping her tunic. "What does that mean?" he asked.

"It means lover," she said. She pulled his head down and whispered in his ear, "It means I am your mistress."

They sank to the floor, and groped and grasped and coupled, consumed and made frantic and clumsy by the sudden desire.

It was over quickly. Toby felt a wave of disgust at himself as he pulled away from her. He sat on the floor and rubbed his eyes and his forehead, as if in pain.

"That was not good, Therese," he muttered. "Not good at all."

"You do not . . . You find me . . . ?" She was stricken by his words.

"Oh God, no, not that," he said quickly. "You are perfect. You are a perfect, a beautiful, an irresistible woman. That's not what I meant. I meant that doing this the way I just did is not the way a man and a woman should make love. This was almost as if I were an animal. It should be more than that."

She got to her feet and began to dress. "But we did not know it was going to happen."

He rose and stood beside her once more. She bent to pick up her bra, and when she straightened up, still naked to the waist, he clasped her to him again. "I want it to happen again, Therese," he said. "But I want it to be an evening where love is the center, not just an accident at the end."

"Yes," she said. "I would like that." Still clutching the bra in one hand, she put her arms around his bare back, and nuzzled the fine hair on his chest.

"I live in a real fishbowl," he said, "but I will find a way. Soon."

"Yes, Mr. . . . . Anh Tho."

She drew away from him until her small, firm breasts barely touched his skin, tickling him, making him tingle. He kissed her again, then pushed her away. "I must go now, before it happens again, right here," he said.

He dressed quickly and stepped to the door. He opened it slowly, peeping out carefully as he did so. The shoes caught his eye.

"Therese," he gasped, "look at that!"

"What is it?" she asked, puzzled.

"Your shoes. They were straight together when we came in. Look at them now!"

One of the small shoes was slightly askew. It was not as she had left it. Something had moved it.

"Perhaps Mr. Dang—"

"He came in from that direction, and anyway, he would not have moved the shoe in that direction coming *in*. I saw him go, and he was not near the shoes at any time."

"Perhaps somebody was watching us." Therese was deeply embarrassed.

"It could be either that, or that somebody was watching our meeting with Dang." Toby peered up and down the pathway, listening for a telltale sound. He looked around the doorway for other evidence, but could find none.

"Now I really am afraid to leave you here alone," he said.

"I am not afraid," she said.

"You must come with me," he insisted.

"No. I will stay."

"But, Therese, I can't leave you after seeing this."

"It is not logical that they would want to harm me," she said.

"Logic has nothing to do with it."

"Nevertheless I will not go."

He could see that nothing would shake her resolve to stay. Reluctantly, fearfully, he kissed her and went down the path to his jeep, his mind racing.

Why did he have to louse things up right at the crucial moment, always? Even if Frankfurt wasn't exactly his fault, things *had* come unglued under his direction. Now here he was in the midst of a delicate recruitment, an agent-in-place in the Viet Cong, and so what did he do? He rutted around on a woman while his agent prospect was under surveillance! Or maybe while he himself was under surveillance.

He did not even make the usual check for bombs or booby traps, but started the jeep motor absently and drove home. He was unsatisfied, troubled. His anger rose at the security problem he now had, and his blood raced when he recollected those moments on the floor.

He had never made love to a woman like her. He had never made love to an Oriental. But it wasn't her being an Oriental. There was a certain hesitant wantonness about her responses that had made him virtually explode. How can you describe that? Of course, he had not made love to any other woman since he had married Mary Lynn.

Guilt, remorse, struck him so suddenly that it took his breath away. He had never before deceived or betrayed her, and now, during this entire evening he had not even once thought of his wife, who didn't deserve this of him.

What was happening to him?

13

Major Thieu was angry, so angry that his English was even more incomprehensible than usual.

"Mr. Busch, *you* not send officers to districts! *I* send! *I* send officers on travel!"

Toby paused at the door of the classroom, stopped dead in his tracks by the fury of Thieu's words.

"It is part of their training," he said.

"But I not said OK!"

"Well, I did not suppose that you would object," Toby replied. Thieu as usual stood so close that he found himself slowly backpedaling. Minnie and Ben, who had come to the classroom with him, kept in the background.

"I not wish. I order them not go!" Thieu insisted.

"Now, wait just a goddamned minute," Toby flared. "Whatever protocol I violated, or whatever quarrel you and I have, can be settled without disrupting the training." In his own anger Toby forgot and spoke words Thieu would not grasp.

"Exactly!" said Thieu. "That is why I tell them not go."

He had not understood. Toby held up his hand. "Major Thieu, let us go sit down and discuss this together, you and I."

This Thieu understood, and he backed off a pace. "We talk," he said, "but my men stay in My Tho."

They went into the empty classroom, and Toby motioned to a chair by the table at the front of the room. Thieu sat down, with Toby opposite him.

"Major Thieu," Toby began, "this is complicated. Can we not have Mr. Minh interpret for us?"

"No," Thieu retorted haughtily. "We will speak in English."

"All right." Toby glanced over at Minnie, who sat down in a chair at the rear of the room and began to look over some papers. Ben sat in a chair beside him, his face expressionless.

"To send men to districts is disturb," Thieu said. "This must be done by my office. Men must not go to districts as *men* wish."

So that was at least part of the problem—Toby had given the men their choice of districts to visit. It was part of the training in observation and reporting. Target analysis, as well. They were to go to the districts and spend two days, then come back and write him a report on their observations, what they could find out about the Viet Cong presence by eliciting information from local citizens. They were to touch base with the district police office, but were to work on their own.

He was getting them off their butts and out in the street where the work was. He had been pleased at their reaction to the assignment. From what he had been able to observe, men in their positions in Vietnam often seemed to feel that their work was to be done at a desk. The results certainly showed it.

Not only was it good training; it would also tell him something about each man, and about the districts, and would serve as a basis for target studies throughout the province. And it would form a squad of men ready for the work of the Phoenix program, to supplement the work of the PRU. That was the way he wanted the program run in his province.

Thieu was reacting to what was a subtle usurpation of his authority. Thieu wanted to run the show, and he would not run it in Toby's way, nor would Toby be satisfied with Thieu's way.

"Major Thieu, I want those men to go to the districts," said Toby evenly.

"No," Thieu replied coldly.

"I have seen your office's intelligence reports."

"Yes, our intelligence reports."

"They are trash, crap, useless garbage . . . What's the word I want, Minnie?" Toby called across the room, aware that it would infuriate Thieu even further. Minnie uttered a sharp guttural sound, and Thieu started, in spite of himself.

"I understand your words, Mr. Busch," he said.

"When the Viet Cong strikes My Tho, and other towns, and Saigon asks, 'Why did not My Tho report about this many weeks ago?' what will you say, Major Thieu? Saigon will say, 'It is Colonel Manh's fault.' Will Colonel Manh say, 'Yes, it is my fault'? No, Colonel Manh will call Major Thieu, and he will say, 'Thieu, why did we not know about the Viet Cong attack? Why did your officers, that Mr. Busch trained, not tell us about the attack? Let us call Mr. Busch and ask him why.'

"Then Colonel Manh will call me and will ask, 'Mr. Busch, you spent many days training these officers, but they produced no information about the attack. Why is this so?'

"And then, what will Mr. Busch say? Mr. Busch will say, 'Colonel Manh, those men were trained. They were capable. But they did not produce information from the districts *because they were sitting on their ass in My Tho!*' " Toby's voice rose to a bellow of rage as he finished. He was not really angry. Impatient, yes, but more amused than furious. Thieu was a bully, and probably a liar. The only way to deal with a bully is to butt heads with him. He was doing it with a lot of words that Thieu would not grasp, but with a tone and an attitude that Thieu could not mistake.

Thieu was confused, but tried to maintain a dignified anger. "You do not frighten," he said.

"I do not intend to frighten," Toby lied. "All I want, and what I demand, is that those men go to the districts assigned to them."

Thieu seemed to be confronting something new to him, and was searching for a way out. He thought for a moment, looked judiciously at Toby as if weighing all factors with complete objectivity.

"You say travel is necessary for training?"

"Absolutely!"

"I would assign men to different districts?"

"No." Toby wondered if Thieu had any special reasons for balking at the freedom of choice he had given to the men, and then decided that it was nothing more than mulishness.

"They will go if I order." said Thieu.

"Major Thieu," said Toby quietly, certain that the moment had arrived to allow Thieu a graceful retreat, "I believe you should order it."

Thieu thought for a moment. Then he arose. "When men come today, I will come talk. *I* will instruct, and *I* will order travel."

"Good! That is all I want. Thank you."

Thieu left the room, and Toby hurried back and sat down in a chair close to Minnie and Ben. There was little time before the men arrived. Ben was watching developments with an intense interest.

"Minnie," said Toby, "we're going to outsmart Thieu, and I'm going to have to depend on you to help."

"I will do whatever I can, Mr. Busch."

"Thieu knows that I do not speak Vietnamese, and when he talks to the men he may give them a frank, or perhaps a subtle set of instructions that will negate what I am trying to do."

"I am sure that is what he intends to do," said Minnie.

"And if that's the case, he will also wait around while I speak to them through you, to make sure of what I tell them."

"I am sure he will."

"Then I won't wait around until afterward, while *he* talks to them," said Toby firmly. Minnie was puzzled. "I am going to speak to them first," Toby went on, "and they'll already have their instructions before he speaks. By then it won't make any difference what he tells them later."

Minnie began to comprehend. A smile came to his lips, and grew wider as Toby talked. "Then we will tell them . . ."

"Minnie," said Toby, "we are going to see if these students remember anything about clandestine communications."

The men assembled, and before they had settled into their seats Major Thieu entered and went to the platform. He sat down near Minnie and waited. The class fell silent immediately, curious.

"Gentlemen," Toby began, "Major Thieu has spoken to me about the assignments to the districts. He is unhappy about this, and I understand why. I arranged the assignments without going through the correct channels, which is not a good or polite thing to do, and for that reason I apologize to Major Thieu."

As Minnie caught up in the interpretation, Toby turned and inclined his head in Major Thieu's direction, and Major Thieu acknowledged the gesture with a similar noncommittal nod.

"The mistake may be attributable to my zeal in teaching you clandestine operations—especially communications," Toby went on. "A large and significant part of this exercise is devoted to practicing the art of carrying out clandestine communications before the enemy, as I have taught you from the very beginning of these sessions." Toby again bowed to Major Thieu, and Major Thieu nodded back. Toby watched the faces before him intently as Minnie translated the words. Minnie's voice was almost expressionless, which in itself was unusual, and Toby was elated to see the looks of comprehension that came to the eyes of the young men. Several mouths looked as if they were struggling not to smile.

"I have explained to Major Thieu what it is we expect to accomplish by this assignment, and he understands and agrees with that. But he points out, with complete justification, that the details of the assignment should not be my responsibility, nor yours. Major Thieu, himself, must make the decisions as to where each of you goes, and when. I am sure that Major Thieu will make an intelligent decision about the places and schedules we have been considering. In any event I know that we can trust him to do what he feels to be right, and that we can all trust you to be on the lookout for opportunities to thwart the enemy in this new training exercise. Thank you."

The men smiled and nodded vigorously. Toby turned to Major Thieu.

"Major, you undoubtedly will want to speak to your men now. Mr. Compton, Mr. Minh, and I will withdraw for a time. Suppose we say that we will reconvene here in half an hour?"

"Very well," said Thieu complacently.

Toby signaled the others to follow him, and they went out and headed for the bar down the street.

"Toby," said Ben admiringly, when they were out of earshot, "that was slick. You've just taken the command of those men away from Thieu."

Toby smiled happily. "What do you think, Minnie?"

"They understand," said Minnie. "You can depend on them. They do not like Major Thieu. He is not a very skillful officer, and not a likable man. They will listen to him politely, but they will deceive him for you from now on, I believe."

"Then you did a good job."

"I think it would be more correct to say that *I* also learned something about clandestine communications today, Mr. Busch."

14

When they returned to the classroom, Major Thieu announced to Toby in a magnanimous voice that he had decided to authorize the men to make the training trips as planned. Toby thanked him ceremoniously, while at the same time observing the faces of the students. They could not understand the words, but they must be aware of the general content of the speeches.

"Men understand," Thieu said, "that reports come to me first. This is proper . . ." He could not think of the word. Toby went to his rescue.

"Of course, that is the proper procedure, Major Thieu. It is exactly what they should do." He looked at Minnie and the students, and then questioningly at Thieu, who with a wave of his hand gave regal permission for Minnie to interpret the words for the students.

There was little change of expression, but something about the slight shifts of bodies in the chairs, the way the eyes rested first on Thieu and then on him, made Toby know beyond doubt that the students had joined his conspiracy. He smiled at them. The Vietnamese, he concluded, were not only a feisty people, they were an astute people. He could not remember ever having worked with any other nationality, even one whose language he spoke fluently, who grasped a situation of this kind more quickly or intelligently than these young men seemed to be doing. They would make formal reports to Thieu, but he knew that when they had something really significant they

182

would pass it along to him directly, by some means.

The students stood up as one man when Major Thieu walked toward the door. He turned and stared at them for a moment before he walked out, as if sealing with this glance his own conspiracy with them.

The class would gather for an hour the following morning for final instructions and briefing. Toby had one more task he must accomplish before they left. He had checked the plans to find out which of the men would be working in the district that contained the village where Dang's man would be on leave. He would have the student verify the visit.

But how to give the instructions? If he passed them along through Minnie, no matter how he managed it, it would have the effect of including Minnie, at least on the periphery, of the Dang operation. Minnie had a quick mind. He would be curious.

There was no natural way he could include Therese personally in the instruction process. A surreptitious meeting with that one student would be difficult to arrange, and would indicate to the student the importance and significance of the task—and that would bring the student into the edge of the Dang operation.

He decided to bury the name.

When he got to the office, he called Therese over to his desk. Nobody was in the room but the two of them for the moment, and he was intensely aware of her presence, but he resisted the temptation to speak intimately with her. Ben or Little Jack might walk through the door at any moment. He contented himself with a broad smile. She smiled back, and he noted with pleasure that the sadness was no longer there in her eyes.

"Therese," he said, "I want you to help me with a job here. Will you bring me the Viet Cong suspect file, please?"

She produced the thick file, and he went to work with her comparing the names with the districts the students were traveling to. He assigned one VC suspect name to each student.

"We will have them use their training in neighborhood checks, you see? Each student will have one suspect to check in his district. They will consider this just a part of their training exercise. But in the case of the student going to *this* district, we'll give him the name Dang gave us. By burying this name among the rest, nobody will attach special significance to it."

"Do you believe the student can do this well?"

"I hope so. Only time will tell."

"Dang might find out that—"

"Yes, Dang might find out how we went about verifying the existence of his test soldier. But I have not told him how we would do it, and there is no real harm in this. Dang is a leader of men, and he must know that one has to train men. He will probably assume that I am just taking advantage of a real-life opportunity to do so, instead of using other, better means of checking up on him."

If the student verified that the soldier had in fact visited his home during the days designated, it would reassure Toby that Dang was still in place and functioning. Whether Dang was under surveillance or perhaps under control of the enemy security service was another question.

Meanwhile, all the information Dang had given Toby was sitting in Toby's safe, carefully drawn up in intelligence reports. Toby was committing the cardinal intelligence sin: sitting on information. But he had no choice. Chet would not pass his reports along until he was able to give reasonable evidence of who Dang was, and whether his information was trustworthy.

This test soldier should help.

By the time the list was ready, and individual slips were made up for the students, it was time to quit work. Therese left. Toby knew that he would not be able to keep his thoughts on business for the rest of the afternoon, and he secured his own desk and safe and got up to leave.

"You haven't forgotten that we're invited over to the girls' house for dinner this evening?" Ben reminded him.

"No, I haven't forgotten. I'm going in to shower and shave now."

He went upstairs. He noted with some wonderment that after that first half-hour or so of remorse and guilt, he had ceased to worry or blame himself about that moment on the floor with Therese. It had happened. Nobody knew except him and Therese. Nobody else need ever know. He had been keeping secrets all his life, most of them from his wife as well as from the rest of the world. One more secret need not be difficult, and would not add measurably to the burden.

But how did it happen that he didn't really consider this secret to be a burden among all the others? And how could he sit and pass along to her by means of one long smile all the electric thoughts that were coursing through his mind, without any hesitation or doubt?

What was happening, he realized, was that his conscience wasn't as strong as he had supposed. The thought that was now uppermost in his mind was not that he should not have done it once, but rather that he might as well be hanged for stealing a flock as for stealing a lamb. It would be no more difficult to keep twice from Mary Lynn than to keep once from her. Whatever the struggle might be, or might have been, in the upper levels of his soul, there was no denying that down there in the lower levels, in the pit of his stomach, the focus of his physical reactions, his desire for Therese had been fanned from a spark to a flame by that first encounter; and he now found his mind straying regularly to plans by which he could spend a night with her. His pulse quickened at the recollection that she wanted a night alone with him, too.

It was an abrupt reversal of all his habits of mind and action. Was it because the profession of spying had already forced him into a mildly schizoid existence? He had spent his entire professional life up to now coolly and consciously appearing as one thing to some people and as another to others. But, then, everybody in the world was slightly schizoid. The intelligence business merely formalized the characteristic, and polished and developed it for the business at hand.

Here on his nighttable were letters from Mary Lynn. Loving letters, newsy letters, with gossip about the town, stories about the kids, plans for what they would do when he got home on leave. She was not a dull wife. She could on occasion be as exciting as any woman he could imagine. And she was bright. They talked. They knew each other as only a man and wife could, and, although he could not expect that their bodies would invariably be a source of mutual joy, they had had enough moments of real passion to judge that their sex life was a good one, probably far better than average. His feeling for her had not changed one bit since Therese.

Had it?

Suppose he found that his response to Mary Lynn had been altered? Sexual stimulus and response can be a mysterious and elusive thing. Suppose she detected something new in him—a difference in his attitudes or his desires?

It could happen. He had discovered within the first few months of their marriage that Mary Lynn had an uncanny understanding of her husband. She read him like a book. In a sense it had always been somewhat of a comfort to him, because, paradoxically enough, it relieved him of the necessity to make any decision about being unfaithful to her. There was no decision to make. He knew that he could not even think of seeking or accepting consummation of any of those fleeting lascivious thoughts that came to him when he peered down a voluptuous décolletage, or watched the inimitable parabolas described by a pair of female hips moving away from him—because Mary Lynn would know. Mary Lynn knew that he had a normal charge of lust in his batteries, but she also knew that he had never gone any further than looking since he married her.

If she did sense something different in him, could he lead her to believe that she was observing the aftereffects, not of adultery, but of simply living in a war?

It *was* a different world, there was no doubt about that. It was another life, a separate life. What he did in this one had only the most tenuous connection with the other one.

And now, here he was, getting himself ready to spend the evening with still *another* woman! He felt so good about that that he found himself whistling as he dressed. For this woman was different. It would be a relief to spend the evening with a woman without complications. He had always been stimulated by conversations with intelligent women. Their range of interests never ceased to surprise him, and it seemed to him that they tended to be more eclectic than men of relatively equal intellect and education. Most men he knew had no inkling of this, because they never really explored the minds of the women around them. Too busy exploring everything else.

And then, of course, there was the sheer pleasure of talking with women, communicating with the only sex that could be mothers, sisters, concubines, or wives.

He liked Louise. She was a woman who put on no acts, had no hang-ups, talked intelligently about interesting things. You could be at ease with her. It would be a pleasant evening.

The three men—bathed, shaved, combed, and smelling of PX lotions—climbed into the jeep and drove out the gate.

As they slowed down for the intersection to the northwest of the house, he glanced up at the wooden utility pole out of force of habit. His heart skipped a beat. There on the pole, at about eye level, was the peculiar slash he had instructed Dang to make.

On the other edge of the town, the woman who put on no acts and had no hang-ups was toweling down after a shower. Out of habit, she made a brief inspection in the mirror, detected no sags or lumps, and was reassured once more. She still had a nice tan, from the last trip to Con Son Island. She always jumped at the chance, when there happened to be a seat on the weekly cargo plane. There was usually a nice crowd for a picnic on the torrid beach, and if it weren't for an occasional day there she would probably be as pale as a ghost from spending most of her daylight hours in the hospital.

She took one more quick look before beginning to dress. It could be, of course, that there were changes taking place so slowly that she wasn't detecting them. Certainly that body was a thirty-year-old body, not sixteen. And the sags would come. She had seen too much bare human flesh on hospital beds to ignore her own vulnerability to the passage of time.

Well, it did no good to worry about it. She began to dress. But she did care. She cared very much. She liked the way a man's eyes flickered when they swept over her body. She knew that when she did meet the man she would want to marry, the least of her problems would be to make him desire her physically. All she had to be alert for was the man whose heart was right, whose mind was in tune with hers, whose tastes were like hers, and who would laugh with her at things that were funny.

It bothered some women that so many men began to think of bed soon after meeting them. It didn't bother Louise. If the guy was a slob, you brushed him off quickly, even brutally if necessary. If he was a decent man, all you had to do was give him the right clues and responses, and he would keep a civilized control over his male equipment. And it was that very tension, the little interplay of clues and responses and control, that gave excitement and flavor to being in company with men.

She adjusted her skirt, and pulled a flowered blouse down over her head. She grinned at her own grinning face in the mirror. *You,* she thought, nodding accusingly at the image, *have on certain occasions given the clues and responses that could lead only to the bed.*

She had no regrets about those times. She was neither virginal nor promiscuous. When she did marry she would do so without guilt or regrets, and she knew that she would have no trouble being a satisfying and faithful wife.

She put on a necklace that set off the pattern of the blouse, and inspected the result critically. Just right.

One thing she was sure about, in this evening to come: Toby Busch was not the one. His eyes had flickered most satisfactorily, and he was a brainy man with a sense of humor, but he was married. She recoiled at the thought of involvement with another woman's husband. The mischief of such a thing was intriguing, of course, and if the wife in question were a shrew it would be less reprehensible. But there was something grubby and unattractive about being the co-respondent, and she was repelled by the idea of troubling or breaking up any marriage, good or bad.

And you could tell by talking with Toby Busch for just about five minutes that he took things seriously. He would not take lightly any liaison with another woman. It would be devastating to his marriage.

Would that intense man, who could be so distant one moment, his mind concentrating on something far away, only to return to you in the next instant with a flash of humor—would he have been the one if he were not married?

He could have been. His life was interesting, certainly. He would probably not take a woman for granted, no matter how long he lived with her. He was the type who would expect a woman to help him change a tire one minute, and then would write a poem to her the next.

She went downstairs. It was still early.

Peggy was arranging chairs, and placing ashtrays and chips and nuts. Bottles and glasses and ice were on a small table to one side. The meal would be buffet style.

"It looks very nice, Peggy," said Louise.

"Yeah, I think it's about as good as we can make this old place," Peggy replied. "This G.I. furniture isn't the easiest stuff in the world to make look homey and comfortable."

"Are you all ready?" Louise asked casually, hoping that Peggy would say no. Peggy was her usual slightly disheveled self, clean as a pin, but somehow not quite touched up and patted into place.

"Yep. All I need is a chair and a whip and we can let the lions in," she said.

"Well, of course," Louise teased her, "we'll let them all in, but there's only one of them that will interest you."

"Sure," said Peggy carelessly, "I always get assigned to that one, and I have to work with the material I get."

"About to get him tamed?"

Peggy looked around at her, shrugged, and sat down on the edge of one of the chairs. "I guess I don't hide it very well, do I?" she said.

"Not well enough for a couple of women who *live* with you."

"Marie Claire notices too, huh?"

"Yes. And we both worry."

"You worry? About Ben and me?"

"Yes."

"What in the world for?"

"About whether you . . . about . . . Gee, do I really have to tell you?"

Peggy sighed. "No. But you shouldn't worry. That thing about the lions isn't too far off the mark, you know? I got him nicely tamed—or maybe he was already tame when I got him, but I can't seem to *train* him to do what I want him to do. But, don't worry, I know what I'm doing—or not doing."

"He was married once before."

"I know. I don't think it had any effect on him at all. She didn't teach him a thing. Maybe she didn't know how to teach him. And he's the kind that never makes the same mistake twice."

"But why is it him? He's nice, but frankly I can't imagine . . ."

"God, I don't know. If I could explain it, maybe I could do something about it. It's got something to do with him being so self-sufficient, so confident, I think."

"But he seems so unapproachable, too. You can never get next to him, never talk on real intimate terms with him. You can kid around, but when you start getting serious he seems to clam up. You can never find out what's really inside of him. Or maybe *you* can?"

"Probably better than others. But still not very much."

"Then you can't really say you know him, can you?" Louise sat down in the chair near Peggy.

"I know him better than you think," said Peggy. "I know, for instance, that he is a rock-bound puritan. That's what makes him a good soldier. He's got his world neatly lined up in categories. He's got just as much dirty old man in him as any man in the world, but he keeps it in its proper military place. He believes there is a time and place for everything—killing, healing, planting, reaping, and sex. And sex is fenced into a special, very narrow cage."

"Really?"

"Yes. And that affects all his dealings with women. There are so few circumstances where it's all right to pull the pants off a woman that he won't ever do anything that might even look like he's thinking about doing it. His idea of courtship is something out of seventeenth-century New England, because he thinks nice girls don't do it, unless they're married, and then they just grit their teeth and think about babies."

"Surely he's not that stupid," Louise exclaimed. "What does he . . . ?"

"He goes somewhere else. I don't know where. But I'm sure he buys it, from girls that aren't 'nice.' And I'll bet he's a real riot in a whorehouse. The time and the place, you know."

"I must say, I never thought of him that way."

"He's that way. But even when he's whoring, it's bound to be a neatly arranged part of his existence, all labeled and scheduled and under control."

"Sounds awful! Doesn't that make you feel any different toward him?" Louise persisted.

"Nope. Because I know Ben has never had a woman *in* his life. He's had women around the edges of it, but never a part of it, never a part of him. If that wall, that shell he's got around him ever gets broken down, he could find out what a woman is really like and she could become a part of his life. And it wouldn't be a bad life, because underneath that rigid outside there's a good man. And I want to be the woman that finds it."

"And you think you've got a chance?"

"I don't know. Sometimes when he looks me in the eye, I want to come right out and say to him, 'Why don't you reach back there and unfasten my bra, Ben?' Or, when we're dancing, you know, 'Go ahead and put your hand there, Ben; I won't fly out of the room like a rocket.' Do you understand what I mean, Louise?"

"No."

"No, I suppose not," Peggy said gloomily. "Maybe I haven't explained it right. Or maybe I don't understand it myself. But what you *can* understand, I'm sure, is that after a day in the hospital, having to be strong and self-sufficient and help other people, it's such a relief to be around a man who wouldn't accept help if you offered it to him."

Louise nodded. "That I can see."

"And Louise, he is a *man.*"

"So is Little Jack."

"Little Jack is a gorilla. If he thought it would be fun, he'd grab you by the heels and bang you against a tree. But Ben is a guy that when you walk down the street hanging on to his arm, you know that if people even look sideways at you, this big goddamned puritan is just naturally going to deck their ass."

Louise burst out laughing. Peggy rolled this kind of thing off her tongue very seldom, and always when you least expected it. Now she enjoyed the effect her words had had on Louise.

"I wish we had talked about this before," Louise said.

Peggy shrugged. "I guess maybe I didn't want to, before this. I guess I hadn't really thought it out before. In fact, I kind of thought it out just now while I was talking about it."

"I'm sort of relieved."

"Relieved? Why?"

"We thought you didn't realize what you were up against."

"I know what you mean, but you said it wrong," said Peggy. "It isn't what I'm up against, it's what I *can't* get up against."

The sound of the jeep coming into the driveway interrupted them, and they went to the door. Marie Claire came down the stairs and joined them just as the men trooped up the steps.

They came in like a prairie gust, full of bellowing good humor, moving in a swirl of the trivia of the first moments of such a gathering. Each man went to the table and fixed drinks for himself and his partner, and they settled one by one into the chairs in the living room.

"I was telling the fellows," Ben said, "that I don't like that little wall you've got around this house. It's made me uneasy ever since I first saw it."

"What's wrong with it?" asked Peggy.

"If I was to look over this neighborhood as a battlefield . . ."

"Good God, Ben," said Marie Claire, "is the whole world a battlefield to you?"

"Yeah," Louise put in. "I know we have to be careful about bombs and things like that—but a battlefield?"

Ben was not at all troubled by the critical tone of their voices. "Of course the whole world isn't a battlefield," he said. "But imagine the surprise of the people of Gettysburg that morning in July. If you had asked one of them a month before, or maybe even a day or so before, what kind of a battlefield his front yard would make, he would have laughed at you."

"You mean you think there's going to be a battle in My Tho?" Peggy asked, frightened.

"No," Ben said with a reassuring smile. "What I mean is that if you wait until it happens, it's too late to get ready.

"For instance, this wall you've got around the house is so low it looks like it must have been built for a rifleman—just the right height and thickness. It's not even waist high. And if you look at the field of fire, you can see that if any action ever concentrated on the Province Senior Adviser's house, this house is one of the most important points in the whole area."

"No kidding?"

"I'm going to get a recommendation through, somehow," Ben went on, "probably to the Province Senior Adviser, to have that wall built up to about seven or eight feet . . . That is, if you ladies won't mind me butting in?"

"Of course not," said Louise, "but what will be the good of that?"

"It will make the house defensible for itself, and less useful as a key point in the area."

"Ben," said Toby, "as long as we're talking along these lines, why don't we set up some communication with this house?"

"How do you mean?"

"I'm getting ready to order a radio net for us, one of the VHF nets, you know—a GE or a Motorola setup. We'll have the base station at the office, with a big enough antenna that we could reach the hand-held sets anywhere in town, and even a few miles beyond the edge of town. I'm going to put a set at the PRU barracks, and one over at the Special Police Office, and at the Revolutionary Development Office, and have one for the jeeps, too. We could put one of them in here."

"Hey, that's a great idea," said Ben. "I'm always kind of nervous for these women. Can you get the equipment, all right?"

"If there is one thing our agency is good at," said Toby, "it's coming up with equipment you need the minute you need it. Our life depends on that."

"I don't know a thing about radios," said Marie Claire. "Do you girls?"

The other two shook their heads.

"You don't have to know anything," said Toby. "You just have to listen, and when you want to talk, you push a button. That's all."

"But won't you be violating regulations or something, to put your equipment in our house? We don't belong to your organization," Louise pointed out.

"You're a taxpayer, though," said Toby. "I may be going against the letter of the regulations, but we've got plenty of the equipment, so we're not depriving anybody else of the use of it. Don't worry about it."

"OK. Whatever you say."

They ate dinner. Afterward they danced, then sat and talked. They knew each other well now, and they enjoyed these gatherings of their group. Even Little Jack seemed to be acquiring some measure of ease and comfort around Marie Claire. She was a quiet woman, and made few demands.

"Louise," said Toby when they were dancing. "I need your help."

"OK. What is it?"

"I've got to go out on some business, but I don't want people to think that it is business. I don't even want them wondering what it is. Would you go along with me, even if I can't tell you what it is?"

"Going to meet Doctor No?"

He laughed. "I've never met anybody even remotely like Doctor No, and I hope I never do."

"Well, whatever it is, I'll do it. Do we walk?"

"No, we'll have to take the jeep."

"Will it take long?"

"Maybe half an hour."

"I hate to desert my responsibilities as a hostess," she said.

"They'll get along. I'll tell them it's something I have to do over at the office, and that you're coming along for the ride."

"You know what they'll think," she said, arching her eyebrows at him. She didn't really care.

He smiled. "In the time we'll be gone, they'd have to think I'm Speedy Gonzales."

"When do we go?" Louise was intrigued by the idea of going along for some spy work, and would not have said no under any circumstances.

"Now," he replied.

Toby told the others, and there were some good-natured remarks and some laughter, but no apparent suspicion. To Louise, they seemed to be taking it as quite a natural thing for a man in Toby's work to do such a thing, and just as normal that she would prefer to be with him rather than unattached in the living room.

They got into the jeep and Toby drove it at a brisk pace through the darkened streets. They went by the government compound, and Toby drove in a complete circle around it, peering carefully through the iron bars that made up the upper half of the fence. What he was looking for she could not tell, nor could she guess as to whether he had found it.

He headed out beyond the outskirts of the town, and drove to the airstrip, where he steered the jeep off the road and onto the end of the runway. He peered carefully through the dark toward the other end of the runway.

"Well," he said at length, "I guess that's it."

"That's it?"

"Yep. Except for one thing."

"What's that?"

"Before we start back I've got to use the restroom over there." He motioned toward the wall of boxes along the side of the runway. "Will you mind? I'll be out of sight, but not more than twenty-five yards away from you if you yell."

"Go ahead," she said, and watched as his figure grew dim in the gloom and disappeared around the end of the wall. "You can write me the poem when we get back."

"What's that?" His voice came to her out of the darkness.

"Nothing. Just talking to myself."

He reappeared, climbed back into the seat, and started the motor.

"Is this what you people do at night?" Louise asked him.

"Yeah! Isn't it exciting?"

"I think I would prefer Doctor No."

"After such an adventure as this?"

"And you can't tell me what it was we did?"

"You mean you don't know?"

"No."

"See? I told you I was Speedy Gonzales! Shall I do it again?"

Louise laughed with delight, and Toby sat grinning at her for a moment before putting the jeep in gear and heading for home.

15

As soon as Therese arrived the next morning, Toby called her into the common room and showed her the envelope with the single sheet of paper he had found in the dead drop the night before. The note was scrawled in pencil.

"It is not very clear," she said. "He must have written it quickly, or with others nearby . . ."

"Tell me what it says now, and then make a typewritten translation, will you please?" Toby asked her urgently.

Therese translated:

"I cannot meet you as planned. I was followed when I left. I am now under observation. I will elude observation once to deliver this message, but I must not do so again because it would confirm suspicions. I will get information and will send it same way as this message, if possible. Do not use other plans to communicate with me until I advise all is safe."

"Of all the goddamned bad luck!" Toby exploded. "Just when we had the guy developed to where he was going to really go to work for us, instead of just handing us a few crumbs!"

"Who is following him?" Therese wondered.

Toby stared at the floor for a moment. "The possibilities are almost limitless," he said slowly. "There didn't seem to be any surveillance of you or me afterward, so we can be pretty sure that the tail was just one person. He probably had specific orders about what to do, unless he was just inexperienced. But I doubt that. I think he knew what he was up to, and he was

198

confident that they could find out about us some other way
. . . Or maybe they already know about us."

"About us?"

"Yes. Who we are, and why we would be meeting Dang.
Maybe what they are after, now that they have made this first
observation, is simply to *nail him,* not discover a network. If
that's what they have in mind, they are watching him for the
next meeting, so they can have witnesses to it, or send a strong
enough force to the meeting site to round up everybody involved."

"Then, if we had gone again to my home to meet him," said
Therese, "that might have happened."

"It sure might have happened. And there is another thing we
must do. We must cancel the neighborhood checks the Special
Police students were going to make." She looked at him quizzically. "Under the circumstances," he explained, "this would be
no test. If the man isn't there, we would have to consider that
Dang might not dare to send him now. If he is there, it could
be that any kind of an inquiry about him would be one more
link in the chain of evidence against Dang."

"Then I will destroy the instructions?"

"Yes. Put them in the burn trash."

Disconsolately, Toby went back to his desk and made a nota-
tion in his log, then wrote out an operations report for the
headquarters record.

He was sitting at the desk, lost in thought, when Ben approached.

"It's almost ten," Ben said.

Toby shook himself out of the trance. He had not realized it
was getting so late, and he had to give the students their final
briefing. With Minnie, they got into the jeep and drove toward
the government compound.

"Toby," said Ben, "I was just now on the sideband with Al
Mallory up at Vung Tau. He wants to know if I can come up
there this afternoon and help them get a new team transported

down to this new village we're opening up, just across the river from Vinh Long Province. The VC have been giving the village fits in the past, and this team is a little edgy. Al thinks it might settle them down if I'm up there to help them move out, and if I go with them to the village to help them set things up."

"Go ahead. Nothing to keep you here, is there?"

"Nothing, except that it will leave you alone, what with Little Jack going down to Can Tho this afternoon for the Phoenix training program."

"Yeah, I had forgotten about that."

"You could probably get some of his PRUs to come up and supplement the guards around the house. They won't be doing anything else."

"Do you think that's necessary?" Toby asked him evenly.

"It's whatever you want," Ben replied.

"That's not what I asked you. Does the safety of the house require extra men?"

"No."

"Then you thought I would want them because I'm scared?"

"Well, no." Ben was embarrassed, and Toby knew he had discovered the truth. "I was just thinking that if you feel uneasy about a lack of experience, or anything like that . . ."

"Forget it, Ben. I've been scared shitless in my life, but it doesn't paralyze me. If the Nung guards and one armed spook are enough to make the house reasonably safe, that's the way it will be."

"OK."

"Mr. Busch," said Minnie, "since there will be little to do after the class this morning, I would also like to leave afterwards, unless you need me for something else. I would like to go to my brother's home for one extra day this weekend."

"Your brother's home?"

"Yes. My brother and his family have a small rice farm north of My Tho. I spend most of my weekends there. This time, with Friday also, I will be able to help him with some repairs to his house."

"Sure, Minnie. You'll be back Monday?"

"Yes. Certainly. As usual."

"I have yet to see a rice farm from close up. Maybe someday you'd take a man who grew up in the corn land of America, to see how they raise rice in Vietnam?"

"I would be pleased to do that, sir. I would have to let my brother know, because he would be embarrassed if a visitor came and we were not ready."

"I can understand that." Toby looked at him thoughtfully. "You are a cosmopolitan fellow, and well educated, and yet your brother is a rice farmer."

"Yes."

"Were you raised on a rice farm?"

"Yes."

The answers were so reticent that Toby wondered if he had hit a nerve of pride or place. He remembered that in Europe or Latin America an intellectual did not find it a matter of pride to come from peasant or middle-class stock. Perhaps it was the same in Vietnam.

A new thought wiped the uneasiness out of Toby's mind. He would be all alone in the house, all night. The guards would be there, and so would Mrs. Chao and Chi Hai, but he had almost come to regard these people as if they were furniture, and so he viewed the prospect as one of being alone.

Alone for one full night. With Therese.

It was with difficulty that he brought his mind to bear on the final briefing for the students, but once into the process, he had no thoughts for anything except the last-minute instructions, and some final advice on common sense and flexibility.

He finished with a short statement about how happy he was with the results of the training so far, and how high a regard he had come to have for them, and how he knew that their work in the future was going to be fruitful for themselves and for Vietnam.

He dismissed them, and they filed by to shake his hand. They were diffident, and tended to bow a great deal, but he caught a warmth, a respect, and an affection from them that he could not have resisted. He liked these young men very much. He muttered words of farewell and good luck, which they did not understand, and they muttered back to him as if they had.

He could detect no change in Minnie's demeanor during the briefing, nor later in the jeep, and he decided that his uneasiness had been needless. They dropped Minnie off at the center of town, where he could get one of the tiny three-wheeled Lambretta buses for the countryside. When Toby and Ben arrived at the house, Ben went immediately to the sideband and called Jerry Burkholder.

"I'm in luck," he told Toby. "Dino's coming along this way at one o'clock, so Jerry's going to have him stop here. He'll be through for the day, and he can take me directly over to Vung Tau. This way I can spend the afternoon with the team, and it will give me time for a little pub-crawling this evening."

"Does Vung Tau have that much in the way of pubs?"

"Night life is where you find it, Toby," said Ben with a grin.

Toby thought with a start that Ben must have gathered something about his own plans for the evening, but a second glance at Ben's face reassured him that the words had contained no hidden meaning.

Ben went to his room to get ready, and Toby opened his safe and put away his briefcase. Therese was typing steadily, her back to him. He looked at her, started toward her desk, hesitated, then sat down at his own desk.

He realized, with wry amusement, perhaps even astonishment, that he was nervous about asking her. Then it came to him that in all his life he had never gone boldly up to any woman and asked her to spend the night with him. Nights with women had occurred as a result of circumstances—usually circumstances that he had carefully engineered—but they had never begun with the bald request.

He fiddled with some papers. He searched in the drawer for a pencil. When he found it, he sharpened it. He replaced some stray paperclips in the little bowl on his desk. Finally, laughing inwardly at his own foolishness, he swiveled his chair around. She was still typing steadily.

He went to her desk and leaned over it.

"Therese," he said quietly.

She started at the suddenness of his voice, and turned to face him.

"I will be all alone in the house tonight," he said. "Will you have dinner with me?"

"Have dinner here?" Her attention had not yet fully shifted from her work to him.

"Yes, here. With me. Alone."

"Oh! Yes, I would like that," she said, almost shyly.

"And we can have the whole night together," he said, almost making it a question instead of a statement.

"Yes."

"Now that you have said yes, please stop looking at me like that, and turn around and go back to work immediately, or I may be on the floor with you again, right behind this desk."

She laughed and returned to her typewriter.

Toby was glad of the distractions that came. He had a light lunch with Ben, then drove him to the airport. Exactly as scheduled, Dino set his little plane down lightly on the runway, loaded his passenger on board with his usual voluble good humor, and lifted them back up into the sky.

Toby drove home and went to the kitchen. Mrs. Chao was lying on the table, composing herself for her afternoon nap. She jumped to the floor with an agility that belied her wrinkled features.

"Mrs. Chao," he said, "Mr. Compton and Mr. Horner will be gone tonight."

"Yes," she replied, bobbing her head. "Gone."

"Miss Therese will be having dinner with me. Miss Therese and I, for dinner," he repeated slowly, and held up two fingers.

"Miss Therese?" She was puzzled.

"Yes. Miss Therese. Secretary." He pantomimed typing. She would know Therese by her Vietnamese name, of course.

"Ah! Miss Therese!" Now she understood. "Dinner here?"

"Yes."

"Good! I fix!" She was grinning broadly.

"Make it one of your good dinners, Mrs. Chao," he said. "Best wine and everything."

"Yes, yes! I fix," she repeated happily. "Chi Hai help. We fix."

There was nothing faked about Mrs. Chao's pleasure. Toby walked out of the kitchen with a sense of well-being. He need not worry about the dinner—it would be excellent. Mrs. Chao and Chi Hai would fix.

Therese brought a small bundle with her when she came back from lunch, and Toby guessed that it must contain night-clothes. He quit work early to shower and shave, and to check over the bedroom and the common room and the bar.

He went back to his desk and tried to concentrate.

After what seemed to him like an eternity, Therese put her things away and picked up the package.

"I will change now," she said to Toby. She had brought something besides nightclothes, evidently.

"I'll be in the common room," Toby said. "Do you like daiquiris, Therese?"

"Daiquiris? What is daiquiris?"

"It's a cocktail. I'll fix one while you are changing. I think you will like it."

He locked up and went into the bar. He had filled the shaker with ice, lime juice, rum, and sugar syrup, and was preparing to shake the mixture when Therese reappeared. She was clad in an *ao dai* of rich red, delicately embroidered at collar and breast. It was perfectly fitted to her form. Its red glow set off the dark flow of hair that cascaded over her shoulders.

As she moved through the room toward the bar, he found himself holding his breath at the serene beauty that was coming into his presence. She sat on a stool opposite him, aware of his rapt gaze, accepting it placidly.

"You are beautiful," he said, still holding the shaker motionless in his two hands.

"I am glad that you think so," she said.

He shook the cocktail, staring happily at her all the while, knowing that the smile on his face must look foolish, and only turned away when it came time to strain the pale green mixture into the glasses on the tray before him.

"Let's go sit at a table."

He led her to one of the low cocktail tables, and extended the tray to her after she was seated. They sipped and looked silently at each other. She nodded that she liked this new taste, and he smiled back.

Chi Hai came in to place a small tray of hors d'oeuvres before them. There were the usual dips and chips from the PX, but the central tidbit was a dish of *cha gio,* little morsels of shrimp and crabmeat mixed with bean sprouts, pork, and spices, wrapped in a jacket of the filmy rice-gluten *banh trang*, and deep-fried to a crisp brown.

They sipped and munched and talked. Toby felt strangely unacquainted with her. It was almost as if that night at her house had not happened, as if this were a first date. She seemed to feel the same. They talked about the ingredients of daiquiris and of *cha gio* and about why the spirituous beverage of Vietnam was cognac instead of sake or whiskey. They talked about French bread and French cooking, about Fritos and potato chips, and about countless other things that were of no consequence to them. They did not know what they were talking about or why they were doing so.

Therese's eyes, which had already lost most of their look of sadness, now began to sparkle with life and fun, and Toby was so smitten with this new, crimson-clad, effervescent Therese that he did not notice the passage of time.

The sudden tropical dusk descended, and Chi Hai came to announce that dinner was served. Toby offered his hand to Therese, to lift her to her feet, and they stood together in the dim light of the bar as if afraid to break a spell.

He led her to the dining room. Mrs. Chao had set the big table in such a way that they would be close together at one corner, with two candles to give them light. The dinner was exquisite, a delicate meal that seemed designed for the mood and the occasion. Mrs. Chao and Chi Hai bustled quietly about them, as they had never done on other occasions. They spoke in low tones to Therese, but there was no hint of secrets shared among them and kept from Toby. Toby could not understand the words, but he could see the pleasure they were taking in her presence at the table.

After dinner they went back into the common room, and sat on the sofa. Mrs. Chao brought coffee and liqueurs, and bade them good night. Toby poured a tiny glass of Cointreau for Therese, a splash of brandy for himself. They drank and talked some more.

Toby kissed her, a light tentative kiss. Her arms went around him tightly, and then he kissed her with more authority.

"Come on," he said. He switched off the lights, and arm in arm they went up the stairs to his bedroom.

Toby was surprised and amused when he opened the door. The covers of his double bed, usually turned down on one side at this time of night, had been turned down on both sides ready for double occupancy. The air conditioner had been set at a higher temperature, so that the air in the room was less arctic than usual. It would not chill bare flesh.

On his desk was a large vase of flowers, lovingly arranged.

"Mrs. Chao and Chi Hai knew," he said to Therese.

"Yes," she said. "They knew. They are glad."

"Glad? You mean that this matters to them?"

"Yes. They like you very much. They believe you need a woman."

"I'll bet it's more than that," he said. "They like you, too. They don't think I just need any old woman. They think I need *you.*"

"Perhaps that is so."

He kissed her again, and went about the room turning off all the lights except for a small one by the bed. She was undressing, and was almost naked when he had finished. His hands went unwilled to her body and he clasped her to him.

"You must undress, too," she said, pushing him away gently.

He did, and then they were locked together on the bed. There was intense desire, but it was not hurried. Deliberately, savoring every moment, steeping himself in every female curve and every soft hidden secret of her body, he made love to her, and she responded. He could not tell whether her pleasure was from her joy at pleasing him, or from the pure physical sensation of a man on and around and within her, but he did not care. Whatever it was that drove them, they were both abandoned for the time to the primitive, unthinking enjoyment of each other's bodies, to the touch of lips, breasts, bellies, and thighs, to the caress and the grip of hands that roamed incessantly, as if trying to discover and grasp each new ecstasy and hold it like a tangible thing.

Then he was sated for the moment and they were still, tranquilly awaiting the next wave of desire that would come to flood their senses.

Toby had no idea what time it was when they lay at last, spent and relaxed.

"Thank you, Anh Tho," said Therese in a soft, wondering voice.

It was so sudden and unexpected that Toby burst out laughing. He raised himself on one elbow and looked down at her smiling face, framed as it was by the silky hair in disarray on the pillow.

"In all my life," he teased her, "I have never been thanked by a woman for doing that. Is that a Vietnamese custom?"

"I thanked you because you have made love to me sweetly," she said. "It has been many months that I have not been with a man. I knew that I missed it, but I did not realize how much."

"Not since . . ."

"Since my husband died. At first it was the sadness, but then I was not sure whether it was still the sadness or whether it was wanting a man."

"And tonight you knew?"

"Even before I met you, I had come to know. There was still the sadness, of course, but now they were apart. I would long for this, for a man's arms, for his hands, for . . . for everything. But I could not go to just any man. It would have been horrible if the man had been—if he had not . . ." She could not find words.

"I think I understand," he said.

"Yes," she said, placing a hand on his cheek. "Yes, you understand."

"But I may have brought you more unhappiness in the long run, Therese."

"How?"

"Because this can't last. I can't stay forever in Vietnam, and I can't take you with me when I leave."

"I know that."

"And yet you are happy? Even though there is no future in it?"

"One cannot plan for any future in Vietnam," she said, looking away from him. "I am living now. And I am in bed with a man who is good and gentle. And I love him."

He kissed her cheek tenderly. "I love you, too, Therese. I do love you." He was surprised at his own words. "I do love you, and yet . . ."

"You are thinking of your wife," she said calmly, turning her head to look into his eyes again.

"Yes."

"Because you love her?"

"Yes. I love her very much."

"You do not believe that a man can love two women?"

"Therese," he said, frowning thoughtfully, "any time the thought of being with another woman has occurred to me, it was only *wanting* her that I thought about. I didn't even consider the possibility of truly *loving* her."

"You were not thinking deeply, then?"

"No, it's just that in our culture—and I don't know how it is in Vietnam—but with us it is understood that you can only have one woman at a time. If you come to love another one, she has got to replace the first one, or she must move out of the picture."

"Why?"

"Well . . ." He was stumped.

"What do you think now?" she persisted.

"If we were in my country now, I would not be able to do this, because neither woman would put up with it for long, and even if they did, society wouldn't. It would destroy my marriage and ruin my home."

"I see."

"But somehow the distance from her seems to be more than a question of miles in this case. It's psychological, almost spiritual. Somehow I am sure that I can do this without its having any effect on my feeling for her, without its having any effect on that other world."

"I hope that is so."

"But on the other hand, I wonder if I will be able to make love to her when I go back without always remembering how you felt in my arms, and without even sometimes having the sensation that it *is* you, in my arms once again."

"I hope it will be that way."

"Even if it hurts my marriage?" Toby asked gently.

"Oh, no!" she exclaimed. "I do not want to harm you or her in any way, Anh Tho. I only hope that you will remember tonight, and remember me, all of me, with us . . . this way . . . because then I will know that I will always be your lover, wherever you are."

He looked down at her nude figure, a perfect, living sculpture lying motionless beside him.

"A night like this," he said, "becomes a part of a man for the rest of his life, whether he wants it to be or not. There is no way I could erase it now, even if I wanted to. For the rest of my life, you will always be my lover, and I will love you."

"And I will love you, Anh Tho," she said tenderly, yet with a sudden sadness, "for the rest of my life."

"You have many years ahead of you, Therese."

"Perhaps."

"Of course you do." His hand stroked her body slowly, from the delicate breasts downward. "My beautiful, my perfect, mistress," he whispered. His hand came to rest on the flat belly. "You are so young, and so perfect. You will have your choice of men when you decide to choose. And peace will come, and then this flat little tummy will some day grow and grow with a second beautiful little Therese, with big lovely eyes, and a round little body—"

He was cut short by the look of shock and awful hurt that came to her eyes.

"Therese!" he gasped. "You—you already have a child!"

She nodded.

"But, it doesn't seem possible. Your body seems barely beyond your own childhood, so smooth and fresh." He stroked the satiny, unmarked belly again. "I had no idea. Where is the child?"

"I had two little girls," she said. "They are dead."

"My God," he said in a strangled voice. "Oh, my God! Children, too!" The sparkle had gone from her eyes, replaced once again by the deep pain, and by the slight glint of tears.

"I know this must hurt unbearably," he went on after a long time, "but I want to know about them, and about your husband. You belong to me now. You will always belong to me, no matter where we are or what happens. Won't you tell me?"

"I cannot." She shook her head.

"Have you ever talked to *anybody* about them?"

Again she shook her head.

"Therese, you must do what you think is right for you, but I believe it might help you to bear the grief if you talk about it. Perhaps I have come along not only to help you fight your loneliness, and to be a man beside you once more, but perhaps also to help you deal with your sorrow. I would like to try."

She looked away from him again, and was still. He waited. She felt for his hand, and he grasped her searching hand in both of his own, kissed it, and held it tightly.

At length she turned her face to him again, and said, "Then, I will tell you." She closed her eyes and drew a deep breath.

"My husband was a good man, a thoughtful and gentle man, and I loved him. I was happy with him. He was educated and seemed to have a good life before him. His family was well respected, and they had enough money to live well. But they were Catholic, and the Secret Police accused them of counter-revolutionary activities. Their money and property were taken from them slowly, and then they were taken to prison, although they had done nothing. My husband was then in danger, and we escaped with the help of a Catholic friend."

"That was when you came to the south?"

"Yes. We went to Truc Giang, because there were some friends of his family who had already escaped, who lived in Truc Giang, and they could help my husband find work. We were poor, but we had enough to eat, and we were free.

"We had two little girls. Chi Hai was almost three years old."

"Chi Hai?"

"Yes," she said. In spite of the glistening eyes, a warm smile of recollection came to her lips. *"Chi hai* means 'number one sister' in Vietnamese. The oldest girl in a family is called Chi Hai."

"I like that. It makes her special, doesn't it?"

"Yes. Our Chi Hai was just as you said, very large eyes, round body, and so happy. She always looked . . . looked surprised . . . because her eyes were . . ." Therese's lips quivered, and she had to pause to regain her composure.

"Little Chi Ba was one year old," she continued. "She was just beginning to walk."

"Chi ba is . . ."

"Number two sister."

Toby's throat tightened, and he swallowed hard.

"The Viet Cong had told neighbors that my husband was working against them, and that they would kill him someday. My husband told all the neighbors that this was not so, that he was not working in any political or revolutionary way at all— which was true. He said that the Viet Cong were just trying to frighten him and the neighbors, that this was just part of their terror, that they would not do anything to him. He was a brave man. He continued to live and work as usual, and he did not show fear.

"Our house was small. It was built partly out over the river on logs that stand on end, I do not know the word."

"Pilings."

"Yes. We all slept in the back room over the water. It was cool and quiet. One night, when the others were asleep, I heard something . . . a noise along the bank of the river, and I got out of bed and went to the other room. I could see nothing, and I stepped out the door to see if I could see better from the outside.

"The Viet Cong had put some plastic in a sampan."

"Plastic explosive?"

"Yes."

Toby was horrified. He knew what a small amount—a few ounces—of plastic could do.

"They were letting the sampan float down in the water under our house. They made it explode just as I went out the door. I do not remember the explosion, but I remember getting up from the ground many meters away and running back to the house. My husband was lying there . . . He could not possibly still be living.

"I never again saw little Chi Ba. After the explosion, there was no more Chi Ba."

Therese's voice was shaking, and tears were streaming from her eyes. "I found Chi Hai in one corner of the front room, covered with broken things. She was crying, and her arms and legs were crooked, and she was blind."

Toby waited, gripping her hand.

"I picked her up and held her," said Therese, "and then she died."

Toby could not speak. Therese lay still, her eyes tightly shut, her lips quivering; then from the depths of her came an unearthly wail, half groan, half sob.

"Oh! Oh!" she moaned. "Oh, my babies . . . my babies . . . my babies . . ."

He gathered her swiftly into his arms and held her close, held her while the storm of pain wracked her body and contorted her beautiful face, caressed her wordlessly, grieving with all his heart over a hurt he was so powerless to soothe.

He turned off the light, and for much of what remained of the night he held her to him while the passion of remembering and suffering spent itself, and he left her at last lying quietly in his arms, shaken now and again by a small fluttering sigh, as a child will catch its breath when the weeping is over.

16

Of the twelve men Toby sent to the districts, three were killed and two were gravely wounded.

He watched in stunned silence as the three bodies were brought into the government compound, to be claimed by their families. The two wounded men had been taken directly to the My Tho hospital, their lives hanging by a thread.

Gabby had been killed. The other two were average, good guys whose faces had become so familiar to him, whose eyes had so often followed him intently as he lectured or demonstrated. The faces were still now, the eyes dead; as still as that other face, as dead as those other eyes he had seen that morning on his doorstep in Frankfurt.

He wished there were something he could say to show their stricken families how he felt, but knew that he could not have expressed it in any language.

Colonel Manh was calm, but cool. With Therese interpreting, he gave Toby the story as he had heard it. Each man had acquired lodgings that first night as best he could, and had been shot from ambush when he emerged from those lodgings the following morning. The wounds were from heavy rifles, and there were many of them. Instead of individual snipers, apparently there had been a small squad assigned to attack each man, and they had fired devastating volleys from long range. The attackers had not been apprehended. They had not even been seen.

214

"The Viet Cong knew about their missions," Colonel Manh concluded, looking Toby steadily in the eye.

"So it seems," said Toby.

"We should have thought that they would."

"Yes." Toby had never in his life been so nearly immobilized by shock. This was not a chance ambush that could be shrugged off as the fortunes of war, the mischance of being in the wrong place at the wrong time. This was an enemy reply to his efforts in Dinh Tuong Province. *We take you seriously, and you had damned well better take us seriously. We will kill them when we choose, and we will kill you when the time comes.* He shivered.

Major Thieu strode into the office. "Five men!" he shouted in a fury. "Five!" He held up the fingers of one hand for all to see. He turned on Toby.

"You send men! *You* send, and Viet Cong kill!"

Manh spoke sharply to Thieu, and Thieu fired a stream of angry words at him, not disrespectful, but certainly forceful by their sound. He was waving in Toby's direction all the while.

Well, he was right, wasn't he? Toby's career seemed to be taking on a regular pattern of finding men, preparing them, and dispatching them into a storm of bullets. He *should* have considered the possibility that the Viet Cong would learn of this operation, and that they would decide to act. He should have had those young men prepared for such an assault. His European-style professionalism had undermined whatever training and instinct they might have had for an insurgency situation, to the point where they had forgotten the most rudimentary safety precautions.

Dazed as he was, Toby was nonetheless struck by something about Thieu's face. There was a subtle difference in this wrath of today and the tantrum Thieu had thrown over Toby's original plan. That first rage had been so genuine that Toby had thought the man might fall into a fit at any moment. This one today seemed almost to be staged, acted out solely for the effect it would have on the audience. Thieu was not really all that upset about losing those men!

When Thieu had subsided, Manh turned to Toby. "You will understand," he said with studied politeness, "that Major Thieu is extremely angry. We will all be able to think about this more calmly some other time. I agree with Major Thieu that there will be no more teaching."

It was a blow, although not unexpected. The implication was plain that not only would there be no more teaching, there would be no more direct contact between him and the remaining students. The liaison would from now on be with Thieu and Manh only.

Thieu made no attempt to conceal his triumphant, righteous indignation as Toby and Therese left them, to drive back to the office. Thieu had won, and he knew that Toby knew it.

When they got back to the office, Toby could hear the single sideband transceiver muttering in the breezeway entrance.

"Buffalo, Buffalo, this is Volleyball. Buffalo, Buffalo, this is Volleyball. Over." Pause. "Buffalo, Buffalo, this is Volleyball. Over."

Toby recognized Volleyball's voice as that of Bill Voigt. He went to the transceiver and answered the call.

"Buffalo," came Bill's voice, "the regional office of your friends here tells us you had a hell of a night last night up there in your province. Over."

"Volleyball, that's affirmative. Have they given you details? Over."

"A lot of details. I don't know how accurate. But it sure looks serious. Over."

"It is serious, Volleyball. Over."

"Well, we can't discuss it this way. All hell may be about to break loose, so you better get on down here right away. Over."

"I can't make it immediately, Volleyball. Cobbler is not here, and I can't get in touch with him very quickly. And you know where Holiday is. Over."

"Yeah, that's right. How soon can you make it? Over."

Toby thought rapidly. "I can make it on Monday. Over."

"All right. I'll tell Butane he's got to get you here as early as possible. Call him for a schedule later this afternoon. Over."

"Roger, Volleyball. Over."

"Buffalo . . ." Bill's voice was grave. "I say again—this is serious. I need facts, all of them. Everything. Do you understand? Over."

"I understand, Volleyball. Over."

"See you Monday. Volleyball out."

"Buffalo out."

Toby went back to his desk and sat down. He did not know where or how to begin, even to begin thinking things through. Nor did he have any urge to do so. His mind was a blank, his initiative gone.

He sat as if in a trance, until a movement near his desk caught his eye. Therese had come and sat down and was looking at him intently. They were alone in the office. He tried to smile at her.

"Now it is my turn," she said.

"Your turn?"

"Yes. Today it is you who need help."

He blinked and tried to organize his thoughts. "Oh, not really, Therese. I'll be all right. I was a damned fool, and so wrapped up in what *I* knew that I didn't stop to think that maybe somebody else might have figured out some things about this war that I didn't know."

"You believe you have been defeated?"

"Whether I believe so is not the point. I know damned good and well that my *agency* will think so. My agency will see that the enemy has defeated me here in Dinh Tuong, and my superior in Can Tho has been proved right, and these facts will reach Washington. You are now looking at a man who is as high up in his profession as he will ever go . . . a man who will be among the first to go when there is another RIF."

"Another RIF?"

"Reduction in force. When they dismiss a certain percentage of the people of our agency. It happened in the past. It will happen in the future."

"They would not be so foolish! They would not dismiss you!"

"You are prejudiced," he said with a weak smile.

"Yes, Anh Tho, of course I am prejudiced. Anybody who knows you as well as I do must be prejudiced for you."

"The people in Washington don't have quite the same kind of an acquaintance with me that you do, Little Mistress."

She took his hand in hers, pulled the fingers out of the clenched ball, and held the hand tightly. "You will see," she said.

"Thanks. I know better than to be optimistic, but I love you for trying to help."

"You will see."

He took her hand in both of his own, and sat quietly with her for a long time.

"I do not like to leave you alone, Anh Tho," she said at last, "but I must go."

"All right," he said reluctantly. "But couldn't you come back this evening?" They stood up and she put her arms around him.

"No," she said. "Not tonight. Tonight it would not be good."

He knew she was right.

"You will see," she said once again, and kissed him quickly. Then she pulled away from his arms and was gone.

His brain was in no condition to work. He knew that even if he forced himself to stay at his desk, he would accomplish nothing. He went into the house, sat at the bar, and had a beer. Mrs. Chao called him to lunch, and he went in and sat down listlessly at the table. Mrs. Chao was tending to her tasks with a high good humor that showed she had heard nothing of Toby's problems.

"You sleep well?" she asked with elaborate innocence.

The question momentarily lifted the veil of gloom, and Toby grinned at her and wagged his finger accusingly.

"Shame on you, Mrs. Chao! No, I did not sleep. I did not sleep at all!"

Mrs. Chao laughed with delight. "No. Not sleep. I know."

"Of course you knew, you oriental yenta," he scolded her affectionately.

She grew suddenly serious. "You good man for Therese. Therese sad. Therese not happy. You help Therese."

Toby wished he could communicate with this woman with fluency, instead of the pidgin English that gave her speech such a childish sound. He knew that she was an intelligent woman who would have been able to give him a rational and thoughtful explanation of her feelings.

One thing was clear, in spite of the language barrier: Mrs. Chao had not looked upon the night from the point of view of Toby's good, but of Therese's. He loved the wrinkled little woman for that, and Mrs. Chao seemed to understand his feelings. "Good man," she said, and went back out into the kitchen.

Toby picked at his lunch without appetite. Afterward, he went back to the common room and paced up and down. He had a drink, and then another one. He had never used alcohol to forget or to escape, and he was not doing so now. He was merely bored, yet too keyed up to read, or to work, or to do anything except pace and drink. He knew that once he had liquor humming in his veins he would not be able to think clearly even if he tried, but he did not want to try.

He spent the rest of the afternoon in a leaden flush of alcohol. It did not solve his problem, but it made the time pass.

Mrs. Chao was silent when she served his dinner, and he guessed that she had heard the news by some kind of grapevine. By bedtime he was tired of the strain of the idle day, tired of the pacing, tired of the taste of booze in his mouth. He brushed his teeth in a sleepy fog and tumbled into bed. He thought dizzily that he had a right to be tired, after all. He had hardly slept last night—in fact, had expended more physical and emotional energy than a normal working day would require, only to be confronted with another shock when the night was over.

Maybe Therese was right. Maybe he would be able to . . . No, she was wrong. A man who consistently sent agents out to get shot . . . But on the other hand . . .

"Toby, wake up! Toby!"

An insistent hand was jogging his shoulder. He opened his eyes. Daylight was coming feebly through the heavy curtains, and Ben was standing by the bed.

"Ben!" he muttered groggily. "I didn't expect you back this morning. What's the matter?"

"The Yenan Battalion wiped out my team in Phu Binh last night."

"Wiped it out?"

"Killed over half of them," Ben continued bitterly. "Wounded all but three or four of the rest."

"But how did you get here this early?" Toby asked, looking at the clock on his night table.

"Jerry rousted Jess out way before daylight. Jess is waiting for me now. I gotta get stuff to take with me and get up there as fast as I can."

"Give me five minutes to have a shower," said Toby. He needed time and cold water to clear his head.

"OK," said Ben. "I'll see if Mrs. Chao has got a cup of coffee."

Toby knew, even as he stepped into the shower, that his mind was healed, even though a new disaster had struck. The events of these days might ultimately destroy him, but he would sit down at his desk and start the rational process of studying them, and trying to find out the causes, and his mistakes, and what action he must take.

Mrs. Chao had begun preparing bacon and eggs the moment Ben drove in, and he was now wolfing the breakfast down.

"If it's all right with you, Toby," he said between mouthfuls, "I'm going to go down to the PRU barracks and pick out about half a dozen men to take with me to the village. This was without any doubt the Yenan Battalion, and they did such a job on that village that there's a chance they'll still have people around to hit the rescue effort."

"Sure. Take whatever you need. Will they go just on your say-so?"

"Yeah."

"Can you wait till I have a bite, or will you come back by and get me?"

"Suit yourself," said Ben, "but if I were you I wouldn't leave this place empty. The hospital here is already sending a big team up there in a convoy with ARVN troops, and there's nothing you can do."

Toby thought about that. "You're right, Ben. I can't leave this place deserted. Have you heard about the Special Police students?"

"No, what about them?"

Toby told him the story, and Ben's jaw dropped. "Jesus! That was the night before last?"

"No, early morning. Just after daylight."

"What districts were those five visiting?"

Toby looked at Ben with sudden comprehension. "Come on," he said, "let's go look at the map."

They went into the office, and located the five districts. They were clustered in one area due north of My Tho. Phu Binh was in the midst of this cluster, although not exactly in the center.

"Would you look at that!" Ben mused.

"There's a solar plexus somewhere in that area, Ben," said Toby. "We were getting too close to something, and they decided to stop it cold and fast."

Ben studied the map for a time, then suddenly started. "Christ, I've got to get a move on," he said. He hurried out.

Toby studied the map. The excitement of untangling a puzzle was gripping him. He had a problem of terrain in the province that was his responsibility. He also had a unit of more than one hundred crack troops at his command. Their job was to collect intelligence in the province. Well, here was the granddaddy of all targets. He would get together with Little Jack, as soon as Little Jack got back, and draw up a plan to search that area thoroughly. Even if it meant a delay in getting the Phoenix program under way.

There was something in that area that somebody did not want uncovered, and by God he was going to uncover it.

17

Ben had not been gone more than ten minutes when the sound of a motorcycle entering the gate reached Toby's ears. He went to the door. It was Tran Van Qui, one of his Special Police students, the one whom Toby had spotted as perhaps the best mind in the class, although reticent and careful.

Mystified, Toby watched him park his motorcycle and unstrap a cardboard box from the carrier behind the seat. He came up the steps and handed the box to Toby.

"I bring from class," he said.

I'll be damned. He speaks some English, and I never had an inkling.

Toby looked into the box and saw a number of items of office supplies and equipment he had left in the classroom, to be picked up later. He still did not understand.

"We do clandestine communications now," the man continued, with a slight smile.

So that was it! The man wanted to talk to him, and had brought the box as a simple cover for his visit.

"Come in," he said quickly, and ushered the man into his office. "I cannot speak Vietnamese," he said, "and Mr. Minh is not here."

"I speak English," said the man. "Not good English, but we talk?"

"Of course," said Toby. "We talk. I think you speak English as well as Major Thieu."

"Better," said the man calmly, and Toby laughed. This man was quick-witted.

"Since you speak English," Toby said, "we can keep this clandestine communication just between you and me. We will not need anybody else. Not Mr. Minh, nor Therese. Just you and me."

"Good."

It was a struggle for them to get ideas across to one another, and they talked for more than an hour. Toby found himself using Vietnamese words, and learning some new ones, as well as some phrases. He had resolved to study the language eventually, and now he had a tutor for it.

Qui did speak better English than Thieu. He could listen to a fairly complicated English sentence and get the sense of it, although he could not construct complicated answers.

What he had to say added to the optimism Toby was already feeling. Qui had spoken with the two wounded men in the hospital. He could not speak long with them, because of the gravity of their wounds, and he had to be especially discreet because of other ears near their beds. They had told him of their conviction that the districts they had visited held some VC secret. Either a large cache of ammunition, or a secret hideout. Perhaps a transfer depot for the shipment of war supplies. They knew that at the center of this secrecy was the Yenan Battalion. They were certain that the ambushes had been laid by the Yenan Battalion.

Most important and most encouraging of all, they were not troubled by the assignments that had sent them into the ambushes. They saw the attacks as proof that they were right to be snooping around. They wanted the search and investigation to continue. They wanted to be in on the work, although in both cases they had many weeks of convalescence before them.

Qui had discussed the situation with the other students, and found them to be unanimous in the feeling that they must continue to look into the districts in that area. They knew that even if Thieu had been willing for them to do so, he would not have the skill to organize a rational plan of investigation. They wanted Toby to organize it. They had delegated Qui—or, thought Toby with an inward smile, Qui had delegated himself, with their consent—to act as their communications channel to Toby.

"Now, Mr. Qui," he said, "suppose I do draw up a step-by-step plan of action for the men? How can they travel to the districts? Thieu would know, and he would not permit it."

Qui nodded. "Thieu is a fool. But Manh is chief. Manh good. You talk to Manh, show him. We go to villages get information. Information for Manh, not for Thieu."

Toby nodded back. "It might work."

"You ask Manh give *you* information."

"Yeah, if he is running things, he'll give me the information in an official liaison exchange, but . . ."

"We give Manh information—but then I come here."

Toby looked at Qui, and a grin slowly began to spread across his face, reflected by an equally wide grin on the face of Qui. Qui had just recruited himself as Toby's agent, without Toby's lifting a finger.

"Qui," he said, "this is great!"

"You see Manh?"

"Tomorrow. I will have a plan to discuss with him by then. I think we can use the PRUs and the Special Police together in this operation."

"Number one!" exclaimed Qui, the highest encomium a Vietnamese could bestow, Toby knew.

"You and I must set up a system for meetings," said Toby. "Clandestine communications between you and me."

Qui held up his hand. "No problem. I come see you after work. You teach me English, I teach you Vietnamese. You have books?"

"Yes. Tuesdays and Thursdays in the evening?"

"Tuesdays and Thursdays. Good."

"I will tell Manh that the men should not go to the villages at the same time. I will draw up a schedule of villages to be visited. I will give you a copy of the same schedule I give to Manh, but Manh will not know you have it."

"OK."

"The basic instructions will be the same for the time being. Talk to the villagers, find out what's going on in the areas, what the Viet Cong is doing. You understand?"

"I understand. Same as before."

"Right."

"I go now. I come back Tuesday."

"Tuesday evening. Thanks, Qui. Thanks very much."

Qui shook his hand and left.

Ben returned late that evening in a black mood.

"They destroyed the team, all right," he said. "Killed more than half of them, wounded the rest. They concentrated mainly on the team, not on the villagers, and the ones that could move hauled ass out, except for six of them who tried to make a stand. Those six were captured, and the VC marched them out into the street and shot them in the back of the head."

"God, what a war!"

"It's a fact of life, Toby. The Viet Cong can't take prisoners, as a general rule. They've got no way to keep them."

"That doesn't make it any less barbaric."

"No, of course not. Those that weren't killed have been evacuated to Vung Tau or the hospital, and I doubt if you would get many of them to go back to any village, anywhere, with another team."

"You could hardly blame them for that."

"And of course the village people, those that are left, have had the be-Jesus scared out of them. ARVN is up there in force, looking for the Yenan Battalion, but with the Tiger in charge they've got about as much chance of finding it as a bunch of campfire girls. The ARVN also lifted a Ranger Battalion up there with choppers, but they'll have no better luck than the others.

"But all the government troops in the world aren't going to make those villagers feel a bit better, because you can tell when you talk to them that the Tiger made sure that each one of them was given the word. If they let another team come in, or if they have anything to do with the Saigon régime, they'll get picked off one by one, at night, or they'll be assaulted in force one night. Either way, they'd all be killed."

"They believe that, too, of course?"

"Of course! The VC have given them all the proof they need. They wouldn't talk to me, and they wouldn't talk to the soldiers. You can scratch one pacified village from our list, my friend. We've flat lost it. For good. The VC can claim that as their own territory from now on."

"Other teams will hear about that, too," said Toby.

"Damn right!" Ben exclaimed. "For the next couple of weeks, I'm going to have to be out visiting as many of them as I can. A thing like this could spook even the best ones."

"Ben," said Toby, "I'm about to make up some plans that are essentially military, and I need your advice."

"OK. What have you got in mind?"

Toby explained to Ben about Qui's visit, and Ben forgot his gloom for the moment. "Didn't I tell you you had taken those men away from Thieu?"

"What I want to do is carry out a systematic examination of this entire area," Toby went on, taking Ben over to the wall map. "I thought of using the Special Police investigators, under cover of some kind, without the local police office knowing about it. I thought I could coordinate their work with PRU operations in the same vicinity. I was thinking of setting up a couple of cordon-and-search operations every week, until we've covered this territory from end to end. Maybe coordinate the operations with some work by your teams, when there is a team in the area."

"I haven't got any within the area, Toby, but I've got a couple or three near the edges that might be of help. They're located here, and here and here." He pointed to the map.

"That ought to help some, anyway."

They got a smaller map and spread it out on the desk. "You can ask Little Jack," said Ben, "but I doubt if what you'll want to do is a full-scale cordon and search. They take a lot of time and work. I don't think you'd have time to do as many as need to be done in this situation, and anyway, what you're looking for is obviously something pretty damned big, not just a rice cache or a few rifles or boxes of ammo. Whatever it is is big and important. The Viet Cong have told us that pretty plainly. A sudden, plain patrol, a straight search, by the PRU, ought to be just as effective as a cordon and search, and it'll be a lot simpler. Two of those you could do in a week."

"Thanks, Ben," said Toby. "I'll talk it over with Little Jack when he gets back."

They were mortared that night. The barrage struck their neighborhood, in a fairly even pattern. It sounded like a full-scale battle to Toby, because there were detonations all around them. The only damage to the house, however, was some pock-marks in the masonry walls from fragments and a hole in the upper corner of the roof where a shell had made a direct hit. The sandbag bunker had absorbed most of the impact.

"Things seem to be heating up, Ben," said Toby, trying to hide his nervousness as they crouched on the roof afterward.

"Oh, not really," Ben replied easily. "This is really more normal. There's been a kind of a lull ever since you got here, but the action is about back to where it has been for a long time."

"Even the Phu Binh attack was normal?"

"I told you when you got here, that first day, that they're kicking the shit out of us. This is what I meant. They're hitting our programs and our installations hard, and they're keeping the pressure on the towns in the countryside."

Early Monday morning, Toby was in Bill Voigt's office, with Chet in a chair nearby. Chet was not angry this morning. He was triumphant, and Toby was not surprised.

"Five of them, Bill," Chet was saying. "Five out of twelve is almost half. That's a pretty goddamned high casualty rate for *any* kind of an action!"

"Toby," said Bill, "give me the story."

Toby told him what he knew, and Bill listened intently. When the account was finished, he spoke.

"The Regional Office of the Special Police is on me to shag your ass out of the delta," he said, "and maybe even out of Vietnam."

"I'm not surprised," said Toby with a shrug. He was not repentant, but he was worried that he might not be left in My Tho to vindicate himself.

"It might not be a bad idea," Bill continued.

"I think it would be a *good* idea," said Chet. "If all a man can do is send people out to get shot—"

"Hold it, Chet," said Bill quietly. "Personalities are not going to help us get at a decision." Chet subsided.

"I know it's going to sound like an alibi," said Toby, "but I think it might be pointed out to the regional people that Manh and Thieu agreed to the operation, and in fact it was Thieu that gave the order, not me."

"He got his version of it here ahead of you, Toby. He says you forced him into the decision by threatening to go all the way to Saigon with some story about how he wasn't cooperating with you."

"Oh, Christ!" said Toby.

"I *will* tell you, though," Bill went on, "that we've managed to calm things down a little, and Saigon is going to leave it up to me. Whatever I say, they'll back me up with the Saigon office of the Special Police. And I don't mind telling you that all my instincts tell me to transfer you out of here. It would solve our problem with the Vietnamese. Furthermore, you've got to consider the scapegoat factor. If you stay, they're likely to pile the blame on you for everything bad that happens from now on. Of course, we could fix it up for our own records so that it wouldn't look as bad for you as Thieu makes it sound."

"Sure," said Toby in a taut voice.

Bill looked at him steadily.

"You've got something in mind, haven't you?"

"Yes."

"Let's hear it."

"If you look at the map, you can see a pattern to these ambushes and the attack on Phu Binh. That's Yenan Battalion territory. Now, why would they set up ambushes on those five men in that particular pattern? The Viet Cong don't act out of whim. There must be something in that area they don't want us to see. Ordinarily, they'd be mobile enough so that they wouldn't be that nervous about any particular piece of real estate. But they're building up for their Tet offensive."

"Jesus, here we go again," said Chet.

Toby ignored him. "And whatever it is has got to stay in place there until that time."

"And what do you think it is?"

"It's got to be something big: a hideout, or a supply dump of some kind. We hear down there that they're bringing in thousands of tons of war materiel from Cambodia every month. It's got to go somewhere, and they haven't been using it all lately."

"So?" Bill was listening intently.

"I want to send those Special Police officers out again, and—"

"Why, you stupid son of a bitch!" Chet exploded.

Toby was on his feet in a split second and was reaching for Chet's shirt front, with his other hand balled into a fist and cocked back, but Bill, with reflexes that would have done credit to a younger man, brought his arm down on Toby's with a sharp blow. He then grabbed Toby's other arm in an iron grip and shoved him back toward his chair.

"Chet," Toby rasped, "if you ever say anything like that to me again I'll break your goddamned back!"

"All right!" said Bill. "Now both of you simmer down. I've got enough problems without having to referee a Pier Six brawl."

"Bill," said Chet, "that's the craziest thing I ever heard of. This is the second time he's had men shot on his operations, and now he wants to turn right around and do the same thing all over."

"He's got a point there," said Bill.

Toby, rubbing his wrist where Bill's had struck it, explained his plans to Bill, his use of Manh, his recruitment of Qui, the coordination of all the factors in the search he had in mind.

"Do you think Manh will go along with it?" asked Bill.

"I don't know. I'm going to do my best to talk him into it."

"He'd be putting his own neck on the block, you know."

"I realize that. But this is a war we're in the middle of, and I don't think it's exactly the time to worry about nothing but covering your ass. If he can be shown that there is something big there to be found, maybe he will be willing to risk it."

Bill toyed with a letter opener on his desk and frowned. Chet and Toby were silent.

"All right," he said at last. "I'll go along, too, if Manh does. I'd hate for the VC to think that all they've got to do is shoot up three or four of our people to make us pull back and stop bothering them."

"Thanks," said Toby. "I realize what a risk you'll be running."

"Make no mistake about it, Toby," said Bill, leveling a cool gaze at him, "if this thing blows up, if anything happens anywhere near like what happened Saturday morning, there will be no way I could save your skin, even if I wanted to. And I'm not even sure I'd want to. So don't thank me. I may not be doing you any favor. I may be doing nothing more than giving you whatever rope you need to hang yourself with."

"I'm not asking for anything except a chance," said Toby.

The temptation was almost irresistible to tell Bill about Dang, but he knew that he must not do so. For that information to get to Bill, it would have to come from Chet. Otherwise, Chet would consider it to be out of channels. Bill might think that Toby was merely being spiteful against Chet, especially since he still had no solid proof about Dang. Even the surveillance and the use of the dead drop could be interpreted by a skeptic as skillful trickery by Dang. And, after all, didn't all his training and experience teach him to be skeptical—teach them *all* to be skeptical?

They left Bill's office, and Toby followed Chet into Chet's office, thinking that perhaps Chet might be glad of an opportunity to add one more nail to his coffin.

"Chet," Toby said, when they had closed the door, "whatever we think of each other, this is a point of communications, and we've got to make it work. I've got some more on Dang that I think you ought to consider, and ought to let me submit an intelligence report on."

"What's that?" Chet asked, regarding Toby with a look of frigid hostility.

Toby told him about the latest developments in the Dang operation.

"Busch," said Chet, when the account was finished, "they're playing you like a goddamned Ping-Pong ball. You really and truly believe you've got hold of a VC penetration there?"

"I know it."

"Well then, you just go on and play with it, and play with yourself too, if you feel like it, because one thing's just about as useful to the agency as the other."

"You won't go to Bill with it?"

"No."

"If it's as bad as you say, I'd think you'd jump at the chance to tell Bill about it, and add one more black mark against me."

"You don't know me very well, buddy," Chet sneered. "I'm not going to go around snitching to Papa, because Bill Voigt would assume that's exactly what I was doing. Anyway, I don't need to help you slam the drawer on your own balls, because you're going to arrange that all by yourself, and before very long, too. If you want the story taken to him, you could do it yourself, you know."

"Sure."

"I'm even going to give you a break. When things do blow up in your face up there, I'm not going to even mention this so-called penetration agent of yours. You're gonna be sent to Siberia anyway, but if I told that one too, they'd send you to the funny farm instead."

"Thanks for everything, Chet," said Toby abruptly. He turned on his heel and walked out.

Toby was surprised and elated to find that Manh was an easy mark for the new plan. He could hardly believe his ears when, sitting with Minnie in Manh's office, he heard Manh acknowledge that he himself had figured things out essentially the way Toby had. It was more than just a terrible harassment of the Special Police. Manh was willing to allow his young men to participate, under Manh's personal direction, in a coordinated effort to find out what the Viet Cong were up to in that section of the province.

Toby told Manh that he felt that Manh should set the pattern and pace of the operations, although the rest of them could work out the specific details. Manh nodded.

"Are you aware that the Viet Cong has agreed to a Christmas truce and a Tet truce?"

"I had heard that there was something along those lines being discussed," Toby said.

"I am certain that your MACV forces will respect the truce, and we will join you in that, of course."

"Do you think the Viet Cong will abide by a truce during Tet?" asked Toby.

"Yes. Tet is a sacred holiday. I believe they will respect it."

"I hope you are right," said Toby, hypocritically, aware as he said it that he was now in the terrible position of wishing the worst for Vietnam in order to save his own skin.

"We will have time for perhaps two operations before Christmas," said Manh.

"Very well," said Toby. Together they studied the map, and Manh pointed to an area near the edge of the zone they intended to search. Toby noted the names and coordinates down in his notebook.

"Let us do this one on December 15," said Manh.

"Good," said Toby. Then he continued in a worried voice, "Colonel, there is one matter that makes me very uneasy. What about Major Thieu?"

"Mr. Busch, I will be frank with you. Major Thieu will be opposed to this plan. He will, I know, make certain that his opposition is known to our superiors in some discreet manner. If we are making a mistake, it will be very bad for me."

"I understand, sir," said Toby. "I am in exactly the same position myself." Manh nodded and smiled at him.

Little Jack, back from his Phoenix training, accepted the idea of the searches without comment. He and Minnie briefed his PRUs, and decided to move into each area at night, so as to take advantage of the element of surprise when they began the search at sunrise.

Meanwhile two of Manh's men, Toby's students, would be in one hamlet close to the village to be searched, and two others would be in a village on the other side.

Ben would be spending the night in a third, pacified village, also close to the search area.

And Toby would stay at home. He could not join the Special Police officers, of course, and he would be more of a handicap than a help to Ben or Little Jack.

Moreover, always lurking in the back of his mind was the thought that when the house was empty, he could once again spend a night in the arms of Therese. He felt guilty to be thinking of such illicit joys of the flesh while his associates took the field against the enemy. He had not thought himself capable of such blithe depravity. Now he knew that he was.

He comforted himself with the thought that while he was actually in bed with her, the others would just be getting into position—that whatever action there was would take place the following morning.

He had a crazy impulse to try to cross every finger and toe as he watched Little Jack and Minnie drive out the gate that Friday evening, to go to the PRU compound and get underway. Ben had choppered up to his village during the afternoon.

Therese had stayed, happily, matter-of-factly.

"You are happy again, Anh Tho," she said, as they sat sipping a drink in the common room.

"Yes, I am, Little Mistress," he said. "I am at last making things move, instead of merely sitting back and studying them. I have a chance to repair a lot of damage from the past."

"Yes. That is so."

"But let's not talk about business. Most of the happiness I'm feeling now is on account of us, tonight."

"Yes. I am happy, also."

"Good."

"Tonight will be good," she said with a shy smile.

"But it is a sad sort of happiness, I'm afraid, because whatever we do, we can't make it last forever."

"But, Anh Tho," she said, "you, yourself, have said that what we have *is* forever."

"Yes," he replied softly. "Yes, I did. And I meant it. And do you know something else? For some reason, I am almost comfortable with that. I wonder why?"

"Perhaps because it is not complicated?"

He thought about that. "By golly, I believe you are right!"

"I think so."

"*It* is not complicated. *You* are not complicated. That must be the reason. You are here with me. There is no doubt about us. We know exactly what we are doing and where it will lead, or not lead, and so we don't waste time or energy worrying about other days. We enjoy this one."

"Yes."

The meal was another study in moderation and good taste. The matter-of-fact attention of Mrs. Chao and Chi Hai somehow seemed to give this affair a rightness, a total acceptability, and Toby abandoned himself to the enjoyment of it.

In his room, which had once again been prepared by the affectionate schemers from the kitchen, Toby was happy to find that nothing had changed. They made love again, and the enchantment was still there.

"Anh Tho," said Therese afterward, snuggling close to him in the dark, "I have discovered something."

"Have you?"

"I have been thinking about it for many days. I have discovered it tonight."

"M-m-m-m. I wonder what it could be? There is certainly nothing about *me* that you haven't discovered and ravished completely by now." He patted her bare bottom.

"No," she said, settling her head more comfortably in the hollow of his arm, "it is about you and me."

"What is it?"

"I do not believe that I have ever loved a man as I love you."

"Haven't you, Little Mistress?"

"Yes."

"You are going to make me sad," he said softly, his lips near her ear.

"But it is not sad," she said quickly. "Why should I be sad to discover such a good thing?"

"I love you, too, Therese," he said hesitantly. "I love you in a way that—" Her small hand suddenly covered his mouth.

"Do not say it," she said. "I do not want you to say something just to make me happy, something you do not mean."

"All right. But if I just say, 'I love you,' will that be all right?"
"Yes."
"I love you. Little Mistress, I love you."

The operation on Saturday morning was uneventful. The PRU search revealed nothing. Elicitation by the Special Police officers brought only some names of suspected Viet Cong collaborators, which Toby incorporated into his new file of suspects.

On Tuesday, December 19, they repeated the operation in an area to the north of the first one. This time Little Jack's men discovered a rice cache, and exchanged a few shots with two men who were nearby, but there were no casualties.

At this point, the war strangely came to a halt. Peace and relaxation were in the air.

"It's the Christmas truce, Toby," said Ben. "Even the people in the villages are less uptight than usual."

No more military operations were scheduled for the Christmas season. Little Jack would leave on Thursday morning for Rest and Recreation in Hong Kong. From the look in his eye, it was evident that he expected this R & R to be a most satisfactory time of "having fun with 'em and then laying 'em." Ben would depart the same day for his own scheduled visit to Vung Tau, undoubtedly to do something similar to what Little Jack had in mind, although perhaps more elegantly described and less blatantly announced. Minnie, with almost no responsibilities left around the office, asked permission to take the days off to go to his brother's place.

It was as if the war were a grammar school, letting out for Christmas.

Toby's own R & R would be to be alone in the house. He had not been in the country long enough to be eligible for leave of any kind, and would not have felt comfortable going on leave so soon, in any event.

He was keenly aware, moreover, that being alone in the

house would permit him to be alone with Therese again. Thus, in his own way, he thought guiltily to himself, he could be said to have plans not essentially different from those of Ben and Little Jack. But before he could broach the subject to Therese, she came to his desk with a request that dampened his spirits.

"Mr. Busch, I have been invited to Saigon to spend Christmas with a family of Catholic friends from the north," she said. He wondered at this formal approach, but decided that she must want others in the office to see that her leave was proper and formally arranged.

"When would you go, Therese?" he asked, with equal formality.

"I would leave Friday morning, with your permission."

"And you would be back . . . ?"

"I would come back the day you suggest."

"Would the twenty-seventh suit you?"

"Yes, certainly. I can come back sooner if you wish."

"No. Make it the twenty-seventh, Therese. And enjoy yourself."

She went back to her desk, and he turned and surveyed them all: Little Jack at his desk, Minnie at his side looking at some manuals, Ben at his desk, and Therese settling herself once again to work.

"Fine bunch of troops I've got," he chided them. "Every single one of you off to have a good time, leaving poor old Busch here all by himself!"

Ben looked up in surprise. "Hell, Toby, I don't have to go! I can put my trip off until—"

Toby laughed. "Not on your life! Give up Vung Tau for me?"

They all saw that he was joking, and his mock martyrdom had put them at their ease. The teacher was sending them away without any homework.

18

Therese was alone with him in the office for the final two hours of the Thursday workday, but she was busy at her desk, and was so engrossed in whatever she was doing that Toby did not disturb her. He felt somewhat uneasy about it, but told himself that he should be pleased with an employee who lost herself in her work that way, even if she was his mistress.

When she finally put all her things away and rose to leave, she stopped by his desk.

"I am sorry to go, Anh Tho," she said.

"Sit down, Therese," he said, much relieved by her genuine reluctance to leave him.

She sat down in the chair by his desk. He was on the point of urging her to stay the night with him, but somehow he knew that it would not be right. The whole thing was already too much like smoking behind the barn, and for him to take her to bed at every slightest opportunity smacked more of pure appetite than love.

"I hope you will not be lonely," she said.

"I will be. But it's nice to know that you will miss me."

"These friends made plans for this Christmas many months ago, and I said that I would be there, and so I cannot . . ."

"I understand. You needn't apologize. But I must say that I didn't realize Christmas was so important to the Vietnamese."

"For the Catholics, it is," she said. "It will be especially

. . . what is the word you use . . . touching?"

"Yes, touching."

"It will be especially touching for this group of Catholics, because we are all far away from our homes in the north."

"But it will be a good Christmas, anyway, with friends."

"Yes. It will be good. Except that I will be wishing that I were here with you."

"But you will be back next week," he said. "We still have many times together in the future."

"Yes."

They stood. Impulsively, she threw her arms around him and kissed him, then slipped quickly from his embrace and was gone.

An hour later Qui appeared for his first Thursday visit. He brought nothing new with him, beyond the official information which Manh had already passed to Toby, and that information was of little consequence. Qui said that the morale among his group was high, and that they were certain that after these two preliminary operations, which were by way of testing the water, they would be closing in on something important. They were enthusiastic about the prospects.

The rest of Qui's visit turned into the language lesson that the visits were purported to be, and Toby was glad to be doing something about his ignorance of the language, although he could tell that this oriental system of speech was going to be difficult to master.

Qui gone, and dinner over, Toby set himself to another task. He made a test of each of the instruments of the new Motorola radio net that had been delivered that week. The net consisted of his base station, a small flat console with a pedestal microphone, and eight handsets, each about the size of a lunch box, with a telephone-type receiver clamped to the handle on top.

He drew a chart of the net, which would consist of his base station in the office, a handset in each of the two jeeps—which would be taken to his and Ben's bedrooms at night—one in the Province Senior Adviser's office, one in the PRU barracks, one in the Special Police Office, one in the Revolutionary Development Office, and one in the house of the three women. He named his net Victory, and marked each set with its own call sign. His base station was Victory-1, his jeep set was Victory-2, the Province Senior Adviser's was Victory-3, and so on.

Friday morning he installed the spidery antenna for his base station on the roof. He led the coaxial cable down from the antenna along the inside walls and through the breezeway to the office, where the base station console was located on a small table near the door.

He loaded the remaining sets in the jeep and set out to deliver them. His first call was the Province Senior Adviser's office. Marie Claire was there, and she listened intently as Toby explained the radio net to the Deputy Province Senior Adviser, a young army lieutenant. The lieutenant had used such equipment before, and understood the mechanics of the network without much explanation.

"I'm putting one of these in the house where Marie Claire lives with two other women," Toby said to the lieutenant. "In a sense it's beyond my authorization, but I've got a spare set, and it might as well be in their house as sitting idle on a shelf."

"That's a great relief," said the lieutenant. "I've been worried about them in that house."

"One of my people had an idea to try to do something about that wall of theirs, too," Toby went on.

"What about it?"

"He thinks it ought to be built higher—about eight feet."

The lieutenant was interested, but had heard nothing. Perhaps Ben had forgotten.

"Well, anyway," Toby continued, "it is understood that this net has several Vietnamese stations, and it is strictly for business. No social calls."

"Of course."

"Is anybody at home over at your house, Marie Claire?" Toby asked. "I can go over and deliver it now."

"No, Peggy and Louise are at the hospital," she said. "Why don't you come over later on, some time this evening?"

"OK. What time would be best?"

"Why don't you just come for dinner?"

"Oh, I wouldn't want to put you to any trouble," Toby said, not even trying to hide his pleasure.

"It's no trouble. If you don't mind being alone with three women."

"Being alone with crowds of women is one of my favorite pastimes," said Toby. "If you ladies won't mind dividing me into three, I'll be there."

"Peggy and I will be lucky to get a tenth each," said Marie Claire.

At dinner, the women served him and made over him with smiling, outlandish concern, and he soaked it up with a self-satisfied expression on his face. It was a welcome change to be in a home where the feminine was in evidence wherever the eye came to rest, after a masculine dormitory such as their own house, with weapons and manuals and the easy blasphemy of male talk.

Peggy and Marie Claire made some gestures about leaving him alone with Louise, but they were easily talked out of it, and they ended the evening sitting in the living room, listening to soft music, sipping coffee and talking.

The Victory-5 set installed in their living room, with instructions to take it to their bedrooms at night, and some demonstrations in how to use the equipment, Toby was ready to leave.

"If I could be sure of an evening like this every time," Toby said, "I'd send all my associates away every few days."

"You're going to be kind of lonesome for a while, aren't you, Toby?" asked Louise.

"No," he lied. "I've got so much work piled up that I'm really glad of the opportunity to be by myself to do it."

"Well, if it gets to be more than you can bear, let us know," said Peggy. "We'll come over and put cornflakes in your bed, or something."

"I'll remember that gracious offer," said Toby. "By the way, when I get home, I'll give you a call to see if the signal reaches both ways."

"Standing by, Victory-One," said Peggy.

The reception and transmission by Victory-5 proved to be loud and clear, and Toby went to bed, having passed his first day alone without feeling alone. But the coming days loomed large, especially Christmas. If his own family in Iowa had been feeling especially lonely, it might have been a rather perverse and selfish consolation to him, but they would be in the midst of the larger family, and although they would miss him, they were far from being lonely. Their Christmas would be joyous, old-fashioned, probably even white, whereas his would be spent in an empty French-colonial house with guards around it, and a generator roaring ceaselessly out in back.

He didn't even have the fear of attack to occupy his mind now, because of the Christmas truce.

After breakfast the next morning he began to realize what it was going to be like to be alone. He wandered into the office, went over some reports, read a mass of material that had come in some days before in the pouch, most of which he would have glanced at and thrown away at any other time, but which now provided a means to spend an hour or so.

After lunch, he looked through the disreputable collection of books that had accumulated in the house, more by accident than by design. Most of them were paperbacks, of the kind one forgets within an hour of finishing. In addition to these, he found hardback copies of Arthur Schlesinger's *The Coming of the New Deal* and Truman Capote's *In Cold Blood,* attesting to an unusual catholicity of tastes on the part of some collector.

He decided to try Schlesinger, and labored over the book for about an hour before giving up.

He wrote a letter to Mary Lynn. He had to be extremely careful not to let his mood show. By sunset he was looking forward to the warmth of a drink at the bar. But alcohol seemed only to sharpen his despondency. He ate his dinner, hardly noticing the food.

He took his coffee back into the common room, and sat gloomily in the emptiness. The selection of records and tapes on the shelf consisted of music that either irritated him or faded innocuously from his consciousness and went unnoticed soon after the first syrupy chords. He decided to forego music.

He made a decision, a minor decision, to be sure, but in a nothing day it took on the characteristics of urgency and importance. He went to the radio set and called, "Victory-Five, this is Victory-One. Victory-Five, this is Victory-One. Over." He repeated the call once more, and heard Louise's voice.

"Victory-One, this is Victory-Five."

"Victory-One, if it's convenient for you, I think I should repair that defect in your set immediately. Would it be convenient for me to do it right away?"

"Can you wait just a minute, Victory-One?"

"Victory-One standing by."

There was a pause, then Louise's voice returned to the air. "Victory-One, we all believe it's important to get it fixed right away. In fact, we're having a great deal of difficulty with it."

Her voice was flat and calm, but Toby knew her eyes would be dancing with fun. "I'll be over as soon as I can make a place in my schedule," he said, in a voice equally as flat. "Victory-One out."

"Victory-Five out."

His gloom gone, he drove across town. Louise met him at the door and led him into the living room.

"Where are the other two?" Toby asked, looking around the room.

"They're both in housecoats and bare faces," said Louise, "and they have no intention of letting a man see them that way."

"You mean, I drove them out of their living room?"

"Only about half an hour before they would have left anyway, Toby. They don't mind. In this country and this war, a woman has got to take any chance she can get to be with a man, and they're happy that you've come, even if it's just for my sake."

"Well, but I didn't intend to come just to see *you*— Er, that is, what I mean is . . ."

"What you mean is," said Louise dramatically, "that this is the end between you and me?"

Toby laughed. "Dammit, Louise," he said, "that is the one thing I would hate more than anything else I can think of, for this between you and me to end. What I meant was . . ."

"It's too late to apologize for such heartless cruelty as that remark shows," she said with a twinkle in her eye, "but I'll do my duty and try to be a gracious hostess, anyway. Can I fix you a drink?"

"If you're not too overwrought to be trusted with strong potions," said Toby, "I would like a gin and tonic."

"OK. You're the only man I know who drinks gin and tonic at any hour of the day or any season of the year."

"It's a rut I can't seem to get out of."

She went over to the portable bar and mixed drinks for them.

"By the way," she said, handing him the glass, and settling herself beside him with a small glass of whisky and water, "what set was it you came over to repair?" Her voice was expressionless, but there was laughter just below the surface.

"Louise," he said, with mock humility, "I have a confession to make."

"Tell me, my son," she said, blessing him with an upraised hand, "what have you done? Have you been using bad language? Have you been thinking impure thoughts? Have you been unfaithful to your wife?"

The remark hit Toby so suddenly that he almost lost his composure. "No," he said carelessly, "it's none of those things. Or, rather, I should say that in *addition* to those things, and almost everything else, I want to confess that there's nothing at all wrong with your set."

"Nothing wrong with my set?"

"Nothing. Not a thing."

"In other words, my set has been OK all along?"

Toby was grinning happily. "As far as I can tell, it's absolutely perfect."

"Then, sir, why did you come under such false pretenses?"

Toby turned to her, and was serious. "I came over because I was bored to death, and because it's the Christmas season."

"I'm glad you did, Toby," she said softly. "Do you know, I've never really had a chance to sit and talk with you quietly?"

"Yes," he said. "I *have* noticed."

"I have a thousand things I want to talk to you about."

"Me too," he said. He leaned back in the sofa. "You first."

"OK. First, why did you come to Vietnam? The CIA isn't like the army, is it? They can't force you to take an assignment like this?"

"I'll try to give you a satisfactory answer," he said, "but first, I want to ask you a question. Why do you ask me that?"

"I have just wondered, that's all. Ben told Peggy you came over here because you wanted to. And that could mean that you're trying to get away from something, or prove something, or who knows what else?"

Toby told her as much as he could of the Frankfurt incident. "It's all in my record," he said. "In a bureaucracy—and even our agency is a bureaucracy—you don't attack a bad mark headlong. You try to make it less evident or less important by surrounding it with a consistent record of good marks."

"But it wasn't your fault?"

"No, but that's of very little consequence, sometimes, in the official record."

"I know you can do it if you get the chance," she said. "And I hope you get the chance."

"You are a sweet woman," he said. "Now tell me why *you* are here."

They talked until late, and Toby relaxed in a mood of ease and contentment. Louise had a way of massaging his ego, and showing her regard for him, by gentle, sometimes almost tender words and inflections, while at the same time she teased him playfully and kept him always aware that he was sitting beside a vibrant woman.

"I must go," he said, looking at his watch.

"Must you?" she asked, with genuine regret.

"Yes."

"What about tomorrow?"

"Tomorrow?"

"Tomorrow is Christmas Eve. If you were bored and lonely this evening, what will it be like tomorrow?"

"You've got a point there."

"Christmas Eve is a terrible time to be alone. The worst time of the year."

"What you are hinting at," he said, "is that you would like to be asked out tomorrow evening?"

"No," she replied. "As a matter of fact I wasn't hinting at all. I was frankly leading up to a direct request."

"Well, then, let me save your virtue by doing it in a gentlemanly way. Louise, will you have dinner with me tomorrow evening?"

"Yes."

"Have you ever been to the Soong Palace?"

"Yes."

"Like it?"

"Yes."

"Shall we go there tomorrow evening?"

"Yes."

"With you in such a positive mood, I don't think I'd better ask you any more questions tonight." He made as if to rise from the sofa, but she put a hand on his arm and stopped him.

"Stay for just a minute more, won't you?" she asked, turning toward him and tucking her legs under her. "There's one more thing I want to ask you."

"OK," he said, leaning back once more, smiling contentedly. "Shoot."

"I'm dying to know. Who is she?"

"Who is who?" Toby asked uneasily.

"Who is the woman? Is it that pretty girl in your office?"

"What are you talking about?" he asked sharply.

"Toby, you blushed almost purple when I asked that silly question a while ago."

"I've never blushed in my life."

"Then that blush a minute ago must have been all the more significant. It's nosey of me, isn't it? It's a question I shouldn't be asking, but I thought that you and I had somehow gotten on such good terms, and—well, I just couldn't resist."

"But, Louise," said Toby earnestly, "even if what you say is true, you wouldn't expect me to talk to other people about it, would you? What kind of an opinion would you have of me if I did?"

"But this is not 'talking to other people,' is it? This is talking to *me.*"

"Do you know," he said slowly, his eyes searching hers, "I believe you're jealous!"

"Of course," she replied, returning his gaze steadily.

"Well, I'll be damned!" He sat still for a long time, thinking, staring into space. Finally, he looked around at her again with a plaintive expression. "Why couldn't this have happened to me when I was twenty?" he exclaimed.

Louise burst out laughing. "You're an impossible man!" she said. She leaned over and kissed him lightly on the lips. "Go home!"

19

Toby got up late the following morning, and puttered and piddled, trying to keep busy. A boy from the PSA brought a big envelope of mail, and there was a letter from Mary Lynn, timed perfectly, as if she had controlled the delivery system from Iowa. A Christmas letter, with notes from the children. She listed the gifts she had bought for the children and other family members, to be given in both their names. They had prepared a box for him, but it had not yet come. The letter was more important, anyway. He was back in touch with his family, back in a state of normality. The kids were enjoying their new town and school, and were looking forward to his first family leave in February. So was Mary Lynn.

He sat for a long time with the letter in his hand, and thought about himself, and Therese and Mary Lynn. It was as if there were two Toby Busches, both of them nice enough fellows, but not connected with one another. He knew that he should be feeling guilt and shame, but he didn't. He knew that if he were as decent as he ought to be, he would not even be able to perform during those moments of illicit love. But he had performed, and he had reveled in it, and oddly enough, he even had a vague feeling that this affair was broadening him as a man, taking him out of a narrow life, making him more profound, somehow more aware. But what if it turned out to be at Mary Lynn's expense? That would be unbearable. She was as much a part of that other Toby Busch's life as his hands and his eyes, and he loved her and would do anything to keep from wounding her.

Anything, that is, except give up Therese.

He sighed, and went in to lunch. Afterward, he gathered up the Swedish K, the M-16, the grease gun, and his .45 pistol, with plenty of ammunition for all of the weapons, and a set of earplugs, and drove over to the police firing range. He worked with all the weapons, marveling at the perfection of the M-16. The Swedish K was a much more elegant and comfortable weapon to fire than the grease gun; he could understand why the agency had adopted it for their men in combat zones. He dropped some tin cans about halfway to the first target mound, and practiced snap shooting with the .45. It was surprising that one could do that well by just pointing, instead of aiming. With a little more practice, he knew that he could become a deadly shot using that system.

He spent the rest of the afternoon back at the house, happily stripping and cleaning the weapons. He had hunted a lot when he was a youngster back in Iowa, usually for quail or pheasant, and using shotguns. But he enjoyed the feel and the machined touch of any firearm under his fingers, and he was whistling tunelessly to himself as he went about the pleasant chore.

He was still a little clumsy at stripping the pistol. He had watched Little Jack do it, his great paws snapping and sliding the parts with an ease that was astonishing and pleasing to the eye. Little Jack had tried to show him how he did it so smoothly, but Toby knew that it was not a question of knowing a method, but rather of devoting hours to practice.

He put the cleaned and oiled weapons away, scrubbed the oil off his hands, and took a leisurely shower. He rubbed his jaw after toweling it dry, and decided that since he had shaved so late in the morning he need not shave again for this evening.

He pulled into the driveway of the women's house just as dusk was settling. He knew that underlying his uneasiness about

Mary Lynn and Therese was also the fact of Louise, but he put that out of his mind. After all, it did not have to be complicated. A dinner in a restaurant—a Chinese dinner, which would oc- cupy a good part of the evening—and then home. The very fact of Therese would keep him from making a serious pass at Louise. How about that, for irony? He smiled at the thought, just as Louise came down the stairs.

She was dressed in a silk cocktail dress, of the same intense blue as her eyes. It did not seem to be cut to be seductive, but somehow, with Louise inside of them, dresses had that effect anyway.

"You look lovely," he said.

"You are sweet to say so," she replied.

"I would say it more often," he said, "except that I forget. You see, I really love you just for your mind."

"Yes, I know."

"What about the other women?"

"We were all invited to a Christmas Eve party at the Province Senior Adviser's house," she said. "They're going."

"But did you want to go, too? Would you have preferred that?"

"Don't be silly!"

They drove to the Soong Palace, which was as grand a name as the restaurant was unpretentious. They were greeted by a young Chinese who spoke good English. He ushered them to a small table in one corner of the dining room, discreetly walled in, although not hidden, by plants and screens. He then helped them order the unfamiliar dishes.

"I just happened to think," said Toby, when the waiter had left. "This is our first real date."

"That's true," she said. "Although I did go out spying with you one evening."

"Being in the line of duty like that, it doesn't count."

"Have you been out in the streets at night since then?"

"Yes, but it isn't the same without you."

"I'd go with you again, but I'd want to know what it was you were doing."

"I'd never tell you. It would surprise you, and disillusion you, it's so dull."

They ate a meal of many small dishes, and finished with cups of fragrant tea. Toby paid the bill and looked at his watch.

"It's early yet. Shall we go to my place for a nightcap?"

"I'd love it."

They drove to the house, and he fixed them a drink. They settled down on one of the sofas in the common room. Toby put on a record, and they sat and looked at each other placidly.

"This is nice," she said.

"Yes. Nice."

"I'm curious about something."

"Now, Louise, I—"

"Don't worry, it's not what you're thinking."

"OK, what is it?"

"Have you ever written a poem?"

"That's a strange question. Why do you ask?"

"Don't answer a question with a question."

"It's part of my training and my profession," he said with a smile.

"Answer the question," she commanded.

"No," he said. "I never have. I've tried, though."

"You have?"

"Yes. But what comes out always sounds like an intelligence report written by Gilbert and Sullivan."

She giggled. "But the fact that you've tried proves my point."

"What point?"

"You're a romantic."

"I am?"

"Yes. I mean romantic in the classical sense, you know, not amorous."

"You think I'm not amorous?"

"On the contrary, I'll bet you're a regular fireball, but even for that you'd be a romantic. I'm sure of it."

"I'm not understanding you very clearly," he said, wrinkling his brow.

"I'll give you an example. Take Marlene Dietrich, on the observation platform of the Orient Express, putting on a man's hat and looking sultry. That's just super-romantic. *That* kind of a woman would just give a man like you a case of the fantods."

"Marlene Dietrich was before my time," he laughed, "but I think that train was the Shanghai Express, not the Orient Express."

"Well, whatever train it was."

"Come on now, Louise," he said, "I have never found myself getting one bit excited by a woman putting on a man's hat."

"Never?"

"Nope. And I have never lit two cigarettes and handed one to a woman with a masterful stare, either."

"All right," she said, "maybe you're not *quite* that romantic. Maybe Camille is not your ideal sweetheart. But what I want to know is, did you ever *play* with a woman?"

"Now that," he said with a wide grin, "is such a loaded question, and such a beautiful straight line, that I'm not even going to answer it."

"But I mean it," she said. "I'm sure you've had a fair amount of experience with women, including recently"—she stopped Toby as he was about to protest—"but I'll bet every one of them has been a case of grand passions and emotions, you know, making the earth move in a sleeping bag. But without it really being very much fun."

"Well, now," he said, "I don't ever recollect being exactly bored by the experience, and I've certainly never done it just out of a sense of duty or self-sacrifice."

"Let me prove my point," she said. She took his glass out of his hand and set it down beside her own on the table. "This is what I mean." She put her arms around him and pressed her lips to his with an evident burst of passion. In an instantaneous reflex, Toby's arms locked around her, and then she began to tickle him. It jarred him loose from her with an explosion of laughter.

"Now," she said, "did you ever kiss a girl that way before?"

"I didn't really kiss the girl, you know. I was kissed."

"You're stalling!"

"No," he admitted. "I never did, that I can remember."

"See what I mean? You've never really played with a woman."

"Maybe not. I'm not exactly sure whether you mean the same thing I do when you say 'play.' Is what you have in mind Indian wrestling, and King-of-the-Hill, and two falls out of three? Things like that?"

"You're getting the general idea."

"You and me?"

"Yes."

"This is just going to play hell with our beautiful platonic relationship. You know that, don't you?"

"Yes. Won't that be a shame?"

"You don't want any more of that drink, do you?" he asked, nodding toward the half-empty glasses.

"No."

"Come with me. I'll bet I can pin your shoulders to the mat in ten seconds flat." He took her hand and led her to his room, shut the door behind them, and kissed her—a long, hungry kiss. She pulled away from him.

"There comes the grand passion," she said, "whistling down the track toward Istanbul."

"Shanghai," he corrected her, not letting her go. "Sorry, but there are some things a man just naturally gets serious about."

"You *have* got a lot to learn," she said. "But I'm here to teach you. And the first thing is to get into uniform. You mustn't play in your good clothes, you know." She began to unbutton his shirt.

"When I'm on the Shanghai—well, all right, the *Orient* Express," he said, "I don't waste any time with buttons and things. I just reach out with one hand and rip the clothes right off of old Marlene."

"This is one of my best dresses," she said, "and it will come off without ripping, and I know how to do it. You wait right here."

Toby undressed quickly, his eyes glued to her all the while. She went over to his desk and stood with her back to him, not out of modesty, but because she was putting her garments on the desk as she took them off.

She unzipped the dress and pulled it up over her head. Then the slip came off, and his heart thumped with what he decided was the purest lust he had ever known. He was sitting now on the edge of the low bed, oblivious of everything around him except the body that was being uncovered before his eyes. The bra came off, and then the panties. This was not a striptease. It was simply a woman taking her clothes off, and it was infinitely more tantalizing than the unimaginative bumps and grinds of what few stripteases he had ever tried to sit through. He had mentally undressed Louise often in the past, but he could see now that even an imagination as active as his own could never have done justice to the real thing.

She turned and revealed the rest to his staring eyes. She had a golden tan, except for the parts of her that had been covered by a moderately brief bikini, and the unburned skin was fair and satiny. It said mutely: *This part is never shown to anybody. This part you can now look at—and touch—but only you, and only here, when we are alone.*

He was suddenly aware that she was standing there flat-footed, at ease under his rapt gaze, smiling unabashedly at the effect she was having on him.

"Well," she said, "do I pass inspection?"

"You most certainly do," he breathed. "I was just trying to figure out where to put the seal of approval."

"Oh," she said, "I thought you would know. It goes right

here." She pointed to the border between tan and white, just below her navel, and walked to where he sat on the bed.

"Just the place for it," he agreed.

He put his hands on her hips, pulled her to him, and kissed the spot firmly.

"Ouch!" she exclaimed, and drew away quickly.

"What's the matter?"

"That beard," she said, feeling his jaw with her fingertips.

"Oh," he said. "Sorry about that."

"Sorry isn't enough," she said. "I have no intention of being sandpapered down to the quick tonight. Come here." She grabbed his hand and led him over to the easy chair. "Now, you sit right there," she commanded him.

She went into the bathroom and came out with a basin of water, soap, a can of shaving foam, a towel, and his razor. He was so entranced with the movements of her nude figure about the room that he paid little heed to what she was doing until she pushed his head back and began to rub his beard with a soapy washcloth.

"You're going to shave me?" he asked, straightening up in the chair.

"What does it look like?"

"But what do you know about shaving? You'll scrape me raw!"

"I'm a nurse, my dear. I've shaved hundreds of men. Even in other places besides their jaws." She leered playfully down along the length of his body, and he covered himself quickly with his hands.

"The jaws will be quite enough, thanks," he said.

"Lean back and be still."

She lathered his face with the foam and began to shave him. He had to admit that it was not bad. Not as nicely done as a barber would do it, and her hands did pull and tug his head in strange ways, but she moved the razor gently with the grain of the beard, and it was not at all painful. It might even have been relaxing if the barber had been anything but a naked woman.

He opened one eye and peered down the length of one of her arms. There below, perfectly framed in his field of vision, was one creamy breast, floating and swaying ever so gently with the movement of the arm. He could no more have controlled his hand than he could have floated in the air. The hand came up automatically, and his fingers brushed lightly across the coral tip.

"Didn't you see the sign on the wall, sir?" she asked sternly, without pausing in her work.

"What sign?"

"Touching the barber is not permitted."

"Oh, but this is an absolute necessity," he said. "I'm conducting a test."

"A test?"

"Yes." His hand moved across her body, out of his line of sight, and stopped. "Aha!" he exclaimed, through lips she was distorting to tighten the skin on his jaw, "I thought so!"

"What?"

"You've got another one!"

The breast he could see jiggled deliciously as the barber laughed under her breath. "I must remind you again, sir, about that sign," she said.

"It was the only way," he said in a tight voice, because she was pinching his nostrils together to shave around them, "that I could confirm what I told you last night."

"What was that?"

"You've got a perfect set."

Again the breast jiggled. Now she moved to the other side of him, and all of her was in his field of vision. His other hand took over the exploration, and traced the line of her waist, down over the hips, over the thighs, and back up to where the white skin began.

"If these were the days of the straight razor," she said, "you wouldn't dare defy the rules of the shop that way."

"Come back tomorrow with a straight razor and see," he challenged her. His fingertips were moving lightly across her lower abdomen now, and up to where the tanned skin began. There was the slightest difference in texture between the skin of the tan and the white areas, and the velvety feel of the forbidden zones sent tiny lightning bolts of anticipation through his fingers and coursing out along his entire frame.

She finished shaving him, took the things to the bathroom, and brought back a bottle of lotion. Almost suffocated by the sight of that voluptuous form, which he had not yet been suffered to enjoy, moving back and forth across his room, he did not notice what she was doing with her hands until she was uncapping the bottle.

"No lotion, please, Miss Barber," he said.

"No lotion?"

"No."

"But won't your face feel dry and tight?"

"Probably. But if you put that stuff on, the only thing my nose will detect for the next two hours will be lime shaving lotion. When I am in the altogether with a woman, I want every one of my senses at its best."

She stepped back from him, puzzled. Interested.

"You really mean that, don't you?"

"I certainly do. If there is ever a time when all of a man's faculties ought to be sending him signals, this is the time." He got up, took the bottle from her, and put it on the lamp table by the chair.

"This, for example," he said, touching her neck just below the ear, "is one of the nicest places to kiss that you can find on a woman, and when I kiss her there I like to catch the fragrance of her. Because it's always there." He took her in his arms and bent down to kiss the spot, which was just as he had expected, soft, and warm, and fragrant, with a wisp of fine golden hair to tickle his nose. "Yes," he murmured through the kiss, "it's here." One hand, stroking the curve of her flank, detected sudden gooseflesh as she stood strangely still in his arms.

Then she jumped away, and sat on her heels in the middle of the bed. "That's an illegal hold," she said. "If you do that again, I'll have to penalize you."

Toby never recollected being so aroused in his life. He lunged at her, and she giggled, and bit him lightly on the nose, and they rolled and wrestled and laughed.

And it was over in ten seconds.

"Well!" she exclaimed, sitting up on her heels beside him once more. "Speedy Gonzales is back in town!"

"You *knew* that was going to happen!" he said accusingly; and her laughter was so spontaneous and free of malice that it healed his slightly bruised male ego, and he laughed with her.

"I must say that I'm improving, though," she said.

"You're improving?" This was beyond him.

"Yes. Don't you remember the other evening in the jeep? It happened and I didn't even realize it?"

"That's right," he grinned. "I remember."

"Well, this time, do you know what? I had a strange sensation, there for a while. Maybe it was an intuition. But whatever it was, somehow I knew for a few seconds that *something was happening!*"

"Oh, hell!" he said disgustedly. "If this gets out, my reputation for speed will be shot."

"Señor Gonzales," she said, pulling his ear gently, "after tonight you're going to be known as Slow-Talkin' Jones."

"Hah!" he snorted. "Just wait till I get my wind back."

"For that," she said brightly, "I've got just the thing. You need yoga."

"I do?"

"Yes. Quiet meditation. Awareness. Deep breathing. Things like that."

She ordered him to assume the seated position, legs crossed like a buddha, which he did as well as he could with his long, muscular legs. She sat in the same fashion, facing him, her knees touching his, arms relaxed at her sides.

"Now," she said, "watch me while I show you how to breathe."

He watched her. She ordered him to meditate as he did so, and he tried, but found it impossible. The deep-breathing display before him was much too spectacular.

"You have to blank everything else out of your mind," she insisted.

"Yes," he said obediently, making his voice sound cavernous and far away. "I am blanking everything out of my mind."

"It would be obvious to anybody who looked at you right now that you are doing no such a thing," she scolded him. "Now, forget about everything else, and try to do as I say."

"I am trying," he intoned, in the same hollow voice.

"Hush up and meditate."

Their meditations were soon interrupted by the arrival of the Orient Express, and shortly thereafter, Louise, her voice muffled by a welter of pillows and sheets, announced that she was absolutely certain something was happening.

They played on, and Toby found that he too could invent silly games, and that she played his just as enthusiastically as she elaborated on her own, and seemed to welcome each new arrival of the train, until at last, in the early morning hours, they lay facing each other on opposite sides of the bed, panting and grinning. He was aching, almost trembling with fatigue, and drained dry of all physical desire.

"Ma'am," he said.

"Yes?"

"Ma'am," he said, in a painfully slow drawl, "my name is Jones, and I've got something I want to ask you."

"What is it?"

"First off, would you come over here, please? I'm too tired to move, and I haven't got the strength to talk across all that distance."

She wiggled herself over to him and into his arms.

"Now," he continued, "I just wanted to tell you that I never knew games could be such fun. I've really enjoyed the ones we've played tonight, and I've learned things from my coach that I never dreamed of before."

"I told you so," she said, squeezing him gently.

"And now, I wonder if the coach would mind if I just held on to her like this for the rest of the night?"

"Give up?" she asked him sleepily.

"I give up."

"All right, then," she replied. "Let that be a lesson to you." She settled herself snugly against him, her tousled blond hair brushing his nostrils, and they slept quietly until dawn.

20

Monday, January 1, 1968. Toby still had not been able to set up a single test of his operations to discover the security leak; still had no idea where the leak might be; had still not found out anything significant about the Yenan Battalion; had not had any further word from Dang; had obtained no solid information from his Special Police students; had acquired nothing that he could label as real intelligence; had, in fact, accomplished nothing he was supposed and resolved to accomplish in Vietnam. Tet was four weeks away.

Four weeks. The Christmas truce was over. It had been observed by both sides, violated only sporadically by unintended skirmishes or clashes. The calm had extended through the following week, and seemed to have imbued every human soul in the delta with the hope that perhaps the war, itself, was winding down.

The search operations resumed after Christmas, but Toby had the impression that he alone felt the sense of impending disaster, the need for speed. It was not that the other participants were unwilling to carry out the operations, or uninterested in the results. It was just that they approached the work as routine assignments, upon which, after all, nothing very important depended.

The first one after Christmas began on the evening of Tuesday, January 2, and it would be the only one for that week. Toby watched the men set off at dusk, to be in place and ready by dawn of the following day. He went back into his office and sat down, intensely aware of Therese's presence behind him, at her desk.

She had arrived back from Saigon on schedule, radiant at the prospect of being reunited with him. He did not know whether she detected any change in him, but he certainly felt changed, and he was uneasy about it.

Before driving Louise home early Christmas morning, he had paused by the door and taken her hand.

"You were right," he said. "I had never played with a woman. Never in my life had a night like that one. Let's play again, soon?" And then he laughed at his own words. "That's the dumbest-sounding proposition I've ever made to a woman."

She smiled, a rather strange smile, almost a sad one. "I'm not sure, Toby," she said. "I'm not sure I ought to, or want to."

"Not sure you want to?"

"That's right. And I'm not going to try to explain that to you." She put her arms around him, inviting him to bend and kiss her, which he did. It was a loving kiss, and was on the way to becoming a passionate kiss, but she turned her head then, and whispered, "Take me home, Toby."

He had slept a good part of that day, Christmas Day. As the exhaustion and aching gradually drained away, he had taken stock of himself in wonderment.

Somehow his life had become so tangled and topsy-turvy that it was *Therese* he felt guilty about deceiving, not Mary Lynn. Well, of course, Therese was right here, not twelve thousand miles away. But he knew that the reason was not that simple. Moreover, he knew that, whatever cultural conditioning Therese might have about a rather free and casual sex life on the part of her man, she would not easily forgive such a swift and insouciant move from her arms into the arms of another woman.

My God, this was something you only read about! A normal, decent man didn't have this kind of problem. Toby had always considered men who moved easily and quickly from one woman to another to be stupid, thoughtless, self-centered.

But he must do something like that now. He knew that even if he had no immediate desire for *any* woman, he had to take Therese to him again, as soon as the opportunity presented itself. If not, she would be confused and hurt.

This evening, the opportunity had come. The house was empty for the night. She was finishing her day's work. He had tried to show her by quiet glances and smiles since her return from Saigon that his feeling for her had not changed, but he was not sure that his signals had been very convincing.

A year ago, if anybody had told him that he would one day be suffering pangs of remorse and doubt about having committed adultery against his *mistress,* he would have laughed.

If the night with Louise had been simply a pickup, a call-girl kind of thing, induced and fueled by loneliness and alcohol, it would have presented little difficulty. But he knew that underneath the lighthearted romping, the hilarious games, the challenge of her flesh against his, there was a strong current of something else, something he had not examined, did not even want to examine. His life was already complicated enough as it was.

Therese closed her desk and safe, and came to where he sat. She paused. He turned to her. She looked puzzled, hesitant.

He took her hand. God, if only he didn't have such an active imagination, or conscience! The very thought of the word "conscience" in this context was so incongruous that it made him smile in spite of himself, and she smiled back.

"Will you stay, Therese?" he asked, trying to make it sound urgent. He must not *worry.* Worry would make him impotent, would grow on its own effects.

"Yes, Anh Tho," she replied.

"Come on," he said. He led her into the common room. As they went through the door his arm automatically moved around her, and his hand came to rest on the curve of her waist just above the hip. The flexing of that curve as she walked beside him triggered a familiar tightening in his gut, and he knew that he would be all right—but he was torn between amusement and exasperation at his heretofore unsuspected priapic capacities.

The reaction was fleeting, nevertheless. As he walked by her side it came to him in a sudden insight that this small, slender woman had stealthily slipped into his heart, into his very being. He wanted to protect her, love her, possess her, belong to her. He had said as much while making love to her, and now he knew that the words had not been merely sparks struck by the physical contact. He meant them. He had fallen in love with Therese.

Whatever this might mean to his marriage, the damage was already done, and nothing could be gained by worrying about it now. He would live this love while he could, knowing that there would be a reckoning, a price to pay, and knowing that that price would in large part be paid by innocent people.

But that accounting was due in the future. Nothing was to be gained by worrying about it now. He would love Therese while he could.

As to the search operation that night, it was even more uneventful than the previous ones.

They carried out two more the following week, each time working inward in the territory toward a central point somewhat arbitrarily established on the map.

"Toby," said Ben. "It's not my place to butt in on Little Jack's business, and maybe he already knows it, but you might be wise to talk to him about the morale of his men."

"What's wrong with them?"

"Nothing that I have exactly detected, but if I know soldiers, this going out time after time for nothing but a walk in the sun is bound to affect their fighting capabilities. They tend to get loose and relaxed. They tend to start bickering among themselves."

Toby asked Little Jack.

"Oh," the big man answered with a shrug, "there's been little problems now and then, but they'll be all right."

Only one search operation was made the following week. Another walk in the sun. Toby began to wonder if their theories had been crazy. There didn't seem to be any Viet Cong in that area at all. No caches of food or ammunition, no evidence of bivouacs—nothing.

Minnie seemed puzzled also. "It is strange, Mr. Busch," he said, in answer to Toby's question. "Perhaps you are right. Perhaps the Viet Cong are not there. We never find anything at all, and that is unusual. But perhaps we are looking for a complicated explanation of a simple fact."

"You may be right," Toby said.

Ben did not believe that a simple explanation was possible. "There is something unusual going on there, Toby," Ben said. "Believe me, this lack of reaction is not normal."

It was Friday, the nineteenth. Tet was ten days away. Toby was now often troubled by a feeling almost of panic. He couldn't make things move as he wanted them to move. He couldn't find out things he must know. He couldn't get a grip on the situation.

He found solace in Therese's arms at each opportunity, aware that their love affair must by now be common knowledge among their friends and associates.

That same Friday, Qui came to him unexpectedly, off schedule.

"I know!" he exclaimed, when they were alone in the common room. "The secret! I know!"

"You found out what's there?"

"Yes."

"How? What is it? Tell me, for God's sake!"

Qui extracted a small map from his pocket, and pointed to a village near the center of their search area. Through much stumbling talk, Toby learned that Qui had spent a night in that village on his own, after having been there on assignment during a previous search. He had discovered that in a village near that one there was a cousin of one of his associates, and he had worked on that cousin all night. The cousin did not have information from personal observation, but he finally told Qui what was fairly common knowledge among the villagers, and among the farmers in that area—which they would never reveal, on pain of death at the hands of the Viet Cong.

The Viet Cong had an underground hideout there. The Yenan Battalion and many other troops spent most of their time holed up in the tunnels. Qui pointed on the map to where the main access to the maze of tunnels was said to be located. The access was inside a small structure supposedly used for rice storage.

Toby had thought that the entire delta area was too wet for underground concealment like that. Qui said that apparently the Viet Cong had had the advice of a hydraulic engineer, who had shown them a place where the groundwater was far enough below the surface to make tunneling feasible.

Toby knew that this was the breakthrough he had been looking for. All he had was a vague report of rumors about a village, but it coincided so well with the facts as he knew them that his mind simply would not doubt the accuracy of the report.

He thanked Qui, and Qui left with a look of happiness, of accomplishment, on his face. Toby wrote up an intelligence report. This would be a legitimate report, because it came from an agent whom he had already made a matter of record.

It was, of course, an intelligence report of interest only to his own province, and to the American and Vietnamese military forces in the area, and would not be disseminated beyond those customers. But at least he had begun to produce.

He told Ben about the report, without revealing to him the source.

"It could be," Ben replied, intrigued. "That would explain everything all right. They are not attacking the search operations because they don't want to tip their hand. They may think you'll figure there's nothing there, and quit searching. But the day the search hits *that* area is the day the shit hits the fan."

"Well," said Toby, "I'm going to persuade Manh that this is where we've got to run the next operation. That'll be on the twenty-sixth."

"It will have to be the last one before Tet, then?"

"Yeah. I don't see how we can do any more before the thirtieth."

"So this one will tell the tale, or not," Ben mused.

"Yes, and I'm going along this time."

"You're going along?"

"Yeah. I know what's there, but I don't intend to tell anybody until we get there. That way I'll know there won't be any leak."

"Christ," Ben said earnestly, "that's likely to turn into a real fight."

"I suppose it could. But with all my big talk about testing for leaks, this is the first real test I have made on our operations."

"Well, it's your funeral."

"That was not a very felicitous choice of words." Toby grinned at him.

"I intended it that way, my friend."

"Why don't you come along, too?" Toby suggested impulsively. "I've let you watch me be an intelligence officer, maybe you could let me watch you and learn how to be a combat soldier."

"No," said Ben. "Not this time. I don't think you're wise to go yourself, but that's your decision to make, not mine. At any rate, if you go, you'll have to go without me."

Toby was about to ask him why, but decided against it.

Little Jack was not altogether pleased with Toby's decision, especially since he could not be told the specific reason why Toby wanted to go along.

"The one thing I can tell you, Little Jack," he said, "is that this time we're going to hit a VC nerve. We may run into a real fight."

Little Jack shrugged. "That's what we're here for. But I'm not gonna lie to you. If we're going to a place where we'll have a fight, I don't want to have an inexperienced civilian around getting in the way."

"I won't get in your way," said Toby. "There's a reason I have to go along."

"You could get killed, you know."

"I know. And the idea of getting killed is not one of my favorite daydreams, but I've got to go with you."

"OK. Suit yourself."

Toby willed himself to work on other things that afternoon. He knew that the first few hours after making his decision would be the time of the most pressing doubt and uneasiness about it. He was certain that he was consciously, and with a calm logic, willing himself into a battle. Somehow, his life had become so much of a turmoil that the fear of battle had become less urgent. When he worried, it was not out of fear of being hurt or killed, but rather from a fear that he would be less than a man when danger came.

There was a space of about two hours, right after lunch, when he was alone in the office with Therese, and she asked him if they might talk alone in the common room. Something about the intensity of her words made Toby wonder, and he forgot his thoughts of combat for the moment.

They settled themselves on the sofa. "What is it, Therese?" he asked.

"Anh Tho," she said with a smile, "I am going to have a baby."

"You're what?" His reaction was so sudden and explosive that it made her start with surprise.

"I am going to have a baby."

"Is it—is it *my* . . . ?" Toby began, and caught the hurt that came fleetingly to her eyes. "I almost asked the stupidest question of my life, Little Mistress."

She smiled, but said nothing.

"But," he continued fretfully, "I had thought that you would, you know, that you would have taken some means to avoid it, Therese."

"No," she said, visibly disturbed by his reaction. "I did nothing."

"Well, then you must do something now."

"Do something now?"

"Yes. You must do something to get rid of it."

"Get rid of it?" she gasped. "Why?"

"But, Therese," he said, "don't you see? I have made love to you, and I love you, but I cannot be your husband. You will have a baby that is part of my flesh, and I could never acknowledge it. The child would never know his father. The idea that somewhere in the world I have left a part of myself that way, who will never know me, and I will never know, is something I don't even want to think about."

"But, Anh Tho," she said softly, her voice freighted with the shock of what she was hearing, "the baby will be mine, too. I will care for him, and he will grow to be a man you would be proud of."

"But a man I would never know."

"A man who will be the only part of his father that I can have as my own."

"A man who will show by his features that his mother went to bed with an American. A man who will be half European and half Asian. A man who will be illegitimate. A bastard." Toby shook his head stubbornly.

"I will not mind," she said. "If people wish to think bad things about me, I will not care, because I know that what I have done is not wrong."

Toby sat in silence. Dammit, he had assumed that Therese was taking some kind of precautions. It had never occurred to him that she might *want* a child by him. It was ironic that before he was married he had always been uneasy about fathering a child, for fear it might force him into a marriage he did not want or was not ready for. Now he had begotten a child in the body of a woman he *would* have married instantly, but *could* not.

As for Therese, he was afraid that she was not looking squarely at the problems she might encounter, at the prejudices she would face, during a period of reconstruction.

"Anh Tho," said Therese timidly, "is it that you are afraid that I will cause difficulties for you after you leave Vietnam?"

"Of course not!" he exclaimed. "You could never do such a thing."

"Then, *please,* Anh Tho," she pleaded with him, "please tell me that you want me to have our baby."

"I am sorry," he said gently. "I am so sorry, Little Mistress. I don't want to hurt you. But I can't tell you truthfully that I want you to have the baby. I want you *not* to have it. I will try to find out how and where you can have it taken care of, if you like, but . . ."

"No," she said. "I only want you to say that you want me to have your child, but you will not say it."

"I can't say it, Therese. It would not be the truth."

Therese got up and went back into the office. When he got back to his own desk, she was gone. She returned to her desk from the bathroom after a long time, her eyes red, her head erect, staring straight ahead.

Well, goddammit, here is another *problem!*

But he didn't have time or energy to spare for this one right now. It could wait a few days. On Tuesday morning he spoke to Minnie about his plan.

"But why do you wish to go, Mr. Busch?" Minnie asked. He was obviously quite concerned about Toby's plan.

"I can't tell you exactly why I want to go on this specific operation, but I think the reason will be clear to you when we get there."

"Where is it to be?"

Toby pointed to the map on the wall. "It will be in this

general area," he said. "This is the last operation before Tet, and the logic of the previous ones puts us right in the middle of the territory."

"That is true," said Minnie. "But I believe you should not go."

"Why not? Do you know something about the place that I don't know?"

"I do not *know* anything, but I have been drawing some conclusions from what has been happening in the past. Either we will find nothing, or we will find something that will cause a battle."

"I think you're right, but I intend to go."

"Of course, you must do what you believe to be right."

Thursday evening he dressed and armed himself under Ben's advice and instructions. He had a flak jacket hanging on a hook on his wall, but when he found that none of the others would be wearing one he abandoned all thought of taking it along. Foolish pride, perhaps, but in a company of eighty or ninety men he would not under any circumstances be the only one to wear protective armor.

On Ben's advice he left the pistol at home. He took along an M-16 rifle and a bandolier with a basic load of eighteen clips of ammunition.

"Knowing what you're going after," Ben told him, "I think you'll want to take a claymore sack full of grenades too. Ever use a grenade?"

"I had some training with them years ago."

"And take along a medical kit. Two canteens. Be sure you wear a helmet. Anything else in the way of survival gear— knives, things like that."

"Survival gear I know about," Toby said.

"Little Jack and his men will undoubtedly take along plenty of smoke and CS," said Ben, "and they'll know how to use it."

He filled his canteens at the house, and took along a box of C rations for the morning.

He was nervous. Little shivers of fear caught up with his muscles once in a while, and coursed along his frame. He kept his mind busy with the mechanics of hauling his body around with the unaccustomed gear, and when the empty, bottomless feeling suddenly came, he turned his attention, by a sheer act of will, to other simple things in his immediate vicinity.

In the jeep, moving along a dark, rough road, with one of the PRU soldiers at the wheel, he had little that he could occupy himself with except the problem of keeping his seat. Three jeeps, followed by four two-and-a-half-ton trucks, carried their search force. They moved through the night with a purposeful rumble.

What in the name of God was he doing here? What kind of insanity had come over him some months ago to volunteer for this kind of duty in the first place, and what climactic bit of craziness had impelled him to come on this night's specific expedition into war? He could certainly have told Little Jack the secret. Or perhaps Minnie. He could have changed his mind ten minutes ago and told Minnie, who had been sitting beside him in the jeep from the start; but that would mean getting out of the jeep in front of all the other men and going back to his house. He could not have done that.

And Therese was pregnant. He had always prided himself on keeping his life free of unnecessary complications. In his business there were a lot of necessary ones you could not avoid, and things were always complicated enough without making them any more so. But he *had* made them more so. When confronted by a nude Therese, there was only one thing he could think about. In fact, even when he was only *imagining* a nude Therese . . .

He turned his thoughts elsewhere, in reaction to this antic lust that had suddenly taken possession of him.

And Louise? He had not even spoken to her since that night. He should have given her some kind of a call, or a note, or something. She might think that . . . But hell, she was much too intelligent to read anything into his silence except—except what? Why had he not communicated with her in any way?

Well, what would he have said? But, for Christ's sake, he should have said *something!*

He decided what he would do when he got back: He would go to her house in the evening, knock on the door, and have two cigarettes lighted in his mouth when she came to answer it, whereupon he would take one of them out and slowly place it between her lips, with a steady, lascivious stare. The image pleased him, and would, he knew, break Louise up, especially since she didn't smoke.

And then there came dancing before his eyes a picture of that incredible body, the gently swaying breast as she shaved him; the hips, white on tan, undulating as she moved away from him; her sudden moments of submission as they played riotously in the confusion of sheets and pillows.

They pulled the vehicles off the road and left three men to guard them. The rest of them set off on foot. They walked along the road for about three miles, then Little Jack halted them, and set up guards around their makeshift bivouac.

"We're gonna wait here till daylight," he said. "The target area is right ahead of us. Better get some sleep."

"I'll take my turn at guard duty," Toby offered.

"No," said Little Jack. "Let the men do it. They've had experience, and if what you say is true, we're probably in a pretty touchy area here."

"I want to do my share, though," Toby protested.

"Sure," said Little Jack absently. He held up one of his canteens. "Speaking of experience, you'd think I was a goddamned recruit myself. I came off without filling my canteens. I'm gonna have to take some water from that shell hole over there."

"You can share mine."

"It's gonna be hot, and you're gonna be in action. You'll use all that water, and still be thirsty."

"But the water in that hole may be—"

"Probably full of buffalo piss and everything else, but it's wet. I'll put iodine tablets in it, and it'll be all right."

He moved off toward the hole, and Toby lay down on the ground and tried to sleep. The sky was clear and moonless, and he stared off into infinity. He knew he would not sleep. He tossed and turn restlessly, his eyes wide, his mind alert. And yet, when the sky began to get light, he realized that the time had passed too quickly for him to have been awake throughout the night. He had certainly dozed now and then.

The PRU knew exactly what they had to do, and they started out with a minimum of talk. They moved swiftly in the spreading daylight, aware that their presence must already be known. Toby kept himself near the middle of their extended line. It did not look to him much like a rational formation, but he knew that these men were veterans of this kind of action, and he was sure that there was a method and a reason for the way they approached the target.

Minnie was among the men at the point. Toby could now clearly make out the line of thatched huts which was their target, structures that almost blended into invisibility in the treeline immediately behind them. He noted that the land was higher here—only a few feet, but perhaps enough to permit tunneling for concealment. The ridges of the thatched roofs were in some semblance of a line, although it was an up-and-down affair. The floors were on numerous short posts or pilings, allowing air to circulate underneath, and the walls were of woven mats, held in place by vertical bamboo slats. These walls were open under the eaves, allowing for the entrance of light and air.

He peered carefully at them, and decided that there could be no tunnel entrance from inside any of these huts, because he could see all the way under every floor. Behind the row, in a small indentation in the treeline, however, was another structure, which was enclosed by a bamboo fence, and he judged that if the entrance were in this little hamlet, it must be inside that fence.

And that was a frightening thought. Here was a company of men approaching what might turn out to be the front door of a Viet Cong stronghold.

As if his uneasy thoughts had given birth to the fact, there came a loud explosion at the point and several of the men crumpled before it. A claymore. He heard something swishing through the grass near him, and wondered dully if these were fragments from the mine, dropping from a high trajectory.

Evidently on signal from the claymore, Toby heard a sound like a giant motor starting up. In the split second he wondered what in the world there could be in this place with such an engine, and then he realized that the motor sound was really a blast of fire from rifles and machine guns along two lines—one line ahead of them, and another line off to one side of their own line. He fell to the ground in an automatic reflex, as had the others.

They had been ambushed! His hands trembling, he brought his rifle around and joined in the firing with his companions, although he could not see the enemy. He could tell where the hostile fire was coming from, however. The ambush was L-shaped, with the apex on the road, so that both lines could fire on the raiding party without danger to themselves.

Toby suddenly realized that his rifle was not firing, although he was holding the trigger down with desperate strength. He laughed hysterically at himself. He had put it on semi-automatic, and had fired one round, and was now holding the trigger down tight on a silent weapon, trained steadily on the enemy. He loosened the finger and began to work it back and forth to fire repeatedly.

For the second time in his life he heard B-40 rockets detonating near him. He was new to combat, but he was certain that they had struck an overwhelming enemy force.

Out of the corner of his eye he saw Minnie moving swiftly about near the point. Minnie was gesturing to some men who were carrying an M-60 machine gun and ammunition, and they took up a position facing the short end of the L. Other men crouched near Minnie, and Minnie suddenly led them in a dash toward the apex of the lines of fire. Toby saw the point of the maneuver instantly. If they could get close enough, the enemy could not fire at them without danger to the other line of the ambush. But he could also see that it was insane even to *try* to move through that intense concentration of fire.

"You goddamned fools!" he screamed at them.

The M-60 opened up a covering fire, but it seemed to have little effect. The firing from the ambush got heavier. Two of the men with Minnie threw grenades, and two others fell heavily and lay still. Then the others dropped to the ground, enveloped in a curtain of flying metal, far short of their objective.

A B-40 rocket struck the men with the machine gun, and sent gun and men flying apart. Toby was paralyzed with the impact and astonishment of the insane violence that had suddenly torn across the world around him.

One of the men to his left gestured to Toby that they were going to withdraw, firing as they did so, to hold the ambush in its position.

"What about Minnie?" Toby shouted at him.

The man looked questioningly at him.

"Tran Van Minh!" Toby shouted, gesturing toward the point where Minnie was lying. The man shrugged and shook his head.

"Well, by God I'm not going to leave them there without at least *trying* to do something!" Toby bellowed, more to himself than to his companions, who would not understand his words. Surely a comrade would not leave his fellows behind—combat has got to be something besides eighty individual battles.

He rose to a crouch and rushed forward, until he stumbled, or was knocked down by some instinctive bodily reaction. His move had provoked an increased chatter of firing, and he felt a sharp pain in his right arm near the shoulder. He could feel the bullets hitting the ground and slicing through the grass around him, and the pop of their individual little sonic booms as they sped through the air above him.

His sleeve had been torn by a bullet, and an oozing of blood had discolored it. He pulled the sleeve up and saw that the bullet had only grazed his arm, that the blood was, in fact, oozing and not flowing.

This was no good. Two of the men in Minnie's group began to wriggle on their bellies toward him, but the rustling of the grass brought a stream of bullets, and one of the men stiffened, half rose, and fell on his face.

Now Toby noticed an ominous change in the sound of the firing before him. It was coming closer. He heard a different kind of explosion, and saw that it was the sound of PRU grenades being hurled at the advancing enemy. He threw two grenades himself, and then turned and ran to where he had been stretched out prone a moment before—and made it without being hit. The remaining PRUs were beginning a systematic process of firing and moving back. They worked in such a way that the firing from their retreating line was constant, although not all of them were firing at once. The advance of the ambushing forces had been halted for the moment. Toby fell into the rhythm of the retreat, aware suddenly of having become so engrossed in the action that he had lost the nervousness, the trembling, that had beset him before the engagement. Fear was still in him, but it was now fear that compelled him to act, that held up no logical measures of risk and safety.

He saw that the maneuver was going to pull them free of the ambush. The two lines could not close on them fast enough to catch them, although the firing was having a deadly effect, nevertheless; for as they moved back they left behind ever more of their number, dead or immobilized by wounds. He wished that he could help those who were hurt and still, but knew that if he stopped, both he and the object of his pity would be killed.

He wondered where Little Jack was, and whether he was leading or ordering the men in any way. There was no evidence of it. Toby was thirsty, but did not dare to make the moves that would have brought his canteen to his mouth.

A man beside him motioned toward the rear and gestured that they were going to make a run that way. Toby looked and guessed that a faint line he could see there in the grass must be a ditch of some kind, although he did not remember having crossed it when they moved up a few minutes ago. All the PRU opened fire at once, and Toby joined them. Then they turned and ran as fast as they could go. He was right. It was a shallow ditch, and they tumbled into it gratefully. Toby almost fell on top of Little Jack, who was lying on his side, doubled up in an agony of pain.

"Were you hit?" Toby exclaimed.

Little Jack opened his eyes, his face white as a sheet. "No," he said. "It's my gut. I've never had a pain like this before in my life."

"Your gut?"

"Yeah," he replied, through clenched teeth. "I think it must of been that goddamned water I drank a while ago."

"Jesus Christ, Little Jack," he said, "we've got to bug out of here! Can you move?"

"Yeah," the big man gasped. "Yeah, I can move."

Toby was going to ask him what they should do, but saw that Little Jack was so wrapped up in his pain that he would be of no help.

"Come on," Toby said. "We're heading for that line of trees, and I'm about to run like hell!"

He shouted the last words at the top of his lungs as he sped out toward the rear. The rest of the company were with him, and he managed to stay slightly ahead of them. He was taller, had longer legs than they did, but he was encumbered with a bag of grenades, the canteens, and the bandolier, as well as the rifle, and none of these things seemed to find a good or comfortable place on his frame so that he could run properly.

He leaped another shallow ditch, which ran diagonally to his line of flight, and continued running pell-mell for the trees.

The gigantic motor started up again, dead ahead of him. A blocking force had moved in behind them, heavily armed and well concealed. The gate had been closed. They were trapped.

He knew, afterward, that it was a foolish thing to do, but instead of dropping to the ground he turned tail and ran back to the diagonal ditch. He could not believe that so much metal had flown at him without hitting him. He fell into the ditch and found that Little Jack had made it this far too, although he was still in agony. It had never occurred to Toby that a simple thing like a bellyache could even *happen* in a battle, to say nothing of affecting the outcome. He crouched in the ditch, trembling, wanting to weep with rage and frustration. They were obviously surrounded by a force many times larger than their own —probably at least a battalion, perhaps more—tough veterans, he was sure, to judge from the systematic and persistent way they had fired at him and his companions, and pursued them into the trap. It was a force that had not been reported in this area, and had no business being here. It had to be the Yenan Battalion. He had found the secret—found what he was looking for—and he was going to pay for it with his life.

He panted heavily, and watched the big man beside him grit his teeth against the pain. Most of the PRUs had taken cover in the ditch, and were spread out in a line along its length. One of them came crawling along, stared for a moment at Little Jack, shook his head, and gestured for Toby's benefit toward the line of the ditch.

No firing came from along the direction the ditch lay in. Surely the enemy would not have been stupid enough to leave that obvious exit open!

Two others joined this man, and Toby followed them. They inched forward along the line of the ditch, through manure and mud, paying no heed to either. Toby could hear the men behind him keeping up a steady fire at the enemy, holding the ambush line back. Grenades were once again exploding here and there along the line.

The ditch curved, and Toby for the first time actually got a glimpse of one of the enemy. It was a small man, lying prone in the ditch, facing them, a rifle at his shoulder, aimed toward them. The man in the lead fell like a stone as the rifle cracked, and the others moved back quickly to the protection of the curve.

One of the men behind Toby immediately pulled the pin on a grenade and threw it in the direction of the prone Viet Cong. They crouched and waited. The grenade exploded with a loud *whump!* and they moved quickly up to the curve. The grenade had landed in front of the man, and he had apparently tried to reach it before it exploded.

Firing broke out from beyond the dead man, but it was scattered and hesitant. The PRUs with Toby spoke softly to one another, passed a word urgently down the line, and presently they gathered in a tighter clump along the ditch. Toby could tell that they were preparing to assault those few rifles in front of them with a sudden rush. He knew that he would go with them. He didn't know where Little Jack was, but he had no time to spare for Little Jack now. If they were to have any chance of getting out of this alive, it was by an immediate rush, before the rest of the blocking force could move laterally to intercept them.

They sprang to their feet and ran, firing as they went. Their appearance seemed to catch the enemy by surprise, and once again Toby got a glimpse of the men who were firing at them. Even as they appeared before him, he fired his rifle, along with the PRUs charging with him, not aiming, not even sure what he was doing, or why. He thought he might have killed one, but others were firing as well and he would never be sure.

Their sudden rush had rolled over a small squad of men who had been placed at that point, and the rest of the PRUs came swiftly into the opening, rifles ready, Little Jack running among them.

And then Toby realized that they were free. Free of the trap. Not safe yet, but now with a better than even chance of getting away, for all the points of enemy fire were behind them. There was no enemy between them and their vehicles.

One of the PRUs, seeing that Little Jack was not going to take charge of their retreat, called the remaining force together quickly and gave some terse instructions. Tired and winded as they were, they accepted the orders without question and deployed themselves in a scattered line, similar to the one they had formed on their approach to the trees. The men bringing up the rear were doing so by a system of leapfrogging, so that there were always some riflemen in position, facing the rear, while the main party made good its retreat.

Out of a force of eighty men they had left eighteen behind, including Minnie. Remembering An Loi and Phu Binh, Toby knew what would happen to any of those left, if they were not already dead. If Minnie had not been killed in his futile assault, and if the Viet Cong knew who he was, they might try to keep him alive for questioning. But Toby knew that this was not likely. He had a conviction that Minnie was dead. He was still too stirred by the action to be able to comprehend the deaths it had included, but he knew that later he would feel the loss of Minnie very deeply.

They climbed into the vehicles and drove carefully over the bumpy road, so as not to cause needless pain for such wounded men as had been able to run and escape.

Lassitude now began to spread through Toby's body. He had been in a combat situation, and had given a reasonably good account of himself, although he was a far cry from a hero. He knew that what was behind this violent action was significant for his operations in the delta, but he also knew that an analysis of what it meant would have to wait until he could think with his brain, instead of his racing blood.

Might they have done something besides run away? He didn't see how. It was obvious, even to an inexperienced ear like his own, that the force that had ambushed them was large and well prepared. It was a daylight raid, and the PRU skills as night fighters gave them no advantages in this case. At any rate, the PRU soldiers themselves seemed in no doubt about the best course of action, and who was he to gainsay their judgments?

As for Little Jack, he had been worse than useless.

He wondered if a military unit ought to discipline a sergeant who forgot an elementary thing like a canteen and who, as a result, had taken himself out of action at the crucial moment. He might have felt lenient toward Little Jack if he had merely heard about the episode, instead of being involved in it, having his own hide risked by it; but the memory of those moments of danger, almost of panic, with the key soldier writhing in pain on the ground, served only to infuriate him right now.

But he must not take any action, or make any reprimands, while he was as wrought up as he was now. *Calm down, and take action from a cool and objective point of view, if any action is in fact necessary.*

They dropped Toby off at the house, and Little Jack went on with the rest to take stock of the situation and get details for the formal report of the action. His pain had subsided to some extent, he said, although he was still having occasional stabs in the belly. He would get some medication for it after he had tended to the business of his unit.

Ben had heard the vehicles coming down the street, and was waiting at the door.

"Eighteen," he exclaimed, with a low whistle. "If you lost eighteen of those tough little characters, it means you ran into some ambush!"

"Well," said Toby, taking off the battle gear and piling it on the desk, "I've never been in any ambush before, but this one sure sounded like a big one to me."

"You got yourself nicked a little bit, too," said Ben.

"Yeah," he said, with a wry smile. "Only a hero would have lived through that."

Ben pulled up the sleeve and looked at it. "Well, even if you don't consider it crippling, it would be a good idea to put something on it. In this climate . . ."

"First," said Toby, "I'm going to drink two gallons of that lovely cold water in the refrigerator, and then I'm going to take a shower, and then I'm going to fix this horrible, gaping wound. First things first."

He blessed the feel of the hot water. It soaked the tension out of his body and made him feel clean and sane again. Ben came to the door of his room.

"You'll have trouble taking care of that with one hand," he said. "Let me fix it up for you."

He brought a medical kit and put some strong disinfectant on the wound, which was more of an abrasion than a cut. "Fact is," he said, "in the tropics, this kind of a scratch is more likely to get infected than a deeper cut." Toby didn't know whether Ben was right, but the sting of the disinfectant was reassuring, and after Ben had taped a bandage over the wound, he put on his shirt and they went down to the office.

Toby gave him a full account of the action, and it was only then that Ben found out about Minnie.

"That's a shame," he said, genuinely moved by the loss. "That little man was a bright guy, and brave as they come."

"Well," said Toby thoughtfully, "I had never before had any doubts about his brain, but what he did this morning didn't look to me like a very bright thing to do." He told Ben how Minnie had reacted to the ambush.

"He jumped up and tried a head-on assault the first thing?" Ben asked.

"That's right. It couldn't have been more than half a minute after they first opened fire. He was on his feet, and got a machine gun going, hollered at the men around him, and ran right into the fire."

"Never had a chance, huh?"

"Not a chance."

"As I've said before," Ben remarked, "I never like to judge another man's battles if I wasn't there to see them, but what Minnie did may have been the best thing to do."

"I don't see how," said Toby, with a shake of his head.

"Usually the right thing to do in an ambush is just that: make an immediate assault on it, firing every weapon you've got as you go. The ambushing force is not bullet-proof, and they're just as susceptible to surprise and fear as the raiding force. With good men like the PRUs, well led, you could break up a pretty good-sized ambush force."

"They weren't well led today," Toby reminded him. He had not spared Little Jack in his narrative of the action.

Ben shook his head in disgust. "Big dumb jackass," he said. "I'd bust his ass to private if he was in my company."

"Anyway," said Toby, not really interested at this moment in the big sergeant, "we've proved that the Yenan Battalion is there. And as far as I'm concerned, we saw enough to be sure that the entrance to their tunnels is right there." He went over to the map and pointed to the village. "Now we can report this, and the ARVN can go in there and clear it out. They probably don't realize that we've discovered where their hideout is. They'll still be there."

"Lotsa luck, Toby," said Ben.

"What do you mean?"

"You might get an air strike, or maybe some guns to fire a few rounds on the place, for whatever good that might do, but it would take a couple of days for the ARVN to set up an operation against that area, and a couple of days is going to put us right into the middle of the Tet truce."

"But if they don't do something, all those troops are going to be available to hit My Tho during Tet."

"You think they're going to do that?"

"I *know* they are. Believe me, I know something about intelligence, and the intelligence I've got is good. The Viet Cong are going to blast this country with everything they've got during Tet."

"From what I know of you," said Ben, "I'm inclined to believe every word you say, but I doubt if other people will. All you can do is try."

"I'm sure as hell going to do that."

"And we can at least have our own place ready. If it does come, we may be one of the prime targets."

21

Therese was at her desk as usual the following morning, and Toby was dismayed to see that something of the old look of haunted sadness had returned to her eyes. He ached to have her alone, to talk with her, to comfort her. He had thought about it last night. He had been foolish and selfish. It was obvious that she was clinging to the idea of this child, that the pregnancy meant something out of the ordinary to her, anchored her in some way in a world that had used her badly.

Later this afternoon he would talk to her about it—repair the wrong between them, bridge the gulf, be her lover again in every way. But now he had other things to do, more urgent than that.

He went first to the Province Senior Adviser's office, to report on the action of yesterday, and to warn the PSA that he should prepare his people for an attack on My Tho at the time of Tet. The PSA was dubious.

"They're pledged to observe a truce during Tet, Toby," he said.

"They're going to violate it, sir," said Toby.

"Well . . ." The PSA did not believe it.

"Whether you believe it altogether or not," Toby went on, "I certainly would recommend that you alert all your people, and have plenty of emergency equipment, and food and water ready."

"Oh, yes, of course," said the PSA cordially. "We'll certainly do all that."

Toby asked if they had an interpreter he could borrow for an hour or so. They did, a serious-faced middle-aged man, who climbed into the jeep without a word and rode to Manh's office with Toby.

There Toby gave his report, making no apologies or boasts about it, but indicating clearly that it had been worth the effort. He had found out where the Yenan Battalion was holed up, and he could advise ARVN and the American forces in time to be on the alert for a move from that area during Tet.

Manh was also skeptical of the Tet danger.

"We are instructed to be liberal in granting our men leave to go to their homes for Tet," he said. "Many of them will be gone."

"You cannot cancel those leaves?"

"No."

"Colonel," said Toby earnestly, "I urge you to take every possible precaution with the men you will have left. There is going to be a massive attack, perhaps even a popular uprising, during Tet. If the Viet Cong catch us off guard they can do us tremendous damage."

"We will, of course, take customary precautions against surprise," said Manh.

Toby knew that this meant they would take no real precautions at all.

He went to Louise's house. None of the women was home, and he drove over to the hospital.

Louise came to the reception area to see him. He had never seen her in her uniform, but he was not surprised to note that the white blouse and slacks were no more successful than other garments in suppressing the richness of the lines underneath.

She gave him a quiet smile, almost shy. He felt equally as awkward at first.

"I just came to warn you," he said. "Nobody seems to believe me, but the Viet Cong are going to hit this city hard on the day of Tet. I think you women should plan to stay somewhere where you will have some kind of defense and protection."

"Where would that be?"

"You could come to our house. Or maybe the Province Senior Adviser could make room for you. He at least has a more defensible place, and plenty of guards."

"The hospital is probably the safest place we could be, don't you suppose? Even the Viet Cong won't hit the hospital."

"Don't be too sure of that."

"Well, I'll talk it over with the others, and we'll let you know," she said.

"Don't let anybody persuade you that there's not going to be any trouble. Nobody believes what I'm saying, evidently, and they'll try to persuade you too."

"I believe you."

He turned to go, and then paused. "Louise," he said in a voice that was muffled by hesitation and doubt, "I want to see you again . . . and I'm not talking about wanting to play, either. I just want to be with you, to talk."

She smiled. "I guess I ought to be flattered. Someone wants me for my mind."

He couldn't help grinning back at her. "I'm not going to play around with words with you, ma'am," he said. "I can say it all very simply. I miss you."

"That's nice."

"I'll talk to you later this evening."

"All right."

He went with the interpreter to the PRU barracks. Little Jack was not there, which was just as well. He called to one side the man who had been near him during most of the action the day before. He explained that although they had had to run away, they had nonetheless succeeded in their mission, because they had found out something very important. He was sorry that it had cost the lives of so many good men, and wanted the rest of them to know how much he appreciated their good work.

The man nodded and acknowledged his remarks with a few words. Toby thought he was pleased, although there was little expression on his face.

"Be sure that you keep somebody posted by that radio from now on," Toby instructed him. "The Viet Cong, including those forces we met yesterday, are going to attack My Tho on the day of Tet. I don't know how your unit will be used or deployed, but this city is going to need every experienced fighting man it can call up. Mr. Horner will be advised, and may have to contact you by that radio."

The man acknowledged the instructions. Toby had a sense of triumph in this case, for this man seemed to believe his warning without any reservations.

Toby went back to the house and had lunch; afterward he sat at his desk and prepared reports about yesterday's action, and the significance he attached to it. He didn't know how he was going to get the information to Can Tho, but figured he would fly down and back, if necessary. He gave his rough draft to Therese to put into a clean copy, and went back to join Ben, who was checking their supplies of weapons, ammunition, food, fuel, and water. Ben might have some doubts about the information, but he was going to be ready anyway. He helped Ben rearrange the supplies, to make them more easily available in a hurry. They took some additional ammunition out, to have ready in their rooms and on the roof.

Toby realized that in the urgency of the day's business he had neglected to make his daily check for Dang's signal, and he strolled out the gates and took a walk around the block.

A new curved mark had been scratched in the post, just under the first one.

Dang had loaded the dead drop once again. The material might have been in there all day yesterday, since Toby had not checked it then.

He hurried back to the office and called Therese to tell her what he had found.

"I don't know how long the material has been there—maybe all day yesterday, since I didn't check for the signal yesterday."

"I looked," said Therese. "It was not there yesterday."

"Good girl!" he exclaimed, trying to cheer her up. "It will be dark in about two hours, and I will go bring the material back. Could you come back to work this evening to help me with it?"

"Of course," she said.

"If you would like to leave now and rest for a while," he suggested. "The work tonight might be long and hard."

"Then I will leave now."

Toby was distressed by the coolness in her voice, but felt that after the work was out of the way this evening he could talk with her and bring her back to a happy mood.

He asked Mrs. Chao to prepare his dinner earlier this evening, so that by the time it got dark he would be free of all other activities. Mrs. Chao did as he asked willingly enough, but she was not her usual cheerful self, and Toby guessed that she must have heard, or sensed, Therese's troubles.

As soon as the streets were dark, he drove as fast as he could to the airstrip. In the dead drop he found a big bundle of papers, wrapped in a plastic sheet and tied with a string. He rushed back to the office and found Therese already waiting for him, her desk and typewriter ready for work.

They opened the bundle, and even Therese seemed to forget her troubles in the excitement of the moment.

"See if there is a note or any kind of a personal communication from Dang, first," he said.

"Yes. Here is a letter from him."

"Will you read that to me now, to see if it contains any instructions or explanations about the other material?"

Therese read:

"My Friend: I go soon to My Tho for final study of our target for Tet. There will be others in the city at the same time. I do not dare to meet with you. I will leave package of papers with information in the box as you directed.

"I conclude your officials have not understood or believed my information. They have not prepared against Tet attack, and it will therefore be carried out as planned. You must warn them, however. The attack is ready. It will be carried out all over South Vietnam. I do not know details of plans for other areas, but I give following general information about all of South Vietnam, in addition to the enclosed detailed plans about operations in Dinh Tuong Province:

"(a) The false information from COSVN has reached highest American and ARVN levels, and is believed.

"(b) At least one important American place will be attacked in Saigon. I do not know which place, but Americans should put extra defense at BOQs, at Than Son Nhut, and at Embassy.

"(c) Three officers of your agency are to be killed or captured, but I do not believe you are one of these targets. They are in the north.

"(d) The attack will begin early on morning of January 30. *All* Viet Cong forces will participate. *All!*"

Therese put the paper down on the desk.

"There's something significant about his attitude this time," said Toby. "He is intelligent enough to know that as late as it is we can't possibly take defensive measures that would show the Viet Cong we are ready in time for them to call it off. He knows that the attack is going to be made, that there is no stopping it now, and yet he has sent us information to help us *defeat* the attack. He has come over to our side, even if he hasn't yet admitted it to himself."

Therese set to work typing out a translation of all the other documents, and Toby took the notes he had made from her oral translation of the letter and typed up an intelligence report. *One more,* he thought grimly, *for Chet Wolleson to put in a file and forget.* Well, by God, he was going to see that this one was not put in a file, even if he did have to go out of channels and work around Chet.

Therese worked steadily, often asking Toby for a precise English word when it would not come to her, exploring their mutual knowledge of French where all else failed. The picture began to emerge of a comprehensive battle plan for the city of My Tho. Toby could see that the value of this information was not for the upper levels of the CIA, nor of either government, although its wealth of detail about the plan would add authenticity to Dang's general information about the rest of the country. The principal use of these meticulous details was going to be to prepare My Tho for the attack.

Toby knew that it was now time to bring Ben into the picture. He went into the house and asked Ben to come into the office. With Therese still hard at work on the translations, Toby gave Ben a brief account of the Dang operation: of the first reports, which were still sitting in Can Tho, and of the receipt of the material they were working on now.

Ben was interested and excited by the operation itself, but that interest was quickly replaced by an intense desire to study the details of the battle plan. He was impressed with the military skill that had devised it.

"There is only one thing wrong with it, Toby," he said. "Even if all the forces he lists are really available, they still aren't enough to capture and hold a city like My Tho. They can do a lot of damage, maybe hold parts of the place for a long time, but unless ARVN and our own people make some crazy mistakes, the VC haven't got a chance. And yet, here they are, coming out of hiding all at once for a face-to-face battle, in the open field."

"But they're expecting that this attack is going to be accompanied by a mass uprising of the people," said Toby.

"Oh, sure, they're talking about the struggle of the masses and all of that, but they always have that crap in their papers."

"If I had the time," said Toby, "I could show you that in this case what they're saying is not just Communist jargon and slogans, Ben. There's a difference that you don't catch, unless you've been studying and living with it for years. In this case what they're saying is not just a bunch of Marxist-Leninist catch phrases. These words mean exactly what they say. These guys are really depending on the people all over South Vietnam to rise up and help them fight."

Ben shook his head. "I didn't think they were that stupid. It'll never happen. You can't make a crowd of people fight a battle. You can't even make them fight back when you attack them, unless they're an organized military unit."

"That's what Dang says."

"All the more reason why you should trust Dang."

"That brings up a worrisome point," said Toby, fingering one of the translations. "I'm still a little uneasy about how Dang came to know all the things he gives us in these papers and his note. After all, he's just a battalion commander, and I doubt if the high command at COSVN takes him into their confidence. Especially about a thing they want to keep a secret."

"I wouldn't worry about it," said Ben cheerfully. "If he's got enough common sense to see the basic flaw in their whole plan, he's got enough common sense to find out a lot of things from the rest of those dummies. This information is so good, it's just *got* to be right."

The picture emerged clearly and completely. The Yenan Battalion would be charged with occupying the provincial government compound and the tactical operations center. One platoon would be detailed to go through the dense residential neighborhoods, to carry out missions of "control and security," whatever that meant. Whatever it was was bound to be unpleasant. The central command post for the Viet Cong attack on the city would be a big pagoda in the center of town. Supplies of weapons and ammunition had already been accumulating in the pagoda for many weeks. The 23rd Local Force Battalion would be responsible for the sector of the city in which their own house and office compound was located. The nearest specific target for a part of the 23rd was a house one block down the street from Toby's compound, which would be occupied by

a platoon shortly after midnight. Its task would be to ambush a
South Vietnamese Ranger Battalion, which would come along
that street into the city at the first news of a Viet Cong attack.
Dang's report indicated that the Viet Cong had detailed knowledge of the South Vietnamese military plans for the defense of
the city. The rest of the 23rd would close the trap around the
Ranger Battalion, and destroy it.

Dang's Determination-to-Win Battalion had the sector of the
city near the airport. Other local force battalions had been
moved into place and were assigned specific areas of the residential and business districts of the city. Infiltration of troops
would begin the day before the attack was to be launched.

"Toby," Ben repeated, leaning back in his chair thoughtfully,
"this information can't possibly be false, or a plant. It rings too
true. You've got the truth here, and you've just got to persuade
Can Tho and Saigon to believe it and spread it around. This
whole goddamned country is about to blow up in our faces."

"OK. Now, we've got to make up an intelligence report from
this that will give enough of the facts to help people get ready,
but written so it won't point to Dang as the source. A report has
got to go to Manh, and Manh's office is probably penetrated by
the VC. If Dang comes through this alive, he may be able to get
back in touch with us, and become a regular agent. In any
event, I don't want to get him shot.

"It's too late for me to call Jerry to get a plane up here, and
when I call him tomorrow I'm going to have to take pretty
much what he'll let me have as a matter of routine."

"Christ, Toby, this is *urgent!* Tell him it is! He'll have a plane
up here in an hour."

"I can't do that. If the VC aren't monitoring our single sideband transmissions they're more stupid than they've given any
sign of being. Suppose you had an action like this scheduled, and
then a person in my profession and location suddenly puts in a
scream for immediate transportation, and then preparations
start all over the country—"

"I get it," Ben stopped him with an upraised hand. "OK, so you get to Can Tho as soon as you can, and then beat it back up here, right? We're gonna be busy as hell around here, you know."

"I know. It'll be down and back for me, nothing more. When I get down there and can talk to Jerry in person, instead of on the air, I can persuade him how urgent my needs are."

They worked until the early hours of the morning, and at last Toby had reports prepared for Manh, and for Can Tho to put into the official channels for dissemination through Vietnam and back to Washington. Nothing more could be done until the working day began.

"Therese, it's late," said Toby. Ben was within earshot. "You could lie down and sleep somewhere in the house until daylight, if you like."

"No, Mr. Busch," she said. "I would prefer to go home."

"I'll take you in the jeep."

While she was putting things away, Toby called Louise on the Victory net. They double-talked briefly, and Louise managed to convey to him that she and Peggy would be at the hospital if trouble started. Not only would it be as safe or safer than other locations, but there was also their own usefulness and professional responsibility to be considered. Marie Claire could do as she wished, and would be guided by her own supervisor. Toby could not argue with that. He hung up the microphone grudgingly, and went out to the jeep with Therese.

He was tired, and it was cool. He drove slowly, enjoying the quietness of the nearly spent night, curiously relaxed and relieved now that they had done everything they could do at this stage of developments. Now he could speak to Therese about her pregnancy.

"Therese," he began, "will you forgive me for what I said about the baby?"

"It has . . . been difficult to—" she said, slowly, measuring her words.

"I wasn't thinking," Toby interrupted her. "Or, rather, I was thinking, but only of myself and my own feelings, and I see now that I was being terribly selfish. I still won't like the idea of being the father of a child I'll never know, even though you are the mother. But I do know that you will care for it well. What I'm trying to say now is what I refused to say for you the other night. Therese, I do want you to have our baby."

He had reached her pathway, and he drew the jeep to a halt by the curb. She sat still, staring straight ahead.

"What's the matter, Therese? Don't you understand what I've been saying?"

"It is too late," she said tonelessly.

"What do you mean, it's too late?"

"It is too late to save the baby. I have already done as you asked."

"You had an abortion? Already?" he gasped.

"Yes. Two days ago."

"Oh, God."

She turned and stared at him with burning eyes. "The Viet Cong killed my other babies," she said, with a harshness he had never before heard in her voice. "This one I killed myself."

Toby sat, thunderstruck, as she slipped out of the jeep and ran down the path into the gloom.

22

The slackness of the season made it possible for Toby to get a plane for Can Tho promptly the following morning, and he was in the ROIC's office by ten o'clock.

But Bill Voigt was not there. He had gone to Saigon, and would be back late in the evening or early the following morning.

Toby swore to himself. It must be some kind of a macumba, or a hex—something that was conspiring to prevent him from getting his intelligence across to the right people and making them believe it.

Chet was still contemptuous. Chet had now reached a point where information that should have made him doubt and reexamine his position only made him all the more stubborn, more resolved not to let any of today's nonsense upset the logical conclusions of the past.

"Chet," Toby told him, "this information is accurate. It has *got* to get to Saigon and Washington!"

"Not until we've got an approved agent or project to attribute it to, it doesn't. How am I supposed to evaluate what you've got here? Do I say, 'Busch says this information is true'?"

"Don't give me that!" Toby retorted. "You know exactly how to word a report under circumstances like these, so it will get read and accepted."

"Sure," said Chet. *"If* I believed it myself—which I don't."

"But look at the details, goddammit!"

"So what we say, then, is: 'This report has got to be true because there's so much of it!' Right?"

"Oh, Christ!"

"Now, look at something else, Busch," Chet went on. "The high-level penetration Saigon is running against COSVN says this is all a deception operation. These guys learned deception from the Soviets. They're good at it. We've got to be just as professional in our response to it. Do you think this office, or the station in Saigon, or headquarters, is going to want to circulate in official channels one report with detailed information that other reports in the same channels say is false?"

"It isn't false, goddammit."

"*You* say it isn't."

"Ben Compton has seen it. He believes it."

"Oh, well, that's different," said Chet, his voice heavy with sarcasm. "I didn't know that. Then all we've got to do is send it in with a little note at the end saying, 'Ben Compton believes this information.'"

"OK, Chet, have your fun," said Toby, getting up abruptly. "I've got to get back to My Tho, because I know what's coming and I intend to have my town ready for it. I'm leaving these reports right here on your desk. What you do with them is up to you. I've got copies of them in my safe in My Tho, and when I get back I'm going to note on those copies that I have delivered the originals to you at ten o'clock A.M. on January 29."

"Be my guest," Chet sneered.

"I would advise you to show those reports to Bill Voigt as soon as he comes back, if you're not going to transmit them electronically through channels before then. If you don't tell Bill, you're making a decision on your own that may haunt you for the rest of your life."

"I've done exactly that before, in your case, don't you remember?"

"Goddammit, can't you forget Frankfurt for one minute? This is Vietnam. This is the biggest action the Viet Cong have ever tried. This isn't one agent, this is a whole country, two whole armies!"

"Two whole armies and Ben Compton," Chet grinned.

Toby ignored the gibe. "Will you tell Bill?" he insisted.

"If he isn't too busy, I may."

Therese had not come to work when he got back, but Toby had other urgent matters on his mind, and he gave her absence only scant attention. She had worked late, after all, and she was emotionally overwrought, as he would be if he were to let himself stop and think about their problems. Let her have time to rest and think.

He picked up the reports they had made up for Colonel Manh. They were in orderly array, and impeccably neat, just as she had typed and arranged them. He drove to the PSA's office to borrow the interpreter once more.

How he did miss Minnie! The soft-spoken, quick-witted man had become such an indispensable part of his day and his work that his absence made a real physical gap. But it wasn't only that. It was the sadness—no, the tragedy—of the death of a man like Minnie. He was a loss to his American friends, and a loss to the Vietnamese.

And surprisingly brave. Toby had known that Minnie was courageous, but he had not expected the automatic, almost insane heroism of that moment of the ambush, when Minnie was the first to react, was the only one who had the automatic reflexes to oppose an enemy ambush with immediate, aggressive action.

The longer he lived, the more Toby perceived that the world is full of great men who are never recognized publicly for their greatness. He had to place Tran Van Minh among those unrecognized heroes. The only award or monument Minnie would ever have would be in the memories of the friends he had left behind. That was the case with many of the world's true heroes.

But why should that be the only recognition? He suddenly

knew that there was something he could and must do. He must set the wheels in motion to have Minnie decorated posthumously for his bravery.

The idea awoke him to yet another thing, and he cursed his thoughtlessness. He had not taken any steps to notify anybody about Minnie's death, and it was *his* responsibility. The PRU had its own machinery for that, but Minnie was *his* employee, and it was up to him to advise the next of kin. He didn't know who that would be. Perhaps the brother he went to see. He would have Therese help him with that as soon as she came in.

He couldn't blame Therese if she hated him. But he couldn't believe that she ever would. Everything seemed to be piling up on him at once, and things were in such a process of telescoping urgency that he had little time to think calmly and sensibly about any single problem, or to try to deal with it serenely.

He and the interpreter got an immediate audience with Manh, and Toby gave him the reports about the preparations for the assault on My Tho. He apologized to Manh for not yet being able to reveal to him the exact source of the information, and lied to him that he hoped and expected to reveal that source to him in due course.

Manh gave the papers a quick glance, and Toby sensed with a sinking heart that he was not immediately impressed. He was seeing in the policeman the same reaction he had witnessed everywhere—what seemed to be an almost willful refusal to believe, a desire *not* to believe, buttressed by soothing press and governmental releases that the truce was to be observed.

Toby even toyed briefly with the idea of trying to go personally to the various unit commanders around the city, to alert them, but knew that even if they believed him, which they would not, they would never take orders from him or make preparations that were not in accordance with the orders and policies of their own chains of command.

All during the next day Toby thought repeatedly of the phrase "the calm before the storm," and decided that he had never before fully appreciated its significance. Everything around their house and office had taken on a tranquility and a slowness of movement and reaction that seemed to his keyed-up senses nothing short of surrealistic. And yet the day passed swiftly.

The first thing he did was to drive to the women's house before time for them to leave for their work. He repeated to them his warning of the impending attack, told them he had had additional confirmation of the information, and demanded from them a careful schedule of their plans for the following day. He wrote out this schedule on a sheet of paper and made a copy for them.

"If you're going to deviate from this in any significant way," he said, "call me on the Victory net. I'll try to be near a set all day, and I'll answer to Victory-One, whatever set I'm near."

The women were impressed by his seriousness, and promised to do as he said. Marie Claire would be at work in the Province Senior Adviser's office during the morning, but they were scheduled to take the afternoon off because of the Tet holiday. The two nurses would be on duty from 8:00 A.M. at the hospital. They did not think that they would have any time off, but said that if they did, they would spend it at home, and would advise Toby.

The rest of the morning Toby and Ben spent in preparation of a map and a Viet Cong battle plan for the city of My Tho, based on the information supplied by Dang.

"Although," Toby said dubiously at one point, "I wonder what good it's going to do? We can sit here and watch the battle develop, but if Manh and Can Tho and Saigon don't believe the information, the plan will be carried out without a hitch. Very little we could do about it."

"You might be surprised," said Ben. "Having a complete set of the enemy's plans may be better than having several hundred troops."

"How do you figure that?"

Ben straightened up from the map on the desk. "Those Viet Cong troops are going to come out of the woodwork for the first time and stand up straight and fight a full-scale battle in the field. They've never done that before, and they're going to find it quite a bit different than hit-and-run attacks, ambushes, sapper squads, and things like that. In this case they're going to be committed to win, not just do damage and run. They're not going to be able to get away from us this time."

Toby looked narrowly at Ben. Ben's eyes were shining with an expression Toby had never seen in them before.

"Jesus, you really mean that!"

"About them not getting away from us?"

"Yes."

"Damn right! Tomorrow we're going to see if the VC are men or boys."

"Just you and me and Little Jack?"

"Yep, and anybody else that wants to get in on the fun."

Toby laughed mirthlessly. "You've got a weird idea of fun. With you in that kind of a mood, I sure hope the ARVN and everybody else is ready. You're likely to get us killed."

Therese had not yet appeared by lunchtime, and Toby spoke to Mrs. Chao. Mrs. Chao was also concerned, and dispatched Chi Hai by cyclo to see what was the matter.

Ben and Toby had a light lunch, and then, after putting the finishing touches on the map, they set about cleaning and oiling every one of the weapons, from handguns to the heavy machine gun on the roof.

"The middle of a battle is no time to find out that a bolt on an automatic weapon won't slam back and fire the next round," Ben said. Toby had had one hands-on session years ago on the firing of the M-2 machine gun; so Ben took him to the roof and drilled him repeatedly on feeding ammunition, aiming, firing, handling.

"If it fails to fire," Ben told him, "wait for about five seconds, then pull the bolt back this way, let it go, re-lay the weapon, and fire it. You've always got to be sure this cover here is latched, and make sure the belt is straight. Got that?"

Toby nodded, and they went over the drills several more times.

Chi Hai returned. Therese was not feeling well, she said, and could not come to work today.

"Therese very sad," Mrs. Chao told him. "Therese sick here." She placed a hand over her heart.

"I know," said Toby. "I am sad, too."

"Today, she not want see you," Mrs. Chao went on. "I know. But one week, maybe two week, she feel right, she love you again. This very hard for woman."

"I know, Mrs. Chao. Thank you."

He sensed through the simple, halting speech a fund of sympathy for himself as well as for Therese, and silently blessed the little woman for understanding. He knew that she would be an ally when the time came to make amends.

He spoke to Little Jack about what they should do with the PRUs.

"We ought to wait," said Little Jack. "Manh has got first call on them, and if we give them an assignment beforehand he'll be madder'n hell. If he hasn't given them some mission when the attack comes, if it comes, then we can do anything we want to with 'em and always have the excuse that we saw he wasn't using them anyway. Know what I mean?"

"Yes. I guess it's the only thing we can do."

"Well," said Ben about the middle of the afternoon. "I think we've got things in pretty good shape. Now, to judge by past performance, Ski will be popping in on us before long."

"You think so?"

"Yep. Ski usually comes down here the day before a holiday, and I'm damned sure he will before this one. He missed Christmas and New Year's, and except for that dust-up you guys had with the ambush, things have been awfully quiet all over the delta. When the rest of the country is quiet, Moc Hoa is stone-cold dead. Ski gets too bored up there to even play with himself, and so he comes down here, or goes over to Vinh Long, to drink and tell lies."

"Yeah, but when Bill Voigt saw that information I left," Toby said, "I'll lay you ten to one he sent word out to everybody in the provinces to be ready. Ski wouldn't leave Moc Hoa in that case, would he?"

"No, not Ski. He may not be the greatest brain in the world, but he would never leave his duty post during an emergency or an alert."

"Furthermore," Toby went on, "I don't know what he'd eat. Mrs. Chao and Chi Hai are going to spend the night with relatives and celebrate Tet with them tomorrow."

"If there's food around, Ski will take care of himself. He doesn't set that much store by elegance or good cooking."

They went over to the RD offices in the government compound to a Tet party. They went out of a sense of duty, a social obligation to Vietnamese counterparts and associates, and watched while a collection of small men drank themselves into a frenzy of camaraderie and good spirits with expensive French cognac. It didn't take long. An hour and a half later, Toby and Ben took their leave and returned to the office.

"Boy!" Toby exclaimed, "getting smashed on something like cognac—you know their heads are going to be busting tomorrow morning."

"Yep," Ben agreed.

"And I didn't see a sign of any preparation for the attack."

"No," Ben said. "But then, the attack is scheduled for tomorrow morning, so Manh may be waiting until later this evening, after dark, to get his forces organized."

"Do you think that's the case?"

"No."

Toby looked sharply at him, and Ben shrugged. "Toby, I don't think anybody in the whole country believes you. Those guys there today didn't act like they did, although I've passed the word through their upper echelons and I've tried to impress on them the necessity to be alert. Of course, they're not combat soldiers, so they don't have much of a sense of urgency, but they're going to be in the battle anyway."

As if to reinforce Ben's pessimism, they found Ski sitting at the bar when they got back to the house.

"Hey, Ski!" Ben greeted him airily. "VC chase you out of Kien Tuong?"

"Whattaya say, fellas," Ski said. "I helped myself to your beer, because I knew you'd want it that way."

"Didn't Can Tho tell you about the attack?" Toby asked him.

"What attack?"

"The Tet offensive."

"Tet offensive? Never heard of it. Hell, there's a Tet *truce* going on!"

Ben explained briefly to Ski, and led him into the office and showed him the map and the battle plan. Ski whistled softly.

"Christ, Toby, is this for real?"

"I got this from a good agent. It's for real."

"Then how in the hell come Can Tho didn't say nothing to me about it? My house up there in Moc Hoa has got nothing but a handful of Nungs, and with me gone God knows what kind of a watch they're going to keep on things. I gotta get back—" He strode to the single sideband by the breezeway door, then paused and looked back. "You're sure, Toby? This is not just a 'maybe'?"

"No maybe about it."

"Because there sure ain't any sign that anybody else knows about it. Dino was happy as a clam on the way down—going to a big party up in Can Tho when he gets back. He's gonna love me for making him come back and get me. . . . God almighty, this don't hardly seem possible, that they got good information and nobody is doing anything."

"It's the history of the intelligence business," said Toby. "We never seem to have the effect we ought to have, and half the time it's because we don't have the information, and the rest of the time it's because we've got information and nobody believes it."

Ski grinned. "Like seeing tanks."

"Exactly."

"Yeah, and those tanks aren't there anymore, and now I know that nobody is ever gonna believe I really saw 'em."

"I believe you, Ski."

"Thanks. How can I doubt your information after that?" Ski laughed and called Jerry, and was troubled to find out that Jerry had no way to send for him before dark. Ski would have to wait until morning.

The four of them, Ski, Ben, Little Jack, and Toby, ate a cold supper Mrs. Chao had left, and sat at the bar with cans of beer, waiting. Explosions started up in the street, and Toby was on his feet in an instant.

"Relax, Toby," said Ben. "That's firecrackers. They keep it up all night during Tet."

Toby sat down with a feeble grin.

"Ben," said Ski, "the only weapon I brought is this pistol. You better fix me up with something, don't you think?"

"Sure, Ski, come on," Ben said. He led Ski out to the storeroom, and Toby went along. There was something reassuring about being in the presence of these two men, who knew what to do at times like this, who took so much in their stride the prospect of a battle in the morning. It calmed his own seething insides, gave him some measure of confidence.

But he knew that he would never again volunteer for an assignment "where the action is."

23

It was midnight, and the Tet party in Can Tho was at its peak. Bill Voigt stood by the bar of the little lounge in the compound and looked foggily at the crowd of merrymakers. Dino was dancing with one of the nurses. Jerry was shaking a set of liar's dice with Russ, the commo man. A couple of people from an Ohio State University Research Team that was quartered at the far end of the compound were sitting with several of the USAID public relations people, who also had offices in the area. All of Bill's regional staff were there, as well as the Phong Dinh Province staff, and Wilbur Hamilton.

Even Chet had unwound more than Bill had ever known him to do; had, in fact, gotten somewhat bagged on CC and water.

The Christmas truce had been peaceful, and things had been quiet ever since, except for that astonishing ambush Toby Busch's people had run into. No question about it, they had uncovered an important hideout, probably of the Yenan Battalion. He would make sure Toby got full credit for that. Although, on the other hand, Little Jack surely ought to have handled that search operation better than that. *Christ, eighteen men killed!*

He looked at Chet, who was leaning on the bar beaming at nothing.

"Looks like our uneasiness about Viet Cong action during Tet was off the mark, Chet," he said. "Everything's calm and peaceful."

"Yeah," Chet replied. "Except for Busch, I guess. He's got his own private Tet offensive going."

"His Tet offensive? What's he doing, planning another search operation right away?"

"No, it's what he says the VC are planning. He's hollering that the VC are going to attack us tomorrow."

"Oh?" responded Bill idly, toying with the glass on the bar before him. "What's he got, some kind of a crystal ball?"

"No," muttered Chet, with something that sounded like a cross between a snort and a giggle, "I don't think either one of his balls is made of crystal, but I think his head is made of Jell-O."

"Well, you gotta admit he found a VC hideout the other day."

"Yeah, and got eighteen more men killed."

Bill did not respond. There was no point in arguing with Chet, especially about something he had such unreasoning responses to, and most especially when he was drunk.

"Him and his goddamned penetration," said Chet, taking a drink from the nearly empty glass.

"Penetration?"

"Yeah. Wunnerful great big goddamned penetration he says he's got. Brings me all kinds of crap from it."

"What's he been bringing you?" Bill asked, suddenly sober. "I've never seen any of it."

" 'Course not! Why should you be bothered with it? It's a whole pisspot full of stuff, but he never was able to get enough information on his agent so we could clear him, and then he said the agent was under surveillance, and he was out of touch, and then he was back in touch with a dead drop, and he comes down here with a great big goddamned battle plan of the Viet Cong and expects me to put that out in an intel—at the same time the Saigon penetration operation is getting constant take, straight from the horse's mouth, that it's all a deception, and—"

"Chet, listen to me," said Bill sternly. "Did Busch bring reports in about a Tet attack—specific information?"

"Yeah."

"When?"

"Yesterday morning. I looked it over. Bunch of bullshit!"

"Where did he get the information?"

"I just told you. From some guy that says he's a local force battalion commander."

"Come on," said Bill. "I'm going with you to your office. I want you to get that stuff out and show me."

Chet shrugged and walked behind Bill across the driveway into the ROIC offices.

Ten minutes later Bill was leafing through the papers Toby had left, his eyes wide with astonishment, sweat starting from every pore.

"Chet," he said, looking intently at the other man, who was sitting drowsy-eyed across the desk, "at the very best, what you've done here is the stupidest thing I've ever seen, and at worst it's downright criminal!"

"Come on," said Chet indignantly. "That stuff—"

"This stuff may be true, or highly exaggerated, or even false, but it is intelligence that should have been disseminated with IMMEDIATE precedence the minute you got it. You've got all the elements necessary here for the customer to study the information and judge for himself. And yet *you* interposed your own judgment that it is is false, and stopped it cold."

"It *is* false," said Chet.

"You'd better be saying prayers for the rest of the night that it is," said Bill, "and even if it is false, this action of yours of sitting on a report is going to go into your record. You've let a personal feeling about another officer distort your judgment and get in the way of your professional obligations."

"Now, just hold on a goddamned minute!" Chet exclaimed. "How in hell can they do anything to me for—"

"And," Bill continued, "if the information turns out to be true, you're going to spend the rest of your career running errands in headquarters, unless they decide to fire you. So, as I say, you better hope it isn't true.

"Now I want you to get every one of the officers in here, and Laura too. We're going to have a staff meeting, and I'm going to do as much as possible to get us ready and warn the rest of the country."

Chet rose and made as if to protest.

"Move!" Bill said coldly. "Move your ass like you've never moved it before!"

The staff assembled with the boisterous good humor of the party they had left, but Bill's steely purposefulness brought them around quickly. Each man was ordered to check the locations of the persons under his supervision, and do whatever he could to alert them, all over the delta. They must not give out any specific information over the single sideband, but the matter was urgent enough, and far enough along, that they would allow the Viet Cong monitors to conclude that something urgent was causing a great deal of traffic.

Having energized and dispatched his staff to alert the entire region, Bill dictated a paragraph that was to accompany the cabled intelligence report the reports officer was even now preparing.

"Make this FLASH precedence," he said to Laura.

Chet protested. "Christ, if you alert the whole world that way, and then it turns out—"

"Come here, Chet," Bill said, leading his deputy outside, where nobody could hear them. When they were alone, he grabbed Chet's arm.

"Next time you butt in on this," he rasped, "I'll say whatever I've got to say in front of anybody that's around. But this is one more time I'm going to answer you in private. If it hadn't been for your stupidity, I wouldn't be having to lay my own reputation on the line by putting out a FLASH message. This information could have gone with nothing but a priority, or maybe an immediate precedence if it had been handled the minute you got it. As it is, FLASH precedence may save something, maybe not much.

"Now, if you can be of any help around here, pitch in. If not, get the hell back to the bar, or to bed."

Bill marched back into his office and dictated the cable.

His reports officer was just coming in with the finished intelligence report when he was signing off on the operational information to go with it.

"Thank God Busch is a pro," said the reports officer. "That report was a beauty just as he turned it in. All I had to do was look up some references, and fix up the dissemination line."

"It looks serious, doesn't it?"

"I gotta say that that report is damned convincing. Chet must have been out of his mind—"

"Here is the ops information to go with your intel," Bill said, handing the page to the reports officer just as the commo man came in to pick up the material for transmission.

THE FOLLOWING INFORMATION WAS OBTAINED FROM A SOURCE AT THE MIDDLE LEVEL OF THE VIET CONG MILITARY COMMAND. HE IS A NEW SOURCE, AND UNTESTED. THE RELIABILITY OF HIS INFORMATION CANNOT BE JUDGED, AND WE REALIZE THAT IT CONTRADICTS THE VOLUMINOUS REPORTING SAIGON STATION HAS BEEN RECEIVING FROM A HIGH-LEVEL VIET CONG SOURCE IN THE PAST (SEE REFERENCES), BUT FIELD ASSESSMENT BOTH OF THIS AGENT AND OF HIS INFORMATION LEADS ROIC TO BELIEVE THAT THIS REPORT IS ACCURATE. THE WEALTH OF DETAILS WITHIN THE AREA OF AGENT'S KNOWLEDGE, THE TENOR OF HIS JUDGMENTS AND SPECULATIONS IN AREAS BEYOND HIS COMPETENCE, AND THE COINCIDENCE BETWEEN HIS INFORMATION AND THE RESULTS OF A RECENT SEARCH OPERATION IN DINH TUONG PROVINCE, WHICH THE AGENT COULD NOT HAVE KNOWN AT THE TIME OF HIS REPORT,

ARE ELEMENTS THAT INVITE CAREFUL CONSIDERA-
TION. THIS REPORT IS MORE, AND IT IS BETTER, THAN
WOULD HAVE BEEN LOGICAL OR REQUIRED BY A DECEP-
TION OPERATION. ROIC BELIEVES IT TO BE TRUE, AND
THIS REGION IS BEING PREPARED FOR ACTION AS WELL
AS POSSIBLE AT THIS LATE HOUR.

FOR REASONS THAT WILL BE CLARIFIED ELSEWHERE
THIS REPORT IS LATE GETTING INTO CHANNELS. IT IS
FOR THIS REASON THAT IT IS BEING TRANSMITTED
WITH FLASH PRECEDENCE.

"OK," said Bill, signing off on the documents and handing
them to Russ. "Let's get this on the air, while the rest of us get
some weapons issued and get set for whatever is coming."

24

Toby was not sure whether it was good news or bad, when the single sideband began to chatter with messages back and forth across the delta. It was obvious that Can Tho had at last gone on the alert, which was good; but if they were so late that the warning was coming only now, it was bad.

Well, that was Bill's problem. From here on, Toby had to concentrate on My Tho.

"Toby," said Ben, "I think we ought to turn that generator off. It's like a beacon to anybody around."

"You're right," Toby replied. "Will you attend to it, please?"

Ben went out, and the deep roar of the diesel engine ceased abruptly. The lights went out, except for two or three small fixtures that were on the city circuits.

"I'm going up on the roof," Ben said, when he came back in. "I think we'll want to set up watches for the night, before any of us hits the sack."

"I couldn't sleep right now, anyway," said Toby. He followed Ben up the stairs. Little Jack and Ski stayed at the bar, cans of beer in their hands.

It was the night of the new moon, only the light of the stars and the zodiacal light to see by on the roof, although the streets were dimly lighted by streetlights. The two of them sat down on sandbags near one corner of the roof. Everything was quiet. They could make out the shadowy forms of the guards below, each in his place. Ben had seen to that.

"Sure doesn't seem like any attack can be coming right away," Toby murmured.

"No, but a good part of their forces were going to infiltrate during the day, remember. As far as I know, nobody has done a thing to prevent that."

"Not that you could tell."

"I don't think anybody even went over to look at that pagoda," Ben went on.

"No. I understand they're awfully touchy about messing around with pagodas," Toby said.

"Who, the VC?"

"No, the South Vietnamese government."

Ben shifted his weight and peered idly down the street. "I don't see any sign that that platoon has moved into the house down there," he said.

"No. No sign yet," Toby agreed.

They were silent for a time.

"You don't get nervous, or scared, when you know a battle is coming?" Toby asked.

"Oh, sure, you get nervous," Ben said. He understood and sympathized with Toby. "I'm always nervous until it starts, because up till then I don't know what's going to happen, or how or where. After it starts, you're too busy to be nervous."

"I'll try not to get you killed, but you're going to have to teach me. You remember we said I'd teach you intelligence work, and you could teach me combat?"

"Yeah."

"I was kidding at the time."

"I thought so."

"It's not a joke, though."

"No, but you'll be all right, Toby. I understand you did real well with the PRU ambush the other day."

Toby was pleased, but dubious. "I've been wondering ever since if I shouldn't have done something, instead of just firing a couple of rounds and running like hell."

"From what I hear," Ben said, "you all walked right into a real sweet ambush. By the time they pulled the chain there was only one smart thing to do, and that was get the hell out."

"I hope you're right."

"I'm pretty sure I am."

"It still leaves me feeling guilty and unsatisfied. We lost eighteen men, including Minnie."

"I know how you feel, Toby. No way to overcome those feelings. What I meant to say about it was that a man without experience couldn't be expected to make a judgment about what to do. The main thing was, you kept control of yourself, you didn't panic, you didn't bug out and leave a buddy exposed. Things like that."

"Running away isn't much of a test, though."

"Oh, well . . ."

"And there's not going to be any running away tomorrow."

"You're right, there, pardner. What we're gonna do tomorrow is run *at* 'em, not *away* from 'em."

"You know you're crazy, don't you?" Toby said. Ben chuckled. Then he straightened up.

"Toby, look!" he said softly.

There in the street more than a block away were shadowy figures moving toward them.

"That must be the platoon that'll occupy that house down there to ambush the Ranger platoon," said Toby.

"Yeah," Ben replied. "The problem is, they're coming on past the house they're supposed to take over."

Ben was right. The figures moved silently toward them, across the intersection.

"Keep an eye on them," said Ben. "I've got to go make sure those guards don't open up on that bunch unless they start firing first, or unless we start it from the roof. I'll send Ski and Little Jack up."

Ben slipped away in the dark, and Toby chambered a round in his rifle. He sat motionless behind the low revetment, watching the enemy draw near.

The shadowy figures grew in number as their line snaked up the street. From what Toby could make out, they seemed to have no intention of doing anything to his own house, and it was a consoling thought. But that they were Viet Cong troops there was no doubt. He was now peering down at his enemy, a sizable number of armed men, bent on some business that Dang's report had not described.

The other three joined him on the roof, and he was greatly comforted by the presence of three combat-wise veterans.

The figures in the street formed a knot directly across the street, and then began to fade into the darkness around the big house that stood there.

"What the hell are they up to?" Toby whispered to Ben.

"Damned if I can figure it out. Wait a minute. That's the platoon that ought to be occupying the house down the street, all right. They've got the wrong house!"

"Damned if I don't think you're right," Toby said.

"Maybe they were told to home in on our lights and generator, a block away, and didn't find them. Anyway, if they know anything about our house at all, they'll think we're a block farther up that way. They'll have no idea we're right across the street from them."

"So, what whould we do?"

In answer, Ben quietly summoned the other two, and they sat close together and talked in low voices. "Fellows, that Ranger Battalion hasn't been alerted to this, it's a leadpipe cinch. They're gonna be coming up this street when the fighting starts, and they'll run into an ambush right here."

"I'll be goddamned!" exclaimed Ski.

"All right, then," Ben went on, "if that's the way it is, here's what we've got to do. We'll keep a constant watch on that house from now on. If we open fire on them we'll ruin their ambush, but they might get away."

"Jesus, Ben," said Ski, "you can't let the Rangers walk into an ambush."

"I don't intend to. We'll wait until we can see the Rangers

coming down there, way down the street. As soon as they get to a certain point, we'll open up on that house with everything we've got. That'll alert the Rangers, and if I know that battalion they'll fan out and come on up here ready for some fun, and we'll just naturally pound the piss out of our friends over there."

"Yeah," said Ski. His voice was steady, but emotionless.

"And they won't get away," Ben added.

Ski and Little Jack moved to the far corner of the house, and Toby sat with Ben, their eyes keeping constant watch over the house opposite them. For a while they observed the arrival of dark figures, the movement around the forecourt of the house, the placement of a machine gun near the street. Toby could make out several of the men holding a well-known weapon faintly outlined in the dim light: B-40 rocket launchers. There was no doubt at all that this was the platoon they had spoken of, and that it had occupied the wrong house.

At last the enemy was prepared, and settled down to wait. Toby could not fathom their obtuseness in not noticing that the house across the street from them was walled and bunkered, but then realized that most of the bunkering would not be visible from the other side, especially at night.

The minutes dragged by slowly. Ski came creeping up to where they were and whispered, "Wonder what happened to Little Jack?"

"Isn't he over there with you?"

"He had to go down and take a leak, but he didn't come back."

"Go down and see, will you?" Ben asked.

Ski moved away. He was back within minutes. "He's layin' down there on the couch. Got a bellyache!"

"A bellyache?" Toby exclaimed softly. "Christ, another one?" He went down to the common room. There was Little Jack, curled up on his side, just as he had been in the field the other day, his face pale with pain.

"Is it the same as the other day?" Toby asked him.

"Yeah. Hurts like hell."

"Did you take anything for it?"

"I took some aspirin, but it didn't do any good yet."

Toby went back up to the roof. Ben and Ski were sitting close together, conversing in low tones.

"It's just like it was the other day," said Toby. "He's out of action."

"I figured as much," said Ben.

"Hell of a note, isn't it?"

"I guess the pain is real enough," said Ben, "but I don't think it's caused by the belly. It's caused by the balls—or the lack of them."

"Doesn't seem possible," Toby replied. "A guy that's seen as much action as that."

"What action has he seen?"

"Well, he's got scars and he says he was in Korea, and was a prisoner."

"That's what he says," said Ben drily. "I'd want to look at his service record."

"Some things are beginning to clear up here," Toby mused. "His operations with the PRU, for example."

"Yeah."

"But I never heard of him getting a bellyache on those operations before."

"He never before seems to have gotten into a real fight on any of those operations. One shot and they bugged out."

"But how could a guy be a professional soldier all his life like that and get scarred up, and still . . .?"

"Some of 'em are real artists," said Ben.

"Yep," said Ski. "You find one of 'em once in a while. You learn never to put too much trust in what a guy *says* about his soldierin'. If you depend on that, you can end up just like we did tonight. And that reminds me that I better get back over there to my side and start actin' like a soldier instead of an old woman." He crept over to the other corner and took up his position.

"Maybe I ought to go down and see if there isn't something Little Jack can do in this business," Toby suggested.

"Leave him alone," said Ben. "Even if he agreed to do something, you couldn't be sure he'd do it. Better to have nobody than somebody you can't depend on."

The hours of darkness dragged on. Ben made another tour of the premises, instructed the guards in what he expected to do, told them to open fire when the firing began from the roof.

About an hour before daylight, heavy explosions began to occur in other parts of the city. "Probably satchel charges," said Ben, "or maybe B-Forties. They won't use mortars much in this action, because they've got their own troops so scattered around the city. Our friends across the street don't have any satchel charges, apparently. They're not expecting to hit any buildings—they're just waiting for the Rangers."

Ski now moved over to the machine gun and checked it. He assumed a position behind it, businesslike, calm. Toby felt an impulsive surge of admiration and affection for these men, who knew what had to be done, set about doing it calmly and matter-of-factly. These were great men.

"Toby, can you throw a grenade that far?" Ben asked.

Toby measured the distance with his eye, was sure he could.

"All right then," Ben continued, "when Ski starts firing with that M-Two, they're gonna be real surprised. They won't react all at once. You put a grenade right in the middle of that little yard, huh? Be sure to get down after you throw. We could get some fragments even up this high. Then we'll open up on them with our rifles. Just keep up the fire is the main thing. Pattern your firing on Ski. OK?"

"OK," said Toby, his throat taut, his ribs tight with fear.

"You're gonna be all right," said Ben, settling himself against a sandbag, his rifle at the ready, his eyes glued to the scene across the street.

"I may die trying," said Toby, "but I'll never in all my life understand why a man would choose a profession that would subject him to this kind of a thing."

"A man doesn't have any other moments in his life that will compare with what's coming," said Ben quietly.

"You love combat, don't you?"

"I don't think you'd call it loving combat. But I do know that there's something about this, it's a kind of coming to life. You live more in a few minutes than most men live in a lifetime."

"Do you enjoy the killing?"

"You can't have combat without killing, but it's more than that. Right now, for instance, what's best about this thing is that they're going to fight. We've got the bastards where they can't get away. We're going to measure them."

"And measure ourselves."

"Yeah. And that's another good part of it. You measure yourself against another man. But this measure is the big one. The big test. You kill him or he kills you."

"I'll never understand it."

"I can say one thing," Ben went on, shifting his weight slightly to find a more comfortable position, "I could never be a pilot, or a gunship man, or I don't even think I'd like artillery. That all puts you at a distance, and then combat becomes a question of accidents."

"You want to kill each man personally?"

"I think a war where you don't look the man in the eye when you kill him is not war. It's just a kind of butchery. The side that kills the most wins."

"I'd think it would be the other way around. To be able to look a man in the eye, and then kill him . . ."

"If you have to kill him, you should honor him," said Ben.

"Honor him?"

"Yeah. For instance, Ski is about to kill that man over there with the machine gun. I've got two men in positions close to him that I'm going to kill. I don't hate them. I almost have a kind of an affection for them. Can you understand that?"

"No."

"Those men and you and I have a lot more in common that we have with the guys in the spookies and the F-104s and the gunships. If we sat down together and talked, we'd find them a lot easier to talk to, to get next to, than we'd find the pilots to be, even though they're our enemies and the pilots are on our side.

"And," Ben went on with a quick gesture of his hand, "I sure am glad as hell that there wasn't a newspaper reporter or a television team around to hear me say that."

"Yeah, I guess they wouldn't understand, even as well as I do."

"Understand?" Ben said derisively. "They wouldn't *try* to understand. They wouldn't even *care* about understanding. They'd just report it, and it would sound like hell, and they'd have a headline."

"Yep."

"Remember that thing about 'We had to destroy that village to save it'?"

"Sure. That's going to be just as famous as 'Remember the Maine!' or 'Damn the torpedoes!' "

"Don't you feel sorry for the poor bastard that said it?"

"Sorry for him? I never thought about it," said Toby, puzzled.

"Can you imagine any soldier, even the dumbest one in the army, being stupid enough to say something like that and meaning it just that way?"

"No, I guess not."

"If you stop to look at it, you can figure out exactly what happened."

"What?"

"Well, this guy has just burned a village down. I don't know what the real reason was, but I'll assume there was a legitimate military reason for it. I've been in exactly the same situation myself. Now, even the biggest prick in the world won't burn down people's houses without feeling something about it, some kind of regret, you know?"

"I wouldn't think so."

"So here's this guy, looking at the village he's just burned down, feeling like eight kinds of a shit heel for it, and a reporter comes up to him and asks him how he feels—you know how they do, like they go up to a woman who's just had her husband killed in a car wreck and ask her how she feels about it?"

"Uh-huh."

"So the guy is upset, and he says those words, 'We had to destroy it to save it,' and he was being, you know, sarcastic, facetious . . . what's the word?"

"Ironic?"

"Ironic! That's the word. He's being ironic. Now, if you quote that statement in print, without any explanation, it sounds like the guy that said it must be a mindless, heartless son of a bitch. But you've quoted him exactly. See what I mean? What can he complain about? He said the words, and there they are in the paper. And then you have all kinds of editorials and commentators hollerin' about what a monstrous war this is when men can say things like that, and that isn't what the guy really said at all."

"It's a shame you can't get that across to the public."

"Yep."

"But not what you said about liking those guys across the street, and then killing them."

"No. You couldn't really explain that on the printed page," Ben continued. "We're going to kill them, and they would have killed us if it was the other way around, and we know exactly what kind of things they're feeling down there, waiting for the fight. It's almost like you were in church. We don't make the wars, but we fight them. We test ourselves against each other, and if we live through it . . . But then, I always know I'm going to live through it."

"You know?"

"Yeah. When the firing starts, there's a kind of a feeling of invulnerability that comes over me. Hell, I can't explain it."

"Never been wounded?"

"Oh, sure. That doesn't count."

"Doesn't hint to you that next time you might really get it?"

"Nope."

"I can explain it," said Toby.

"How?"

"You're out of your mind."

"I guess maybe I am," Ben chuckled softly.

There was enough daylight now to outline objects in the streets clearly, and they had to be extremely careful not to give themselves away to the enemy.

"Did you ever meet that Ranger Battalion commander?" Ben asked him.

"No."

"He's a little bit of a guy, with a voice like a foghorn. When he yells, you'd think the recoil from the voice would knock him on his back. But he's the fightingest ninety pounds of man you'll ever see. He wears a big forty-five revolver. I don't know where he got it. It isn't military, and it's a foolish weapon for combat, and especially for him—it's so long and he's so short that it almost drags the ground when he walks. But he'll size up the situation within half a minute after we start firing, and you'll see those Rangers deploy and come around that house like a swarm of hornets. You'll have a chance to see a good military operation."

As if on cue from Ben's words, they saw the first vehicles of the battalion appear far down the street. Ben moved over to the other corner. Toby extracted a grenade from the bag by his feet, and waited.

Ben watched as the vehicles drew nearer. "Now!" he shouted, and Ski began to fire. Toby saw the man behind the machine gun across the street start, kick slightly, and then lie still. Others were being hit, and all of them looked in astonished bewilderment in the direction of this murderous fire. Toby pulled the pin on a grenade, waited, then threw it. He watched long enough to satisfy himself that it would reach the yard, then ducked behind the sandbags. The crump of the grenade brought him up to look, and he could see more still bodies.

"Keep firing," Ben shouted. Toby brought his rifle up and began to fire. By now, they were receiving answering fire from the upper windows across the street, and Toby aimed at those windows. His ears rang. A B-40 rocket entered the room below them and exploded with a shattering crash. Grenades came from across the street and fell in their own courtyard, forcing the guards to crouch even farther down in their bunkers.

Another rocket struck the outer wall around their yard, and went into the guard bunker near the gate. Toby saw the explosion, but could only imagine how the men inside must have been mangled and macerated by it. A ricochet sang off the parapet near him, and he ducked reflexively. Just like Hopalong Cassidy. Even as a kid he had known that if you hear it, it's too late to duck it.

From the courtyard, a small squad of men came sprinting for the gate, to make a charge on the house, and at that same instant every weapon on the Viet Cong side opened up at once on Toby and his comrades.

"That's the way to fight, goddammit!" Ben bellowed. "Come on, Charlie, we're fightin' like men today!" Ski had to crouch down, away from his machine gun because of the intensity of the fire, but Ben threw a grenade at the gate opposite them. It slowed the squad only temporarily. Ski straightened for a moment at the explosion, fired off two short bursts at the approaching squad, and sought cover again. Toby saw that the fire was concentrated on Ski's part of the roof. Plaster and brick dust hung in the air from the metal that was striking the wall of the house up that high. Toby leaned around the edge of his own small revetment and fired at the squad, his rifle on semiautomatic. He hit two of them, before the fire from the upper window across the street veered over to his corner. He flattened himself behind the sandbags and felt the impact of the bullets on the bags.

"That's the way to do it, Toby," Ski roared. As the stream of fire left his location he straightened up, and his machine gun chattered again. Another of the squad fell, and the rest retreated back into the yard.

A lull came in the firing, interrupted only now and then by the pop of a single rifle from across the street or from the guards below. When the firing revived a moment later, it was with a new intensity, and from a different direction. Toby had paid no attention to the Rangers after the firing had started, and he realized now that the Ranger Battalion had read the situation accurately and had already come up behind the Viet Cong's ambush site. A heavy explosion struck the Viet Cong house from somewhere. Now a squad of Rangers came around the corner and moved toward the front of the house, but were driven back behind a low wall next to the house by heavy firing from within. They held there, and from that position kept up a constant fire.

More intense firing began at the rear of the VC house, and it was evident that a massive assault was being made from behind. The squad by the low wall now renewed its own attack, and was soon inside the building.

It was all over. Some of the Rangers came out with several prisoners, stripped to their shorts, and herded them into a truck. A jeep with a heavy machine gun fixed to a frame behind the driver's seat pulled up before the house, and a diminutive man stood up and waved up to Ben.

"Thank you, Major," the man roared, and Toby thought he was hearing an old movie of the booming voice of Eugene Pallette.

Ben shouted something in Vietnamese, and the little colonel laughed. With much waving and shouting, the Ranger convoy resumed its ride up the street.

25

When they got downstairs they found the guards tending to their dead comrades. Three had been killed by the rocket. They were being carried gently to the rear of the house and covered with a tarpaulin. Two others had minor wounds.

Little Jack was sitting on the sofa, his face white, his jaw clenched.

Ben went into the office to look at the battle plan. "The government compound is one of the main targets, and it was supposed to be occupied by now," he said. "That will mean the Special Police Offices, the RD building, the works. If anybody believed you, Toby, they were ready for the VC down there, and may have given them a fight. Let's see if they were."

He went to the Victory base station and called the RD office. There was no response. He called the PRU barracks, and got no response.

"Jesus, sounds like they got the whole town," said Ski.

"No," said Ben. "They may have the compound, but not the PRUs, I'm sure. More than likely Manh went down to the PRU barracks and got all the men for himself. They'd be the quickest troops he could lay his hands on, and he'd be after them, first thing. But I am worried about that RD office."

He went to the storeroom and got more ammunition and grenades.

"According to our map," he said, "I can make almost a straight run down to the compound from here without hitting any VC. Toby, you stand by that base station until I get back, will you? Ski, will you get things squared away on the roof, in case we get hit again? The rest of that Twenty-Third Battalion is still down there somewhere wondering what the hell went wrong with their ambush, and they may decide to make our house a secondary objective."

Ski went to the storeroom for more ammunition for the roof, and Ben climbed into the jeep and sped out the gate. Toby went immediately to the Victory base station and picked up the microphone.

"Victory-Five, this is Victory-One. Victory-Five, this is Victory-One. Over."

There was no answer. He repeated the call, to no avail. He hoped that meant that the women were at work, but he was troubled. It was earlier than they should have left the house. If they were at work it was because somebody had summoned them early, which of course was possible in a day that was already full of battle.

Again he repeated the call. This time he was rewarded with two short blips, the breaking of the squelch, the sound that was made on the receiving end when the talk button was depressed on the other end. What could that mean?

"Victory-One, this is Victory-Seven," came Ben's voice. "I caught those blips. Something may be wrong over there. I'll drive by and see."

"Roger, Victory-Seven."

Louise and Peggy and Marie Claire were huddled in Louise's room, terrified, desperate. Louise had taken the radio set into her room before going to bed, as Toby had ordered, and she had been awakened at dawn by the sound of rifles and explosions she could not identify.

The other two women had burst into her room as she ran to the window, to see a squad of Viet Cong finishing off the four guards at the front of their house, and then calmly killing the last two, who came speeding thoughtlessly around the side of the house from the rear.

The Viet Cong squad had then entered the ground floor. The women heard gunfire, and presumed that the housekeeper and her husband had been killed. Then the trampling of feet as the invaders explored the house. They chattered to one another as they searched. They had entered the other rooms on the second floor, tried Louise's door, and found it locked. They paused awhile, exchanged words with somebody on the ground floor, then descended. There was the sound of other feet in the corridor now and then, and Louise was certain men were stationed upstairs, some probably near her door, but she could not believe that they even suspected the women's presence in her room.

Through the window she watched the Viet Cong preparations. It was as Ben had predicted. They were not interested in *this* house, except as a vantage point. Their attention was mainly centered on the Province Senior Adviser's house, which was already under attack. They took up positions behind the low wall, and elsewhere around the structure, she assumed, although from her window the only VC men she could see were those around the wall. She counted them. Six men, whom she could see, well armed, loaded down with ammunition.

Evidently the women were going to be safe, so long as the battle for the PSA house continued.

Peggy turned to her and began to speak, but Louise quickly clapped her hand on Peggy's mouth and shook her head frantically. They must not make any sound. Peggy pointed to the radio set. Again Louise shook her head. If they spoke, it would alert the Viet Cong to their presence. She was sure that the Viet Cong would eventually discover them, but their only hope was to delay that discovery.

Louise went to a drawer and took out a small pistol, and held it up ruefully. It was the only weapon she had in the room.

They waited. Louise thought about the poor couple downstairs, killed without hesitation; about the guards, all of them killed in a sudden, surprise attack. She didn't remember that Toby had said anything in his intelligence reports about their own house being a target. If it had been, he certainly would have told them. But, on the other hand, Ben had said long ago that their house was a key point in the area.

The radio came to life, and she could hear Ben calling somebody. Quickly she silenced the speaker, and they waited tensely to see if there was any reaction from outside the door. There was none.

Louise held the telephone-type receiver to her ear and listened to Ben's futile calls. The temptation to speak was almost irresistible, but she knew that they would be dead before help could get to them.

He called another number, and she looked on the card. The PRU barracks. *Ben, for God's sake, call Victory-Five! Victory-Five!*

But what if he did? She couldn't answer. Well, if she didn't answer he would know something was wrong, wouldn't he?

She got out the schedule Toby had made her prepare. According to that schedule they should be right where they were, for at least another hour.

Now it was Toby's voice, and she looked at the other women and gestured with frantic joy. They understood.

Toby called twice, and she could tell by the tone of his voice that he had not reached any conclusion. Then she noticed that each time he began to speak there was a slight click or blip as the transmission began. It was when he pushed the talk button, obviously.

When he called the third time, she pressed the talk button twice. That caught their ear! Now it was Ben's voice replying, wondering about the blips. He was out in the street, apparently. He must be in the jeep with the radio set. And he was coming by.

She looked at the other two and formed the word "Ben" soundlessly with her lips, steering a car in pantomime with her two hands. They crept quickly to the window.

Minutes passed.

"Victory-One, this is Victory-Seven," came Ben's voice. "I have their place in sight now. They've got some Charlies around the front of it, and as near as I can tell the whole place has been taken."

"Victory-Seven, we did get that response from Victory-Five."

"But no voice," said Ben. "Just a couple of clicks. It could be anybody. Let me try again. Victory-Five, whoever you are, are you still on the air?"

Desperately, Louise pushed the button twice again.

"They're there, One," said Ben. "But who they are is another matter."

"Seven," Toby's voice sounded again, "will you stand by for a minute and let me give them a test. Victory-Five, I am going to give you a list of five names. When I come to the name of somebody you saw at Christmastime, give me two clicks. Do you understand, Victory-Five?"

Louise pressed the button twice.

"All right, Victory-Five. Do not break the squelch—that is, do not press the button until you hear the name of the man you saw. Here are the five names. Joseph Murphy . . . Mr. Clean . . . William Voigt . . . Señor Gonzales . . ."

In a rush of relief and silent, hysterical laughter, Louise pressed the button twice.

"Victory-Seven," came Toby's voice, "the goodies are in the package all right."

"Roger, One," Ben replied. "Stand by and let me talk to them now. Victory-Five, listen to me carefully and answer with the button. Twice for yes, and once for no. Understand?"

Louise pressed the button twice.

"Are all three of you together?" Two blips. "Are you up-stairs?" Two blips. "Do the Charlies know you're there?" One blip. "Are there Charlies in the house?" Two blips.

"All right. They're busy now with their main target. We've

got very little time. I'm coming to get you, and there's going to be some shooting. All of you get down flat on the floor and stay there. Don't make any noise, and don't come out until I tell you. Understand?"

Louise pressed the button twice.

Instead of lying flat on the floor, they all went to the window. Louise motioned them to keep back out of sight. Up the street they could barely make out the outline of the jeep. It was moving slowly in their direction.

The man was insane! He was all by himself, against this heavily armed house. He had been right about one thing, though: the Viet Cong she could see were all intently watching the PSA house. Nobody was paying the slightest attention to anything else, and Ben's approach went undetected.

From midway up the block Ben accelerated suddenly, then slammed on the brakes as he approached the wall, headed the jeep straight for it, was standing up in the seat as it struck with the front wheels. The momentum propelled Ben forward, but he was prepared for it, had calculated it, and he came over the hood of the little vehicle and leaped the wall all in one strenuous motion. He landed on his feet in the courtyard, spraying fire from his machine gun as his feet hit the ground. The men crouched behind the wall, astonished, struck dumb and motionless by the speed of the assault, turned their weapons inward, but too late. Five of them fell, one by one, under the long burst of fire, and the sixth started to crawl away behind a raised flowerbed. Ben strode toward him relentlessly, ruthlessly, and sprayed him with bullets. He paused, pulled the magazine from the machine gun, snapped a fresh one in place, and moved toward the door. He disappeared from view then. A loud explosion followed. A grenade, Louise guessed. Silence, and then a rush of footsteps and voices. Firing from machine guns and rifles. Another grenade.

All was still as death now, and the women waited, their

hearts pounding. From near their door they heard a series of shots, a muffled shout from below. A bullet struck their door, and then another. The house was full of a violent storm of fire and metal.

A movement outside the window caught Louise's eye. One of the men Ben had first shot had arisen, and was running toward the door with his rifle ready. He was bleeding, but still active and ready for a fight. Louise was about to scream a warning, but before she could find her voice a rattle of gunfire from downstairs told her that the warning would have been too late, anyway.

There was a rustle of feet outside their door, then footsteps up and down the corridor, then silence. A silence that seemed to last an eternity.

A knock sounded on the door and they heard a familiar voice.

"Peggy! Louise! Are you all in there?"

"Ben!" Peggy screamed with joy and relief. She flew to the door, frantically fumbled with the key until she had unlocked it, and threw herself into his arms, oblivious of the fact that she was dressed only in very sheer short pajamas. The other two clustered joyously around their rescuer, dressed no more modestly, laughing and weeping, and clinging to him in the inexpressible relief of liberation.

"OK, ladies," Ben said soothingly, "it's all over. Everything's all right now. You're OK. You're safe." His arms had closed around Peggy, one hand still clasping the machine gun. His face was powdered with plaster dust, and the air around him was filled with the smell of ordinance and broken masonry.

"Come on, now," he said at last. "I'm going to take you somewhere safer than this."

Only then did Louise realize the state the three of them were in.

"First we've got to get some clothes on, Ben," she said, trying to draw the nightgown around her more modestly.

"I should say so," Ben laughed. "Give me that radio, and get yourselves fixed up and downstairs as fast as you can."

He took the radio downstairs, and stepped outside the door.

"Victory-One," he called, "the goodies are safe. I'll be back there shortly."

"That's good news, Seven," came Toby's voice. "Thanks."

26

"The VC have got the government compound," Ben announced to the others upon his return to the house.

"What about the women?" Toby asked.

"I took them over to the hospital," Ben replied. "The nurses will be needed there, and Marie Claire wouldn't be safe at her office, even if I could have gotten her over there. So I left her at the hospital too."

"So now what, Ben?" asked Ski.

"That's what we've got to figure out. Whatever it is, we've got to do it quick. These guys are new at taking and holding positions, and they haven't had time to get themselves all set yet. Now is the time to hit them, and hit them hard. A few hours from now it will be too late."

"So?"

"OK. I'm going to take Toby with me. He fights like a tiger, but he's green, so he needs to be with somebody. I want you to stay here and get this house back in shape, and repel any attack that comes. I'm still uneasy about the rest of the Twenty-Third being around here somewhere."

"OK, Ben," Ski replied. He obviously would have preferred to go with Ben, but he did not question the orders. "Where are you going?"

"We'll go down to the government compound and see if we can help out. If they keep hold of that, they've psychologically got control of the provincial government, and that's bad. Let's go, Toby."

They loaded the jeep with weapons and ammunition and sped out the gate. It was a wild ride, with Ben at the wheel. Twice they came under fire from machine guns, and they were regularly shot at by individual riflemen. The vehicle was struck twice by bullets, but the two men came through without a scratch.

Ben stopped the jeep in a side street out of sight of the compound, and they went on foot to the street that bordered it. An ARVN officer whom Ben knew had taken cover inside a small store across the street, and Ben spoke to him, gesturing toward the compound.

"They're waiting for an ARVN regiment that's supposed to come and retake the place," Ben said to Toby, not concealing his disgust. They heard scattered firing from along the street to their left. Ben spoke again to the officer.

"Well, whattaya know?" he said, returning to Toby. "Our friend Thieu has got a little squad of men and he's checking out the houses around the square. Finding a sniper here and there, apparently."

Ben signaled to Toby, and they moved around the square from tree to tree, house to house, while Ben looked the situation over.

"Toby," Ben said at last, "those guys had a little bit of a firefight with somebody in there when they took the place over, and they're acting like the battle is over and it's a big, final victory. They haven't got set yet against any counterattack, probably because they know that the only units that could counterattack them are still way the hell outside the city."

"I'm afraid to ask you what you've got in mind, because I think I already know."

Ben grinned back at him, a bright gleam in his eyes. "You and I," he said, "are going to go in there and chase the bastards out."

"How come?" Toby asked sharply. "I thought you wouldn't want them to get away?"

Ben laughed. "Most of 'em won't."

"How many are there?"

"That lieutenant says about a hundred. That means there may be as many as fifty. What did Dang's report say?"

"He didn't specify any numbers, as far as I can remember."

"Come on," said Ben. He led Toby at a trot back to the jeep. Toby followed unwillingly. He was now deeply afraid. This battle-hungry man was going to lead him into a fight that they could not win—a fight that would surely get them both killed.

Although the fear was mounting, and seizing his chest, threatening to suffocate him, his leg muscles kept churning. He knew that terrified as he might be, he would follow Ben. If he refused, he was joining Little Jack on the sofa. He would rather die than do that.

Ben slung a Swedish K over his shoulder, and instructed Toby to take more magazines for the Swedish K in his own hands. Ben then picked up an M-79 grenade launcher and a bag of grenades.

"We're gonna be looking 'em right in the eye this time, Toby," he said. "We want handy, automatic weapons and grenades. We're gonna hit 'em hard and fast."

Toby had never seen the grenade launcher in use, but he had heard much about it. It looked something like a single-barreled shotgun, but fired a projectile forty millimeters in diameter. In this projectile was a charge of a quarter-ounce of plastic explosive, wrapped in finely serrated wire. When it exploded, it filled the air with a lethal cloud of almost microscopic fragments of that wire, and nobody within five feet of such an explosion would live to tell about it. The fragments did not make wounds one could see, or count. They dusted a body with thousands of tiny punctures, and the blood and the life oozed out.

"Let's go," said Ben. "We don't want them to get set."

He started out at the same trotting pace, and darted across

the street to a small gate in the rear of the compound. Toby had not known this gate even existed. It was locked.

"You've got a K ready," Ben said. "See if you can bust that hasp." Toby studied the angle for a moment, trying to figure whether a ricochet might come back to strike them. He fired a burst, and the hasp broke loose. They rushed through the gate and took cover behind a tree. Ben's target was a small, one-story building behind the RD offices. Its shutters were closed, at least on this side, which was the rear.

"Get over behind that tree," Ben said, pointing to a big tree nearby, "and give those windows a burst from your K. See if we can make them open one of the shutters. If we can, I'll drop a grenade in."

Toby darted over to the other tree, sprayed one of the shutters with bullets, and waited. The shutters opened almost immediately and Ben, with a wide grin, stepped out into the open for a moment, aimed his ungainly weapon carefully, and fired. He immediately reloaded, and before the occupants could have recovered from the first explosion, he had lobbed another of the deadly little projectiles into their midst.

"Come on," Ben shouted, "let's get around in the front."

His mind a blank to all sensations except the voice of Ben, and the need for speed, Toby raced around one side of the building, while Ben went around the other way. The front door was open, and Ben motioned Toby in frantically. Toby understood. He was the one who had a machine gun at the ready. He hurried in, went through a small anteroom, and came to the room that looked out over the back fence. Four men were peering cautiously out of the window, their backs to Toby. Two others lay motionless on the floor.

The four heard him, all at the same time, and turned. For the fraction of a second, Toby looked full into the eyes of the men he was about to kill. He pulled the trigger and held it, and the Swedish K chattered. Three of the men fell. The third came toward Toby. Toby gave him a burst, and could see the impact of the bullets in the clothing over the man's belly, but he kept coming. Desperately, Toby fired again, emptying the magazine, but the man still moved toward him. Toby leaped back and grabbed for a new magazine from the satchel at his waist, and heard a burst of fire from his side. Ben had brought his own machine gun around, had fired at the man and finally brought him down.

"I don't think I'll bring these Ks to my next fight," Ben said grimly. "They don't seem to stop a man very well."

His Swedish K had killed the other three without any problems, Toby thought. It was just that one . . .

"OK, Toby," said Ben. "Now we're gonna clear out the RD cadre building. What I want you to do is find a place where you get a full view of the ground between the RD building and the main building. I'll work on it with this M-Seventy-Nine from a distance, but I want to make sure they don't get any reinforcements from the main building. I'll depend on you to keep up a fire that will keep them busy and keep their attention, and keep anybody from making it from one building to the other. OK?"

"OK, Ben," said Toby.

Ben had not told him exactly where to go. Ben now assumed that Toby could figure that out for himself.

Toby looked the terrain over. There were no trees that seemed to offer any view of the area he had to cover. A jeep was parked to one side of the building, which would have afforded cover, but somehow he didn't trust the vehicle to stop bullets. Then his eye fell on something he had never noticed before. There in front of the jeep was a greasepit, which the mechanics used to service the government vehicles. It afforded the field of fire he needed. He caught Ben's eye and motioned toward the pit. Ben nodded, pulled his Swedish K up, and fired at the building. Toby realized that this was covering fire for his own run, and he sprinted out the door. Somebody was shooting at him from the main building, and he heard Ben's gun continue its intermittent fire.

He reached the greasepit at a dead run, leaped into it, and fell heavily on a crush of living bodies. The greasepit was crowded with people, mostly women, unarmed, who must have been caught in the early-morning assault. Toby's fall had hurt some of them, and he apologized wordlessly to them as he gathered his wits. Carefully he positioned himself against the concrete wall, peered up over the edge of the pit, and saw Ben signal. Some of the shutters of the RD building were closed, but there were enough of them open to give Ben ample targets. He began to fire the grenade launcher, and as if on signal two men came running from the main building toward the RD building. Toby fired at them and they fell. For good measure, he fired several more rounds at the door they had come out of. That magazine was empty, and he snapped another one into place. While he was doing so, he heard firing from the upper floor of the main building, just as more men came from the lower door. The shots sounded like carbines. Two of the men fell, and the other one hesitated, then ran back into the main building. Ben had not fired, and neither had Toby. The carbines were in the hands of friends on the second floor.

"We got company, Ben," Toby shouted.

"We sure have," Ben shouted back. "Let's treat 'em nice!"

Now the lower floor of the main building seemed to burst into sound, and bullets splattered and sang around the rim of the greasepit. Every weapon in the main building was apparently trained on his greasepit, and the firing kept up. Fragments of cement splattered, one of them striking his cheek, and he felt the sharp sting and a trickle of blood. Some of the women around him were wailing in terror.

He thought with sudden fright of enemy grenades. If they threw one into this pit, nobody could live through it. Why hadn't he thought of such an elementary thing before he selected this hole in the ground? He forced his brain to consider the problem calmly, and decided that he was out of the range of grenades from the main building, although perhaps from the RD building . . .

A familiar tremendous crack shook the universe around him and left his ears ringing and dead. B-40. Now another one. They were trying to make the rockets strike the inner edge of the greasepit, but did not succeed.

Toby found that he had to make a choice: either keep down and be relatively safe from the firing, or take a look and reassure himself that his little concrete trench was not being approached by the enemy on foot.

He took a quick look, fired some more, then realized that the fire from the main building had turned to concentrate on Ben. This would not do. He sprayed the building with his machine gun, and ducked. More heavy fire struck around him, including more rockets.

The morning took on a dreamy quality—a nightmarish quality. He wanted to wake up. He must wake up. But he couldn't. He was trapped in an eternity of shooting and being shot at, of explosions that shook the world around him, of automatic responses that followed the orders he had been given. He was down to two magazines now, and some hand grenades, although what the hell he could do with hand grenades from this hole in the ground . . .

He realized that during his nightmare, Ben had been lobbing grenades into the building, one after another. Now, he also realized that the firing from within the RD building had ceased.

He peered out at Ben, who motioned with his hands. Ben wanted him to come to him! He was overcome with a sudden rage at that cool, smiling, killing machine, who had brought him into this mess and was now calmly instructing him to come out of his shelter and get killed.

"What I'm going to do, goddamn you," he muttered to himself, "is do exactly as you say, and if I get over there to you, I'm going to club you right in the goddamned head."

He looked around and noticed the jeep. A quick run to the

shelter of its chassis, and he would be within another short dash to Ben. One thing he had caught from his smiling mentor throughout the morning: When you decide to do something, do it immediately and fast.

He ran up the steps at the rear of the pit, heard the firing begin and knew it was pointed at him, made the safety of the jeep, paused for a moment, and when the firing had ceased, made another spring and reached Ben's side.

Ben clapped him on the back and grinned. Toby knew that he didn't hate him after all.

They made a rush at the door of the RD building. There were few men alive inside, and those few were suffering from the shock of Ben's relentless grenade bombardment. They killed these men quickly and paused in the wreckage to take stock.

"Jesus," said Ben, "we're about out of ammunition. We haven't got enough left to take on that main building."

Yesterday, taking that main building full of Viet Cong, with just the two of them to assault it, would have struck Toby as mad. Now it seemed to be the logical thing to do. Of course they would assault the main building. They would capture it.

Ben was invulnerable.

Toby was invulnerable.

"What'll we do," Toby asked, "go out and get some more and then come back?"

"It's either that, or give up the job, I guess," said Ben. "But if we leave, it'll give them a chance to retake these places, and then we'll have a hell of a time getting back in through that gate."

"Maybe I could go and leave you to hold on here," Toby began, but he was interrupted by a familiar voice.

"Resupply!" came a cheerful call.

"Ski!" shouted Ben. "In here."

Staggering under a load of ammunition, Ski came through the door.

"Nothin' goin' on up at the house," he said. "So I came on

down here. Brought a lot of stuff with me in the jeep, and I watched you fellows for a while from over yonder, and wondered how I could come in and help you without you shooting me by mistake. And then, the more I watched, the more I figured you must be running short of everything except the runnin' shit, so I come in with a few groceries for you."

"That's great," said Ben. He began to fill his satchels, and Toby followed suit.

"Ski," said Ben as he worked, "we got a couple of friends up on the top floor there. Don't fire at them."

"I noticed that," Ski replied. "What's next?"

"Let's have a look," Ben replied. He motioned Toby over to a window facing the main building. Toby crouched on one side of the window and Ben crouched on the other. Ski went to the next one. Before Ben could speak, a crackling, screaming *whoosh* sounded between Ben and Toby, and the wall on the other side of the room was shattered by an explosion.

"B-Forty," said Ben with a grin. Toby would swear for the rest of his life that the rocket had brushed his ear. Their enemy was still very much alive, and with a lot of fight left in him.

"Toby," he heard Ben say, above the ringing in his ears, "grenades, hand grenades, are what we want in there. What we'll do is this. Ski and I will take up positions so that between us we've got all four walls in sight. When we're ready, you get up there close to the walls of that building. They can't get to you then, and you can flip grenades in every window you can reach. Just keep the grenades going. Anybody that shows up to try to take a shot at you, Ski and I will get. OK?"

"OK," said Toby. "What about the ones upstairs?"

"If our friends up there can't take care of them, we'll have to do it later. They can't do too much to us right now."

Toby picked up a large sack, heavy with grenades. Quick action was important, as usual.

"Give us time to get set," Ben said. "Ready, Ski?"

"Let's go," Ski replied.

The two of them darted swiftly out the door, and moved to trees, to vehicles, around any object they could find to provide momentary cover. Their progress was followed with such a fierce fire that Toby wondered how they could survive it, and then remembered that he himself had survived it only a moment ago.

Ski was soon lost from sight around one corner of the building. Ben took up a prone position behind a small piece of statuary, a pagoda-like structure, a shrine evidently, off one corner of the building. Ben motioned to Toby, and Toby took a deep breath and shot out the door. He ran straight to the back wall of the main building, the heavy bag of grenades banging clumsily against his side, and he had a passing thought of what might happen if a bullet hit that bag.

He was soon pressed against the wall of the building. The windows were at a height so that the sills were about even with the top of his head if he stood erect, which he did not do. In a semi-crouch, he began a systematic progress around the building, searching for open windows, and at each one he lobbed in a grenade. He waited each time before throwing, waited longer than was really safe. He did not want to see one of his own grenades come flying back out the window. He was naked there, with no place to hide.

Almost in a rhythmic dance, he moved along and sent charges of explosive and metal into the ground floor of the building. Ben and Ski fired steadily at the windows above him, and he knew that they were holding the enemy back from striking at their tormentor below the windowsills. On and on he went, flipping grenades in—he lost count of how many. He was down to three or four and paused, his eye caught by a motion from Ben. Ben was crawling carefully on his belly from behind the stone shrine toward a big tree near the front of the building. Toby watched for a moment, and then realized that he had a duty to his friend. He tossed another grenade. And then another.

Ben made it to the tree, waved cheerily at Toby, and pulled his weapon around to begin firing.

Toby heard the angry *whang* of a heavy rifle from a new direction, across the street from the compound, and at the same moment he saw Ben's form leap with the shock.

He waited, stunned by the knowledge that his friend had been hit. Ben lay quietly for a moment, then lifted his head, waved again at Toby, and began to fire at the building.

Ben was invulnerable, just as he had said, Toby thought, and picked out another grenade. Then the sound of the carbines upstairs began again, but he could tell that they were turned inward. Shouts and more firing, and suddenly it was all over. About a dozen men straggled out the front door of the building, unarmed, their hands clasped over their heads. Toby learned later that about a dozen more had escaped out the back way, the same direction from which Toby and Ben had mounted their attack.

Toby could not bring himself to believe that the battle was over. His ears rang, his whole body was tingling as the fear and the blood lust drained away. He was suddenly very tired.

He looked over at Ben, who brought the palms of his hands to the ground under his chest to push himself up, and then collapsed.

Toby rushed to his side and saw a hole in his trousers just over the left buttock, where a bright patch of blood was soaking the cloth in an ever-widening circle.

"Shot right in the ass," Ben murmured weakly. "First time in my life."

Once again Toby was confronted with a gravely wounded man and did not know what he should do. Before he could make a decision, a small figure, clad in white blouse and slacks, came running through the front gate and fell to her knees beside the prone man.

"I knew it had to be him," she said to Toby, "when they told me that some crazy Americans were attacking this place." She leaned over and looked at Ben's face, lying on one cheek in the dirt. "You goddamned oaf," she said. "Why do you always figure you have to fight the war all by yourself?"

"Hi, Peggy," said Ben drowsily. "I'm feeling kind of poorly."

She looked up at Toby. "Help me turn him over, will you?" she said. Her voice broke slightly, and Toby could see the anguish in her eyes.

Gently they tugged at the limp body. A groan of pain escaped from Ben's throat, and a sobbing gasp from Peggy showed where the pain had struck home. "Easy now," she said. "Let's take it real easy. Don't hurt him! Don't hurt him! That's the way." They got him over on his back, away from a pool of blood that had gathered under his belly. The clothing was soaked and torn.

Peggy unbuckled his belt and Toby handed her a knife. Quickly she cleared the clothing from his belly.

"Holy Mother of God!" she cried, her voice choked with horror. "That bullet must have hit bone somewhere and tumbled."

It did not seem possible to Toby that one bullet could have caused such massive damage. Ben's entire abdomen was a greenish-blue, and there was a jagged tear in it beside the navel. Bits of intestine were protruding from the tear, and blood was flowing steadily.

Peggy jumped to her feet. "Ski," she said, "do you know where the hospital is?"

"Sure."

"Get in that jeep of yours and go over there and bring Dr. Greevey back with you, and dammit, don't you take no for an answer. You tell him I said it is the most important man in this province, and he's got a bad abdominal wound. Bring him, do you hear?"

"On my way!"

Peggy took some gauze from Ben's own first-aid kit, and began to try to staunch the flow of blood. Then she spied the morphine in the little packet. With a cry of joy, she extracted it and gave him an injection.

"Toby," she said, "I need gauze and tape, and everything else. Do you suppose there is any of it in these buildings?"

"There ought to be," said Toby. "I'll go see."

He went in the door as the last of the prisoners were being herded out, prodded by carbines in the hands of Qui and two of his associates.

"Qui!" exclaimed Toby. "It was you up there?"

"Yes, sir."

"Thanks for your help."

"*We* thank *you*," said Qui. "If you had not—"

"Do you have medicines, bandages, cotton, things like that? Mr. Compton has been wounded."

"Mr. Compton? Yes. I bring."

Qui turned the prisoners over to his comrades and disappeared into the building. He came back with a big medical kit. Peggy grabbed it and went instantly to work. Ben was lying quietly, his eyes glazed with shock and morphine.

"You big dumb oaf," she crooned to him, as her hands cleaned and dressed the wound. "You hardheaded stubborn jackass. Had to go and get yourself shot in the behind, didn't you? Too bad, because there's still a few Viet Cong around town that you haven't shot yet. But maybe we can patch you up so you can go take care of them, too. We don't want to spoil your fun, now, do we? Too bad they shot you in the butt and the belly. If they'd shot you in that hard head, the bullet would have bounced right off."

Qui caught Toby's attention. "You and your friends kill Tu Binh," he said.

"Tu Binh?" The name was familiar to Toby.

"Tiger," said Qui. "Commander. Yenan Battalion."

"Where?"

"Inside."

"Show me."

Qui led him into the building, and Toby had his first look at the devastation caused by the grenades. They went into a corner room, which was littered with corpses, and Qui motioned across the room at a figure propped against the far wall.

"Oh," said Qui, "not dead yet!" He brought his carbine up. Toby stepped over to the figure, his eyes wide with disbelief.

It was Minnie.

His body was so badly torn that Toby wondered how he could still be alive, and knew that he could not live long. Both legs were lifeless, blood-soaked. His chest had been crushed by something powerful. A grenade?

Blood streamed down one side of his face from a scalp wound.

"This isn't the Tiger, Qui. This is Tran Van Minh."

"Yes," said Qui politely. "Tu Binh. Tiger."

Minnie tried to smile.

"Is it true, Minnie?" asked Toby.

"Dang did not know?" Minnie asked, his voice faint and breathy.

"Dang? Minnie, you knew about Dang? That means it was *you* at Therese's house. It's been you all along?"

Minnie closed his eyes, as if to nod.

"Then, you didn't really *charge* that ambush; you were leading us into it."

"I did not . . . did not like to be . . . your enemy, Mr. Busch," said Minnie weakly. "It is so strange. You and I are friends . . ."

"Minnie, don't talk anymore. I'm standing around here like a fool, when you need help. I'll go get help."

"Go if you wish, but it is of no use. I will not be alive."

"And I'm the one who killed you," said Toby bitterly.

"Mr. Busch," said Minnie, "remember . . ." He managed a genuine smile, and traced a large circle in the air with his index finger.

Toby stood motionless for a long time, his heart thumping

with grief and regret. Then he turned and ran out the door.

"Peggy, can I stay here and watch Ben for a minute while you have a look at Minnie?"

"Minnie?"

"He's inside. He's been a VC all along. Will you look at him?"

Something about his tone sent Peggy into the building. She had placed big swatches of gauze over Ben's wound, and there was nothing to do now but wait for the doctor.

Peggy was back in a moment.

"He's dead," she said.

A sudden burst of fire from an upper floor across the street made them all start. The firing came from the direction of the rifle shot that had struck Ben, but this fire was within the building. Toby went to the fence and looked over. A figure appeared in the window, and Qui came to Toby's side.

"Major Thieu," said Qui.

"So I see," said Toby. How could you predict the fortunes of a battle? Thieu had killed the man who had shot Ben.

Ski slid his jeep to a stop, leaped out, and ran to Peggy and Ben.

"The doctor's coming," he said. "He said it would take him about three or four minutes before he could leave, but then he would come as fast as he could."

"Did he ask who it was?"

"No. He already knew."

"He already knew?" Peggy was astonished. "How?"

"I told him just what you said," said Ski. "I said that you had told me to tell him that the most important man in the province had been hurt, and right away he says, 'Ben's been hit? Where?' "

"Boy," said Peggy with a sheepish grin, "I don't hide it from *anybody*, do I?"

Toby sat down on the ground by Ben and waited. He felt suddenly weak with the letdown. A young American doctor sped up in a jeep and ran up to them, carrying a heavy black bag. He lifted the gauze and looked at Ben's belly. He prized Ben's body up slightly and explored the hip with his hands, feeling and prodding gently. He peered at Ben's eyes, felt his pulse.

"Did you give him anything?" he asked Peggy.

"Morphine," she said.

"All right," said the doctor. "Get him ready for plasma, will you? Everything you'll need is in the bag."

The doctor stood, and spoke to Toby. "You're his associate?"

"That's right, Doctor. Toby Busch." They shook hands.

"Toby," the doctor said gravely, "Ben is in danger. We don't have the means of handling a wound like that in this hospital. That bullet has tumbled all through his gut, and he's going to need extended surgery, probably some of it pretty delicate. I can't even get in there to stop the internal bleeding without putting him in a danger I can't cope with. Is there any way you could get him up to Dong Tam?"

"I don't know. I can try."

"You'll have to do better than try. If he isn't up there in an hour, two hours at the very most, it will be too late."

Peggy had heard, even as she was setting up the apparatus for the plasma, and for the first time Toby saw tears start to her eyes. He squeezed her gently. "We'll get him up there, don't worry."

Peggy nodded quickly and kept working.

"Come on, Ski," said Toby. "Let's go get on that single sideband."

They ran to Ski's jeep and went careening up the street. The battle for My Tho was still raging at other points of the city, and they came under fire once, but made it home, and Toby rushed to the shortwave radio. It was not working.

"Well, shit!" he bellowed. "Of all the times for this goddamned thing to be on the blink."

"No electricity, Toby," Ski pointed out. The generator was not running.

"Oh, Christ, I forgot," said Toby. "Do you know how to start that generator?"

"Sure," said Ski. He hurried out the back door.

With a rumble the big generator came to life, and lights came on all over the house, refrigerators began to hum. The indicator lights on the transceiver winked on, and Toby waited for the tubes to heat. Then he grabbed the microphone and began to call Jerry Burkholder in Can Tho.

27

None of the Vietnamese employees had come to work in the CORDS compound that morning, and Bill Voigt and his staff had made a big pot of coffee, and were trying to get things organized in the midst of the battle that was swirling in the streets of Can Tho. The Tactical Operations Center had almost been lost to the Viet Cong attack in the early hours of the morning, as well as Eakin Compound and some of the dormitories. ARVN 9th Division Headquarters had come under heavy attack, but there was never any danger of losing that.

The two nurses, Cynthia and Sheila, who had not been able to get to their hospital, went back into the kitchen at the compound dining room and discovered a plentiful supply of bacon and eggs, coffee, milk, and other staples. They set to work cooking a great quantity of scrambled eggs and bacon, and hungry people came from all over the compound to eat.

Dino and Jess were among them. No Air America planes were aloft today, and the pilots had been told to stay on the ground until Saigon advised that they could resume operations. Jess and Dino were not unhappy.

"The fraternity of the unmitigated cowards, that's us!" Dino said. "Our motto is 'We fly anytime except when the bullets do.' "

"Right!" Jess exclaimed. "And our song is 'Here we stay, out of the wild blue yonder . . .' "

Bill was worried about the unprotected flank of the compound, which fronted on the Bassac River. An assault could be launched by sampan, if the Viet Cong considered the compound to be a worthwhile objective, but there had been no sign of that yet.

Jerry came into the dining room. The breakfast had been so late that the coffee loiterers were almost into lunchtime by now.

"Bill," said Jerry. "My Tho is on the horn. They want to know if we can get a chopper up there to them."

"You told them no, of course. You told them everything's grounded until Saigon gives the word?"

"No, I didn't. Before I could tell them that, Toby told me that Ben's been wounded so badly the doctor says he's only got an hour or so to live if he doesn't get to Dong Tam."

"Ben!" Bill exclaimed, all attention now.

Dino and Jess looked at each other, and shifted nervously in their chairs. "What's the situation up there in My Tho for flying?" Dino asked.

"Toby says the airstrip is in Viet Cong hands, and there's pockets of 'em all over the town. They've got small antiaircraft guns here and there around the town, too, to keep gunships and Spookies off. The fellows over at Paddy Control tell me they've already lost two gunships over My Tho."

"Wow!" said Jess softly.

"You say Ben will die . . ."

"That's what this American doctor up there says. He's got an hour to live, maybe two."

"And he called for help in plain English over that radio?" asked Jess unhappily.

"No other way to do it, Jess."

Jess and Dino looked at one another in silence.

"It's old Ben, Jess," said Dino, quietly.

Jess nodded, and looked at Jerry. "Tell Toby I'm on my way," he said.

"I'm going with you, Jess," said Dino.

"What the hell for? What do you know about choppers?"

"I always wanted to keep it a secret," Dino said, grinning, "but I had some hours in 'em once, before I decided they wouldn't fly. I could probably get us out in case you get shot in the ass."

"Come on, then," said Jess. They went out the door to a Bronco parked near the door. Before they could get in, Cynthia joined them and unobtrusively but unhesitantly climbed into the seat, a medical kit under her arm. They looked questioningly at her for a moment, then climbed in and drove away.

Bill and Jerry went into the little room off the air ops office where the single sideband transceiver sat. Jerry brought Toby back on the air and told him the chopper was on its way.

Bill grabbed the microphone. "This is Volleyball, Buffalo. How are things up there?"

"We're pretty well infested," said Toby. "But we cleared the government compound, and I think we're going to kick the hell out of them."

"Good."

"You got my reports?"

"Great stuff, Buffalo! I got to them late, but it wasn't your fault. It was a real godsend, all over the country. Things could have been a lot worse without them. I'll fill you in completely later on."

"OK, Volleyball. I'm going to get the hell on down there to the compound now. Buffalo out."

"Volleyball out."

Toby hooked the microphone back on the set and came through the dining room. Little Jack was sitting at the bar, staring into space, apparently drunk. Toby shook his head, and he and Ski got back into the jeep. Everything seemed calm enough here at the house. They drove recklessly through the streets, back to Ben's side.

Ben had been eased onto a stretcher. Plasma was dripping

into his arms and his eyes were open. He was drowsy. Peggy was holding his hand, stroking it lightly, scolding him lovingly all the while.

The beat of the fan of a Huey reached their ears, and they soon saw the Air America helicopter, up high, directly above them. Suddenly, the awkward machine banked until the blade was almost vertical to the ground, and came tumbling down in a tight, dizzying spiral. Toby would not have believed a helicopter to be capable of such a maneuver.

"Boy," exclaimed Ski, "old Jess can really fly that thing!"

There was a sound of machine guns from several directions, and the helicopter came abruptly out of the bank and flew away.

"They chased him off," Toby muttered.

"Yeah, those crazy things will only go eighty miles an hour. You can't face antiaircraft fire with that kind of speed."

The clatter of the fans came closer once more, but they could not see it this time because of the trees. He was somewhat lower than before. They listened tensely, but heard the noise begin to fade after a moment. He had been driven off again.

"I guess he must have given up," said Ski sadly.

"Looks like it. You can't blame him, really. He won't do Ben any good by getting *himself* killed. Maybe he'll try to land somewhere else, and see if we can get Ben to him by car."

Without warning, they heard a deafening clatter, and the blades of the chopper were beating the air only a few yards above them. Jess had come barreling in from the edge of town, so low he was almost dragging the trees, and then had set the strange machine back on its tail in a Bugs Bunny stop. He set it down like a feather on the ground in front of them.

Ski and Toby grasped the stretcher handles and lifted their friend carefully, while Peggy walked beside him, holding the plasma bottle. The door slid back, and Cynthia and Dino jumped to the ground. Dino helped ease Ben into position on the floor of the helicopter, and strapped him down securely.

"I thought it was just us fliers that got shot in the ass, old buddy," he said to Ben as he worked. "You got some explaining to do after we get you up to the repair shop." Ben smiled up at him dreamily.

"I'm almost sorry you came," Peggy said to Cynthia, as the two of them settled their patient comfortably and secured the plasma bag to the back of the front seat.

"Why?" Cynthia asked.

"I wanted to go with him. Now I've got no excuse. Our hospital has got people waiting in the corridors. I've got to stay here."

"We'll take care of this fellow," Cynthia said. "We'll have him in Dong Tam in a few minutes, and I won't leave him till he's safe in bed up there."

Peggy felt Ben's bare feet, and tucked the blanket around them snugly. Then she bent over and patted his cheek.

"You come back, do you hear me, you big jackass?" she whispered into his ear. "You and I have got some things to settle."

"Thanks . . . Peggy," he said. "Thanks for the help."

She kissed his pale forehead, and jumped down and ran out from under the whirling blades. She stood there quietly, her hands to her face, her shoulders heaving.

"You certainly had problems getting in, didn't you?" Toby asked Jess through the door on the pilot's side.

"Sure as hell did," Jess replied, watching attentively as Dino checked the passenger space, and settled himself in the copilot's seat beside him. "We took several rounds, and I think one of 'em hit a blade, but she still flies. All set, Dino?"

"All set."

"OK." Jess grinned at him. "We came in *that* way, but we're gonna fool 'em and go out *that* way." He gestured in the opposite direction. "So put your hands in your pockets and lift up, 'cause here we go!"

The blades whirled faster and began to generate the typical

slap-slap of the Huey, and Jess set the blade angle to bite the air. The machine lurched upward and hung suspended for a moment. Then Jess pointed the nose down, and they darted away, seeming to scrape the leaves of the tall trees with their skids. The downdraft caused the branches to whirl and sway violently.

Toby listened until the sound faded away, and its gradual fading reassured him. They had made it. The Dong Tam airstrip would be no problem, right in the middle of the U.S. 9th Division as it was.

"I'll take you to the hospital, Peggy," he said.

"I can take her," said Ski. "You get on back to the house, why don't you?"

Toby was too bone-tired to argue. He climbed into the jeep he and Ben had left on the side street, and drove home. The fighting had died down for the moment, and he ran into no hostile fire on this trip.

Mrs. Chao and Chi Hai were there. They had come home from the Tet celebration that had never happened. Mrs. Chao's face was drawn with fear.

"Viet Cong try to find us," she said. "Viet Cong send many men, send everywhere. Find Vietnamese work for Americans, and kill. Look for us. We run!"

Toby was alarmed. "They are out looking for Vietnamese who work for Americans, you say?"

"Yes."

"To kill them?"

"Yes. Already kill twenty, thirty."

"Therese!"

Toby raced back out the door, his fatigue forgotten, his muscles in the grip of a new terror.

He did not even notice whether he was being fired at as he drove back across the town and pulled up in front of the familiar pathway. One of the small dwellings was on fire, just off the path by the street, and neighbors were trying to save what had been inside. Otherwise, the neighborhood did not seem to have been touched by the battle.

He ran down the path, his Swedish K grasped purposefully, the bolt back, ready to fire. He passed a small clump of people, the women weeping. A teen-age boy came hurtling down the path in the opposite direction, and sped past him.

The area he was entering now seemed deserted, and he slowed down to a walk. It was eerie. He edged slowly up to Therese's little house. It was empty. He walked on, seeing a small cleared area through some spaces between the houses. There were people standing dumbly at the edge of this clearing.

He came out into the clearing from between two shacks. There, in the little bare-earth plaza was a line of bodies, more than a dozen. They had fallen at different angles, but always forward on their faces. They had passed the last moments of their lives kneeling before their assassins, their hands tied behind their backs, a pistol at the base of their skulls.

A small black object caught his eye. It was resting on the back of the body at the near end of the ghastly line. He moved closer, and saw the object more clearly. It was a SONY television set, smashed and ruined, but still recognizable.

He went up to the body and stood looking down, his mind not yet receiving or accepting what his eyes saw. He laid aside his weapon. He did not know if there were any enemy around. He had forgotten the enemy.

He picked up the smashed plastic box and set it carefully to one side. As he did so, he noticed the shoes. They had come off in the last seconds of violence, and were lying askew nearby. She would have hated that. *One should be tidy, whatever the circumstances.* He picked them up with a tender smile and set them, neatly together, by the motionless feet. He straightened her tunic, and his swimming eyes fell on her hands, twisted and swollen because of the fetters fashioned from the television power cord, its European adapter plug still attached, dangling from the knot. It was hurting her. He pulled out his knife and cut the cord from the wrists. As he did so, he heard a faint moan from nearby, and looked up.

A middle-aged woman had come, and was squatting there. She was dressed in black rayon trousers and a white blouse. She was watching him intently, her cheeks wet with tears, her hands clasped tightly together. She was shaking her head slowly and rhythmically. The neighbor in the next house, perhaps. Toby nodded and managed a faint smile at her.

He placed the arms carefully beside the body, and moved to straighten the hair. He stared vacantly at the horrible, gaping hole at the base of the skull, the fine hair around it matted with blood.

Gently, he turned her over and pulled her to him, heedless of the blood, cradling her head in his arms, kissing her soiled cheek, caressing her, kissing and caressing as if he could thus bring life back into the still, fragile form.

It was the Day of Wrath. He knew. The Day of Wrath, and now it began to cave in on him . . . the noise, the fire, the killing, the screams, the blood, the terror.

And it all ended here, on the hardpacked dirt of this clearing in a slum.

"Oh, God. Oh, my God. Therese, Little Mistress, what have they done? What have they done?"

He lifted his gaze and looked at the sobbing woman, and back down at the quiet face before him.

"God damn them, Therese," he said, his voice hoarse and deliberate. It was not an oath of exasperation, but a curse, a holy malediction, pronounced out of a limitless rage. The woman did not understand his words, but she knew what he was doing, and she joined her keening to his invocation of the powers of heaven and hell.

He looked up at the afternoon sky.

"Whoever did this, whatever man has done this, may God damn his soul to eternal hell!"

For some time he continued to stare at the sky, calling down curses on the enemy, curses on this war, and curses upon his own thoughtless, selfish soul for what he had done.

Then he bent his head, and buried his face against the breast of his dead mistress, and wept.

28

The Tet offensive continued for many days, as the Viet Cong, with incredible, reckless bravery, dashed themselves to pieces against the greater numbers and firepower of the South Vietnamese and American military forces. The "masses," from whom they had expected enthusiastic help, had stood by and watched, or had cowered in fear in the midst of the battles and the destruction, or, toward the end, had for the first time in the history of this war begun to report to the government about the location and the operations of the insurgent forces.

As the days passed, Bill Voigt heard and read reports from the provincial offices under his supervision, and smiled with pleasure. These tough young men, wise in the ways of their enemy, unflappable in the face of attack, had stood like rocks throughout the delta, and had more often than not provided the one hard nucleus around which government forces began to re-form and halt the attacks, and destroy the attacking forces.

And especially Toby Busch, who wasn't even a soldier.

Bill had gone to Dong Tam two days after Ben had been taken there. Ben was weak, and under sedation, and soon to be flown to Tokyo for surgery, but he was cheerful and optimistic.

"Hell yes, Bill," he said. "I'm coming back to My Tho. Don't let anybody else have my programs. Unless you're not satisfied with my work?"

"Oh, for Christ's sake," Bill snorted.

362

"Because now is bound to be our best opportunity. After this big attack the VC are going to be as weak as kittens. We'll have them on the run. With them all chopped up, the Phoenix program is really going to pay off, because now the farmers and the villagers will tell us who the secret ones are, and we can round 'em up. The farmers won't be afraid of them anymore. I want to be there now that this is happening."

A nurse came by and scolded him for getting excited, and he waved her off with a grin.

"Toby has sent Little Jack out of his province," said Bill. "I'm sending him back to the States."

"Yeah," Ben nodded. "Poor bastard."

"He was paralyzed the whole time."

"Has the CIA got medals for bravery, Bill?" Ben asked him abruptly.

"Yes, we have."

"Get one for Toby. The highest you've got."

"I was already thinking about something for his reporting on the Tet offensive."

"Well, I'm no judge of that, but I can tell you that he's one of the finest combat men I've ever fought with."

"When you get back on your feet, if you'll give me an account of the action, I'll pass the recommendation along."

"Get me an army clerk or a stenographer in here tomorrow, and I'll dictate it while it's fresh," said Ben.

"Sure you're strong enough?"

"Yep." Ben lay back easily for a moment. "We finally got 'em out on the battlefield, toe to toe," he said contentedly, "and we kicked the shit out of them."

"We sure did," Bill agreed. He didn't tell Ben that the American public did not yet know about the victory; that the American news media, with their relentless determination to doubt everything except their own judgments, seemed to see only a violent attack against the American Embassy's sacred premises, not the lifeless bodies of the attackers strewn around the grounds; seemed to see only the devastation of cities throughout the country, not the countryside, which had at last been relieved of the burden of a ruthless insurgent army that had for years been hidden in its reluctant breast; seemed to see only the mangled bodies of American soldiers, not the smashed and bleeding battalions of the rural insurgency forces, who had destroyed themselves in urban combat; seemed to see only the venality and treason of many South Vietnamese officials, instead of the steadiness and sacrifice of the ARVN soldiers; seemed to see only an unmitigated disaster in what was in reality, to any thoughtful man on the spot, the most important and significant victory of the American and South Vietnamese forces of the entire war.

Ben would find all this out soon enough.

In My Tho, Toby kept busy. He had to keep busy. He must not stop to think. He engaged in no further combat; for ARVN forces and the U.S. 9th Division took over the task of eliminating the pockets of Viet Cong that clung stubbornly to parts of the city, and Toby had only to tend to the repair and reestablishment of his office and home.

It dawned on him only gradually that he was the only one left. Except for the guards and Mrs. Chao and Chi Hai, he had to start all over, although he had heard from Ben that he expected to be back at work within a couple of months.

He had met with Manh and Thieu, and restored amicable relations, even with an unexpected overlay of mutual admiration, and he had taken advantage of the moment of cordiality to ask to be permitted to hire Qui to replace Minnie. He knew that Thieu would suppose that Qui would constitute a penetration of his office, but he didn't care. Qui was a sharp man. He would be about as good a replacement for Minnie as one could find.

"We will learn each other's language together, Qui," he said.

"Yes. And learn also each other' work," came Qui's quaint reply, which Toby understood.

Can Tho was sending an assistant regional plans officer to handle Toby's office while Toby was away on family visitation. Some North Vietnamese friends of Therese, whom he had met at the simple Catholic funeral, had sent him a timid young girl, who spoke good English and could type. She was rather pretty, but did not even approach the beauty of her predecessor, which, Toby thought sadly, was a good thing.

Now he was ready to go home to his family for three weeks. He looked forward to it with relief and trepidation. It would be heaven to spend some days in absolute relaxation in a small Iowa town—in a countryside at peace. The coming reunion with Mary Lynn presented his mind with so many unknowns that he didn't even like to think about it; in fact, he consciously blotted it out of his mind for the time being, to be coped with when the moment came.

Tomorrow the Can Tho officer would arrive, and Toby could brief him. Fortunately, the man already knew almost all he would need to know, from having been in the chain of command for these many months.

And tonight the women had invited Toby to a farewell dinner. He was glad. They were almost his only link with the days before Tet, the days that seemed almost like an ancient dream.

They were old comrades, and although the dinner was not the lively party that their past gatherings had been, it was pleasant. They spoke pityingly of Little Jack, and wonderingly of the pugnacious Ben Compton. Peggy was certain that she had at last begun to penetrate that outer shell of the reticent soldier, and she did not try to conceal her sense of triumph.

And then the other two had, without any apologies or dissimulation, left Toby and Louise alone.

"I won't be here when you get back, Toby," said Louise quietly, when they were alone.

"You won't? I thought you had another year here."

"I've asked for a transfer, and they're going to send me up to Two Corps."

"I guess I know why."

"Of course you do. But there are some things I want to explain to you, anyway." She tucked her feet under her on the sofa and sat facing him.

"I guess I ought to try to explain some things, too," he said.

"I know about them already."

He shook his head with a smile. "There doesn't seem to have been one single secret in My Tho in all the time I've been here."

"We can even say her name out loud," she said gently. "You loved Therese very much."

"Yes."

"And now you're worried about going home?"

"Terribly worried. I don't know how I will . . . This world is so far away, it's as if I had taken up a whole new existence that has no connection with that other world. But I know it has all made such a deep impression on me that going back home to Mary Lynn may turn out to be a problem for me, and may hurt her terribly."

"But you still love her?"

"Yes. In that other world, I love her more than I can ever say."

"I was sure of it. That's why I'm transferring out of here."

"I wish it didn't have to be that way."

"When I first met you, I could tell that you would take things seriously. And I didn't even let myself *think* about loving you. All I could do would be cause you trouble, and I could never have you for myself."

He was surprised. "But I thought—I just had an idea that when we were playing, the way you—"

"You really didn't think I was serious?"

"No."

"Well, I hadn't intended to be, had thought I wouldn't be. But then I got jealous."

"I caught a little hint of that, but mostly I thought you were just kidding."

"I was kidding for real. You have no idea what it did to me when I found out about Therese. Here I had kept myself in a very careful relationship with you because I didn't want to be a part of anything that might make a mess of your life; and then I knew that you had made love to her, and I was sure you weren't doing it in any casual way. A man like you couldn't be casual about an affair like that."

"I think you're right. I don't believe I ever could be."

"And so I thought, Well, I can never have him, but as long as he's already taken that step toward problems at home, I might as well have at least one night of fun."

Toby gazed intently at her.

"I wanted to play that night, Toby," she said, "but there was nothing casual about it. I wanted to roll and laugh and have fun and forget everything in this whole horrible damned world, except just us, and the night, and the games, and the love."

"Yes," he said. "That's the way it was. That was exactly the way it was."

"And," she went on, "if I stayed here in My Tho, we'd do the the same thing again."

"Yes. I could never resist it."

"And we must never do it again."

"I suppose you're right."

"But not just for the reason you're thinking about."

"No?"

"No. It's me that couldn't bear it. *I'm* the one who would be destroyed."

"You?"

"Yes. I let down the barriers, thinking I could share a little part of you without it mattering very much. What I was not admitting to myself was that I began to fall in love with you that very first night when we sat and talked nonsense to each other.

And after that, every silly game we played just pulled me in more and more hopelessly. And the same thing is happening to me right now." She looked away from him abruptly.

"Louise, I—" he began.

"You don't have to make any kind and gentle remarks," she said. "That's not what I'm telling you this for."

"Goddammit, listen to me," he said roughly. "You're acting as if I were some dumb pet that you had to handle in a certain way so as not to upset him. You said you didn't want to cause me trouble, but you haven't the faintest idea of exactly what it is that's troubling me."

"What do you mean?"

"I mean that those games weren't just a casual night of fun to me. I mean that I love you, too, and if that sounds like the craziest thing in the whole crazy world, I guess it is, but it's true. If we had been back in the United States I would never have found out, because I would never have allowed myself the opportunity. Tell me, do *you* think a man can love more than one woman at the same time?"

"I don't know. How could I know?"

"It's crazy. It's insane. Back in that other world I would never have believed it. I would have said he was just fooling himself, that he was reacting with his glands, not his heart. But here, in this world, I could look at Therese, and say to myself, 'If I had met her first, I would have married her, and would have been happy all my life, and considered myself to be the most fortunate of men.' And then I can look at you and say, with all my heart, 'Louise, if I had met you first, in that other world, you would have been my only love, for all my life.'"

"Why do you have to say that?" she exclaimed, tears glistening in her eyes. "Why don't you *help* me?"

"Because I've got just as much right to give you the burden as you have to give it to me."

"It's not right."

"Louise, the only thing we will have of one another from now on is remembering that we made love, and that we were in love, and that we said it to each other. I'm glad we said it."

She rubbed a tear from her cheek. "I think you'd better go now."

They stood by the door and he held her in his arms. Then he drew back and smiled down at her.

"You asked me once if I had ever written a poem."

"Yes," she said, her eyes smiling back at him.

"Now is a time when I wish I could. More than any other time I can remember. Because I don't think there's any other way to express what I'm thinking now."

"What are you thinking now?"

"I've been thinking that that night with you told me something about myself that I had never realized, never seen in myself, never thought about. I tend to be serious and solemn most of the time, I guess, maybe even gloomy. And then I played that night with you, and you are so fair, and so bright, and so clear-eyed, and so luminous, that it made me seem stuffy and dull in comparison.

"If I could write a poem, it would be something about how impossible it is to hold sunshine in your arms, but how warm and good the sunshine makes you feel when you try."

Her breath caught in her throat, and she stopped him. "Please don't go on."

He kissed her gently and held her close, saying nothing, deeply moved by her silence and the trembling of her body.

"Señor Gonzales," she said at last, in a small, pinched voice, "something is definitely happening to me, and it's the most horrible thing in my life. Please leave, while I still have the strength to let go."

He left, and she stood for a time, leaning against the closed door. "Sunshine!" she whispered to herself. "Oh, damn you, Toby Busch. Damn you, damn you!"

29

Bill Voigt drove into the compound shortly after dawn. The Viet Cong had mortared Can Tho in the early hours. Mortar attacks against the towns were about all they had left in them now. He had not been able to get back to sleep. The house he shared with Chet, on the airport road, was not a target, and the noise was not what had kept him awake. He was worried almost to the point of illness. He had puttered around, brewed a pot of coffee. He almost wished Chet were around, although he had no regrets about having demanded Chet's immediate transfer back to headquarters.

As he drove through the gate, he realized that the neighborhood around the compound had been the target of the mortars. You could see some of the destruction.

He saw movement through the door of the dining room, unusual for this time of the morning, and he went in to investigate. Cynthia and Sheila were there, and Jerry. Jerry had had the guard duty last night. The three of them were scrubbing the floor and the tables, and setting things back to rights.

"What's up?" Bill asked.

"I never had a night like this in my life, Bill," said Jerry. His face was pale and drawn.

"What happened?"

"The mortars made a lot of direct hits across the streets. We had this place full of wounded. That American doctor that lives down the driveway there came in and everybody in those houses over there heard that he was here treating people. The worst was the woman that brought her family in. Four kids. One of them died, and one of them lost both feet. And there were others."

"Yeah," said Sheila. "We see it all the time at the hospital. But this was bad, all right."

"Bill," said Jerry, pausing in his work to look up at him, "I don't know whether I'll be able to eat off of these tables again. The doctor used them to work on. And I've actually been picking up *pieces* of those children off of the floor. Picking up *pieces* of children! Can you imagine that? We're all a bunch of goddamned sonofabitching animals, that's what we are! Blowing little kids to pieces!"

He went back to work.

Bill went into his own office. He knew how Jerry must feel, but his own personal worry was occupying all of his thoughts, and right now he could not manage Jerry's as well.

At the commo room, he found that Russ had just come in. "I'm bringing the machines up on the air right now," Russ told him. "Last night's traffic will start coming in on them pretty soon."

"Let me know the minute anything comes in, will you?"

"Sure."

He went to his office and opened his safe. There on top of his in-box was the cable that had occupied his thoughts for the past eighteen hours, almost to the exclusion of everything else.

FOR BILL VOIGT. ALL YOUR FRIENDS AND ASSOCIATES HERE IN FAR EAST DIVISION GRIEVED AT LOSS OF YOUR SON AND EXTEND HEARTFELT CONDOLENCES.

It had to be a mistake. The army might be inefficient, and mix-ups were always possible, but it was not conceivable that his friends in headquarters could have heard that kind of news without his having the slightest inkling of it yet. He had cabled immediately to ask about it, but had had no reply so far. The answer was undoubtedly in the night's traffic, which Russ was only now receiving on his machines.

Lying in the in-box, under the cable, was a galley proof of an article that was soon to appear in a national magazine. He did not know how Washington had gotten hold of the proof, but it was obvious why they had sent it to him. It was entitled *The PRU: The CIA's Murder Incorporated.* It was written by Chris Christopher. It had a picture of the author in her baggy fatigues, standing by Wilbur Hamilton and some of his men. There was also a picture of a small stick of wood, with a date on it, "carved," the caption said, "by a knife that had only moments before been sunk into the heart of a Viet Cong soldier."

The article left no doubt in the reader's mind that the primary mission, and virtually the only activity, of the PRU, was to move out into the countryside and murder people it suspected of being part of a Viet Cong cadre or sympathizers. He had not yet shown the article to Wilbur. It would be a blow to that fine young officer.

Russ came in with a message, and Bill could tell by his face what the message contained.

"I am very sorry, Bill," Russ said, and quickly left.

REGRET TO INFORM YOU THAT YOUR SON, WILLIAM VOIGT, JR., WAS KILLED IN ACTION ON FEBRUARY 26. ALL CONCERNED DEEPLY DISTRESSED THAT REFERENCE MESSAGE REACHED YOU BEFORE OFFICIAL NOTIFICATION, WHICH WAS INEXPLICABLY DELAYED.

The phone rang, and Bill picked it up with a trembling hand. It was the adjutant at the Regional Adviser's office. "Bill," he said, "I've just received a message from Two Corps . . ."

"Yes, Hank," said Bill. "I know what's in it. I've just had the news from my own people."

"I don't know why this was delayed."

"It's all right. Those things can happen."

"I'll send this one right over."

"I'll appreciate it. How did it happen, do you know?"

"Yes. Apparently he did a brave thing, and it's not just the blah-blah that usually comes in these messages."

"What did he do?"

"He was trying to rally a remnant of Rangers after a bad ambush, and he went into one of those mud forts to bring some of them out."

"He went into a mud fort?"

"Yeah. A B-Forty hit it. He was killed instantly."

Bill sat as if frozen, the phone still in his hand.

"You still there, Bill?"

"Yeah. Sorry. Yeah, I'm still here."

"You OK?"

"Sure."

"There's nothing a fellow can say, Bill. Awfully sorry to give you such news."

"That's OK. Listen, do you think arrangements could be made for me to take him home personally?"

"I'm sure it could be arranged, if that's what you want to do."

"Will you work on it, then? I'll have to get my own people's permission for leave of absence, but I don't think that will be any problem."

"Leave it to me, old friend. I'll see that this doesn't get delayed. I'll be in touch with you."

Bill hung up the phone and sat motionless. He was feeling nothing yet. It was too soon. Such a calamity takes time to begin shaking a man's soul. He had had experiences in the past. The worst time was yet to come. He would weep for Will later today and tomorrow, but the real trial would come when he went home to his wife, bringing her only son back to her in a coffin.

He called Laura in and dictated a cable asking headquarters' permission to accompany Will's body to Massachusetts for burial. He also cabled headquarters to ask that his closest friend through all the years, a man whom he and his wife had known

and loved since the old Burma days, be the one to go to her now
with the news.

Then he went to the dining room. It was back to normal now,
and the Vietnamese employees were serving breakfast to a
capacity crowd. Bill sat down at a table that he was sure was the
one that had held the dying child. The crowd was unaware of
what had been going on in this room only three or four hours
ago.

Two navy public relations officers, whom he knew by sight,
came to the table with another man and asked if they might sit
there. Bill motioned them into the chairs. The other man was
a reporter.

"My paper printed the story, and it looks like a couple of
others might pick it up, too," he was saying. "But it wasn't really
as bad as it sounded to you when I told you about it yesterday."

The navy men smiled politely.

"It was worse," the reporter continued, wanting to give everybody within earshot the benefit of his witty attempts to
needle his hosts. Bill regarded him blankly, not really paying
attention.

"And so, I went out on that carrier, you know, and what do
I have to put up with but an escort. It was a young jg that
wouldn't let me out of his sight."

"Well," said one of the public relations men, "that's standard
operating procedure, you know."

"Yeah, I know. I also know that what they wanted was to keep
me from moving around the ship and talking to the people I
wanted to talk to, and getting the story I was after. But I got
away from the stupid son of a bitch anyway, and found just the
guys I was looking for, and got the story I wanted."

"What was the story you wanted?"

"I wanted to find out what the morale really was like on that
ship. Whether the guys were smoking a lot of marijuana,
whether there were many of them that had deserted or wanted
to desert."

Bill could not resist interjecting a comment. "I'd think you could find a better story where the fighting is still going on. There's plenty of it."

"You're wrong, my friend," said the reporter. "The news isn't here in Vietnam. The news is back home. People are sick and tired of this stupid war, and what the people are interested in hearing is that their army and navy feel the same way. These kids want out. Now.

"Canada and Sweden are full of 'em, you know. At least there are *some* young guys in our country that have got enough brains and guts to figure out what's right and do it."

Bill stood up as if to leave, but instead of turning to go, he brought his fist around in a crunching haymaker that caught the reporter full in the mouth. The reporter's head snapped back and he flew backward against a nearby table, knocking it over and scattering the startled occupants in all directions. Bill moved over to where the man sat, groggy from the force of the blow. Blood from a cut lip was dripping on his fatigues.

"You slimy bastard," Bill snarled. "You've got a war that's tearing millions of lives apart on land and what do you do? You go on board a ship to look for drugs and deserters. That's all this war means to a chicken shit like you—a chance to beat the competition with a story of how worthless and demoralized our soldiers are, and how great and noble the Viet Cong are. Money and fame, that's what you're after, and you don't care how you get them!"

Everybody in the dining room was sitting in silence, staring at the scene. The reporter made as if to rise.

"If you get up now," Bill said, "I'll finish the job on you. You better sit there and listen, because it looks like the only way the press is ever going to get the truth is to get their hard heads beaten in.

"You're sitting in the middle of a battle that's been won, won flat and hands down by us and our allies, but do you print that? No, you sure as hell don't, because that message, even though it's the God's truth, that everybody in this room knows, doesn't happen to agree with the gospel according to Saint Walter.

"Now, buster, if you want to tell your editors who punched you in the mouth, and who would be glad to kill you if you were worth killing, tell them it was the CIA Regional Officer in Charge, and that if they want to ask me why, I'll be glad to tell them.

"And what I'll tell them, you miserable chicken shit, is that our soldiers have won this battle, and this war, but you and your smart-ass friends, and your wiser-than-anybody editors, have lost it. And so every single death and every drop of blood through all these years, that you've had so much fun showing on the screens with your snide remarks, it's all been for nothing.

"And that is *your* fault!

"I hope you and your friends can live with that, because there is no forgiving it, and twenty years from now you're never going to be able to explain it."

He stalked out.

The rest of the people in the dining room, who had been frozen into immobility by this sudden violent drama, began to straighten up the furniture and get back to normal. The public relations men helped the reporter to his feet and took him into the bar, where Sheila brought a basin with some water and some first-aid supplies, and began to treat his cut lip.

"Jesus Christ," said the reporter through his swelling lips, "what kind of Neanderthal is that guy?"

"He's a very sweet man," said Sheila. "You just caught him at a bad time."

"I've known a lot of hawks in my time," said the reporter, "and I've seen a lot of love-it-or-leave-it flag-wavers, but I never had one come at me that way, for nothing."

"He didn't like your remarks about the army and navy," said one of public relations men.

"In case you gentlemen didn't know it," Sheila went on, still swabbing at the cut lip with a piece of gauze dipped in disinfectant, "that man about half an hour ago got word that his son was killed in action up in Two Corps, day before yesterday."

"His son was in the army?" the reporter asked.

"That's right."

"With his old man here, he wouldn't have had to come to Vietnam," the reporter mused.

"He came because he believed in it," Sheila replied. "He volunteered."

"The boy seems to have had about as much brains as the old man," said the reporter.

Sheila put the gauze down and stepped back. She looked the reporter in the eye.

"You know, you really *are* a chicken shit," she said, and walked indignantly out of the bar.

"Toby," said Bill, later that afternoon, "this is the only bright spot in what has been a bad day for me."

Toby had arrived from My Tho, on his way to Saigon and home for his leave. He looked gaunt, and the killing and grief had left a dark shadow in his eyes. Bill was glad he could give this man something pleasant for a change. He handed Toby a manila folder.

"This has got a whole stack of messages to and from headquarters about you, some that are addressed directly to you, and some that are not to or about you, but that will interest you nevertheless. But I'm going to take the selfish pleasure of being the first to tell you right now, instead of letting you get it from the written messages.

"First off, kind of a sad note, that I think you already know. Ernie Free was captured and taken north. You knew that, didn't you?"

"Yes. I'd heard it."

"Your intelligence report sort of predicted it, in fact. He was in a daze. The Tet attack caught him with his pants down, almost literally, and he never recovered. He never fought, never resisted."

"Poor guy. Believed his own reports, I guess."

"Not only *he* believed them. *Everybody* believed them."

"Yeah, I guess so."

"But you don't know the big part of it. That so-called penetration of COSVN . . ."

Toby's eyes widened with a dawning realization. "You're not going to tell me that that high-level penetration was Ernie's?"

"It sure as hell was. But there's more. After about a week of the fighting, when COSVN began to wake up to the fact that they had lost the battle, and the masses hadn't risen up, and the VC had been destroyed in the south, well, one of their high-level leaders defected to our embassy, and this was a sure-enough defection. The station debriefed him for several days. That's how they confirmed that Gypsy-One was a deception operation.

"Ernie was their patsy. As soon as he hit Vietnam, the word came down along the VC channels that here was a guy that they had already worked a double-agent operation on in Europe. They sent along an analysis of just how to go about hooking him again. He fell for it, and built up such a convincing project proposal that after a couple of cycles of reporting and assessing, his product was considered to be extremely valuable, and extremely high level."

"Jesus, you don't suppose he was *theirs,* do you?"

"No," Bill replied, "and neither does headquarters. He was an easy mark, and they knew him, and knew exactly where he was, and knew he was vulnerable and gullible, and knew exactly how to play him. But he wasn't a traitor. They probably figured he'd be an ideal man to debrief on CIA operations, and that's why they decided to pick him up, alive, and take him with them. Headquarters figures he's in the Soviet Union by now. They're in the middle of a damage assessment, and they'll probably have a lot of questions to ask you about him."

"He may have been foolish," said Toby, "but he didn't deserve that."

"Well, this straightens out the Frankfurt incident," said Bill, "and I don't have to tell you that your fitness report from me will tell the complete story and get the record straight. Not that it will really be necessary, because there's also a cable of commendation in there from the director, which will go into your record."

Toby smiled, and nodded his head with pleasure.

"And there is an acknowledgment of my recommendation that you be awarded the Distinguished Intelligence Cross for your performance during Tet."

The highest award the agency could give! It took Toby by surprise; left him speechless.

"From the wording of that message," Bill continued, "the recommendation has got enough high-level support that the award could be made within a week or so. If so, they'll want you and your wife to go to Washington for the ceremony."

"What can I say, Bill?" said Toby. "Nothing like this has ever happened to me before. But what about Ski and Ben?"

"I've sent recommendations through army channels to give Ben the Distinguished Service Cross, and a Silver Star for Ski," said Bill, "and I understand that those recommendations will get immediate and unqualified endorsement all the way up the line."

"Good," said Toby. "Those are two of the greatest men . . . you know . . . the most . . ."

Bill smiled at his struggle for words. "Combat friends, Toby. Comrades in arms. You don't have to explain it to me."

"But, on the other hand," Toby said, suddenly sober, "somehow there is something kind of horrible about me getting a medal for killing people, and in the middle of all the destruction, and so many other people being involved in so many ways. Some of them are dead, and my staff down there pretty well wiped out . . ."

"Yes, I know about that, too," Bill said with a sympathetic smile. "I think I know quite a bit about your staff, and what you thought of them."

Toby looked at him closely. "Yes," he said, "I expect you do."

The door opened, and Dino poked his head in, then opened it wide and walked in.

"My supersonic Spad is waiting at the airfield, Toby," he said. "The propeller is spinning, the wings are waving, all just itching to take off for Saigon."

"Another of our resident heroes," said Bill to Toby, grinning affectionately at Dino.

"I heard about him," said Toby.

"Hell yes," said Dino. "I'm a certified hero. We're all heroes. There ain't anybody in this ROIC office that isn't a goddamned hero."

"OK, Dino," said Bill, "see if you can get this hero to Saigon without getting him shot."

"Oh, he may get nicked in the butt," said Dino. "But why should he be any better than anybody else?"

Dino went out, and Toby grasped the hand Bill proffered. "I won't have time to read all this stuff, Bill. Can you hold it for me till I get back?"

"Sure. It'll wait. You get the hell on home."

"Bill," said Toby hesitantly, "I know this is going to be a terribly sad time for you. When you see your wife, if you think it's OK, tell her that I met your son, and had some good talk with him, and that I can't think of any better way to tell her how he impressed me than to say that I hope my own son will be half as good a man in every way."

"Thanks, Toby. I'll be sure to tell her. She'll like that."

Toby left, and Bill sat for a long time staring at the door. That young man had come through days of shock, and he probably had no inkling that others had had the same experiences: bloodshed, separation, loneliness, love affairs, emotional turmoil, bereavement. Bill understood, remembered. Toby and Ben would be back together in My Tho in a couple of months, taking up where they had left off, picking up some of the pieces of things that had shattered, starting afresh on a difficult and exciting task, not even dreaming that others had been down the same road before them.

Bill glanced at the file folder on his desk, and over at the newspaper clippings in his in-box. He shook his head. There was one road he had never been down that Ben and Toby were going to have to travel, and he wondered how they would cope with it.

For the next year or so, Ben and Toby would be fighting and winning a war that was already lost.